The Brittle Star

Davina Langdale

The Brittle Star

SCEPTRE

First published in Great Britain in 2017 by Sceptre
An imprint of Hodder & Stoughton
An Hachette UK company

A CIP catalogue record for this title is available from the British Library

Hardback ISBN 978 1 473 62203 6
Trade Paperback ISBN 978 1 473 62204 3
Ebook ISBN 978 1 473 62205 0

Typeset in Sabon MT Std
by Palimpsest Book Production Ltd, Falkirk, Stirlingshire

Printed and bound by Clays Ltd, St Ives plc

Hodder & Stoughton policy is to use papers that are natural, renewable
and recyclable products and made from wood grown in sustainable forests.
The logging and manufacturing processes are expected to conform to the
environmental regulations of the country of origin.

Hodder & Stoughton Ltd
Carmelite House
50 Victoria Embankment
London EC4Y 0DZ

www.hodder.co.uk

For B.R.S.

For time at last sets all things even –
And if we do but watch the hour,
There never yet was human power
Which could evade, if unforgiven,
The patient search and vigil long
Of him who treasures up a wrong.

–Mazeppa's Ride, *Lord Byron*

Part One

In a White Wood

1860–1861

I

Deep among the white-armed sycamores, there was a pool where the river bent back upon itself. It was fine for fishing, and John Evert was there that day, with a rod made of willow. He wore faded breeches and a blue cloth shirt, open wide at the neck, and the bar of his collarbone shone with perspiration. A haze of midges clouded about his head, but he paid them no mind, keeping his eyes upon the dark brown shape of the fish that hovered in the outer tendril of the current. He could not see the speckled pink and lilac stripe that ran down its side, but he knew well what it looked like. He kept his body right still, only his forearm and wrist moving back and forth smoothly as he worked up a flat cast, making allowance for the low-hanging branches overhead. His line, when it spun out, cast a sickle shadow over the amber water. The mayfly trembled upon the surface before the fish, which moved its tail a fraction. When the fish came up to take the fly, it was lazy as all hell, gulping it down exhaustedly. He set the line with one stiff jerk and hooked it cleanly. There was little fight; he had it on the bank and dead in a matter of seconds. Afterward, he took off his clothes and swam naked in the river.

He walked back through the woods, the same way he had come, ascending the steep slope of the back pasture up to the ranch house. He left the bucket there on the stoop, removed the wooden lid from the water barrel, and took up the wooden scoop to his mouth. The water was as warm as he was. Over the lip of the scoop, his eyes travelled slowly across the pastures.

Like most of the properties in southern California at that

time, the Burn ranch was mired in litigation. The sheriff held a writ of ejection, but out of respect for John Evert's mother, or some other mysterious principle, he had not seen fit to issue it. John Evert's father had been a Scotsman, by all accounts a fine man, a decorated soldier of the Mexican War, a hard worker who had transformed the fertile but unruly land of the ranch into a going concern. A man of vision, he had diverted the course of the river, damming and dividing its flow, so that it flooded and watered a greater area of pasture. Yet he had made sure that the tributaries he had broken were re-joined to filter back to the original path where the river left his property. A fair man, he took for himself, but never at the expense of another. He had passed when John Evert was five years old. Now, at the age of fifteen, John Evert possessed but one clear memory of him: a large, steady hand in the small of his back, supporting him as he rode a horse for the first time.

According to John Evert's mother, his father's death had had a profound effect upon him. Prior to it, he had been a happy, laughing child, gregarious with strangers. Afterward, he became silent and taciturn, and never quite recovered from this early loss. Perhaps it might have been different had he a brother or sister but, as it was, he was never again entirely at ease in company. Yet whatever his reservations when it came to people, he had a way with horses, and with all things that loped and scuttled and flew. Where words might fail him, sensitivity did not: he could read the thoughts of animals and knew their goodness, and they, in turn, were drawn to him. His mother's temper had been sorely tested by the baby possums and fallen fledglings that she would come across in makeshift nests within her laundry. She had forbidden him to bring any more animals into the house, but when one of the mares disappeared and later returned in foal, John Evert had spent twenty-four hours with her, first in the blazing sun, then out in the dark, delivering the foal single-handed by the light of an oil lamp. After that, his mother no longer chastised him.

At one time, the ranch had boasted a thousand head of cattle, but now there were just a few hundred, while their mounts consisted of a few sway-backed, slab-sided mustangs, sorry excuses for horses. The fields of wheat had been reduced to a fraction of their former size and wild mustard now grew taller than a man in many areas, amid the Indian paintbrush. John Evert was not concerned with what the ranch might once have been: he lived in the present. He knew every inch of the ranch and loved it all, but his favourite place would have to be the ancient oak tree that stood hidden upon the back of a rise in one of the far pastures. Some time, long ago, it must have been struck by lightning, for the enormous bull-thick trunk had split through the centre and peeled down to either side, so that the still-living branches rested their wearied finger tips upon the ground. Up through the centre of the trunk had sprung a holly bush, which burst out like a wayward cuckoo child. It was a place of special significance for John Evert, of mystery and power, although he could not have said why. He would go there often to sit in solitude, to ask questions of the stillness around him, and listen to the answers in the songs of the grass and the cricket's whir.

A vineyard-owning neighbour, a character going by the name of Phineas Gunn, had offered more than once to buy the ranch, for even in its dwindled state it had the mighty advantage of the river that ran through it, but John Evert reckoned there was more chance of one of Gunn's Indian labourers remaining in a state of God-fearing sobriety on pay day than there was of his mother selling to such a man. Gunn was one of those cultivators to employ Mission Indians who, once emancipated from the iron-fisted rule of the Mission fathers, proved to be good Christians, and nothing short of indispensable as farm labourers and herders. Gunn, however, had taken to paying his Indian workers in *aguardiente*, and as a result, every Saturday they would spend the night in drinking and gambling, fighting viciously with knives until the marshal, with his special deputies, would drive the brawling mass to a corral someplace to sleep it off. In the morning, they would be sold as indentured labourers to pay off their debt to the community, and Gunn would buy them back again, and pay them the following week in *aguardiente*.

'How many innocent souls have been ruined like that?' his mother would ask angrily, of no one in particular. John Evert's mother was Spanish and thus a Catholic. Every Sunday, without fail, they made the long journey to the church at Anaheim, where she would remain, long after the service was over, her velvet-black head bent deep as she spoke to God. Whatever these private conversations entailed, John Evert was of a mind that they did not constitute praying exactly. He had a notion that prayer should involve asking for something, an element of begging. His mother never begged. Anyone who happened to watch her at it would be hard pressed to escape the impression that what she was actually doing was holding God to account. After the service, she would engage the priest in long conversation. The father's face would run through a gamut of emotions: from benign indulgence, to concentration, to uncertainty, to exhaustion. Worse than that, was the reaction of the congregation. None of the women, straw-haired, sallow-faced creatures with crooked teeth, even looked at her, let alone spoke. She stood out like a cactus bloom in a dustbowl: her hair and eyes shiny black as agate; the bright teeth exposed in her smile as unexpected as the white lupins that would erupt in the pastures during a wet spring.

One day, John Evert overheard part of the conversation of some men outside the church. 'Goddamn,' one said. 'I'd like to know what she's got to talk to that priest about for so long. Guess when you got a body made for sinning, you got a helluva lotta confessing to do.' His companions fell about laughing. One clutched at his groin, as though John Evert's mother caused some pain in him. John Evert's cheeks burned the whole way home. His mother said not a word, but somehow knew what had passed.

That night, as they often did, John Evert and his mother played cards. She was expert at every game and he had never beaten her; she was not the sort of woman to play beneath her ability. At a crucial moment in the game, she looked at him over her cards, frowned and rapped the table. 'You remember what I told you about the face, eh?' she said, her inflection particularly Spanish in her annoyance. 'The most important part of any game is to keep your countenance. *Mira!* Look. Don't show your opponent your hand. It bores me if I know what will come next.' Her cardinal insult, this, boredom being, to her mind, the greatest of sins.

She won, of course. John Evert could not disguise the faint twist of his lips when she did so, at which she took hold of his forearm across the table. 'If a man beats you, you never let your anger show, never at the time. You wait, until he least expects it, until nobody remembers that you were angry at all.'

She slapped his face then, only gently, but it felt like a whip. Her eyes glittered in the candlelight, with the flat opacity of a snake's. In that moment, John Evert was afraid of her.

It was at about this time that there seemed to awake in her a new feeling. She no longer drew him to her and hugged him passionately as she had when he was younger, and her unexplained withdrawal was bitter. She expected more from him, without giving any indication of what she wanted. His chores increased. Phineas Gunn paid them a visit, moving stiffly up the steps on his snapping legs. He had a curious gait, Gunn, suggestive of some mechanical delay, and there was a momentary pause before each of his movements. To John Evert's surprise, his mother sent him out to work in the barn while she spoke with Gunn. John Evert brooded on this in the dusty, husk-filled shadows.

A few weeks previously, she had done something else with regard to Gunn that had surprised John Evert. They had been passing along Gunn's fence line when she had spotted a plum tree in early fruit. She slowed the wagon to a halt, and stood upon the edge of the box to pull one from the tree. She winced at the bitterness as she sank her teeth into the bright flesh. 'Hmm, not yet,' she said, wiping red juice from the corner of her mouth with her thumb. All the same, she made a loose bowl of the gathers of her skirt, within which to hold the fruits.

'But, Madre, it's stealing,' John Evert hissed, scandalised. She looked down, haughtily, and threw a plum at him. He watched her, uncomfortably, remembering early lessons in the sacrosanct nature of property, and wondering why none of those rules now applied. She jumped down, and tipped the fruit from her skirt into one of the sacks in the wagon. She held one out to him, but he turned his head away, pompous. She dug him in the ribs and began to tickle him; he was terribly, hysterically ticklish. When his mouth opened as he began to cackle with laughter, she shoved the fruit inside. The noise he was making startled the horse, which began to move off suddenly, and as the wagon made a violent jolt forward, they both fell over backwards, their legs in the air. They lay on their backs and roared, which caused the horse to bolt. Pandemonium ensued as they attempted to quit their laughter, right themselves and get hold of the reins once more. For the rest of the ride into town, they dissolved into occasional guffaws.

Still, whatever her strange behaviour toward their neighbour, when Gunn stepped back down off the stoop that afternoon, he moved even slower, as though she had stuck a splinter in his joints, which was reassuring. And yet his visit unsettled her, for that evening, when John Evert took a pot shot at a bobcat that was creeping up on one of the chickens, and missed, she stalked out to his side, carrying a leather pouch of paper-wrapped black-powder cartridges, a ram rod clamped under her arm. She ranged three cans on the fencepost a long way off, returned to his side, snatched the Enfield from him, bit open a paper cartridge, poured the gunpowder down the barrel, reversed the cartridge and placed the bullet in the muzzle, rammed the cartridge down and then, fully cocked, swung it up in one smooth movement to her shoulder. She set her sight, paused for a moment, then fired, knocking the first can high into the air.

She was an extraordinary shot, an unnatural gift for a woman. It was why she so rarely handled a gun. He began to smile, but her return glance snuffed out the attempt. 'You don't come in for dinner until you have hit those other two,' she said.

He knew she was not joking. He was not a bad shot, but he did not often practise, and he could not vouch for himself at such long range.

A while later, his right cheek was smeared with powder residue from firing cartridge after cartridge, and his frustration began to make his aim wild.

Silently, she reappeared at his side. 'Remember what I have taught you,' she said. 'Never lose control.' She took the rifle from him and reloaded it. '*Mira*. Breathe,' she said, taking a deep breath herself. 'Aim, but don't think about it. Not too much. Feel it. Breathe out, halfway. Go still. Totally . . . still.'

She squeezed the trigger, and the second can disappeared neatly. She did not look at him through the tendrils of smoke that hung in the air from the shot, but handed the rifle back to him and returned to the house.

John Evert kept trying but still he could not do it. He became hot with frustration, even firing into the ground in his rage, taking a savage delight in the clod of earth thrown up by the blast. The light was fading when he took the rifle from his shoulder and held it loosely at his side. He put it on the ground, closed his eyes and took a few deep breaths. Then he leaned down, picked up the rifle and reloaded it slowly, with beautiful care, as though this was the first and last time he would do so. Without looking at the can, he mounted the Enfield up smoothly to his shoulder, breathed in, breathed out, and only brought his sight to bear at the last moment. Time seemed to slow as his eye travelled from the back sight to the pip of the foresight and on to the can. He squeezed the trigger, and the can spun over and over on its end into the grass.

When he returned to the house, there was no sign of her, but on the table was a scalding-hot bowl of stew. He ate it, alone and lonely, thinking that if he had won something, the prize was not the one he wanted.

Not long after this, one of the horses went lame. John Evert brought it in from the front pasture to take a look at it, and found a festering boil in the soft part of its foot. He tied it up close in the barn, but did not use the twitch, his feeling being that it was better to risk a kick than to force an animal into obedience with pain. He whispered to it and ran his hands along its neck and back, massaging its hot skin. The horse exhaled deeply. Its head bobbed up nervously as he felt around the frog of its foot, and it trembled as he lanced the boil and drained it, but it did not pull away, merely releasing a grunt deep in its throat.

'Good boy,' John Evert whispered, 'good boy.'

He poulticed the foot with a paste of herbs that would draw out the rest of the poison, and tethered the animal out of harm's way. He wiped the sweat from his forehead with the back of his hand and felt his hair stick up wet with it.

He walked slowly up to the stoop and filled the scoop at the water barrel, pouring it over his head, running his hair back smooth against his head. Droplets hung upon his lashes. As he blinked them away, his gaze was arrested by a small puff of smoke that had appeared on the plain beyond the ranch boundary. He replaced the scoop and the lid of the barrel, and whistled for his dog, which skittered round the side of the house at speed and came to his heel. He reached down and stroked one long ear as he waited for the riders to appear.

As it turned out, it was a lone rider on a red horse that had clearly covered some ground for the lather at its sides ran in long white stripes, froth dripping from where the heavy bit wrinkled the corners of its soft mouth. 'Morning, son. Is there a Mrs John Burn here?'

'Who's asking?' John Evert replied.

The man tilted his head back to get a better look at him from under the brim of his hat, as his horse twisted about. 'Somebody who's used to being addressed more courteous is who's asking.'

'Who's asking, sir?'

'Marshal Randall,' was the curt reply. The man swung his leg over the back of the saddle, and dismounted heavily. 'Is there any chance of some water and food for my horse?'

'Yessir,' said John Evert as he came down off the stoop to take the horse's reins.

'And to whom do I owe it?'

'John Evert Burn.'

They walked together toward the corral, the man leaden-footed after his ride. 'That's a fine horse,' John Evert said. The man grunted in reply. John Evert got a sideways glance at the marshal, whose beard covered the greater part of his face beneath his wide-brimmed hat. His gaze trickled down to the twin Colts that swung at the back of the man's belt.

When John Evert removed the horse's saddle, he found it had two sores. 'You want me to put some *aguardiente* on those?' he asked.

'That ain't the customary use for it,' the man replied as he pushed his hat back on his sweat-sodden head.

'No, sir, but it's the best thing for those sores,' John Evert replied, and then added awkwardly, 'I'd be glad to offer you a cup of it too.'

The man let out a bark of laughter. 'Well, and I'd be glad to accept one.'

With the horse watered, they took a seat on the stoop in the shade. 'Just you and your ma out here?' asked the marshal. John Evert nodded. 'You know why I'm here?'

'No.'

The man chewed the end of his *cigarrito* and spat. 'There's been some trouble over at the properties east of here. Raids.'

'By whom?'

'Indians. Paiute, I guess.'

'But there's been no trouble with them for years now, I thought.' John Evert frowned.

'No. But something or someone's put the wind up them.'

'Much taken?'

'Cattle, horses, anything they can carry with them. But it's more the manner of the raids I'm concerned about. Listen, is your mother going to be back any time soon? I should really be talking to her.'

'We've a couple of rifles and a pistol. I'm the only one able to shoot them,' John Evert lied – he would never have betrayed his mother's ability to a stranger. 'There's the few Mexicans who work on the ranch, but I wouldn't trust them with a firearm – they'd be as likely to shoot themselves with it. So, if you don't mind my saying, sir, it's best you just tell me whatever it is you need to tell.' John Evert blushed at the length of his own speech.

The marshal looked out at the pastures and leaned back in his chair, so that it balanced on two legs. He rocked back and forth a little. 'You got any brothers or sisters?'

'No.'

'The places that were raided, things were done. Two girls were taken.' John Evert said nothing. 'Could you go to town for a visit, or is there a neighbour you and your ma could stay with for a while? Over at the Gunn place, perhaps.'

'No, sir. I know my mother and she won't go staying someplace else and leave the ranch unprotected.' As far as John Evert was aware, his mother only went to Los Angeles under sufferance: to consult a lawyer, for medicine, or to attend the occasional funeral.

The marshal dropped the butt of his smoke on the floor, and brought his heel down upon it. 'I hear there's a writ out on this property,' he said.

'Yes, sir, but the lawyers are taking care of matters, and we're sure to be winning on that score,' John Evert said firmly.

'I'm glad to hear it.' The marshal stood, and pulled his belt up a little. 'Give my regards to your mother. I'm headed to the Gunn place now. I'll ask for some men to be sent over here.' He put up a hand to silence John Evert. 'That's my decision as marshal.'

'Yessir,' John Evert mumbled.

The man saddled up his horse and John Evert handed up to him a full canteen. He looked down at John Evert. 'Keep your eyes open, son. The first sign of trouble, you and your mother get out of here, you understand? No playing heroes. The trouble with dead men is, they may feel mighty righteous themselves, but they're not a whole lot of use to the living no more. You catch my meaning?'

John Evert nodded. The marshal swung his horse's head about and loped away at a slow canter, his blanket roll bouncing behind the saddle. Soon, horse and rider returned to the shifting heat haze whence they had come.

John Evert went into the house and shut the door behind him. On sunny days, the inside was dark as pitch and might have been called oppressive, but at night, with the fire alight, with every door and window sealed tight, and the place smelling lye-scrubbed clean, it was the happiest of refuges. But just now, he could barely make out the black stove as he passed by it to take out a key from where it was hidden in one of the storage jars. He went through to the back, unlocked the cupboard and then the trunk inside. He took out the rifles and the pistol, and brought them back to the kitchen, where he laid them side by side on the table while he went for the wire brush, patches and some boiling water.

The door opened and his mother was framed in the bright rectangle. She must have been unable to see him for it was not until she was inside and had deposited the packages she held that she became aware of him. 'John, what are you doing?' she asked in surprise.

'Cleaning the rifles.'

'*Ya veo.*' She tutted with a toss of her head as she moved her packages about upon the long shelf at the side of the room. 'I see that,' she repeated in English, as was her habit. 'Why now?' She began to untie the string on a parcel.

'The marshal came by.'

She turned. 'Why?'

'There've been raids at some places east.'

'What kind of raids?'

'Paiute.'

'Strange,' she said, with a frown. 'Some quarrel between them

13

and a landowner, perhaps. These things don't flare up for no reason.' She returned to her package.

'They kidnapped a couple of girls,' John Evert said.

She walked over to the table where he sat. 'What? Which families?'

'He didn't say.'

'*Madre de Dio*.' She took a seat at the table, folding her arms so that her hands cupped each elbow. She wore a cotton dress of very fine blue and white stripe that was full in the skirt, fitted in the bodice, and buttoned all the way up to her neck. Her dark eyes gleamed black and anxious. John Evert's eyes were not dark, they were green. This was considered an oddity, for his father's eyes had been dark also. It seemed he had inherited this rarity from some distant ancestor. 'The Changeling', his mother would call him, in moments of levity.

'The marshal wanted us to go over to Gunn's.'

She was up on her feet again in a flash, with the celerity of movement that was hers. 'Under no circumstances.'

'I told him no.'

'Good.'

'But he's sending some of Gunn's men over here. Said there was nothing we could do about it.'

The quiver of her nostrils was the only indication of the hard-mastered temper beneath. 'Well,' she said, severing the string on a parcel as she might break the neck of a chicken.

Two men came riding in that evening. 'A couple of scrawny *burros* that will be about as much use as a stick,' his mother put it, as they watched them dismount. Despite this opinion, she greeted the men graciously and led them inside.

While they ate the cold meats and bread she had laid out for them, she asked them about their work and the state of Mr Gunn's grapes that year. Jack and Aubrey were their names. Aubrey was small and wiry, with a foxy face that seemed to be glancing in all directions at once. The one named Jack was nice-looking, with very straight black eyebrows that framed wide-set brown eyes. He had a quick smile that would flash across his face sometimes, disappearing just as swiftly.

The two men were very polite to John Evert's mother and seemed a little in awe of her. John Evert could hardly have been described as worldly, but he was not stupid to the fact that many more men called at the ranch than women, and the men who did would sit around dumbly, like they had a dumpling stuck in their gullet. All except Phineas Gunn, who never ran out of things to say.

When John Evert was much younger, he had overheard Gunn and his mother discussing the legal contest relating to the Burn land, land, Gunn claimed, that was rightfully his, due to the way the boundaries had been drawn up when it was first settled. John Evert had not understood much of what Gunn said, but he remembered the conciliatory tone in which he had spoken when he had told John Evert's mother what a great thing it would be if they were to combine their land, how with one fell swoop it would make them both rich and cause all the legal questions to disappear. At the time, John Evert had figured that Gunn wanted to go into business with her. It was only when he was older that he understood he had accidentally witnessed a marriage proposal. John Evert thought again about how tired his mother had looked after Gunn's last most recent visit. A quiver of anxiety fluttered through him as to whether she was not, quietly, by slow degrees, being worn down. What would happen when the day came that she was simply too tired to say no one more time?

John Evert and Gunn had had dealings once. He had never spoken of it.

He had been way out, on the trail of some cattle that had broken off from the herd, when movement caught his gaze far down the track that led toward the Gunn boundary. He rode there, and found a mule deer that had got its antlers caught in the whippy branches of a tree. The animal had been that way a while; a wolf or coyote had had a go at it and its haunches bled from ragged wounds. It trembled at his presence but it was so exhausted that it could do little more than sidle its back end to and fro, its head held fast in the vice of greenery.

John Evert dismounted slowly and removed his knife, with a view to cutting the animal free. The vegetation was so thick that there was no way to get to the other side of it; he would have to go up close to cut it loose. He made soothing noises and was taking his time in approaching it, when a shadow fell across the animal. Startled, he turned about quickly. His sudden movement alarmed the deer, which bucked and caught him in the side with its hoof, felling him to the ground.

From where he lay, he looked up at Phineas Gunn, astride his horse, laughing.

'Haha!' Gunn chortled. 'What are you about, young John Evert? That beast'll kill you given half a chance.' Gunn studied the animal critically as John Evert got to his feet. 'You'll never get in there to cut it loose,' he said. 'Make it do the work.' He unfurled the long bull whip in his hand and cracked it on the deer's flank. The animal reared up and backward, lost its footing and fell over, only its head held up by the branches, its legs galloping air. Heat flared in John Evert's belly. Without thinking, he shot forward and grabbed at the length of the bull whip and yanked on it as hard as he could. Unprepared, Gunn was half unseated but, quick as a flash, he righted himself, snatched further down on the whip and pulled back with all his force. A yard or so of rawhide whistled through John Evert's tight-closed fist, taking the skin with it. He cried out at the pain. Gunn's face was contorted with anger. He took out his pistol and shot the deer in the back of the neck. It struggled no more, just lay heavy, swaying slightly, hanged by its crown of green.

'Why'd you have to do that?' John Evert said, his fire gone and turned to pity.

'Those wounds were rotten,' Gunn snapped. 'It would have died anyway.'

'You had no right,' John Evert said. 'Not on our land.'

'*Your* land?' Gunn said. '*My* land,' he objected, pointing at a marker post hidden among the trees. 'My land. My deer. To do with as I choose. You want this to be your land? It can be, easily – if you persuade your mother to consider my suit.'

He returned the pistol to its holster and studied John Evert with his pale, mocking gaze. He picked up his rein and began to move off. Over his shoulder, he called back, 'Take that deer to your mother – a gift from me. The hide'll make fine shoes and breeches for winter.'

John Evert had kept his fist closed. When he looked down, he saw blood trickling from it.

He had given his mother some excuse about his hand. She had been glad to have the deer and had shown him how to tan the hide. He had been reluctant to do it and she had chastised him for being soft. He was still not sure why he had never told her how he had come by it. Maybe it was that her protectiveness worried him sometimes; what she might do if she found out someone had hurt him.

When it was time to turn in, John Evert took the two men to the barn and showed them the rough beds that had been made up for them there. 'Shall I take first watch?' he asked them, as they tossed their blankets on to the beds.

'You sure?' Jack said. 'Mr Gunn said it was for us to do the job.'

'You've been working today,' John Evert said.

'Sure.'

'I haven't. You could get some rest and I'll come wake one of you in a few hours.'

'Thanks, kid,' he said gratefully, as he took off his boots. John Evert nodded to them, checked on the lame horse, and returned to the house.

He knocked at the door of his mother's bedroom and entered to find her still fully clothed, propped up on the bed, with one of the rifles next to her, its muzzle upon the pillow. John Evert smiled faintly. 'Anyone'd think that gun was Pa,' he said.

She snorted and returned to reading the journal she held towards the lamp at her bedside.

'I'm taking first watch,' he said.

'*Bueno*,' she said, without looking up, 'I feel safer with you out there than one of them.'

He watched her for a moment. '*Madre*,' he said, '*tienes miedo? Are you scared?*'

She laid the journal in her lap and studied him calmly. 'No. I have never been scared.'

'*Buenas noches*,' he said. He closed the door behind him. He suspected that she would not continue reading and that she would go to the window to keep watch instead, but he admired her defiance. He, on the other hand, did feel scared, but it was a fear tinged with anticipation.

He went out to the rocking chair upon the stoop and laid a blanket over his legs, with the rifle balanced across his knees. His dog curled up against his feet and he tickled it with the tip of his boot. He sat back and rocked gently. He could just make out the murmur of the men's voices in the barn, but soon they fell silent and the only noise was the wind and the occasional clack of a chain against a gatepost. The temperature dropped steadily, and the white pinpricks of the stars brightened until the sky was one giant, moth-ravaged blanket. The wind brought with it the scent of dust and wild sage. At one point, there were rustlings away to the side of the house, and John Evert held tight to the cold metal of the rifle, but it was just a possum that came snuffling around in front of the stoop, scented the dog and scuttled away. With his nerves on edge, his watch passed quickly and he jumped with surprise when the barn door opened and one of the men came out to relieve him.

'I was going to come wake you,' John Evert said.

'It's all right. I was awake anyway,' Jack said, rubbing the heels of his hands into his eyes. 'Aubrey snores like a hog with its face in a pile of shit . . . Scuse me,' he said apologetically.

''S all right,' John Evert said, pleased at being spoken to in that familiar way.

John Evert bolted the door of the house behind him and felt

his way in the darkness to his bedroom. He took off his clothes and crawled under the blankets, listening to the sound of his dog's claws clicking back and forth at the side of his bed. 'Come on, then,' he said, and the dog hopped on to the bed, turned around twice, settled into the curve of his side and sighed. He stroked its head and looked up at the blackness. He did not remember falling asleep.

2

Jack and Aubrey turned out to be handier about the place than John Evert's mother had supposed. They were, Jack in particular, awful willing: only an hour after breakfast they were attending to wobbly fenceposts and helping the Mexicans clear out a clogged stream. Jack entered the barn, where John Evert was changing the poultice on the mustang's foot, and came over to watch.

'What's that in there?' He sniffed.

'Herbs,' John Evert replied.

'Does it work?' John Evert nodded, as he squatted with the horse's heavy leg bent in his lap. 'Where'd you get it?'

'I made it.'

'Bully.'

When John Evert had finished tying the bandage, he replaced the horse's hoof on the ground and stood up, red in the face from the effort. Jack was rolling himself a *cigarrito*. John Evert watched him, standing with one hand on the horse's withers. Jack noticed him watching and held out the *cigarrito* out to him, with raised eyebrows.

'Oh . . . no, I didn't. I mean, I don't . . .' John Evert stumbled.

'You ever tried one?'

'No.'

'Try one.' Jack leaned forward in a friendly way, holding out the thing until John Evert took it. Jack struck a match upon a medallion that he wore about his neck. John Evert reckoned he was just about the slickest fellow he had ever seen. He breathed in a big lungful of smoke, felt it claw at the back of his throat, and swiftly exhaled with a racking cough. He looked at Jack through watering eyes, embarrassed. Jack did not laugh, he simply lit his own, and blew one perfect smoke-ring that drifted out toward the sunlight, faded and vanished. They leaned against the wall of the barn in silence, Jack smoking, John Evert just holding a bit of smoke in his mouth. The horse rested its muzzle on John Evert's shoulder, until the smoke bothered it and it limped away.

'Your ma said it might be an idea to go check on the cattle, maybe bring them closer to the house,' Jack said.

'Did she?'

'What do you think?'

John Evert, shy at being asked his opinion, did not answer for a little while, but then said, 'Yeah, I think that's an idea.'

'Well, let's go, then.'

John Evert, Jack and Aubrey rode out together, John Evert leading the way. The two men talked, mainly about work at the Gunn ranch. Neither spoke in complimentary terms of Gunn, but John Evert still had a notion they were curbing themselves because he was there. He did not pay them much mind for he was more interested in studying the land, enjoying the feel of the wild mustard trailing along his ankles as his horse pushed forward through it, parting it like water. The sun was relentless, a gold disc in the sky. The breeze was hot and dry, banishing the sweat that clung to his body.

They came upon a string of cattle, the animals looking up dozily at the horses. They got up behind them and the cattle trundled ahead of them, so little bothered that the horses' noses almost touched their dusty black flanks.

'Wait,' John Evert said. Jack reined in his horse next to him. 'The bull's over there.'

'Where?'

'There.' John Evert pointed.

'I don't see 'im.'

John Evert rode close to Jack, stood up in his stirrups, leaned in toward him and pointed again. 'There, in the shade of those willows. You see him?'

Jack squinted. 'Damn, you've got good eyes. Come on. Aubrey, you stay with these.'

The two of them cantered over to the narrow strip of shade where the black bull lay with his eyes closed, his head nodding slightly. They rode right up to him before he opened one eye in a halo of flies.

'Come on, you lazy son-of-a-bitch,' Jack said, taking his lariat off the pommel to hit him.

'No, no, there's no need,' John Evert said, dropping down from his horse and approaching the bull. He patted him on his huge boss and rubbed his face, then leaned over the creature's head, massaging its massive neck with both hands. The bull's breaths were vast and deep as a pair of giant bellows. When the animal lifted its head slightly, John Evert's feet clear left the ground. 'Come on, Samson,' he said, making chucking noises as he slipped down to one side of the bull, leaned against his massive shoulder and rocked him. The bull sighed. His damp breath made the thick ring in his nose gleam in the sunlight. He tried to ignore John Evert's pestering but, eventually, he got to his feet laboriously and shook himself with a great muscular ripple, so that the dust cascaded off his huge bulk. John Evert beamed at him affectionately. To John Evert, he was still the calf that he had met the day it was born.

'I'll be damned,' Jack said, sitting back in his saddle. 'Is he old or somethin'? He doesn't look old.'

'No, he's six. He's just lazy.' John Evert took a hold of one of the bull's horns and walked alongside him, his horse on the other side, trailing its rein in the long grass.

When they reached Aubrey, Jack said with a laugh, 'You ever seen such a soft roundup?'

'No, I ain't,' Aubrey said, with a shake of his head. 'Is that a tame bull?' he asked.

John Evert tilted his head. 'I guess so.'

'Well, I ain't getting down there to check,' Aubrey said, then looked at Jack with a questioning expression. Jack shrugged at him. John Evert remounted his horse and they drove the herd slowly toward the house.

They spent the rest of the day collecting up loose groups of cattle in this way, and by the time the sun was drooping low in the sky, they were thick with dust-crusted sweat. When they rode back to the house, John Evert's mother was there to greet them.

'You've done well,' she said. 'Here, the men will take your horses. *Vamos*,' she said to the two Mexicans, who were waiting nearby. 'I've filled the tank for you, so you can bathe. There's soap and all you need.'

John Evert walked toward the large wooden trough that stood to one side of the house, stripping off his shirt as he went. By the trough were buckets and small blocks of the lye soap that she had boiled down from potash. There was a metal hand pump for filling the trough, and he gave it a couple of hard pumps, just for the pleasure of seeing the bright water gush out. He took off his breeches and turned to find Jack and Aubrey hesitating. His mother laughed behind them, saying, 'It's all right, I'm not planning to watch you. Throw your clothes in the bucket. I have fresh ones inside that should fit you.'

She turned on her heel and returned to the house, closing the door firmly behind her. Jack and Aubrey looked back at John Evert, who was pouring a bucket of water over his head, and began to strip off their clothes, hurling them aside. The odour from their bodies was rank and spicy, of leather and sweat and toil. Unlike John Evert, who had kept on his under-linen, the men stripped naked. John Evert tried not to let his curiosity at their bodies show: all the hair and muscle, the swinging, lifeless appendages. Jack threw a bucket of water over himself, took hold of a block of soap and rubbed it up into a fine lather, coating himself head to toe until he resembled a giant head of cotton flower. He let out a whoop and jumped right into the trough, so that water splashed over the edge and down the sides. He went under and then surfaced, spouting water out of his mouth. John Evert laughed at him. It was as if he had never bathed before.

'Damn, that is good!' Jack cried, his dark hair swept back against his head. Aubrey picked up his bucket and threw the contents of it at Jack's grinning face. Jack ducked, then burst out again, the water streaming off his shoulders and chest, and used both hands to sweep water over them. John Evert hurled his bucketful too and they had a happy time being ridiculous and very noisy until they were exhausted and John Evert was panting with laughter. He did not know when he had had so much fun.

'Boys!' John Evert's mother called invisibly from a window. To John Evert's amusement, both Jack and Aubrey hid themselves in the water. 'It'll be dark soon, come inside.'

They wrapped themselves in the cotton cloths she had left out for them, and entered the house. Behind them, the pastures fell into dark blue shadows, and the sky began to set a fiery orange. Two neat piles of John Evert's father's old clothes were laid out for the men. John Evert went to his room to dry and change. His mother entered and sat upon his bed, watching him. He did not pay her much attention as he hopped on one leg, struggling to get his clean breeches on quickly, so that he could go back to Jack and Aubrey.

'You like having them here, eh?' she said.

'Yeah. We had a fine time getting the cattle. You know that Jack, he—'

'I didn't realise how much you'd missed having a man in your life,' she said.

He studied her face, worried that she was somehow offended. '*Non, Madre.* I like things just as they are. It's only . . . it's nice to have them here for a visit.'

'Maybe you'd like to have a man here all the time?' she asked, studying him closely.

'I don't know,' he said, with a shrug.

'*Ay*, don't go and sulk now,' she said. '*Anda*, go to them.'

He kissed his mother's cheek, then dashed to the main room where Jack and Aubrey were standing, clean and slightly awkward in the unfamiliar clothes.

They sat down at the table in the dusty glow of the oil lamps, and John Evert's mother served them thick T-bone steaks, marbled with rich veins of fat. There were slivers of potato that had been fried in oil, garlic and handfuls of the rosemary that grew thick about the stoop of the house. When his mother leaned across him to settle a bowl, she smelt of the same spruce greenness.

'There's wine,' she said, putting a pitcher in front of Jack. He poured three cups and handed one to her. 'No, not for me, for John,' she said.

John Evert looked at her in surprise. He had never tasted wine, and its unfamiliar tartness stung his tongue. He put a forkful of green beans into his mouth, which tasted a lot better.

'I never saw such a thing as that there bull of yours, ma'am,' Aubrey said, as he attacked the meat upon his plate.

'How so?' she asked.

'Well, it came with that boy like it was a big dog. How'd you get him like that?'

'Oh, I couldn't do that with him. He's only like that with John.'

The three of them turned to study John Evert, as though he were some novelty. John Evert rubbed at a mark on the table top with his sleeve.

'We'll go out again tomorrow and see if we can't bring in some of the other stragglers,' Jack said. 'There's one of them with a gammy wound that'll need looking at.'

'Yes, thank you. I admit I didn't approve of you being sent over here by Mr Gunn, but . . . well, you are a great help.' Jack smiled at her. She stood and went to tend things at the side of the kitchen. 'What would you like to do now?' she asked them.

'We could play cards,' John Evert blurted out. She raised an eyebrow at him and he realised he had said the wrong thing. 'Usually, I read aloud to John,' she said. 'You may listen, if you like.'

She left the table to take a chair by the wood-burning stove. The three pushed back their chairs and joined her in the circle of warmth. John Evert took a seat on a blanket next to the foot of Jack's chair. His dog came and lay by him, its head upon his thigh.

Jack picked up one of the books on the stool by the fire. 'Honoré de Balzac,' he read, and opened it. 'Oh, it's . . .'

'French,' she said.

'I guess it is.'

'We had just started reading some Dickens. Do you know Charles Dickens?'

'He a local man?' Jack asked.

She smiled. 'No, he's an Englishman. It's called *Bleak House*. You'll like it. We will return to the beginning. We had only just begun.'

She read beautifully, with fine expression. Soon, the four of them were no longer in the open spaces of California but in the narrow streets of London, in Chancery, in the fog.

Later, John Evert saw that Aubrey was fast asleep, but Jack was listening, with rapt attention, his eyes never leaving John Evert's mother's face. When she finished reading, and closed the book, he seemed sorry. 'That was real pretty, ma'am,' he said.

'I'm glad you liked it. John, time for bed.'

'Oh, but—'

'No. Bed. Jack, will you take the watch?'

'Yes, ma'am.'

John Evert reluctantly went to his room and listened to his mother talking to Jack a while longer, until she, too, went with soft tread to her room.

John Evert did not sleep. From his bed he could hear the soft creak on the stoop as Jack moved around from time to time. An owl hooted now and then. A couple of hours must have passed, for he heard Jack moving around restlessly and figured he was trying to stop himself going to sleep. John Evert rose, put on his clothes, and went outside.

'Sorry, kid, did I wake you?' Jack said blearily.

'No.'

'I'll get Aubrey.'

'It's all right. I can sit up now, if you like. I'm right awake.'

'Okay. You call us if you need us.'

'Yeah.'

Jack stumbled off to the barn. John Evert took a seat in the still-warm chair and pulled the blanket over his legs. His dog had followed him. It stood, staring out into the night, sniffing gently. Clouds had gathered, obscuring the moon.

'What is it?' John Evert asked. The dog came back to him and took a seat in front of him. He could feel its eyes on him in the darkness. 'Possum?' he said. 'Go see.'

The dog padded away from him and bounded off the step. It was gone a while, circling the house, he figured. When it had been noticeably long, he let out a low whistle. There was nothing. He got up from the chair, holding the rifle loose in his hand, and went down the step. The moon was hidden and there was nothing to see, but the patchwork of clouds was shifting slowly, opening small pockets here and there, so he waited until the hidden glow of it brightened and he could make out the sharp angles of the fence line. The light grew steadily and he was able to see the outbuildings and the dark masses of the trees. There was no sign of his dog. He let out another whistle and listened. In return, there came what he thought might have been a distant whine. The moonlight was now bright enough that he felt confident to walk out. He strode some distance away from the house then paused and listened. It seemed strangely quiet – no wind, no insects, nothing. As he stood there, the light began to fail. He looked up to see a heavy bank of cloud moving across the moon again. All at once, he felt very vulnerable so far away from the house, and he turned to walk back in the darkness. As he did so, he could swear something moved in the trees behind him. It was no noise, just a sense of something shifting. He turned about quickly, the rifle tight in his hands.

'Who's there?' he said in a whisper. He waited a full minute, his heart beating thickly in his chest. He did not know why he was so nervous. If he shouted, the men in the barn would surely hear him. He turned back in the direction of the house and began to jog toward it. His footfalls thudded against the sun-baked ground, and they were joined by echoes. Something was running after him. He stopped dead in his tracks and whirled around to face the night. Whatever it was, it was coming at him at speed, its feet beating a tattoo upon the ground. He raised the rifle, although he knew not where to fire. Something passed very close by him, and then something else, almost touching him, the freight of its passage a rush of warm air. He was disoriented, lost, and when his dog barked somewhere out in front of him, he nearly fired at it in sheer terror. To his intense relief, the moon appeared again, and suddenly the scene was laid out in silver for him – his dog, hot on the heels of three deer, which rose in quick succession to take flight, clearing the fence in a black, liquid wave, rippling off across the pasture.

'Jesus,' he said, dropping the rifle from his shoulder. His hands were trembling. When his dog gave up the chase and came trotting back to him, its tongue lolling, he said furiously, 'I nearly shot you, you stupid dog. Get back here.'

The dog dropped its head low and followed him obediently to the stoop, where he sat down and chided himself for his fears. He did not move again, and forbade the dog to do so either. His body was tired from the day's riding but his mind was awake.

He reckoned it had been three hours when he stood up, stretched and went to the barn to wake Aubrey. It smelt thick of sleeping bodies. Aubrey snored rhythmically, his breath heavy with the acidic odour of wine. John Evert shook him gently a few times but the man was like a corpse. He went to Jack and shook him also, but he merely grumbled and turned away with the blanket over his face. John Evert figured he might as well keep going. It must have been about three in the morning – it would be light before too long anyway. He went back to his chair, and his dog thumped its tail on the floor as he settled down again. He tutted at it, still embarrassed at his silly display earlier. The dew was already forming, for the arms of the chair were wet to the touch. He huddled back into the warmth of the blanket and soon his eyes began to feel heavy. He shifted about, trying to get some life back into his tired legs, and crossed them at the ankle.

He must have dozed off because when he jerked awake the moon was out again and he could see mist lying heavy upon the ground to a depth of ten feet or so. It uncoiled in front of him, as though feeling its way along the stoop. Somewhere out there an owl called, and another answered. He felt dreamlike, as though the mist had curled itself into his sleeping nostrils and come to live in him. His dog raised its head and looked out intently at the mist.

'Don't you start again,' he mumbled. The dog let out a long, low whine. 'Stop it! No more deer!' he whispered sharply. The dog made no more noise, but it quivered at his side. He stared out into the swirling grey ahead and then, what seemed a terribly long way off, came the very slow sound of a horse's hoofs, but too slow to be any real horse. He frowned, squinting out into the impenetrable shifting screen ahead. Deep in the grey, it seemed for a moment as though a white streak appeared, but it disappeared just as fast. Then, there it was again, larger now, a white column sailing toward him. He sat up properly, blinked rapidly, frowned and realised, simultaneously, that the hoof beats were much closer together. He shifted forward in his chair and was getting to his feet when, out of the grey mist, careering toward him, came a horse and rider, but not like any he had ever seen. His breath, his heart, actually stopped for a few seconds as a white horse catapulted out of the bank of mist, surmounted by a white rider. It galloped toward him, and just as the strange hoof beats that had been distorted by the mist caught up to match the thundering feet of the horse, the white rider raised one arm up into the air and behind his head. All at the same time, John Evert awoke from his deceptive dream, his legs tangled in the dropped blanket, and understood that it was a real man atop the horse, all painted in white, and that the hand he was bringing back from behind his head held an arrow, which he was fitting into a bow.

John Evert just had time to duck as the arrow sang past his head, and embedded itself with a thump in the wall. The Indian let out a piercing cry that ricocheted between the ranch buildings. John Evert raised his rifle and fired but the white rider flew past the house, the white flag of the horse's tail streaming out behind. At the same moment, a volley of arrows thudded into the house and his dog let out a cry. John Evert reloaded as fast as he could.

'John!' his mother's voice called from the side of the house. She must have been at her bedroom window.

'Get away from the window,' he shouted, as he dug for cartridges in the pouch at his belt.

'Hey!' one of the men yelled from the barn, and John Evert saw the door swing open as Jack hobbled out with his boots half on. He was silhouetted in the lamplight from inside the barn and he was fumbling with his rifle. 'You okay?' he shouted.

John Evert signalled at him with his free hand to be quiet. He beckoned at him but Jack could not see him in the darkness. 'Jack!' John Evert hissed. 'Don't stand out there in the open.' Jack's movements were confused and he half turned as though to go back into the barn. 'No!' said John Evert, but there was a rapid tattoo of hoof beats and, with supernatural speed, another horse burst out of the darkness, its rider a low mound against the horse's withers. It shot between Jack and John Evert and, after it passed, Jack was standing curiously still until, slowly, he collapsed to his knees and fell face down in the dirt.

'Jesus Christ,' John Evert said, his body trembling. A shot rang out from the side of the house as his mother fired and there was a squeal from a horse in the darkness.

'John!' she cried. 'Are you all right?'

'Yeah, I'm fine.' He did not have time to say anything further, for another volley of arrows hailed into his side of the house, the tail of one splicing his cheekbone. 'Ah!' he cried out, more in shock than anything else. Furious and terrified, he reloaded his rifle and fired off another shot into the night. After that, much of it was a blur. Horses flew out of the night and he aimlessly fired shot after shot into the mist and darkness. He reloaded as quick as he could and his mother did the same. He brought down two riders and was reloading when a burning missile flew past him, shattering the window and bursting into greater flames inside the kitchen with a sound like a gasping intake of breath. His mother screamed at the noise.

'*Madre!*' he cried.

'What's happening?'

'Kitchen's on fire. Get out of the house.'

'*Ay . . . coño—*' Her voice was cut off as she fired and an ungodly howl went up as she hit her mark.

Smoke was billowing out of the broken window next to John Evert. The fire within illuminated the whole of the porch and, he realised, himself. A whooshing sound made him instinctively duck again. A small axe thumped into the wall where he had just been standing. He was coughing at the black smoke, his eyes streaming, ears ringing from all the shots he had fired. The barn was on fire, too. Through the ringing, he heard screaming. Running past him in the now bright moonlight went Aubrey. The back of his scalp was missing. Blood poured out of his head – his shirt was black with it. There was an unearthly howling of the Indians, interspersed with the sound of shattering glass.

'Ma! *Madre!*' he roared. 'Get out here.'

'I can't!' she shouted back, letting off another pop of shot. '*El fuego*, it's outside the door.'

'Then get out the—' he fired at a figure that whipped past '—window.'

'John!'

'Ma! Get out the window. Jesus!' He cried out as an arrow plunged into his left shoulder.

'John! What's happened? Are you hurt?'

'Yes. Jesus,' he said again. He was coughing so much from the smoke, he could hardly speak now. 'Ma,' he croaked, 'get out the window. Ma? Ma!' He staggered down off the stoop, the pain in his shoulder knocking him off balance. He was aware of how terribly hot it was by the house now, how bright and orange everything was as the building was consumed by the flames. He was stumbling around the side of the house when he felt the beat in the ground through his feet. He turned around, clumsily raising the rifle to his shoulder with just one hand, but he was not fast enough. The white-painted man, his eyes black and terrible as Hell, his lips stretched open in a rictus grin, thundered toward him. From his forearm, the painted man let drop an axe into his hand so that, as he gained upon John Evert, he held the very end of it. When he reached John Evert, he swung it viciously upward. The axe smashed into his face, and for John Evert everything went black.

3

It took John Evert several minutes to realise that he was neither dead nor blind. He was hot, blistering hot, and all he could see was yellow. He put a hand to his face and felt his eyelids, shut tight and crusty. His head was pounding so hard he did not dare sit up. He felt around the crust of his eyes and began gently to pull his eyelids apart. He cried out, first at the pain, then at the light that scalded his eyes. He put his hand up against the brightness. He could just about see now, in a blurry sort of way, but the edge of his vision was feathered with black spikes. Something had dried hard and crisp around his eyes and nose. He put his fingers into his parched mouth and moistened them before rubbing his eyes. When he looked at them, he found dark brown smeared across them. That was when he understood that he was caked with dried blood.

He let out a sob and sneezed, at which black phlegm flew out of his nose. In dismay, he felt his face again. His lips were fat to the touch, and his nose felt very wrong in some way; he figured it was broken. Finally, the pain in his face and body started to register, and he became frightened. He tried to speak and found he could not. He tried to sit up and found he could not. But just as the sensation of panic threatened to overwhelm him, he heard a voice in his head. He did not recognise it, and all it said was his name, but it was enough to check him, and he lay still. He tried to remember what had happened. He lay there for a long time, breathing through his open mouth. He held up one of his hands and looked at how black it was. Fire. There had been a fire. That would explain the awful stuff coming out of his nose. He could feel something looking at him, and he shifted gently on to his right side, coming face to face with a large crow that was inspecting him hopefully. Looking past it, he saw the gate to one of the pastures, and realised where he was. Something made him stay like that for a long while. He had a terrible feeling about what he might see if he turned the other way. He groaned softly, before rolling on to his belly, wincing at the pain. Carefully, he raised his upper body, with the aid of his forearm, and slowly turned his head toward the house and the devastation that awaited him there.

Where once the house and outbuildings had stood, there were now serene black mounds of charcoal. Constructed entirely of wood, the house had given itself up completely to the flames. The only shape that broke the shimmering heat haze was the metal flue of the stove, which pointed aloft crookedly, like an arthritic finger. Just beyond the remains of the house was the small oak tree, which had also been set alight. It resembled now a black crucifix, for splayed within its branches was the body of a young steer. The scene was so dreadful that he could not stop staring, from one awful end of it to the other.

Eventually, he became aware not only of the sun hammering down upon him, but of his intense thirst. He managed slowly to push himself up into a sitting position, and then shakily got to his feet. His head throbbed viciously and his vision was stabbed with black and gold dots. He took a few wobbly steps in the direction of the house, but then stumbled and veered off lop-sidedly, so that he bypassed the house and headed toward the river. He took the shortest route, but, even so, it took him a long time to get there.

After the bright sunlight, the cool gloom of the woods blinded him; when he reached the river he half fell into it, wading up to his thighs. He scooped handfuls of the water to his mouth, gulping greedily. He drank without pause until his breath gave out. Then he promptly vomited it all back up. He tried three times, taking in just sips, before he could keep it down. His shirt was stuck to his back and shoulders. He knew that if he were to remove it, he would take some skin off, too. In the end, he lay down in the water, and, despite the burning, he managed to peel the shirt off. The whole of his left side was so heavy and numb that it was not until he felt around his upper body that he located the source of all the swelling: an arrowhead lodged in his left shoulder. The shaft must have snapped off when he fell. He knew that it would be best to leave it there for now. After soaking in the water to take the heat out of his body, he felt less lightheaded, and made his way back toward what was left of the house, his wet clothes squelching.

He approached the ruins cautiously. When his feet reached the black edges of the burned remains, he stopped and trembled, reluctant to cross the threshold. When he did so, he could feel the heat of the cooling embers through his wet boot soles. Around the shiny black wood, pieces of glass sparkled in the sun, beautiful against the darkness, like precious stones. Among the wreckage, he found the odd piece of metal. He used his boots to turn over the charred wood, and located a small metal chest and some items from the kitchen. It did not take long to find the body of his dog where it had fallen on the stoop. All the hair was burned off it but its carcass was intact. He knew he had reached the bedroom when he came across the iron bed frame, but even as he looked for the body of his mother, he did not believe that she would be among the remains. She was not.

He ran his shaking hands through his hair several times, then left them atop his head and turned around in a circle. He barely knew what he was doing. As his gaze travelled hopelessly around the place, he saw through the wreckage of the house into the yard, where the trough had been. It was now a pile of cinders, but the metal hand pump for the water still stood. At the sight of this, and the realisation that it had been but the day before that all had been as it once was, he dropped slowly, first to his knees, then his haunches, and wept bitterly. When he could cry no more, he sat and hugged his knees to his chest, rocking back and forward, unable to stop, or think, or stand.

Darkness fell, bringing with it the chill and terrible recollections of the previous night, but he kept his vigil upon the cracked surface of the rock-hard earth. Deep in his heart, he hoped the cold would kill him. All night long, he was racked with shivering. With the pain in his body and the lack of water, his mind uncoupled from reality and rattled loose like a box car down a railroad track. He was visited by strange hallucinations of the white rider as clouds passed over the marbled face of the moon.

When dawn broke, he was disappointed to find himself still alive. He spent all day asleep, in the shade of a tree. By the time the second night fell, he was delirious and his shoulder was hot to the touch.

And yet another day did dawn, and the dawn brought with it something else. Overriding the concentrated buzzing of the flies that were busy feeding and laying eggs in the dead steer, and the bodies of Jack and Aubrey, which lay where they had fallen, was the sight of something trotting toward the ranch. It was no horse for it was too small, its gait too elastic. As it drew near, he knew what it was. The ripe smells emanating from the corpses would have been quite enough to entice it. It trotted all the way to the pasture fence, then skirted along it, its long muzzle low to the ground. At the gate it halted and slowly walked in.

John Evert kept quite still and watched the coyote, which gazed back at him calmly through yellow eyes. He moved slightly, but it showed no alarm at this evidence that he was alive. It looked away from him, to right and left, surveying the wretched scene, then put its nose down to the ground again and padded toward him. It came right up to within three feet of him and stared at him. It was close enough that he could see the individual white hairs around its eyes. Hardly knowing what he did, he slowly extended his hand to it. In turn, it stretched forward its muzzle, its nose twitching at the smell of his fingers. Its pointed ears swivelled back and forth as it carefully stuck out its tongue and, very gently, touched his fingers with it. He stared at it until something seemed to startle it for, with a sudden growl, it drew back its head, turned tail and cantered away. 'Don't . . .' he croaked after it, his own voice strange to his ears. It did not look back.

Real or imagined, the appearance of the animal acted as a spur upon him, reminding him that he, too, was still alive. A short while later, he got to his feet and made his way down to the river again. While he was drinking, he became aware of the presence of something moving in the trees. He was filled with sudden terror, and hid himself behind the widest tree trunk as whatever it was flattened the undergrowth. His fear was greeted by the honking wail of the mule that belonged to the Mexican labourers, of whose existence he had quite forgotten. One look at the jerky creature was enough to tell him what had befallen the Mexicans. Certain that the creature would bolt at the sight of him, he called to it softly. The animal appeared relieved to hear the familiar voice, and trotted raggedly to his side. With shaking hand, he took up the rope of the head collar that it still wore, and led it in the direction of the Mexicans' huts, which lay further downriver.

There was no sign of life, but there were beans and tortilla and dried beef, which he fell upon. He took everything that would be of use, canteens and a saddlebag, and blessed the chance that had given rise to a bridle and a worn-out saddle being hidden under a heap of blankets for mending. There was a broken piece of mirror hanging from a string upon the wall, and he was able to take a look at himself. His nose had been slashed horizontally and was clearly broken; his top lip was badly cut through the left side; he would not have recognised himself. He was not able to get a good look at the arrowhead still buried in his shoulder, but he took with him a knife that had been overlooked. All his thoughts now were of his mother. If she was not in the house, she had been taken by the raiding party, which meant she was still alive. It was this thought that had finally roused him from his helpless state. The only thing to do was set off in pursuit. He knew very well that the most likely outcome was that he would be killed on sight but the thought of any other course of action was impossible. He did consider riding to Anaheim for help but he had lost a lot of time already, and thought it better to follow the trail of the raiders alone. His faint hope was that he might be able to offer himself as some sort of bargaining piece. His exact value as a prize was hazy in his mind, but he would rather find her and be killed than do anything else.

He returned to the house with the mule and looped its rein over a fencepost. He walked to the edge of the cinder remains of his home and looked around one last time. He closed his eyes for a few moments and prayed. He was not at all sure what he was praying for, but when he opened his eyes, a flock of birds took flight from a distant tree, as though the tree's answer had been whispered to the sky, and he took this as a promising sign.

He went to Jack's body, where it still lay, undisturbed, upon the unforgiving earth. He had thought about burying the bodies, but he had hesitated, recalling a half-remembered story about Indians and how they often returned to the scene of a raid, so he left the bodies where they lay. He stood over Jack now, and looked down at the corpse of the man he had liked so much. The sting of loss was surprisingly strong, considering how little he had known him.

Having filled his canteens and buckled down his saddlebag, he led the mule to a boulder and mounted it gingerly, keeping his left arm as still as he could at his side, taking up the reins with his right. He turned the animal's head east and started to ride out in the direction the Indians had clearly taken, for they had made no effort to cover their tracks.

It was hard to maintain his seat at first, for his wounds gave him much pain, but after a few hours numbness fell over him, and he was able to ignore the discomfort. He rode through the verdant pastures that bordered the river, then up over the rocky bluffs that led to the plain. He passed through velvet layers of rust-coloured dust that exploded softly upwards, coating the mule's legs and settling upon his clothes. He had with him only a knife, and a flint and steel, but it was enough to make fire and to dig up tule roots, which he would roast. He had found some prickly pears too. That night, he burned the thorns off in the fire, scraped them clean and split them in two, leaving them face up on a clean piece of cloth he had spread upon the ground. He took off his shirt and put the knife's blade into the heart of the fire and allowed it to get red hot. He opened the canteen that was filled with *aguardiente* and took a couple of long swigs, which made him cough. Then, before he could consider too much what he was doing, he took the knife out of the fire and stuck the red-hot point of it into the weeping wound in his shoulder. He screamed at the pain but dug in deep and, with astonishing accuracy, found the arrowhead. He leaned back upon the knife, feeling the triangular head tear backwards through his flesh toward the surface, but before it reached its point of entry, he fainted from the pain.

When he came around, he was lying on his back and the mule was breathing gently upon his cheek. As though reassured that he was still alive, it walked past his head into the darkness beyond the firelight, and continued to crop the grass there. He felt crazy for what he was doing, but there was a vicious pleasure in the pain and the sensation that he was doing something. He felt disconnected from himself, as though he were merely a spectator, hovering above, watching. He returned the knife to the fire until he was sure all the dirt had burned off, then shut his watering eyes as he stuck it, shallower this time, into his shoulder, and got the arrowhead half out. Panting, he pulled on the tiny bit of protruding shaft with his fingers and, eventually, the bloody thing fell into the fire with a hiss. He poured a good slosh of *aguardiente* into the wound, which stung like hell, then took up half of a prickly pear and bound it face-down to the wound. With that, he collapsed on to his back and fell unconscious.

The next morning, he awoke in pain, but it was a cleaner pain of torn muscles and blood, rather than swelling infection. His head felt clearer and he was able to take note of his surroundings. There was no longer an obvious trail to follow, but he figured that if he continued riding east he would eventually encounter something that would give him a sign as to the route he should follow. The vague notion of his mission had solidified into something more real, and had become more positive: he decided that if he, too, were captured he would stand the best chance of being reunited with his mother. That was his only goal.

As he rode slowly east the landscape hardened and crystallised. He left behind the fertile ground that was softened by the life-giving presence of water, and entered a land of wind and desert, where only snakes and birds survived.

After two days of riding, he and the mule were making their way through tall, sandstone cliffs, the wind having carved numerous tunnels and narrow crevasses out of the soft rock. At noon, they reached a natural crossroads. There were two forks ahead, each sheer-walled. John Evert stood up in his stirrups and looked down each high-walled crevasse, then at either side of his saddle: one canteen was empty; the other half full. He figured he should be all right, provided he found water soon, but he had no way of knowing how far the crevasses ran, and, once he was in them, there might be no turning back. The only alternative was to loop back and ride around the place, but that did not provide any guarantee of finding water any sooner. He decided to ride the mule into the entrance of each to see what it would do.

In the first ravine, it simply ambled on when he took his leg away from its side. In the second, it turned awkwardly, reluctant to go forward. He took it back to the first crevasse, hesitated for a moment, then pushed it on gently. The gulley swallowed them in a matter of seconds, so that when he turned to look behind him, all that met his gaze was a wall of solid orange sand. The path looped, sinuous, through the rock, at places so narrow that his stirrups scraped against the walls. Eventually, it widened but just as he thought the ground was rising, it dropped again, into a rabbit warren of crisscrossed paths. He just rode on in the same direction. When dusk fell, he stopped and made a fire with kindling he had gathered on the ride. He tethered the mule's reins to his ankle for the night, lest it wander off down one of the paths. The wind got up and made mournful music along the pipes of the tunnels. He shivered in his sleep and longed for the morning.

He awoke at dawn, cold and disoriented. His stomach fluttered and a bitter taste filled his mouth. Before the nausea could rise and overpower him, he mounted the mule and rode on. In one clearing there were clumps of grass; the mule made eagerly for them, tearing up the blades with blunt ripping sounds. He allowed it its head, grateful for the opportunity for the animal to eat, and also at this sign that somewhere, deep down, there was water. It was dusty in the tunnels, and with each breath he took, his nose and throat felt more and more parched. He resisted taking a drink from the canteen as long as he could, but eventually he had to, for his tongue was so swollen he was having trouble breathing.

Later that day, he ran into a solid wall of rock. He and the mule looked at it and he could swear he felt the animal's shoulders drop. The only option was to retrace their steps and take another parallel path. This they did, but any sense of an improved position was short-lived. He was aware they were being pushed west and the path never did seem to turn east again.

By the next day, his water was finished and, once or twice, a feeling of heat flowered across his breast. He knew what it was: it was fear. He looked down at the dark ridge of cropped hair that ran down the back of the mule's narrow neck and said, 'I'm sorry, boy. We shouldn't have come in here. We shouldn't have come in here at all.'

The mule was in a better state than he was as it was able to scrounge the odd blade of grass here and there, while his tule roots were all gone, and he knew that hope was going too. He made camp that night, half delirious from the lack of water. The mule, also exhausted, lay down. Unable to gather the strength to build a fire, he lay next to it, his body pressed to its leathery hide for warmth.

His head, when he woke the next day, throbbed violently. The light around him was flat and white as bone. The mule got to its feet as he did and when he stood in front of it, it leaned into him. He patted either side of its neck and let it rest its long forehead against his chest. He knew what he had to do and it made him sick. 'Goddammit,' he said quietly into the dusty fur of the mule's head. Then he put a hand under its muzzle and raised its head up. The animal looked him in the eye. He put one arm under its neck, so that it rested its head on his shoulder. With his free hand, he took the knife from his belt. The mule stood perfectly still as he whispered soft nothings to it, its liquid brown eye quite calm as he plunged his knife into its neck. Its breath was sweet and grassy in his face. John Evert wept as he felt the animal's blood flow hot over his hands. Truly he hated himself in that moment. The mule rested the great weight of its square head upon his shoulder as he put his mouth to the wound in its neck and quenched his thirst and hunger. He filled his canteens with the animal's blood. Not until he was finished did the mule sink down to its knees and breathe its last in his arms. He held its head a long time, and stroked its soft muzzle until he was sure it felt no more pain.

He wept as he walked away from the body of the mule, but on the back of those blood-filled canteens he was able to make his way out of the tunnels on foot. He was lucky, for he ran into two rancheros on the trail of some lost steers just beyond the tunnels, one of whom caught him as he collapsed, gibbering nonsense.

4

After a life lived entirely on the land, the thing that most struck and unsettled John Evert about Los Angeles was the noise. His ears, accustomed to the harmony of wind, rain, birdsong and but one voice, were now assaulted by the thunder of wagon wheels thudding into sun-baked potholes, the jarring ring of a black-smith's hammer, and a multitude of voices that chattered, shouted, cursed and sang all hours of the day. He found it deafening. There were moments in which he had to place his fingers in his ears simply to hear the rhythm of his own breath, to still the beating of his frightened heart.

Los Angeles was both perplexing and disturbing to him, and for good reason: in the year 1860, there were more desperadoes in Los Angeles than anywhere else. All the unsavoury characters that had been driven from the gold fields once the money ran out took refuge there; welcoming its proximity to Mexican soil, they used it as a stage upon which to settle differences with a knife or a revolver.

To John Evert's untutored eye, the town itself consisted of rows of one-storey adobe houses and dusty streets, while around a plaza stood the church and a few important buildings. One structure that stood out above the rest was a two-storey, flat-roofed adobe, with a corral to its rear and a large Spanish portal above the door. It was named the Bella Union and boasted rooms for guests. The clientele consisted of rancheros, each with a pair of Colts swinging at their rear and a bowie knife, and, today, John Evert.

He studied the men around him, and thought of the two rancheros who had rescued him in the desert and taken him to the house of a priest, who had nursed him back to health in an isolated village. At John Evert's request, he had been moved on to Los Angeles, and entrusted to the pastoral care of the Mission fathers there. John Evert knew how lucky he had been. The wounds to his face had begun to heal, but his broken nose had been reset too late, and would never be straight again. He would bear a scar to his mouth, too, the tightening of the healing skin tilting up the left side of his top lip. The swelling about his eyes had subsided, but still dark circles underscored them.

It had now been approximately one month since the raid upon the ranch, and the reason for his visit to the Bella Union was that he sought the marshal. The Mission fathers had done all they could for him; his plan now was to gather his wits, and all the funds at his disposal, to mount a search for his mother; there was yet hope, and if his upbringing had taught him anything, it was that hope must be pursued at all costs.

While lost in thought, his gaze had dropped hazily to the earthen floor, but now it came back into focus. He looked up to the bar, where a grim bartender presided, wearing an old military overcoat, a red hat and open-legged Mexican trousers with jingling buttons down the seams.

'Excuse me,' John Evert said. 'Can I go up on the veranda if I want to look for someone?'

The barman tossed his head in assent. John Evert took the uneven stairs and opened the door on to the railed veranda, which commanded a decent view of the main street. The traffic below consisted of covered wagons drawn by oxen, and spirited horses, their riders wholly unconcerned at the danger their steeds posed to pedestrians as they pranced sideways and kicked out. It was a busy river of many cross-flowing currents: a woman in a bonnet watched carefully for two girls at her side; packs of caballeros cantered along, in suits that must have cost five hundred dollars apiece. It seemed to John Evert that there was a lot of money swilling about in Los Angeles, and a lot of activity, although to what end he could not say.

He would not be able to tell the marshal from any other man

upon the street, but he would certainly recognise his horse, and, after an hour or so, he made out that particularly fine example of horseflesh, loping athletically down the street as its rider gave it a long rein, sitting loose in the saddle. John Evert descended the stairs, jogged off the front step and trotted awkwardly alongside the red horse and rider. 'Excuse me, Marshal.'

The man squinted down at him, allowing his horse to continue walking. 'Yes.'

'We, uh, we met . . .'

'Can't say that I remember,' the marshal admitted, when John Evert went no further.

'You came to my ranch to warn me and my . . .' stumbling over the word, he found it easier simply to remove his hat and reveal the mess of his face '. . . came to warn us. The name's . . .'

The man sat back and his horse halted abruptly. 'Burn. Of course I remember you, but it was reported that you and your mother were missing. In truth, I expected dead. What in Hell's name happened to you?' he asked, studying John Evert's face. John Evert opened his mouth to speak, but nothing came out.

After his rescue from the desert, when he had first come round he had been unable to say a word. As he had drifted in and out of consciousness, he had been aware of bright white light upon whitewashed walls, and the rhythmic sweep of a broom upon an earthen floor. Wondering where he was, he had overheard the priest and the women who cared for him discussing whether he was dumb. 'No, it's the shock, I think,' the priest had said, and John Evert had experienced a moment of pique, convinced as he was then that his silence was because he *chose* not to speak. Only later did it become apparent to him that that was not the case, which frightened him.

'I don't think he remembers what happened.' One of the women had sighed, while John Evert had lain there, eyes closed as the breeze moved through the fine net curtain that encircled the bed like a veil, thinking he did, he did remember – he remembered it all.

'Are you all right, son?' the marshal prompted.

To John Evert's embarrassment, he could not yet respond. He looked up helplessly at the man, who dismounted and put a hand upon his shoulder. 'Here. You come with me and you can tell me what's gone on.'

It was clear from the moment they entered the marshal's office that matters were in disarray: the desk was piled up willy-nilly with yellowed, dog-eared papers. The marshal picked up a chair by its back and gestured at John Evert to take a seat. As he walked around behind his desk there was a metallic chime as his boot connected with something stray upon the floor. He cursed under his breath as he kicked it away. 'Whole place has been turned upside down of late. I lost my deputy who kept it all in order, can't find a damn thing. Now, you go right ahead. Take your time.'

John Evert managed to collect himself and, haltingly, relayed the details of that night. He sat very upright in his chair, his hands squeezing tight his thighs, and found that the concentration required enabled him to recount events well enough. Once he had finished, the marshal considered and sucked his teeth. 'Why didn't you ride to Phineas Gunn for aid?'

'He's the last person I would go to for help,' John Evert replied, noticing the flicker of the marshal's brow at this.

'Well, he's the one who came to me to report you and your mother missing. Says he went to check on his men and found them dead, the place burned and you and your mother gone. What was your plan in pursuing the raiders?'

'I thought I could offer myself as a . . . If I was alone, I figured they might take me, too. If I'd gone with others, I guessed there'd just be a fight.'

'Well, that's not wrong,' the marshal said, 'but I do wish you'd come to me sooner. Phineas Gunn didn't find out what had happened till three days later. He gathered up a posse of his men and they set off after you but they lost your tracks. And by now, well, by now you realise the amount of ground that's been put between us and those raiders? They could be anywhere.'

'I know it,' John Evert said dolefully. 'What'll I do?'

'There's not a great deal I can do for you. Whole town's waiting on the arrival of troops from Fort Calder. Till they arrive it's all we can do to keep the peace, what with Arcadia Alley overflowing with unsavouries and Ricardo Urives loose somewhere.'

'Arcadia Alley?' John Evert echoed, but the marshal gave no answer for he was deep in thought. 'How long till the troops get here?' he asked.

'Mail train brought a message yesterday: about a fortnight. I'll be honest with you, though, I can't say for sure they'll go after those raiders straight neither. They're here to gain the peace first. When they'll be able to go out looking for those lost persons, I don't know.'

John Evert and the marshal surveyed each other unhappily. 'Have you people here?' the marshal asked. 'Family in town?'

'I got somewhere to stay.'

The marshal stood, and extended his hand to him, making clear the interview was over. Desperate for this not to be the case, John Evert blurted out, 'Can I come by for news?'

'Yes, but I'll plain speak with you. You need to prepare yourself for there being none.'

John Evert nodded vaguely, touched the brim of his hat and drifted out into the sand-choked thoroughfare. Four Spaniards done up in their finery cantered abreast down the street. John Evert did not move as they headed toward him. The two centre mounts divided to pass either side of him, and he was caught in a rich eddy of horseflesh and cigar smoke. Thoughts fluttered dimly about his head. He was sensible to the fact that speed was of the essence. He could not wait for the soldiers if they were to be so long in arriving. A half-formed thought led him onward. After a few hundred yards, he paused next to a brown man frying nuts at the roadside. 'Do you know Arcadia Alley?' he asked.

'*Ah, ahi.*' The man gestured.

John Evert negotiated his way down to the narrow neck of the alley. There emanated from the mouth of it the stench of putrescence. He hesitated a moment, then steeled himself and entered the place. After no more than ten steps, he found himself in full-blown pandemonium.

There were several bands playing music of the Mexican-Indian kind, inharmonious. A great squawking went up to his left, and red-gold feathers floated up into the air from the cockfight that was taking place beyond a greasy wall of shoulders. John Evert could smell all sorts of things cooking over the many small open fires that lined the street. The distant scream of a horse was met with the crack of a whip. Several different languages were being spoken by the men and women that jostled past him. Men squatted around in circles, betting. A shot rang out somewhere far ahead. John Evert wandered down the narrow passageway in a state of anxiety and revulsion. He happened to glance inside a dark doorway as he passed, then retraced his steps to look inside once more. The tables inside were covered with green cloth, and in front of the men seated at the tables were heaps of gold nuggets. No one noticed him, so he stood quietly just inside the door, his back to the wall, and watched.

Betting was high. A ranchero, with an immense pile of gold afront of him, nonchalantly smoked his *cigarrito* and bet twenty slugs on the turn, the losing of which produced no discernible unease. Suddenly, at the back of the room, there was the bang of a chair overturned and shouts. A man drew a knife, and the place erupted into feral chaos. John Evert backed hastily out of the door, sweat prickling all over him. He hurriedly retraced his steps to Main Street, where he caught his breath in the shade of a general mercantile store.

He figured that, before he approached any of the characters residing in that place, he had better learn more about the way things in Los Angeles worked, and exactly how much money he had to his name. He walked down Main Street until he found the painted door plaque of Mr Hector Featherstone, Attorney at Law. He knocked. Receiving no response, he opened the door for himself, closed it behind him and stood in a dim room, sheltered from the rumble of traffic without. He removed his hat, and wiped his forehead. His shoulder wound throbbed dully and his bones ached. He longed to sit down, but instead he looked about the room. There was a very large bookcase, every shelf of which was filled not with any old books but with the tallest, fattest tomes he had ever seen. He loved books. He took a few steps toward them and read the gold lettering that gleamed dully against one green leather spine. He stepped nearer, his head on one side, but at that moment a door at the back of the room opened and a small man catapulted through it, a sheaf of papers clutched to his chest. Around his head, he wore a green eyeshade, which cast a pea-green tinge upon his face.

'Well, good day,' he said, in a high chirrup that sounded like nothing more than the call of a startled bird. 'Did you ring the bell, sir? I apologise, I did not hear.'

He trotted toward the desk and deposited his bundle of documents. A long stretch of thin, pink ribbon was wound around his fine wrist. The other documents upon his desk were all tied with the same ribbon. 'Please, take a seat. And how may I assist you?'

'Abraham,' a quiet voice from the further room murmured. 'The door.'

'Oh, yes, sir,' the little man said, as he fluttered across the room and drew it closed. He flew back to John Evert. 'A seat, a seat, please.' He gestured at a chair, into which John Evert gratefully sank. 'Would you do me the honour of relaying the matter upon which we may be of assistance?'

John Evert studied the slight man with some suspicion. He felt pretty sure that this high-pitched speech pertained to some joke at his expense, but as the man gazed at him attentively he decided to trust that perhaps this was not the case.

'My name is John Evert Burn,' he said. 'I come on behalf of my mother, Mrs John Burn.'

The man's mouth formed a perfect circle. He swallowed and

said gently, 'We recently heard that you and your dear mother were presumed dead. What a great relief that we were mistaken . . . Your mother also, she is . . .?'

'She has been kidnapped,' John Evert said dully.

The man stared at him in ill-disguised horror. 'I think it would be best if we sought the advice of Mr Featherstone,' he said. John Evert nodded. 'If you would give me one moment,' he added. He vanished through the door. A few moments later, he opened it wide, making a sweeping gesture to indicate that John Evert should enter.

A much younger man than John Evert had expected was standing behind the desk. He was of slender figure and grave mien, with a cleft chin and dark, high-arched eyebrows that gave him an air of anticipation. He came around the desk and offered John Evert his hand.

'I am Hector Featherstone,' he said, in a clipped, formal tone that was strange to John Evert. 'I am most terribly sorry to hear of what has happened, and greatly relieved that what we heard of you proves not, in fact, to be the case.'

He returned to his desk and they sat across from each other without a word. John Evert realised that the man was waiting for him to speak. He cleared his throat. 'I have come to find out what money there is to mount a rescue party.'

Featherstone did not break his gaze. 'You have been to the marshal, I take it?'

'Yessir. He is awaiting cavalry and I know that will be too long. My mother was taken a month ago. I cannot afford to lose another day.'

Featherstone's face fell. 'Only now you come in search of assistance?'

'The ranch was burned to the ground. I was beaten,' John Evert gestured at his face. 'I gave chase but did not . . . I was defeated by my injuries.'

Featherstone nodded, then said evenly, 'How do you expect a rescue party to pick up a trail that is four weeks cold?'

'I know the direction they headed. I can lead a party there, and then . . . Then they'd have to spread out,' he faltered.

'I see,' Featherstone said, sitting back in his chair, making a temple of his fingers and pressing them to his mouth, his brow furrowed. John Evert waited for him to speak but he did not. He took note of the gold watch chain that hung in a shallow curve across the man's waistcoat. He looked very young to be a lawyer. As though reading his thoughts, Featherstone said, 'You wonder how I find myself here?'

John Evert twitched at being caught out, but Featherstone was unperturbed. 'As you may be able to hear from my accent, I am an Englishman,' he said. 'I was called to the bar, in London, when I was nineteen. I was a member of Lincoln's Inn, and practised there as a barrister for three years before I took the passage here.'

'Why'd you do that?' John Evert asked, sensing something amiss. A barrister was a fine thing to be; he knew that from what his mother had told him. This man was not the usual type to find his way west.

Featherstone paused thoughtfully before replying, and John Evert was aware of having surprised him. 'A good question,' Featherstone said. 'My reason for departing was that I was disbarred for an error of judgement.'

From Abraham's desk, outside the room, came a strangled cry, as of a songbird having its neck wrung.

'Abraham,' Featherstone called mildly through the open door, 'would you look up the Burn file? My clerk is a little eccentric,' Featherstone said, in response to John Evert's glance. 'He also happens to be the most trustworthy man I know.'

Abraham reappeared and placed a bundle upon the desk.

'I am speaking from memory,' Featherstone said, 'but I believe the capital in your mother's account was not extensive. It should be enough to rebuild the ranch house.'

'And to mount a search party?'

Featherstone sat back in his chair and again made a temple of his elegant fingers. 'I would urge you to await the soldiers who are *en route*.'

'What about a bounty? I went to Arcadia Alley to see—'

Featherstone took his fingers away from his lips, and said, in astonishment, '*You* went to Arcadia Alley? That singularly misnamed locale. Are you aware that no officer of the law would attempt an arrest in Arcadia Alley? That no law-abiding man enters there?'

John Evert looked at his feet. Fortunately, they were interrupted by Abraham again. 'Mr Featherstone, sir, you *must* leave for the court now or you will be late.'

'Indeed, Abraham. Bring those papers upon your desk.'

John Evert watched Featherstone as he gathered his things, experiencing a sense of the rug being pulled slowly from under his feet. This crisp Englishman radiated a reassuring calm, and the time John Evert had spent in that room, talking to him, was pretty much the first distraction he had had from the ever-present sliding sense of despair he felt at his circumstance. He found himself blurting out, 'Can I come with you?'

Featherstone, evidently surprised, studied him briefly, straightened the sleeves of his coat, and replied, 'I don't see why not. There is a public gallery. Abraham will send you in the right direction.'

John Evert took his leave. He paused at the door to put on his hat. As he did so, he overheard the voice of the clerk, 'A curious boy.'

'Yes,' Featherstone replied. 'I do not know what we may do exactly, but we must do everything we can.' Then he added, in exasperation, 'Abraham! The papers?'

'Yes, sir, yes. I shall have them *directly*.'

5

The courthouse was easy to find, even for a stranger to the town. The front was thronged with people, all intent upon entering the public gallery. The clerk of the court attempted half-heartedly to encourage a wagon to move on from the entrance, but soon gave up, for people simply poured in around either side of the obstacle. The horse, still harnessed, rested one hind leg upon its toe and slept, swishing its tail at a bothersome fly. John Evert joined the crowd and, with some nervousness at the proximity to his fellow man, squeezed inside.

After the bright sunlight, it was dark and very hot inside. The tiny panes of the latticed windows were old, stained yellow from years of tobacco smoke. The light falling through them cast small amber diamonds upon the floor. All the seats were taken, and most of the company were on their feet. A long table stood beyond the waist-high wooden rail that held the people back, with chairs arranged at one side, facing away from the gallery. Beyond that was an expanse of empty floor and, at the rear of the room, a sort of pulpit. To the right of this, a chair was raised on a small dais. Along the right-hand side of the room, there were two rows of six chairs. The space was loud with chatter, which mingled with the smoke from countless pipes and cigars.

Five suited men entered through a side door, made their way to the table at the front of the room and took their seats. One was Hector Featherstone. The men spoke softly among themselves, Hector turning in his chair and smiling at something one of the others said, holding his hands out to either side in a supplicatory gesture. He must have said something funny for one man stifled a laugh. The clerk entered and called for silence. All stood as the judge entered and seated himself in the pulpit. His stiff shirt front was spotless white; against it a glossy black neck tie hinted at flamboyance.

John Evert learned from his neighbour's conversation that 'Old Horse Face', Judge Ogier, was presiding, and as the judge surveyed the room, turning his elongated face this way and that, he did resemble a horse.

'May we have the jury?' he said to the clerk. From the side door, twelve men, informally dressed, entered. They took seats in the two rows of chairs. The judge watched them benignly until they were settled. 'Bring them in,' he said to the clerk.

Three men were led in. Each wore manacles. The courtroom filled with the sounds of murmuring as everyone craned to get a better look at the prisoners.

'Felipe Read,' said the judge.

A man was led forward to the chair upon the dais. Dark-skinned, his long black hair was tied back at the nape of his neck. John Evert had been eavesdropping on his neighbours, and learned that the case involved horse-rustling and incidental murder, and had been going on for several days. One defendant had taken the stand the day before; now it was the turn of the other two.

'Mr Lyne,' said the judge, settling his glasses upon his nose, 'would you like to proceed?'

One of the men sitting near Hector got to his feet and walked around the table. He was slight of build, with a small head and a dogged expression. 'Mr Read,' he said, 'is it true that you were in the employment of Mr Jennings at a ranch in San Fernando but had been fired for drunkenness?'

'Yes.'

'How long ago?'

Read paused. 'Some time in June.'

'We both know this is not the case. You have not been in employment since May.'

'If you say so, sir. I don't know the dates.'

'How had you been supporting yourself since then, some three months?'

'Buying and selling.'

'Buying and selling of stolen objects.'

'No, sir.'

'What were you doing in San Fernando?'

'Looking for work.'

'And you looked for work at the Thompson ranch, and were declined?'

'Yes, sir.'

'Did Mr Thompson give you a reason for not offering you work?'

'He said he didn't employ half-breeds.'

Lyne continued, 'I put it to you that, having had a good look at the ranch, you assessed the animals there, and having been refused work, you decided to steal some of those horses and engaged the help of your fellow men to do so.'

'No, sir. I never saw these men before that day in the riverbed,' Read replied.

'How do you explain your presence there?' Lyne asked, with a hint of exasperation. 'What were you doing in a riverbed thirty miles from the nearest habitation, at the scene where fifty horses were found, in the possession of a band, which includes the men standing beside you?'

'We were travelling on the same road.'

'So, simply by accident, you happened to be at the scene?'

'Not by accident.'

'Ah, so you were there by rendezvous?'

'No. I was there for a wolf.'

'A wolf?' Lyne repeated with disbelief.

'Yes. That's one of the things I sell. Skins. I had a trap there I went to check.'

'And was there a wolf in it? Were you able to produce a dead animal as proof of a reason for your presence there?'

'No. The trap was empty.'

'So we have nothing more than your word to go on,' Lyne said. 'No more questions.'

Hector got to his feet and walked forward, his step lithe. He looked at the floor as he walked, as though mulling something over.

'Mr Read,' he said. 'Would you tell me about your father?'

Judge Ogier raised his eyes from the papers in front of him. 'Mr Featherstone, I trust this diversion will return swiftly to the matter in hand?'

'Of course.' Hector nodded. 'Mr Read, where was your father from?'

'Edinburgh.'

'He was a Scotsman. And your mother?'

'She was a Seneca,' Read said.

At the mention of Indian blood, John Evert's eyes darted to the man's face, reassessing the swarthy skin. A coal-black lump of anger glowed into life in his belly and his hands trembled as images from the night of the raid crowded into his mind's eye. He was not alone in his suspicion: various whisperings around the room attested to the fact that the audience assumed the half-Indian Read was guilty: what more questioning was needed? John Evert pushed away the horrible memories and dragged his attention back to the scene in front of him.

He noticed that as Hector spoke he kept his right hand behind him. He curled his fingers upward, and in this way was able to fiddle, unseen, with the cuff of his coat sleeve. It was a strange tic, and John Evert considered whether his air of perfect calm belied something less certain beneath. The shadow of a memory skittered across his mind, of a lesson from his mother during a card game, in which she instructed him not to look at the eyes of his opponent to learn his thoughts but to watch the other's hands.

Hector had moved on. 'Who discovered you and the others in the riverbed?'

'Zapatero,' Read replied. 'The chief of the Tejons.'

'What did he do when he came across you, the other men and the horses?'

'Stripped us all naked, tied us up, whipped us, then turned us loose to make the best of it we could.'

The courtroom blew up, and the judge allowed them a moment of revelry before bringing his gavel down.

'Why? Why did he do this?' Hector asked, his left hand outstretched before him, fingers splayed in an imploring gesture.

'I believe he recognised the Thompson brand on the horses.'

'And what did he do with the horses he had found miles away from their ranch? Surely, when they had been stolen by other white men, when there was no danger of being accused of theft himself, he simply rounded them up and drove them off to his lands.'

'No sir. He and his people took them back to the Thompson ranch.'

Hector glanced at Lyne, then said, 'Mr Read, you tell us you are a trapper?'

'Yes.'

'You have sold pelts this year?'

'Yes, sir.'

'And we can prove you sold them because the owners of general stores from here to San Fernando have been buying them from you.'

Lyne got to his feet. 'Objection,' he said. 'How? Are we to drag Mr Read up and down the country to every general-store owner to ask if they recognise him?'

'No, no,' Hector said, with barely concealed pleasure. 'Mr Read, do the general-store owners know you as Mr Read?'

'No, sir. They call me Donehogawa.'

'And what does that mean in Seneca?'

'"He who guards the gate of sunset".'

There was a ripple of displeasure in the public gallery. John Evert overheard whisperings of 'blasphemy' and 'dirty savage'.

'And how does this help us?' Lyne demanded. 'We have a man with two names but the fact remains he is just an Indian.'

'Mr Read,' said Hector, 'would you be so good as to show us your chest?'

'There are ladies present!' Lyne protested.

'But he is *just an Indian*,' observed Hector softly, amused. 'It is not as though I ask *you* to reveal yourself, Mr Lyne.'

'Your Honour!' beseeched Lyne.

The judge ruminated, chewed the inside of his cheek. 'Defence, approach the bench,' he said. He and Hector were involved in some whispering, Hector all the while clasping and unclasping his right coat sleeve. Eventually, Ogier declared, 'The defendant will open three buttons of his shirt.'

There was a furore in the public gallery. Somewhere at the back, a woman fainted. No one went to her aid.

Ogier waved his hand at the clerk, who approached Read and spoke to him. Read opened three buttons of his shirt and spread it wide. Upon his chest there was a large, dark, almost perfect circle. Everyone craned to get a look.

'Is it a tattoo?' asked the judge.

'No, sir. I was born with it.'

'Clerk.' The judge waved him forward. The clerk inspected the thing, even rubbing it tentatively with one finger, to the delight of the gallery.

'It is a birthmark, sir.' He gave his verdict.

'So, he has a birthmark,' said Lyne. 'What does this signify?'

Hector opened the file upon his desk. 'I have here sworn testimonies from general-store owners from Los Angeles to San Fernando, all attesting to the fact that every year they purchase pelts from the Indian gentleman going by the name of Donehogawa, whom they have known for at least a decade. This year, they have purchased the pelts of three wolves, eight grey foxes, fourteen rabbits . . .'

'Meaning?' demanded Lyne.

'That Mr Read is not a horse thief, that he has been earning his living perfectly well and that he had a valid reason for being in that riverbed.'

'And how did you ascertain this information?' asked the judge.

'My clerk rode to each of the stores. I have all the notes to provide you with—'

'No, please.' The judge sighed. 'No more, I beg you, Mr Featherstone.'

Some of the spectators around John Evert chuckled. 'That there Featherstone,' someone said, 'he's a thing to watch, perfooms 'em flowers and paints 'em lilies, and drives Ol' Horse Face half crazy with his digressions.'

'Mr Lyne, any more questions?' exhaled the judge, pushing his spectacles up to his brow.

'No more questions,' Lyne replied. Read was allowed to re-join the other defendants.

'Romualdo Pacheco,' called the clerk. Another man took the stand.

Pacheco spent far less time there. Without the benefit of Hector's attention, and under cross-examination by Lyne and two of the other lawyers, he swiftly gave up and confessed to rustling and murder. The jury listened to the evidence, was advised by Judge Ogier to do its duty, and retired. No one left the public gallery, preferring to discuss the trial at their leisure. The jury took less than an hour to return its verdicts.

'Reyes Cajero . . . guilty. Felipe Read . . . not guilty. Romualdo Pacheco . . . guilty.'

John Evert watched Hector's back, and saw a twitch in the slim shoulders at the verdict. When Hector turned his face in profile to talk to one of his colleagues, his taut, arched brow had relaxed slightly, and John Evert thought this verdict meant a lot to him.

Judge Ogier nodded toward the condemned men. 'I move that Romualdo Pacheco and Reyes Cajero be taken to the hill and hanged by the neck until they are dead. May God have mercy on your souls.'

With that, he tapped his gavel once, laid it down and stood. The court rose with him, maintaining silence until he retired, at which point the room burst into noise and the audience began to filter out of the room. John Evert was one of the last to leave.

He walked out into the bright light and blinked. He would not follow the crowd down Main Street. He wanted to be alone and quiet. He was confused by all he had heard and seen. His feelings had been with the public gallery: that Read was half Indian had convinced him of the man's guilt. For John Evert, every Indian that walked the earth was now a raider. He wondered why Hector Featherstone, that quick and able man, had fought so hard to disprove it.

In the heat of the street, he was suddenly transported to a past winter of biblical rain, when the ranch had seemed in danger of going under, such was the weight of mud and water that spewed across the ground, threatening to submerge the steps of the house. He and his mother had seemed to live in their oilskins as they fought to prevent the cattle becoming stranded upon the desperate islands the flood made of their land. One rough night, in the pale yellow light of the oil lamps, John Evert had struggled to affix a heavy rope across his shoulder before awkwardly throwing open the door to step into the roaring night. He had screamed at the sight that met him. In the gaping doorway, framed in darkness and venomous rain, stood a grey and terrible man, his hair so long and thick it had matted with his beard in a nest of swarming grey serpents. John Evert had fallen backwards, into the arms of his mother, who had thrust him behind her. The old man, for he was very old, had taken two heavy steps inside, bringing with him a dreadful stench that John Evert would never forget. Then his knees had buckled and he had fallen to the floor. John Evert's mother had barked at him to heat water and find bandages, as she felt the old man's clothes and began to pull them from his body, in her urgency tearing a piece of sackcloth that covered his shoulders. John Evert had stood by, appalled, as she stripped the filthy creature naked and examined him for wounds. Finding none, she began to rub his skin with scalding hot towels, discarding filthy, blackened cloths into a pile in the corner, slapping the old man's freezing skin to bring back the circulation. She swaddled the wretch in clothes and blankets, then forced him up into a sitting position, so that he leaned half upon her chest as she dribbled warm broth into his mouth. Finally, after two hours, she had let him rest. As the creature snored upon the floor by the stove, John Evert, who had been no more than ten at the time, had made known his disgust. She had whirled around and caught him by the chin. 'Don't you ever refuse aid to a man in need,' she hissed. 'We are all God's creatures.' With that, she had pushed him away.

In the morning, there had been no sign of the old man in the house, and they had opened the door to find the storm had cleared. The sunlight upon the water all about the ranch house was so brilliant to the eye that they could not look at it. Through his shading fingertips, John Evert could make out no land bridge to the house. The man must have waded away. When they returned inside, his mother had found a perfect white oblong stone upon her table. She held it in her hand and looked out of the window thoughtfully. 'Who was he?' John Evert had asked.

'Jonah,' she had replied, with a faint smile.

The memory of her pierced John Evert with grief and he shook his head vigorously to clear it, then trailed off down the street.

6

'May I ask what you require the money for, Mr Burn?' Hector Featherstone said evenly. They were back in Hector's office, Hector seated behind his desk, John Evert standing, hoping to depart the room with all haste. John Evert had not considered that he might be asked this. He twisted his hat brim around in his hands.

'I plan to offer a bounty and rally a party of men.'

'You cannot be serious. Mount a rescue party? To where? The country is vast. A man could wander for years without hope of discovering them. The marshal tells me that Phineas Gunn and his men lost the trail when they were but days behind. Yet you expect to pick it up now, weeks later?'

'There must be a chance,' John Evert said.

'In the event that you located the party, what then? There could be fifty Indians to contend with. Even the cavalry would hesitate.'

'We would take them by stealth.' John Evert had read this line in a book.

Hector pressed his fingertips against his temples. 'And this *we*. Of whom do you speak?'

'The men I'll raise to assist me.'

'Ah, yes, the men you will raise from Arcadia Alley. You would not be five miles out of Los Angeles before those men would shoot you and take your money faster than they would a drink.'

John Evert gazed at Hector plaintively.

'Mr Burn. John Evert,' Hector said gently, 'such terrible things happen. It is a risk we all take, living in a place such as this. We lead an exaggerated life. Some men make their fortune, others lose everything they have. You must be aware that women and girls have been taken before. They are not . . . They are not seen again.'

'What happens to them?' John Evert asked.

'They are taken as wives. They become a part of the—'

'You don't know my ma,' John Evert interrupted, his voice shaking with anger. 'She wouldn't—'

'Actually,' Hector cut in, 'I do know her. If she were to attempt to escape, if she made things too difficult, they would kill her.'

'But she does.' John Evert's voice cracked. 'She does make things too difficult.'

'I don't believe she will on this occasion. Your mother is a very clever woman. She is also a survivor. She will survive, but you will have to let go of the search. Let her find you.'

'No,' John Evert whispered. 'Give me the money and I'll do it alone.'

Hector sighed, and used his right hand as a prop upon which to rest his brow as he studied the file in front of him. John Evert's gaze rested upon the crown of Hector's glossy head as he spoke from beneath the hand that seemed to shelter his eyes, as though from an impending blow.

'I regret to inform you that the capital remaining is only enough to see you out for a few months, you alone, not to mention the hiring of men.' Hector looked up at him then, with regretful eyes that clearly spoke no word of a lie.

'You . . .' John Evert gulped to catch his breath.

'You may see for yourself,' Hector said, holding out the file.

John Evert's face contorted. He turned away. He went to the bookcase, placed his forearm against it and pressed his face against his wrist. He could not believe it. He simply could not. The hopelessness of his situation was more than he could bear.

Hector allowed him some time, then came to his side and placed a hand upon his shoulder. John Evert jerked away as though burned by the touch. 'You came to me for my advice and assistance, and my advice is this. It is time to put aside childish things, wild notions of the impossible.'

'What will I do?' John Evert murmured, feeling as though his heart were being steadily buried beneath a pile of rocks.

'You will stay here in Los Angeles. You will put your faith in the marshal and the troops, when they get here. Let them manage the search for your mother. Meanwhile, you must find employment. I will assist you all I can.'

'The ranch . . .' he muttered.

'It is still yours, of course, but the house is gone and you cannot run the land alone. My suggestion would be to sell the cattle that remain – I can arrange this on your behalf – and let the land lie fallow for the time being. As you know, there are some complicated claims relating to it, litigation to do with the previous owner and your neighbour, Mr Gunn, but I am confident that I can block any attempt to remove the land from your possession. You have plenty of time to consider, and – who knows? – at some later date you may, nay, you *will* be in a position to return and rebuild . . .'

John Evert might have been in the room with Hector, but his mind had been spirited away to the place he loved so well. In fall, the aspen leaves would simmer to yellow as though toasted in butter. The wind would shake them, too, so that the trees would seem to be laughing, fair bubbling in delight at their own beauty. He loved most specially to walk in the woods at that time of year: following the trails covered with the fallen leaves was akin to walking upon a river of fire. When the wind got up, it would pick up those little flames into small tornadoes, and the words from Revelation 21 would echo in his mind: *And I saw a new heaven and a new earth: for the first heaven and the first earth were passed away* . . .

'I know ranch life is what you are used to,' Hector was saying, 'but I cannot see you being happy as a hired hand, working some other man's cattle. I think you would be better served here in town. The opportunities are manifold, and a clever man may make his fortune. My first port of call would be the *Star*.'

'The *Star*?' John Evert repeated, his eyes drawn back to Hector by the word.

'The newspaper. I know they are in need of a writer who can translate. With your education and your Spanish you could be just the man. Go back to the Mission. Rest, eat – you're half wasted. Tomorrow we will set about your new life.'

John Evert dropped his eyes. After a while, he looked up again. 'All right,' he said, 'but please can I have twenty dollars?' In answer to Hector's raised eyebrow he added, 'I want to make a donation to the Mission, to thank them for all they've done for me.'

'A very generous amount,' Hector said. John Evert held his gaze until Hector continued, 'I will have Abraham draw up a cheque and you can take it to the bank to cash it.'

'Thank you.'

As John Evert made to take his leave, Hector asked, 'When will you make the donation to the fathers?'

'In the next day or so,' John Evert replied. 'Good day, Mr Featherstone.'

It was the first lie he had ever told.

He returned to his bare cell at the Mission. He felt empty as a burlap sack. He sat down upon the hard, narrow bed and looked at the wobbly wooden table with the Bible set square upon it. He was tacky with sweat. He took off his shirt and went to the deep window sill, to the bowl there, and poured water into it from an earthenware pitcher. Dampening a wash-cloth, he wiped the salt from his skin. He glanced down at his left shoulder, to the wound there. With his rough removal of the arrow head, he had torn the skin every which way, and the pinkish lines resembled a broken, many-pointed star. He pressed the washcloth to it. The pain was so intense and pure that he was transported right back to the stoop on the night of the raid, and saw his mother's face. He took his hand away, and shut his eyes to hold back the tears. 'Don't think about it,' he whispered aloud. '*Don't* think about it.'

He went and lay upon the bed, keeping his eyes tight shut. Soon, he returned to where he often found himself: in the red sandstone tunnels where he had lost the mule. In his dreams, however, the animal yet lived, and they walked free of the labyrinth together, their steps growing faster and faster until they took off from the earth in flight.

The next day, Hector came to the Mission to seek him out. John Evert was glad to see him, standing lean and straight, sipping bravely at the grainy, weak coffee that the fathers brewed for visitors.

They walked together along Main Street, sticking close to the frontages to avoid the chaos of the thoroughfare. Hector walked with his hands clasped behind him. John Evert had never seen an American man walk along thus. With his high-stepping gait and oiled hair, Hector seemed uniquely exotic upon the street. Occasionally, he asked John Evert a question, about life at the Mission, about how he found Los Angeles, and would lean in to hear the answer, turning his keen eyes upon John Evert's face and nodding encouragingly at the brief answers, which he seemed to understand did not come without real effort. John Evert, meanwhile, had to contend with the fact that his insides seemed made of lead, so heavy was the misery he carried within.

'Here we are,' Hector said, as they reached a little frame house with the sign *Imprenta* over the door. They entered, the whole structure seeming to shake as Hector closed the door behind them. He rang a bell on the counter and a man with a violently colourful paisley kerchief about his neck came rattling through an inner door, from beyond which came a faint sound of clatter. He was immensely fat, his heavy jowls spilling over the neck tie.

'Mr Featherstone, how do?' said the man.

'Good morning, Mr Rivers. This is John Evert Burn. This is Mr Quincy Rivers.'

'How do?' the man said briskly, and then to Hector, 'I suppose you're here about the Read trial write-up.'

'No, no, I know better than to complicate your fine creative pieces with trivial details, such as the facts,' Hector replied wryly, which drew a smile from Quincy. 'Actually, I'm here about the writer's position you're trying to fill.'

'Hell, I've almost given up trying to find a man who knows his alphabet, never mind translating a sentence into something fit to read,' Quincy said, wrenching his kerchief from his neck and wiping his brow with it.

'Here,' Hector said, pointing at John Evert, 'is your answer.'

Quincy regarded John Evert suspiciously. 'How old are you?'

'Fifteen, sir.'

'Where'd you go to school?'

'I had some schooling, sir, but mostly I learned at home.'

Quincy raised his eyebrows at Hector. John Evert expected Hector to speak, but he did not. 'Well,' Quincy said noncommittally, 'if Mr Featherstone says you're up to it, I guess I'll have to give you a try. Pay's ten dollars a month . . .' He began to rattle off information as he turned to open the door behind him. Hector indicated to John Evert that they should follow. As Quincy opened the door, the faint clattering sound that John Evert had been aware of increased to a loud clank and roll.

In the back room, a man scribbled at a high desk while at another a man was bent toward a small device connected to wires that ran up the wall and out through a hole into the street outside. A little wooden lever on the device tapped back and forth rapidly, apparently all by itself. His ear cocked to the device, the man scribbled words on a piece of paper. John Evert wondered what the man was at with the little machine, but his eye was swiftly drawn beyond it to the wheel of another, much larger, that was being turned by an Atlas-shouldered black man in shirtsleeves, with a blue apron tied about his front.

Opposite the black man a smaller fellow was feeding into the machine big sheets of paper that were sucked along and rolled under a turning drum. They were white when they went under, but covered with black when they reappeared on the other side. John Evert realised, with some fascination, that it must be a printing press.

Hector wandered over to it and bent down to inspect the complex workings of the wheels and cogs beneath. Meanwhile, Quincy kept up his non-stop talk, his voice raised over the clang of metal on metal. 'If I take you on, you'll dorm upstairs with these three: Casey, Meriweather, Victor.' Quincy pointed at each of the men as he named them. 'Work starts at seven. Most important thing for me is a man who's accurate—'

At that moment the building was shaken by an almighty explosion. The black man stopped his wheel, the other men jumped back from their desks, and a surprising hush fell. Dust drifted down from the wooden planks of the ceiling.

'Goddamn it, Bill!' Quincy cried through the wall. 'Mr Featherstone, I tell you, you gotta speak to the man.'

'I'll pass by for a word,' Hector replied.

'Now, sit down here,' Quincy barked at John Evert, 'and copy this out into English.'

John Evert took a seat, and began to read the messily written Spanish that Quincy thrust under his nose. The other men got back to work; the wooden clack-clack of the small machine resumed, followed by the rhythmic clanking and knocking of the printing press. John Evert took up the pen that lay on the desk, dipped it into the ink he found beside it and began to write out a translation, aware of Quincy's stertorous breathing over his shoulder.

'Hmph,' Quincy acknowledged grudgingly. 'That's the neatest hand I ever saw.' He tutted when John Evert made to turn to him, 'Don't stop – get it all down and call me when you're done.'

John Evert concentrated upon his task. By the time he had neatly translated the page, he realised that Hector was gone. He felt a pang of loneliness, which was mercifully short-lived, for Quincy bore down upon him with a bundle of papers.

He put in an afternoon's work and, at day's end, Quincy said, 'See you tomorrow.' So John Evert figured he had the job. He was not sure how he felt about it, but he did notice just then that the past few hours were the first moments in a month that he had not been chin-deep in wretchedness.

He was making to leave when Abraham, Hector's clerk, appeared, his eyes darting about the room. 'Ah, Mr Burn,' he said. 'I am glad I caught you. There is someone to see you at Mr Featherstone's office.'

'Me?' John Evert said. 'But I don't know anyone here.'

'A Mr Gunn,' Abraham replied. At the mention of the name, John Evert's gut clenched. He would have refused to go but Abraham would brook no opposition, gently steering him by the elbow out of the *Star*.

When John Evert entered the room, Gunn, who was seated, hunched forward, his hands hanging loose between his knees, got jerkily to his feet. His eyes darted over John Evert's face, as though to convince himself that it really was him.

John Evert said nothing. His own face, he knew, was stony. He studied the features of the man he loathed: the pallid, flaky skin, cheekbones branded red by the sun; the hair and eyelashes so pale they were almost white. He did not know what it was about Gunn's colouring that was so deep distasteful to him, unless it was simply that it was the human face of the ugly soul beneath. It put him in mind of a hog. It had always put him in mind of a hog.

Hector broke the silence for them. 'Mr Gunn wanted to see for himself that you were alive and well,' he said.

'I'm sorry,' Gunn said. 'I'm very sorry.' And he really did look sorry, wretched, in fact, but that did nothing to soften John Evert's feelings toward him.

'Your men were no good,' John Evert said.

Gunn nodded shakily. 'If I . . . if I could have done things differently . . . Is there anything I can do for you? Anything at all.'

'Yes,' John Evert said. 'You can go out and find her.'

'I tried . . .' Gunn began, looking down.

'Not hard enough. You know where they've gone,' John Evert said. Gunn's eyes flashed to his face. 'You followed,' John Evert added. 'You know which way they headed.'

Gunn's angular shoulders dropped. 'Yes, but we lost the trail. They could have gone any way afterward.'

'We must leave this to the soldiers who are due any day now,' Hector said.

'I want him to go too,' John Evert said coldly. 'If he cared for my mother so very much then he must. Unless all he really wanted was our land.'

'Mr Burn—' Hector began.

'I see feelings are running high,' Gunn said awkwardly. 'I will leave you. If there is anything practical I can do, Mr Featherstone, please tell me. Good day.'

'Thank you, Mr Gunn. Good day,' Hector said.

When the door had closed behind Gunn, Hector turned to John Evert and said, 'It seems to me he is genuinely distressed at your circumstances.'

'And what is that to me?' John Evert replied hotly. 'Everyone says how distressed they are but no one will *do* anything.'

'The soldiers—'

'Yes, the soldiers. Wait for the soldiers,' parroted John Evert.

'In the meantime, I have encouraging news. The two young women who were kidnapped some time before your mother have been found.'

'Where?' John Evert cried, his heart singing at the news. 'And my mother?'

'They were found wandering in the desert. It appears the raiding party may have been alarmed by something and chose to abandon the girls. But I regret that they were not with your mother. They were disoriented and frightened after their experience but both young women say they never saw a third woman. It does give us some hope, however.'

Despite Hector's optimistic tone, John Evert's face fell, his giant hopes extinguished in the course of a moment.

'How did it go at the *Star*?' Hector asked.

'I got the job.'

'Good. Work is the best distraction from despair.'

John Evert nodded half-heartedly, then made to take his leave. When he reached the door, Hector said after him, 'Do make sure you give that money to the fathers soon. It would be an unwise temptation to think it might be used for a bounty.'

John Evert avoided his gaze.

'Your mother gave me power of attorney in the event of her death or absence. I will do all I can to look after your interests, but you must be sensible. You must stay with the *Star* and you must not do anything reckless. If you did, I might be forced to think that my time could be better spent elsewhere, rather than defending your claim to your property.'

John Evert knew what this meant. He departed, heart leaden, and with an overwhelming sense that he had been trapped. The most important thing in the world to him was his mother. The most important thing in the world to her was their land. If ever he had to choose between the two he knew what she would want.

When he was very young, John Evert had been frightened by a sermon in church that had dwelled on the nature of Hell. He had not slept the whole night through for worry about it and had gone tearful to his mother. She had touched him lightly on the brow and reassured him that, provided he was good, he would never have to go there. But this was not true, he now knew. He had done nothing wrong but he was in Hell all the same.

Quincy Rivers was as good as his word. John Evert left his room at the Mission the next day, and moved into the dorm above the print room with Casey, the black man, Victor and Meriweather, who had been using the little machine – the telegrapher, he learned. When John Evert arrived, with his blanket roll and few possessions, his bed had been neatly turned down and a box left open at the foot for his things. John Evert was aware of Casey's eyes upon him, and knew he must have been responsible for the small act of kindness. John Evert nodded at him, but Casey's gaze had dropped already to the floor.

Quincy was pleased at John Evert's ability to translate so rapidly between English and Spanish, and piled him up with work. As well as writer, John Evert was errand boy, and he was sent to and fro about town, carrying messages. Wherever he was going, he always stopped at the marshal's office to ask for news; always, the marshal greeted him with a patient negative. At one point, Quincy caught him coming out of the marshal's office and gave him a clip round the ear and a barrage of abuse about personal business during work hours. Quincy did not appear to know anything of John Evert's circumstances and John Evert was glad of this. He preferred that Quincy treated him as any old body; the idea of being pitied had become unbearable.

The days were easier than the nights, which followed ever the same pattern: he would fall into bed, dog-tired, and be instantly asleep, only to wake in the recesses of the night, beset by images of his mother. His imagination would run wild, and he replayed the night of her capture over and over in his mind. The thoughts threatened to smother him and he would say the Lord's Prayer a lot because it was a small comfort. He also took to cupping his hands together, leaving a space between, as you might cup a butterfly. He would whisper into the air he held, all the while imagining making a skin for it so that it became akin to a delicate soap bubble, and then he would gently release it and blow it away toward the window. He would imagine the bubble sailing outside, over the roofs, out of the town and into the wilderness, crossing many miles of scrub and dust, travelling onward to wherever she resided now, and he felt sure that when it reached her, she would feel it and she would know that he was there.

7

It was Meriweather who learned of the arrival of the soldiers, for he heard it down the wire. He passed the news to John Evert, and before Quincy could forbid it, John Evert had hot-footed it to the marshal's office.

He was disappointed to find them so few; at a glance, he figured they were only twenty in number. But they wore dark blue uniforms, rode good horses and carried guns, and were the most promising thing to have happened since John Evert had arrived in Los Angeles.

The marshal called him in for an interview with the leader of the group, who sat upon the edge of his desk and listened to John Evert's recounting of the raid. The question he asked of John Evert took him by surprise. 'Are you sure they were Indians?' he said.

'I . . . well, yes,' John Evert replied.

The man tapped his whip upon the toe of his boot. 'It seems half crazy them mounting a raid like this when they know what it will surely bring down on their heads,' he said.

John Evert repeated the description of the white-painted man, the other he had seen, the sounds they had made, their skill with bow and arrow, and although he did not actually know it to be the case, he said firmly, 'There wasn't a white man among them.'

The man nodded. 'Very well, we'll see to it.'

Days passed, and John Evert heard nothing. With each day, his faith in what those twenty men might achieve dwindled. Maybe it was something to do with the way they rode out of town, not at a gallop, but at a stately walk, the soldiers talking among themselves, seeming singularly untroubled by the task ahead. It was just a job to them, John Evert realised, not a mission, not a quest upon which life depended. If he himself could not go, and they could not be trusted, then what was needed was a man who shared his drive and desperation.

One night, while the others slept, the dorm room was filled with the opalescence of the full moon. It was what his mother had always referred to as the witching hour. As he often did, John Evert reached under his mattress for the reassurance of feeling the twenty dollars he had never given to the fathers. It was not much, but it was a start for a bounty anyway.

He went to the window, pushed aside the thin cloth that acted as a curtain, and stared at the bone-white disc of the moon. He summoned his mother in his mind, and begged her to speak to him. Suddenly he felt a deep calm pass over him and he remembered her taking his young face in her hands when he sulked upon something, saying, 'Don't brood, *amor*. That way only leads to madness. Action is the answer. Make your thoughts of action only.'

His gaze scoured the moon and he whispered to it fervently, 'If you live, Madre, you see this moon. See it and know that I will come for you.' He put his fingers to his scar and lightly stroked the lumpy, tender skin as though it were some twisted rosary as he prayed, 'God, please, make me strong. I make this vow to you. I vow that everything warm about me will grow cold, that every part of me that has been soft will become hard. Make me strong and, please, God, send someone. Send someone to help me, too.'

He made his body go rigid with the thought and, like the imperceptible freezing of a lake, his soul shuddered and set, with a dull crack and a splinter through the centre.

It was the very next day that Meriweather said the fatal words, 'I see Bill's brought that bounty in.'

John Evert's head came up from where it had been bent at his work and he stared at Meriweather, who was shuffling a sheaf of papers. 'Bill next door?' he asked, pointing at the wall.

'Mm-hmm,' Meriweather hummed, as he glanced at the paper in his hand.

'He's a bounty hunter?' John Evert asked.

'When the mood takes him,' Meriweather replied.

John Evert looked at the wall in amazement. All this time, and the man he needed had been right there all along. He would have charged round there that instant, but something stopped him. He had never spoken to Bill, but he had seen him.

Bill was not tall: he was of medium height, lithe rather than muscular, yet gave the impression of great physical strength. He was of dark complexion and substantial features, his profile magnificent in its resemblance to that of a Roman senator. The nose commenced high in the forehead and passed downward with glorious front, as though he had arrived in the world ready to charge, bull-bossed, against the most unforgiving of surfaces. His eyes were sleepy, the lids so heavy that they seemed in perpetual threat of closing; they were docile eyes, yet changeable, and married to a full and fleshy mouth. The face was an event, something one first glanced at and swiftly turned toward, certain that something important or shocking had just passed there, but which, upon closer scrutiny, gave up merely a not entirely convincing innocence.

John Evert had had occasion to study that face for he passed by Bill's door several times a day, and Bill was often sitting out front of his place, or in the shade just inside the big double doors. It did not look like a house, his place, more of a barn, but Bill surely lived there for his presence at night was attested to by various bangs and rattles. Bill had never spoken to John Evert either, but he watched him as he went by, from under the brim of his hat.

'Who is Bill?' John Evert asked Quincy.

'A student of the true school of philosophy,' replied Quincy, cryptically.

'What's his last name?' John Evert asked.

'Who knows?'

'Is he a Spaniard?'

'No. Seems his mother was Indian,' Quincy said absentmindedly. John Evert let out an involuntary sound of dismay. 'Not redskin,' Quincy corrected him, 'from India, in Asia.'

'Huh.' John Evert was silent for a while. He had seen India on a map but that was all. 'What does he do there, next door? Those noises.'

'Chemistry seems to be his favourite science,' Quincy replied, 'though whether it is the science in which his talents lie, I most seriously doubt.'

'What's he trying to make?'

'Sometimes gold,' Quincy sighed impatiently, 'but most of the time he's doing his best to make first-class cognac brandy out of *aguardiente*.'

'Is he crazy?'

'No, but he has a strange sense of humour.'

'Do you . . .' John Evert was unsure how to phrase his question. 'Is he a man to trust?'

'Trust?' Quincy looked at John Evert now, his eyes tiny in his large face. 'If you have to ask that question then . . .' Quincy experienced a change of temper for he rounded off snappily, 'Why don't you quit these questions and find someone else to bother?'

That evening, John Evert wandered out of the *Star* on to a street striped with the blunted shards of an autumn sunset. There was a pleasant odour in the air, which had rolled down off the mellow hills. A rowdy blackbird was perched atop a flagpole, its voice tumbling up and down its range. The street was quiet, and John Evert walked across the loose brown dirt, turning on his heel to look back at the building that had become his temporary home.

To the right of the *Star*, the full-face double doors of Bill's place stood open. Inside was dust velvet darkness.

John Evert strolled to the wide doorway, put a tentative hand on the jamb and peered in. A little light fell through a skylight in the back, illuminating the outlines of a lot of junk. A movement down upon the floor, just inside the door, caught his eye.

A blue cattle-dog puppy waggled all toffee-kneed toward him and sniffed at his boot. He bent to pick it up. As he stood upright, it breathed on him, with breath that should have smelt milky but did not, and tried to lick his face.

Out of the darkness came the loud clang of metal upon metal, and something smashed into his forehead, just above his eyebrow. The pain of it ricocheted through his head, and he almost dropped the puppy as he reeled off the door jamb into the street once more. His ears rang, and he wondered whether he had been shot.

As he leaned against the outside wall, and his vision cleared, he became aware of a presence next to him, in the doorway. It was Bill, blinking dozily and sucking the end of a *cigarrito* that hung from one side of his mouth. 'Right in the face, huh? Wasn't looking what I was doing,' he said. He bent down, and picked up out of the dirt the thing that had hit John Evert. It was the chamber from a pistol. Bill surveyed the buildings on the opposite side of the street, as though checking for someone.

John Evert, who now had the puppy in one hand and the other hand pressed over his eye, studied the thrown-back head, the profile that seemed carved of basalt. It was hard to drag his gaze away from all those unusual angles. 'Aren't you going to say sorry?' he demanded, pain making him forget himself.

'Lucky you were looking down at that mutt or it might've taken your eye out,' Bill drawled over his shoulder, as he turned away. 'Mind you, seems like it isn't the first time you've been hit in the face.'

John Evert moved his hand from his throbbing brow to his kinked nose. He stood in the doorway, watching Bill lob the chamber into a box. 'This dog wants feeding,' he said.

'The bitch that whelped it is dead,' Bill said. 'It never was mine.'

'Can I feed it?'

'You can have it. I have no use for it.'

'Really?'

'Bitch was wild. The pup will be the same, impossible to train.'

'I don't care.'

'A match made in Heaven.'

Bill disappeared into the back, beyond the clutter. John Evert contemplated the pup, which wriggled in his grasp.

The next morning, John Evert awoke with a purple bruise upon his brow and bed sheets damp with urine. As he lay on his back, the pup, which had spent all night curled in the crook of his arm, and evidently pissing everywhere, hopped up on to his chest, and sneezed in his face. He laughed, pushing its soft head away, wiping his mouth.

He lay there, thinking about Bill, wondering why he had thrown half a pistol at him, why he had given him the dog, and how he was going to talk to him. It was the first morning that he had awoken with a sensation less than the usual gnawing sadness.

Quincy was not at all happy about having the pup in the print room, but John Evert kept it in a box under his desk, so it was out of sight, and the noise of the print machine drowned its whining, so Quincy promptly forgot it was there.

'What happened to your face?' Quincy asked.

'I fell over,' John Evert replied.

Quincy rolled his eyes and muttered, 'Hopeless,' under his breath.

'Meriweather, will you take this round to Bill?' Quincy said.

'I'll go,' John Evert interjected, leaping up.

Quincy waved as though to dismiss this idea but Meriweather, who was nothing if not idle, said, 'Let him go. I'm busy here.'

Quincy handed him a sealed message, and John Evert made his way out with it.

He entered the dark doorway with some trepidation, the bruise on his head seeming pretty fresh again. 'Hello,' he said loudly, to ensure he was heard over the noise of the street outside. It was morning, and Main Street was at its busiest. The dust had been stirred up by so many hoofs and wheels that the air was thick with it.

There was no answer, so he made his way along the path that carved through all the junk to where a dirty curtain hung down, bisecting the room. He lifted it aside and stared in astonishment. The room was rigged up with all sorts of equipment: round and long glass bottles and tubing all linked together; there were books everywhere, their pages propped open with whatever object had sprung to hand; something simmered, releasing a rich smell of baking bread. The light falling through the dirty skylight shone off polished metal contraptions. What in God's name the man was up to in there, John Evert knew not. He jumped when Bill, who had been invisible, spoke from a chair in the corner.

'What do you want?' he said.

'I'm sorry,' John Evert stammered slightly. 'Mr Rivers asked me to bring you this.'

He went and handed Bill the note and turned to leave but Bill said, 'No, wait.'

He read the message, then studied John Evert before saying idly, 'You ever been to San Gabriel?'

'No, sir,' John Evert replied, while completing his survey of the room, which took in a small table with the remnants of a meal upon it and, in the corner, a low-slung bed.

'Good. You'll like it.'

'Pardon me?'

'You'll come with me. I need a pair of quick hands.'

Part of John Evert could not believe his luck at being thrown together with the man so easily; another part was fearful, although for what reason he could not say. 'When are we going?' he asked.

'Now. Here,' Bill tossed a lariat at John Evert, who caught it. Bill came toward him and smiled a lopsided smile.

'I'd better ask Mr Rivers if this is okay,' John Evert said.

'I'll tell him,' Bill said dismissively, as though Quincy were about as much bother to him as a fly.

They walked outside, down the alleyway that ran along the building to a hitching post at the rear where two horses were tethered. Bill saddled the tall grey, and gestured to the roan pony at its side. John Evert saddled it, and they led them out on to the street where Bill leaped on to the grey unaided, though it was some seventeen hands high.

Once astride, Bill leaned towards the small shutter in the side wall of the *Star* and rapped loudly. Casey's hand opened it a few inches. 'Casey, tell Quincy I'm taking this kid on a job,' Bill said. Casey said something in reply and Bill laughed. He turned the grey's head away.

'Wait,' John Evert said, 'my dog.'

Bill turned back to the shutter. 'Casey, you'll feed that dog.'

Then Bill sat back in the saddle, tugged at the grey's reins so that it shook its head in alarm, and slapped John Evert's pony's haunch with the lariat. The two horses, wildly fresh, spiralled and bucketed out into the traffic, with John Evert just keeping his balance, and promptly bolted neck and neck down the street, nearly felling a couple of pedestrians. The roan pony took a great jump over a dropped sack in the road, and Bill roared with laughter as they skittered around obstacles, oblivious to the shouts their passage raised. Exhilarated, and to his own surprise, laughing, John Evert kept his legs pressed in tight to the pony's sides until the town was long behind them and they were trotting over gritty soil and dusty scrub.

In the hazy light, the distant hills seemed painted faint on the horizon, their folds marked by soft shadow bruises. Every so often, the dark shape of a cactus stood out misshapen against the plain. The horses' hoofs fell with muffled thuds upon the sandy earth. John Evert took stock of Bill. He sat his horse as if he were a part of it, barely using the reins, at one point freeing both hands to retrieve a *cigarrito* from his pocket, lighting it as they trotted along. A rifle was strapped behind his saddle, and the customary pistols at his belt.

John Evert had not left Los Angeles since his arrival there several weeks ago, and his eyes trailed greedily over the landscape, the subtle gradations of colour: the ochre of the earth, the silver-grey of the brush, the endless shades of blue as the landscape streamed away from them into the welcome void of the sky. He breathed in deep the familiar scent of dust and brush, and even his heartbeat seemed to have slowed in relief at being back where he belonged.

The roan was a plucky little thing, and strove to keep pace with the grey. It felt good to be back on a horse. It made John Evert remember who he was, or whom he had once been. At the ranch, he would often spend the entire day out on horseback, his lunch packed in a saddlebag. You could ride all day, with no more aim than a closer intimacy with the land, until a time had come when he knew every meander and pool of his river, particular trees, clearings where each year certain flowers would bloom, and yet each year things would be slightly different, as Nature rejoiced in her own creativity, writing a subtle story in the pages of which John Evert's name had been inscribed. He had not realised how much he had missed it. He thought of his mother, and it made him ache.

They rode across chaparral, entered scrubby oak woodland and wove between the trees along a vague path, the grey's haunches dappled with shadowy stripes by the trunks of the trees. Where there were fallen trees across the way, Bill put the grey at them and it leaped over the obstacles languidly. John Evert's pony tossed its head and pranced on the spot. When he put it over anything, it flew at double the height.

'He likes a jump, that pony,' Bill said, over his shoulder.

John Evert patted its iron-hard neck as it snorted with pleasure.

They stopped when dusk fell. Bill made a fire most efficiently. 'Go see if you can shoot something,' he said, handing John Evert the Winchester.

John Evert took it, and went away through the trees. The woods were full of animals and he had no trouble surprising a rabbit. He walked back, holding it by its velvet ears. How was he to bring up the matter with Bill, he wondered. And how much would he need to offer him to persuade him to take on the job of finding his mother?

When he returned to the fire, Bill was sitting cross-legged, his hands upon his knees, his eyes shut. Just like a Goddamn Indian, John Evert thought angrily. In the firelight, Bill's face glowed orange, but his deep eye sockets remained cast in shadow, an echo of the skull beneath. The old boughs in the heart of the fire cracked sporadically, like breaking bones.

'Good,' Bill said, when he saw the rabbit. He skinned and gutted it, rubbed over it a concoction from a bottle, and roasted it. John Evert had to admit that it was pretty fine. After they had eaten, Bill smoked while John Evert listened to the night noises of the forest. Somewhere distant, a coyote called, its howl the slow closing of a creaking door. They did not speak as the fire died down and tumbled in upon itself. The evening was mild, and they slept with their heads resting upon their saddles.

When John Evert awoke, it was just before dawn. Bill had already made coffee, and was stirring beans in a pot over the fire.

They left the shelter of the trees, and rode on through the early morning upon the plain. High above, a buzzard circled, screaming. Bill, deep in his thoughts, said little. He had not yet put on his hat, and his shaggy hair blew free in the breeze, his profile magisterial, minted upon the coin of the rising sun.

A few hours later, John Evert hazarded a question. 'You're not a Spaniard, are you?' he said. Bill shook his head. 'Is it true you're an Indian?'

'I'm not a Paiute or a Sioux, if that's your meaning.'

'No, I mean from India.'

'My mother was. My father was an Englishman. He worked for the East India Company.'

'What's that?'

'A trading company. I was part of it myself for a time, spent years at sea.'

'Why'd you stop?'

'I got sick of the sea. And I'll be honest with you, I never liked the British. They lack imagination, to my mind.' He began to sing then, in a fine baritone, a song about Spanish ladies, the words spilling like wine down to where the horses' hoofs padded the talc-soft earth.

They rode all day until they reached the edge of the San Gabriel valley, which John Evert had never seen before. The distant deep-blue mountains seemed to guard the white walls of the San Gabriel mission, which sat upon a bolt of verdant green. It was the most fertile land in the region, and such was their vantage point and the view it commanded that they could see for many leagues, making out plains, forests, a lake, and the serpentine back of the silver river that looped unendingly westward.

Hundreds of horses ran loose there, and they looked down upon black, brown, grey and piebald animals. Their coats shone sleek in the sun as they grazed among herds of deer. The animals formed a slowly moving carpet that inched ever onward, like celestial bodies in an untroubled sky.

'Beautiful, isn't it?' said Bill. 'It's how I imagine Heaven must be.'

They rode down into the valley, and followed the bends of the river, pausing at a shallow bank to allow their horses to drink. Bill dismounted with his saddlebag, and wandered off toward some willows that grew at the water's edge. John Evert took off his boots, rolled up his breeches and waded into the clear water to refill the canteens. He closed his eyes, relishing the noise of the water babbling at the rocks in the stream.

When he waded out to the bank, he found Bill in full Spanish dress, with a wide black sombrero upon his head, and a patterned blanket thrown over one shoulder. John Evert blinked, but said nothing. At that moment, Bill kicked John Evert's legs from under him and pinned him to the ground, putting his weight on John Evert's chest so he could not breathe.

'Who the hell are you, you little bastard?' Bill demanded.

John Evert shook his head, trying and failing to take a lungful of air. Eventually, Bill took some of his weight off him so John Evert could take a whooping breath.

'I . . . I . . . What?' John Evert gulped, wincing in pain.

'Who sent you? Who sent you, dammit?' Bill cried, his face furious.

'I don't understand,' John Evert stammered.

'You come snooping round my place, then you come with me, without a word, not a question asked. What do you want? Who are you reporting back to? Are there men waiting for us at San Gabriel?'

'No one, I promise, no one.'

'Bullshit,' Bill roared. He pulled a knife and put it to John Evert's throat, his eyes murderous.

John Evert shut his eyes tight and said, 'God sent you.'

Everything went still. After a while, John Evert opened his eyes. Bill was staring down at him with a bewildered expression. 'You're going to have to explain that to me,' he said, taking more weight off John Evert.

'I prayed for someone to come help me and God sent you,' John Evert gabbled.

'Help you do what?' Bill asked, no longer angry but simply mystified.

'Find my mother. She's been kidnapped. I know you're a bounty hunter. I was going to offer you a bounty.' The blood was pounding in John Evert's head but his honesty must have been undeniable, for Bill rolled off him and sat back. John Evert pushed himself upright and gasped for air, clutching his chest where Bill had crushed it.

Bill observed him with interest. 'Well, you're clearly no spy. Are you crazy?'

'I don't think so,' John Evert said.

'You're an original one, kid,' Bill said. He pondered things for several moments, then began to smile. 'And, just so you know, I can assure you of one thing, that if anyone sent me, it sure as hell wasn't God.'

They sat together, in the sunshine, alone in their thoughts. John Evert felt relieved that he was not dead, and that things were out in the open. He figured it was all right now to ask a question. 'Why are you dressed up as a Spaniard?' he asked.

Bill did not answer this. Instead, he said, 'I know Spanish is your mother tongue. The moment we enter this place, you don't speak one word of English.'

'All right,' John Evert said, figuring that he was going to be allowed to stay with Bill a while longer, which was a good sign.

'We'll arrive independently,' Bill said, 'and you are to give no sign that we know each other. I will take one room and you another. Make sure your room looks out to the rear, not the front. I'll explain later. Here, take this.' He handed over a pistol, which John Evert inspected, then tucked into the back of his breeches.

Bill rode on ahead. John Evert waited for an hour before following. He made sure to check the pistol was loaded, and hoped he would not have cause to use it. He had no idea what he was getting into but he did not truly care. He would do as he was told and, hopefully, if he did well enough, Bill might agree to help him.

It was a small outpost beyond San Gabriel, consisting of one large building and a few scattered barns and corrals. The main building was Spanish: two floors, with the ground-floor entrances large and arched, a railed veranda running the length of the first floor, rooms set back beneath the overhang of the roof, which was supported by slim wooden pillars that ran from the roof to the ground. It must have been a place of quality when first built, the window frames huge and solid, jutting out of the adobe, but it had not been well maintained, and the whole place breathed a decrepit air of neglect.

John Evert secured the roan at the rear, far from Bill's grey, and unsaddled it. He got a hell of a shock when he turned around and came face to face with an Indian. He let out an involuntary cry and stumbled backward, half tripping under the weight of the saddle he held.

The Indian, who was small and wizened and wore a brown blanket about his shoulders, widened his eyes at John Evert's reaction. He looked down at the bucket he held and said quizzically, '*Agua?* Water?' nodding at the roan, holding out his free hand in a begging manner.

John Evert, whose heart was pounding against his ribs, fit to explode, slowly realised the man was just hoping for a handout. 'Get away from my horse,' John Evert hissed. 'Don't you come near me, you dirty cur.'

The man's gaze dropped to the ground and he withdrew.

John Evert was left alone, shocked at the violence of his own reaction, at the depth of his hate. He took off his hat and wiped his forehead, then drew a few deep breaths to steady himself.

He returned to the main entrance and walked shakily through the high archway into a central courtyard. It was empty. He looked about him, and turned to where he could see, through a tall door, the edge of a bar and some signs of life. He walked into a high-ceilinged room, with tables and chairs scattered about. A couple of men sat drinking in one corner. They glanced at him in a bored way. He went to the bar and waited until a man appeared. The man was wiping his hands on a rag, but pretty much all of him was unclean. Short, curly hairs grew out of his face and neck in unexpected places.

'*Buenas, tiene una habitación?*' John Evert asked.

The man glanced at him without answering, and John Evert felt himself flush. He placed some of the coins Bill had given him upon the bar and the man awakened. He led John Evert upstairs to a room on the front side. John Evert pointed toward the rear. The man shrugged and they walked around the courtyard to the other side. The door of another room opened and a man looked out, but it was not Bill.

John Evert waited in his room, his stomach in knots. He heard two Spanish men talking. After a while, he heard one descend the stairs, while the other walked in the direction of John Evert's room. It was Bill who entered. Along with his new dress and remarkably fluent Spanish, he had adopted a whole new range of gestures; even his walk seemed different. He sat down on one of the beds, and put his hands upon his thighs. 'Now, listen,' he said, with a sigh, as though he had made this speech many a time before. 'I will leave this here with you.' He placed a watch on a chain upon the bed beside him. 'You will stay here and ask for food to be sent up. At ten o'clock, you get down to the horses. Saddle ours. But no one must see you go down there.'

'How—'

'Through the window. That's why the back room. You'll take this with you.' Bill laid a leather pouch upon the bed next to the watch. 'You'll go round the horses and feed them a couple of lumps. A couple, mind, no more than that.'

'To our horses as well?'

'No, not to our horses.'

'What is it?'

'Never mind.'

'Will it hurt them?' John Evert asked anxiously.

'Only for a few hours.'

'I'm not going to—'

'You will,' Bill interjected, bringing down the syllables like two swift hammer blows. 'If you don't, I will hurt you for a lot more than a few hours.' His gaze was so malevolent that John Evert looked away. 'Once you've fixed the horses, you'll climb back up here and come down the stairs to the saloon. You'll watch the game. The game will start to turn against me. Keep a close watch. At my signal . . .' Bill made a gesture, drawing his forefinger across the bridge of his nose, as though scratching an itch '. . . you'll go out and take both horses to the start of the road. Stay hidden behind that first barn we passed and wait for me. Whatever you hear, you wait for me quietly there. Unless, that is, I haven't come out by dawn. In which case, you get out of here and you ride for home.'

'I just leave you?'

'Yes, but that won't happen.'

John Evert nodded uneasily. 'What if something goes wrong?'

'Improvise,' Bill said, slapping his thighs and getting to his feet.

'One thing,' John Evert said. 'Why did you take me with you?'

'I wanted to find out who you were, and I did need an extra pair of hands. I usually take another boy with me but he's no good any more.'

'Why not?'

'He's dead.'

'Oh,' John Evert said, as though this were quite normal.

Bill departed the room, and John Evert said, under his breath, 'Shit.'

A few hours later, some food was brought to John Evert by a girl about his age. She looked askance at him as she deposited the tray on the table, then hesitated at the door to glance back at him.

'*Que estas mirando?*' John Evert asked. He did not speak harshly, but she ducked her head and disappeared.

John Evert ate hungrily, listening to the growing noise below. It sounded as though there were many people downstairs. Music from a guitar and a penny whistle chuntered up through the floorboards. Down the corridor, a door slammed and a woman laughed. He poked his head out of the window and counted the horses tethered below. A couple of men stood talking, but soon they moved away. He checked the watch very often and wiped his sweaty palms upon his breeches.

At ten o'clock exactly, John Evert pushed open the shutters of the window and scrambled out on to the lintel. It was an easy climb down, with the jutting frame of the window below acting as a step. He jumped the last few feet, landing softly in the dirt. His hands shook a little as he wiped the dust from them. He had no idea what he would do if someone came outside; whatever he was up to, he knew it would seem suspicious to someone else. He went to their two horses and saddled them while whispering soothingly. The horses stood still and silent. Then he went down the row of horses. There were fifteen in all. He wondered how the other people in the saloon had travelled there for there were certainly more than fifteen people inside, judging from the noise, but he guessed that was not his problem.

He took the bag from inside his shirt and felt for the rough pieces. When he took them out, the horses perked up at the smell of sugar. He had to stop a couple gobbling down more than their share, and one put its ears back and tried to take a bite at his arm. He punched it lightly on the nose at which it squealed.

At that moment, a side door opened and light spilled out around the corner of the building. He whipped away from the hitching rail and pressed his back to the wall, into the corner of the window frame. He took his hat off and placed it over his face, hoping it was dark enough that his shape would not be made out, and stayed absolutely still. He heard a man moving about, then loud splashing as he urinated nearby. Then he was gone, and the door slammed again.

John Evert took his hat away from his face and waited a few moments before hopping on to the window frame and scaling back up to the room. When he got back there he was sweating. He poured some water into the large china bowl on the dresser, washed his face, and waited until he had cooled down before he made his way downstairs.

The large room was full. Men stood and sat in every available space, drinking and playing cards. Several women decorated the knees of men, perching like gaudy birds. The room was loud with shouted conversation. Smoke spiralled up to the ceiling, culminating there in a heavy layer, diffusing the light from the lamps. To John Evert's relief, no one paid him any mind.

Bill was playing cards with three Spaniards at the rear of the room. The air around their table was thick with smoke from their cigars, and they seemed set apart from the bawdy crowd by their dense silence. John Evert did not approach the table, but watched from the bar where he drank a glass of water. The hairy man paid him no attention, but the girl who had brought him his supper put a short glass of something in front of him. When he tasted it, he found it was liquor, very strong but not unpleasant. Each time he finished sipping it, it was refilled, and it warmed his belly and steadied his nerves, so he drank several.

As the evening ran on, Bill's game clearly became more serious, for it began to attract some spectators. John Evert's heart sank. How was he to see Bill's signal if he had no clear sight line upon him? He was reluctant to approach the table but, taking his glass, he pressed in behind some of the other people to get a proper view. The other two men were out. It was just Bill and one large Spaniard, with narrow eyes, a heavy beard and a closed expression.

The stakes were high and, finally, the Spaniard sent for a man who brought something in a pouch. It was tossed on to the table. Bill opened its loose flap with one lazy finger, then let it fall. He seemed in danger of falling asleep, as though the game bored him entirely. At one point, he shifted in his chair, and John Evert tensed, but then relaxed. More spectators crowded around. To his dismay, John Evert was pushed back and could only view the game over someone's shoulder, but he was able to note the rapidity with which Bill's pile began suddenly to diminish. And then Bill's hand went briefly to his face. He rubbed the bridge of his nose with the knuckle of his forefinger. A few moments later, he did it again.

John Evert drained his glass, and, feeling surprisingly calm, turned about, pushed past the people behind him, and made his way across the room to the door. He made sure that he kept his walk slow, so as not to attract attention, although he noticed that he was not walking entirely straight.

Out in the darkness, he found two of the horses he had fed lying down. The others held their heads low. They did not stir at his presence. He mounted the roan and led the grey by its reins, trotting swiftly away from the building toward the last barn. He waited there, shivering, although it was not cold.

Suddenly a shot rang out. He and the horses jumped and he snatched at their reins, but they stood obedient. More shots sounded, and shouts. John Evert, his heart hammering in his chest, peered through the darkness trying to see any movement in the building. There was just enough light coming from the place for him to see a figure tearing along the upstairs veranda, with another in pursuit. The first figure spun on to one of the supporting pillars, shimmied down it, and came running across the dark ground in his direction. He saw more figures pouring out of the building. They were all firing blind into the dark, but he did not see how Bill would make it across the distance safely. All too fresh in his mind was the memory of what hesitation under attack resulted in, and without thinking any further, he kicked the roan on madly and galloped across the open space between him and Bill.

Bill could not see them coming in the darkness and he ran smack into them, but he reacted swiftly, leaping up, like he was made of water, on to the grey, spinning it on the spot.

'Ride!' he shouted.

They galloped on to the dark road, John Evert scarcely able to breathe, the thunder of the horses' hoofs keeping time with his thudding heart. They did not stop until they had put several miles between themselves and the outpost, and the horses were exhausted. They brought them down to a heaving walk.

The ride had filled John Evert with a strange jubilation, but Bill said not a word. John Evert sensed he might be angry. He kept the roan behind the grey and watched Bill's dark back nervously, the great courage he had felt dissipating in the cold light of the coming dawn.

The sun had been up for an hour before Bill slowed, allowing John Evert to catch up with him. He took a *cigarrito* from his pocket and lit it. 'What the hell was that?' he asked. John Evert studied his stern profile. 'Why didn't you stay by the barn like I told you?'

'There were so many. I didn't think you'd make it.'

'Don't you ever get sentimental again. Or were you just drunk, you little skunk? Don't think I didn't see you at the bar knocking back what that *señorita* was bringing you. Pah!' he spat, but there was laughter in his voice. He turned to John Evert then and smiled, and a fanfare of tiny lines exploded at the corners of his eyes, deep creases dimpling the sides of his heavy mouth.

It was such a lightning, joyful transformation of the brutal face that it surprised John Evert. 'Aren't you worried they'll be tailing us once those horses wake up?' he asked, unable to keep his jangling nerves to himself.

'No. Not one of them would show their face in Los Angeles.'

'Why were they shooting at you?'

Bill rummaged in his saddlebag, and handed a stained pouch to John Evert, who opened it to find an enormous piece of dirty gold nugget. He handed it back swiftly and said haughtily, 'So that's what you are. You're not a bounty hunter . . .'

Bill halted the grey and, as the roan drew level with it, reached down and got John Evert by the shirt front and yanked him close, almost pulling him clean off the pony, which sidestepped into the grey in surprise. The horses danced sideways together as Bill, his face a furious mask, said slowly, a few inches from John Evert, 'What am I?'

'A thief,' John Evert mumbled against Bill's smoky breath, which mingled with his own smell, which was strong and musky.

'You know the worst thing a man can be?' Bill said. 'Judgemental. 'Tis a fundamental mistake to form an opinion of a situation of which you know naught. Will you take the word of a man who has seen more than you ever will that what you were engaged upon was no simple matter?'

'Why should I?' John Evert said. 'Why should I trust you?'

'You have no reason not to, as yet. And who else is there?'

John Evert looked into those wide-spaced, hypnotic eyes. Yes, that much was true.

'And you enjoyed it, didn't you?' Bill said quietly, his low, rich voice ever so compelling. John Evert thought how, for those nerve-racking, desperately exciting few hours, he had been free, his soul light as a feather. He looked down bashfully.

Bill mouthed the end of his *cigarrito*. 'Good, kid.' He let go of John Evert's shirt front, and seated him back on his pony. 'You can rest assured that gold didn't belong to him, any more than it belongs to me now,' Bill added, spitting in the dirt. 'And to put you out of your moral misery,' he added, 'here!' He tossed something bright at John Evert, who instinctively threw his hand out for it and caught it. He opened his fingers and looked at the oversized silver coin with a five-pointed star cut into the centre. 'What is it?' he asked.

'Can't you read?' Bill replied.

John Evert held it close to his face and studied the writing stamped round the rim of the badge. 'You're a Texas Ranger? Does that make you like the marshal?'

'More than that.'

'More than the sheriff?'

'Different.'

'What do you do, then?'

'Well, I was mustered as a ranger to fight in the Mexican War . . .'

'My pa fought in that war,' John Evert said, feeling a rare moment of kinship.

'Most able men did.' Bill nodded. 'Then, when the war ended, I kept on as a ranger. The work suited me, it seemed.'

'How come you're here instead of Texas?'

'Oh, rangers get all over. Outlaws got no mind for borders.'

'Who'd you take your orders from?' John Evert asked. Bill threw him a glance then that suggested he might have crossed some invisible line. 'I'd have you not discuss with anyone in town what went on last night,' Bill said. 'It's ranger business. All right?'

John Evert nodded. He felt much better, knowing now what Bill did. 'So, would you take on the bounty for my mother?' he asked.

'Depends how much it is,' Bill replied.

'I only have twenty dollars just now,' John Evert said.

'Pah,' Bill scoffed. 'I don't get out of bed for less than two hundred.'

John Evert's spirits sank, and he frowned at the roan's mane. He was aware of Bill's eyes upon him and, after a while, Bill said, 'However, I reckon we might be able to work something out. You scratch my back, I scratch yours.'

John Evert's gaze darted hopefully to Bill, but he was rolling a *cigarrito* and saying, more to himself than to John Evert, 'And you *are* half crazy, kid. You definitely are. There's no other explanation for it.'

They rode slowly back towards Los Angeles, John Evert's mind circling around all he had seen and done, wondering how much he would have to do for Bill before Bill would do what he asked, but he did not really care what the answer was. Sent by God or not, here, he felt sure, was the solution to his problems.

8

John Evert found himself in something of a quandary upon his return to Los Angeles. A part of him wished to tell someone about what had happened at that outpost beyond San Gabriel and to ask someone about Bill being a ranger, because something about it did not sit quite right in John Evert's mind. But Bill had made clear to him that if he told anyone he would wind up with a problem. 'Not,' Bill said, 'because you've done anything wrong, but it looks wrong. And that's all that matters to some people, how things look.'

In answer to John Evert's query as to what he should say if questioned about his recent whereabouts and doings, Bill provided him with a simple story involving another place altogether, some horses and an auction. John Evert was not at all sure that this would be sufficient, but Meriweather was the only one to ask where he had been. Casey would never ask anyone a question, and Victor, who was a sulky creature, only ever asked one if it related to how long it was until they could knock off.

While relaying his brief, rehearsed account to Meriweather, John Evert was aware of Casey's eyes upon him, and when he glanced at him, he swore Casey gave him a small nod. He blushed, wondering whether it was very obvious that he was spinning a yarn. Then Quincy cut in, chiding them for wasting work time. Quincy seemed most uninterested in where John Evert had been, which struck him as a little odd. He felt unsettled, and the feeling persisted all day.

'You have to hand it to them, it was a gutsy move. I can't think of anyone who'd have the *cojones* to pull fast and loose with that crowd.'

It was Meriweather who spoke, commenting upon a truncated piece of news that had just come down the wire. Working at the *Star*, John Evert was party to news before the rest of the town, although the only news that had ever been of any interest to him was the arrival of the soldiers. There had been no news of them since they had departed, which boded ill.

'I wouldn't want to be the one to have Ricardo Urives on my tail,' Quincy replied. 'Still, there won't be no tears shed for the loss of that life.'

John Evert was only half listening as he translated a particularly dull piece of agricultural news from Spanish.

'It was a shoot-up in that outpost near San Gabriel. But what's this about it being some character and a kid?' Meriweather asked.

John Evert pressed the nib of his pen so hard into the paper that it split. Black ink spattered bloodily, as though he had killed something upon the page. He did not know a man had been killed that night, and now he was clearly part of the story, too.

'I think that's some mistake,' Quincy said. 'Story's half jumbled anyway, and no one's going to testify. Even if they did, no one will believe anyone from that hellhole. Must be bunkum – leave that out.'

'What I wouldn't give for a man skilled with a pencil to sketch.' Meriweather sighed. 'By the time anyone puts two and two together on recognising anybody they're long gone.'

John Evert nearly jumped out of his chair as Casey's hand appeared suddenly next to his elbow. 'Sorry, sir,' Casey murmured.

'It's all right,' John Evert said, forcing himself to breathe more steadily as he looked up at Casey. 'You just gave me a shock, that's all. And you don't have to call me "sir", Casey.'

Casey's face was impassive. John Evert, on the other hand, was uncomfortably aware of the sweat upon his upper lip. He wiped his face with his shirtsleeve.

He watched Casey as he walked away. Casey never said a lot, but John Evert had the impression that he was a lot smarter than anyone at the *Star* gave him credit for. He just chose not to let anyone know it. Whatever instruction came his way, he simply replied, 'Yessir.' Only, occasionally, he would catch eyes with John Evert, and John Evert thought he detected humour in that gaze, although he had never heard Casey laugh, not once.

'Do you want to help me set the type?' Casey asked. This was one of John Evert's favourite tasks, watching Casey arrange the letters in the print machine. His large hands were amazingly dextrous; he handled the letter-blocks like they were butterflies.

'Sure,' John Evert replied, thankful for the distraction.

They went over to the press, and he took a seat upon a high chair. Casey began to fix the letters, passing John Evert the words, which he slotted into the tiny rails. And that was another thing about Casey, John Evert thought: he was very well-spoken. He spoke just as well as any of the other men at the *Star*, and he could read. John Evert was not sure how he knew this, but he knew that this was unusual for someone who was not a white man.

'What's the name of this type again, Casey?' he asked.

'It's Caslon type. It's what they use everywhere now, even in New York City.'

'Have you ever been to New York City?'

'No.'

'Me neither.' John Evert slotted the last word backwards into the rail, and began the next, the sentences opening like flowers beneath his hands. 'Where did you learn to read, Casey?'

'South Carolina. The man who owned me taught me when I was young so I could keep the books.'

'The man who owned you . . .' John Evert longed to ask more but had a feeling it was too rude to ask. 'Well, it's lucky he taught you,' he said instead. 'There's a whole lot more ways you can get on when you can read,' he said, parroting a sentiment of his mother's.

'He didn't teach me so I could get on,' Casey said slowly.

John Evert observed the shifting passage of emotions across the other man's face. 'What did he have you read and write?' he asked, but something in Casey's expression made John Evert no longer wish to know the answer.

'John!' Quincy said loudly, at which John Evert jumped. 'Letter for you.'

He tossed something on to John Evert's desk. He dropped down off the high chair, went to his desk and looked at the envelope. He did not recognise the hand. The envelope contained a single piece of paper: a banker's draft for twenty dollars, made out in his name. He frowned at the draft, then looked at the hand on the envelope again. Who owed him money and why twenty dollars? Then he realised who it was from and what he was being paid for. Now what he had for a bounty was double, but the money was blood money. With a confused flush of shame and excitement, he stuffed the draft into his pocket.

A growl sounded beneath his desk. He ignored it, until Quincy bellowed, 'John! Will you take that damn cur outside?' John Evert jumped.

'What's got into you today?' said Quincy. 'Jumping about like a jack rabbit. How many times have I told you I don't want that dog in here?'

The dog was standing at John Evert's feet. In just a few weeks, it had grown like a weed. Its limbs promised to be long and rangy, and its coat was darkening to a blue-grey brindle. Its ears were big and flopped about its face. It was not just cattle dog, there appeared to be an unruly mix of blood in its veins. It was tremendously ugly. John Evert loved it dearly. It looked up at him, put its tongue out and yawned, displaying a great number of white teeth. John Evert made for the door, the dog close at his heels.

'You know,' Casey said quietly, as he was passing, and he paused to listen, 'that dog's a wild thing. It'll never be proper tame.'

John Evert looked at Casey, but Casey's attention was on the letters in his hands. He replied swiftly, 'I know it, but he's all right.'

'Sure, but watch yourself. Wild things, they have a habit of turning,' Casey replied.

Once outside, John Evert fell to wondering anxiously about

the story that had come down the wire. Bill had said no one would be interested in what had occurred, but clearly he was wrong, and a man had been killed. And what did Bill think he was doing, sending money? John Evert was glad to be paid for any job but not a job like that. The banker's draft seemed to burn him through his trouser pocket. He could have died of shame. It was his fault he had fallen in with Bill: he had sought him out. Now he was not sure that had been such a good idea. He gnawed at his thumb nail, seized with an urgent need to talk to somebody. He struck off up the street, in the direction of Hector Featherstone's office.

The walk did him good. His mind unknotted a fraction, and by the time he reached Hector's door, he was all ready to confess and throw himself on Hector's mercy. He knocked at the door and let himself in, bidding his dog remain outside.

'Mr Burn!' Abraham said. 'A pleasure to see you. I trust all is well at the *Star*?'

'Yes, thank you. How are you, Abraham?'

'I find myself quite besieged with work, Mr Burn, but who would wish for any other state of affairs? The continual degeneracy of mankind is, after all, our bread and butter.'

'Er, right. Is Mr Featherstone here?'

'He is, but he is with someone. Will you wait? Take a seat. May I offer you tea?'

'Thank you. Oh, and I'll bring that book back to you. I'm sorry, I forgot it.' Hector had told John Evert that he might borrow any book he liked, and John Evert had taken advantage of his generous offer, eagerly ploughing a furrow through Hector's library.

Abraham disappeared and reappeared some minutes later with a cup of black tea that was so full of sugar it had collected like molasses at the bottom. A well-dressed man emerged from Hector's office and took his leave.

'Mr Featherstone,' Abraham said, through the door, 'young Mr Burn is here to see you.'

Abraham showed John Evert in. 'Mr Featherstone,' Abraham said, 'before you commence your interview, may I ask you a few important questions?'

John Evert shook hands with Hector and sat down. Immediately he felt calm and safe, and certain that he had come to the right place. He would tell Hector everything and Hector would know exactly what to do. John Evert sat in silence while Abraham reeled off questions at Hector, the answers to which he scribbled down in a notebook. By the time Abraham had finished this inquisition, he seemed in a state of fine agitation, and flew out of the door.

'He seems busy,' John Evert said.

'Oh, no more than usual. It is his habit to wind himself up like a clock spring. It hurts him to be idle. I wonder whether it's because they focus more on this life than us Christians, with our fascination with the idea of Heaven.'

'They?'

'The Jews.'

'Oh,' John Evert said. He had had no idea that Abraham was Jewish, but then he supposed that was because he had never met a Jewish person before. He wondered what Jewish people were supposed to be like.

'If one believes most in the importance of the here and now,' Hector continued meditatively, 'one could be forgiven for being a little anxious, I think.' Then he collected himself. 'My apologies, you did not come here for my social or theological commentary,' he said, with a rueful smile. 'Before you tell me the reason for your visit, I have some news for you also. A count has been made of the remainder of the cattle on your ranch. Two hundred—'

'Two hundred?' John Evert interrupted.

'Apparently, yes.'

'There was a lot more than that.'

'Some of the herd may have been taken by the raiders?'

'No.' John Evert shook his head. 'They were moving too fast to have taken any with them. Who made the count?'

'Phineas Gunn.'

John Evert stiffened. 'Why him?'

'Because he is the nearest landowner, and the only man nearby with the resources to do so – and he offered.'

'I bet he did,' John Evert said tightly.

Hector did not seem surprised at John Evert's animosity. He paused a moment. 'John, may I ask you a question? Was there really no arrangement between your mother and Mr Gunn?'

'Arrangement?'

'Pertaining to marriage.'

'No!' John Evert replied, so shocked he actually quivered.

Hector held up his hands in apology, splaying his fingers as though attesting to his innocence, 'I am sorry, of course. Thank you for clarifying this. I had to ask.'

'Why?'

'Because Phineas Gunn indicated to me that some sort of promise had been made.'

'Lying bastard,' John Evert breathed.

Hector raised an eyebrow. 'Please moderate your language. Whatever the case, Mr Gunn has offered to be the guardian of the land and—'

'No.' John Evert shook his head.

'There is no one else. We must be grateful for his offer. You are not of the means to do anything else.'

John Evert opened his mouth, then thought better of it, and simmered in silence as his mind darted about fruitlessly.

'Now, what was it that you came to discuss with me?' Hector asked. His face was patient and generous, but John Evert noticed the dark circles under his eyes, the way he blinked often, as though dry-eyed.

'Nothing,' John Evert mumbled. 'I just wanted to say I was getting on fine at the *Star*.'

Hector cocked his head to one side. 'That's good to hear. Is that really all? You know that you can always tell me anything, in confidence, anything at all.'

John Evert looked back at him miserably. Having been forced

to accept a favour from the man he hated most in the world, John Evert felt suddenly that Hector was no longer on his side. He was backed into a corner and, in his confusion, he retreated into himself. 'No, no, that's all,' he said quietly.

Hector studied him. Disappointment hung in the air between them.

'I'd best be going,' John Evert said.

He shook hands most briefly with Hector and went to see himself out. Before doing so, he paused and turned about. 'One thing – does he have Samson?'

'Samson?'

'The bull.'

'There was no mention of a bull, only steers and heifers.'

'Oh,' John Evert said dejectedly.

He closed the door behind him, bade Abraham farewell, and went back out on to the street.

He walked along slowly, deep in thought, occasionally stroking his dog's long ear when its head brushed against his leg. His attention was caught by a bugle as a party of soldiers cantered by. 'Where are they going?' he asked a man standing outside the general store. 'More of them to look for the Indians?' he added hopefully.

'Injuns!' the man snorted. 'They're the least of your worries. It's your fellow American you've got to watch out for, son. Every kind of thieving and looting going on around town, no one safe in their own home at night, hotbed of backstabbing immorality . . .' The man was still muttering as John Evert walked away.

He continued down the street, wondering how anyone was supposed to work out the good from the bad. In the past, at the ranch, he had thought he had known the answer to this, easy, but now, now he had no notion at all.

When he reached the *Star*, he went straight upstairs, and felt under his mattress for his twenty dollars and laid it on top of the mattress. He took the banker's draft from his pocket. A man had died for that, but he had been a brigand. John Evert's mother was missing and his cattle were being stolen by Phineas Gunn.

When he looked at it like that, there was no doubt in his mind. He made a small slit in his mattress with his knife, pushed the twenty dollars and the banker's draft neatly inside, and steeled his heart. He hoped he could do another job with Bill soon. Eight more jobs at twenty dollars and that would do it.

'About time,' Quincy said, clipping him around the ear when he returned to the print room. 'Get down to the courthouse and see what's going on with the trial.'

'You don't want me to get on with the translation?' John Evert asked.

'No, you're taking over some of Victor's work.'

'Where is Victor?' John Evert asked, bewildered by all the happenings of the day.

'He quit. You've been promoted. Congratulations,' Quincy said.

John Evert ran down to the courthouse, so surprised that he momentarily forgot his recent worries. He made it in just before they closed the doors, paper and pencil clutched in his sweaty hand. There was nowhere to sit, so he made his way to the front where he could lean upon the rail. He had no idea what the trial was about. It was not that busy in the courtroom, just the usual old-timers who listened in most days, for want of anything better to do.

'Excuse me,' he said politely, to one of the old men nearby, 'you wouldn't happen to know what this is all about?'

The man removed his long, yellow-stemmed pipe from between his teeth. 'You that boy who works at the *Star*?' John Evert, surprised to be recognised, paused a moment, then nodded. 'Same as usual – a coupla good-for-nuthin's been brawlin' an' fightin' an' shot a man in Arcadia Alley.'

'You got their names?'

'I do.' The old man, gratified to be asked, nodded as John Evert noted down the particulars of the case.

Hector's language was delicate as ever, and despite John Evert's recent frustration, he thought it a pity all that eloquence was scattered on the stony ground of the jury, who listened open-mouthed and confused by much of the proceedings.

It was no surprise when Judge Ogier passed his usual sentence of death by hanging, but then he paused, and said gravely to the courtroom, 'These are difficult times we find ourselves in, but note this – I will not hesitate to mete out the harshest sentence to any man who is under the misapprehension that he may take advantage of these straitened times to break the law and go without punishment. The rule of law shall be upheld, by this court at least.'

John Evert followed the people outside and, for the first time, went with them to where the hangings took place. Previously, he had never wished to see the final justice done, but something about all the confusions of the day made him want to see it through to the end, to know for himself how things were.

He was surprised at the makeshift nature of it all. He had expected more ceremony. As it was, it was a crude scaffold, surrounded by general junk, with a few stray dogs hanging about the place, attracted by the smell of death. A woman in the group gathered before the gallows was crying. The two unfortunates took the stand together and stood looking down at their bound hands, all bluster knocked out of them. They were given the opportunity to speak. The first had nothing to say. He just swallowed a few times and shook his head. The other cleared his throat and proclaimed loudly, 'I'm sorry for the things I done and let ever'one here know. But, most, I'm sorry I got caught. There's every man in this town out for hisself, and there's men in this crowd who's just as guilty as I am.'

There was a bit of cat-calling at this, but others shifted about.

The first man asked for his eyes to be covered, which the hangman did. The other refused the hood. He looked out at the people as the overworked father did a hasty commendation of their souls to the Lord Almighty. He stared directly at John Evert as the noose was settled about his neck. It seemed in that instant that he and John Evert were the only living creatures in that benighted place. John Evert, transfixed, could not take his eyes away.

When they opened the trapdoor beneath him, the noise of the man's falling was a muted thump. He kicked for an awful long time, far longer than John Evert would have expected, twitching horribly until he was finally still. John Evert's mouth filled with a bitter taste and he pushed his way through the people to open ground where he was sick.

He walked back to the *Star* and dropped his notes upon the table next to Quincy, then walked right back out again, his dog hard on his heels.

'Where do you think you're going?' Quincy asked. 'Hey!'

John Evert walked around the back of the *Star*, and came across Bill there, leaning against the wall, eyes shut, basking in the sun, like a giant lizard. He opened one eye, rolled it down to look at John Evert, then shut it again. 'You got what I left for you?' he asked.

'Yes.' John Evert shuffled his feet in the dust. 'I watched a man hang,' he said.

'Hmm,' Bill hummed.

'It's awful.'

'Death usually is.'

'I've seen plenty of animals die. It was never like that. I don't ever want to be hung—'

'Hanged,' Bill interrupted.

'What?'

'Hanged, not hung.'

John Evert blinked. Bill sure was a strange man. 'I don't ever want to be *hanged*. I'd rather go by a gun.'

'A sensible choice.'

'That man you killed. He was a bad man?'

'He was.'

'Doesn't it make you bad to kill a man?'

'Not always. It depends on the circumstances, and the man.'

'How many men have you killed?'

'No idea. In the war, I killed a lot,' Bill said. 'A lot.'

'Maybe my pa did, too.'

'Maybe.' Bill nodded.

John Evert stroked the head of his dog thoughtfully, and squinted against the sun.

'Here, I've something to show you,' Bill said. 'Come with me.'

They went inside Bill's place, and he went to the corner of the room. He threw some blankets off a large wooden trunk, bent down, unlocked the heavy clasp and pushed back the lid, heaving the trunk forward so the brightness from the skylight fell inside. John Evert peered over his shoulder, and took a sharp breath.

Arranged in neat wooden holdings was an arsenal of the highest quality. The silver of the rifles' inlay gleamed like moonstone. Bill reached in, withdrew two flintlock pistols from one side of the chest and held them up for John Evert to see. 'These were made by Joseph Manton. The father of all gunmakers. Master of a man. Here, have a play with 'em.' He proceeded to empty the chest a piece at a time, explaining the history and merits of each. There were beautiful rifles with the most delicate silver filigree on the inlay and glossy walnut stocks; pieces such as John Evert had never seen or even imagined to exist. The last gun that Bill drew out, he hesitated over. 'And this . . . This is a Whitworth. You know what's so clever about it? The hexagonal barrel. It grips the bullet, which is hexagonal, too, see. Gives you a grip you wouldn't believe. No more ball rattling around the barrel. You have to make the bullets, melt down the lead and cast them, but you know how many yards you can shoot accurate with this son-of-a-bitch? Twelve hundred.'

'Really,' John Evert said, with disbelief. Taking the rifle that Bill bestowed upon him, he admired the barrel's polygonal rifling.

'I'll let you try it out, if you like. You're an okay shot, I reckon, but I can teach you how to be better, a lot better than others.'

The mere thought of being able to shoot the beautiful guns made John Evert quiver with excitement, and the notion of becoming a great shot was pretty compelling too. He would become a crack shot, raise the money for a bounty, go with Bill to find his mother and they would rescue her together.

'I have business down south in a week's time,' Bill said, licking the paper of the *cigarrito* he was rolling. 'I'll be needing a hand.'

'You'll pay me for my part?' John Evert said.

Bill chuckled. 'Yeah, I'll pay you. It sounds like it'll be coming back to my pocket in the end, doesn't it?'

'What about Quincy? How's he going to let me go off with you? Who'll do my work?'

'From what I hear there's a new boy starting at the *Star*.'

'How'd you know?'

'Casey told me.'

'Are you and Casey friends?'

'Yep.'

'Will I still have a job when I come back?' John Evert asked, remembering Hector's admonition that he must keep that job.

'Yep. I heard you'd been promoted anyway.'

'Yes, I suppose I have. Did you have anything to do with that?'

'Certainly not. I heard Victor left.'

'Did you have anything to do with *that*, then?' John Evert said. Bill flicked a look at him, which made John Evert decide to quit that line of questioning while he was ahead. 'Well, then . . .' John Evert said, the gleam from the silver-laid breech of one of the rifles playing in the corner of his eye. 'Sure. I'll go with you.'

9

John Evert had hoped it would take a matter of weeks to raise the bounty, but after that second job, Bill did not take on another for a month, and time began to stretch out. Weeks turned into two months. In the meantime, the soldiers who had been sent on the trail of his mother had violently chastised a band of Paiute at Sharps Spring and killed twelve. The severed heads of the dead men had been displayed as a warning. John Evert had been viciously pleased at this news but it did little to counter the fact that the soldiers had failed to uncover any sign of his mother. Eventually, they were posted on other duties.

The marshal imparted this news to him with a heavy countenance and was obviously relieved when he took the news apparently well. Little did he know that John Evert had his own plan afoot and that he had placed all his hopes in Bill, for the more he got to know him, the more John Evert was certain that if anyone could track down his mother, it would be Bill. He had convinced himself that the passage of time was not that important. All that mattered was getting Bill to take the job.

Bill, meanwhile, was making something of a protégé of John Evert. The moment John Evert finished his day's work at the *Star*, Bill was instructing him in the mysteries of tracking and fighting. He taught him how to light a *cigarrito* and fire a rifle accurately while cantering, with the reins jammed under his knees to keep the horse's head straight. John Evert learned the paramount importance of bluffing, the advantages of some well-timed humour, the enormous fun to be had in shooting out the lights at a local fandango and how not to betray emotion while watching Bill fight a duel. Bill, he discovered, was invincible, and quite without remorse, fear or morality. He was the world's own devil.

This was not to say that Bill sailed through life entirely unscathed, but he never seemed to suffer anything more than the occasional flesh wound. If anything, the greatest danger to Bill was Bill.

One hot day, the staff of the *Star* was kicking its heels in the shade immediately opposite the building where Bill was engaged in his scientific experiments for the benefit of mankind when, all of a sudden, there was an almighty explosion. The upstairs windows and the door blew out. Smoke billowed from the empty window frames. Casey, John Evert and Meriweather rushed in, and were in the midst of clearing the smoky wreckage in search of Bill when he emerged from Mr Hardy's drugstore, which doubled as a saloon, where he had paused to refresh himself with whiskey.

There was great relief that Bill had not been killed, but this event put paid to Bill's claim that his laboratory had been set up simply for the distillation of hooch. The marshal was straight down there, demanding to know whether Bill was engaged in the making of gunpowder and other incendiaries. Bill swore this not to be the case, and confused the marshal greatly by reeling off the names of all the possible flammable chemicals that might have been responsible. In the absence of any evidence, the marshal was forced to take his word for it, but he served Bill a notice that he was forthwith banned from the making of anything at all within the limits of Los Angeles, which Bill considered narrow-minded of him, but acceptable in the circumstances.

Apart from liquor, Bill appeared to have only one other weakness: a love of women. Despite his almost total lack of respect for his fellow man, he was possessed of an excess of gallantry when it came to the fairer sex, and they were helplessly attracted to him in return. John Evert could never work out what it was about Bill that the ladies found so compelling, but that lopsided smile of his seemed to bring about the most peculiar transformations. John Evert had been witness to a woman in a store who had been reduced to a red-faced, stammering girl by nothing more than Bill's leaning his elbows upon the counter, gazing up at her and refusing to answer her repeated question as to how she might be able to help him. Eventually, the young lady had retreated out back and fetched an older lady to assist him. John Evert found it all most curious.

The next job Bill took John Evert on was a quiet one. They travelled to Thousand Oaks and hung about, watching the comings and goings along the stagecoach route.

'What are we doing here?' John Evert asked.

'Gathering information,' Bill replied.

'Information about what?'

Bill said nothing. And nothing happened at all that time, but Bill paid John Evert a few dollars all the same, which was better than nothing.

To John Evert's relief, he did not have to think up a story to tell Meriweather about where he had gone with Bill on that occasion as Quincy had announced beforehand that John Evert was being sent to check the crop report and a property dispute in the area. 'John Evert's our new roving reporter,' Quincy said, evidently pleased with the term. When Meriweather snorted at this, Quincy snapped, 'And you, Meriweather, fancy some out-of-town work?'

'No, no, thank you,' said Meriweather, shaking his head. 'I welcome the sight of my own bed more than any sight you can show me.'

'Well, then, you just pipe down,' Quincy said.

John Evert indeed found out about the crop report while he was away, and it did appear in the pages of the *Star*, but he was near sure that Bill had put this notion into Quincy's head, as a way of ensuring no undue attention was called to John Evert's absence. If this was indeed the case, then Bill must have a lot of influence over Quincy, John Evert thought. He did wonder about that, but he knew better than to ask Bill. There were questions it was fine to put to him, but there were plenty that were not, and John Evert was learning where these invisible lines lay.

The next job they did, Bill left John Evert in a saloon house some sixty miles outside Los Angeles, and was gone for more than twenty-four hours. He was beside himself with concern by the time Bill finally sauntered back through the door to tell him they were heading back to Los Angeles. He made a point of saying nothing about Bill's long absence, for if there was one thing Bill hated more than annoying questions, it was a fuss.

When John Evert went to saddle the horses, he found a Spaniard, gagged and bound, tied to the hitching post. 'Who's that?' he asked.

'A good-for-nothing,' Bill replied. 'We're taking him with us.'

Bill slung the man upon a hired horse, which he led by a long lead rein. The man clearly suffered on the ride for Bill made no alteration to their usual pace, and John Evert, who turned in his saddle repeatedly to look back at the man as he lolled from side to side upon the horse, asked if he might give him some water.

'If you want,' Bill said, 'but don't untie his hands.'

When they paused in the shade of a tree, Bill pulled the man off his horse and dumped him on the ground. John Evert untied his gag and the man unleashed a torrent of curses. John Evert was taken aback, but showed the man his canteen. The man ceased cursing, and let him pour water into his mouth.

Afterward, he looked at John Evert, but there was no gratitude in his expression. John Evert knew then that if the man had been able to get free, he would, with no compunction, have slit John Evert's throat. He replaced the man's gag, and did not look at him again.

When they reached Los Angeles, Bill took the man to the marshal and handed him in; it transpired that there was a bounty on his head. The marshal noticed John Evert in the background and, when he recognised him, he said sharply, 'Bill, what is this boy doing with you?'

'Him?' Bill replied, with lack of interest. 'Taking my horse to the blacksmith.'

'He's not been with you . . .' the marshal began.

'Hell, no. You think I travel with green kids, these days?' Bill tutted, turned his horse and walked away.

The marshal continued to gaze suspiciously at John Evert. 'Son,' he said, coming to the roan's side, 'I know Bill must seem pretty smart to you . . . well, he is pretty smart, but I would advise you against becoming too friendly.'

John Evert did not reply, but touched his hat brim politely and led the roan away. He had no interest in the marshal's opinion when the man had failed to do anything useful in the search for his mother. Coming across a stone in his path, John Evert kicked it violently. When he had made the mistake of asking Bill when the next job might be, Bill had snapped at him. John Evert had not mentioned it again.

His spirits brightened upon his return to the *Star* when his dog gave him its usual hero's welcome. It shadowed him everywhere he went, as though determined that he should not escape again. The animal was so jealous of his affections that the only other person who could do anything with it was Casey, who fed and cared for it while John Evert was away.

John Evert had continued to stash his rewards in his mattress, but he began to worry that somebody might find it, or that some terrible accident, such as a fire, would snatch his gains away. He knew the best thing would be to open an account at the bank, so the money was safe, but he was not sure how to do this. He did not want to ask Bill: he had a feeling that Bill would dismiss the idea of a bank when money or gold stashed under a floorboard or tree seemed his preferred method of housing his assets. Hector was the most obvious person to ask but he would want to know how John Evert had managed to accrue such a sum. In the end, he asked the quietest, most trustworthy person to hand: Casey.

'Casey,' he said, when they were alone in the dorm one evening, 'if I wanted to put some money in the bank, can I just go and open an account?'

Casey turned his shiny, serene face to him and said, 'How old are you?'

'Fifteen, nearly sixteen.'

'You'll need someone older to vouch for you.'

'Would you do that for me?'

Casey smiled then, a wry smile. 'I'd have been glad to, but you'll need someone else.'

'Why?'

'You need someone of position.'

'You mean someone white,' John Evert said uncomfortably. Casey nodded. John Evert frowned and fell to thinking.

'Why don't you ask the boss – Mr Rivers?'

'What'll I tell him I want it for?'

'Well, tell him you want to save some of your wages. That must be what you want to open the account for, right?' Casey said slowly, raising his eyebrows.

John Evert flushed a little. 'Yeah, of course,' he said.

Casey nodded. 'And you can tell him the bank's got a prize on – anyone putting down money just now gets their name in a draw.'

'Oh, yeah, what's the prize?'

'A hog.'

'How'd you know this, Casey?'

'I listen to what's going on.'

'Why would the bank be doing that, offering a prize?'

'To get people to put their money in there. Too many folks keeping their money under their floorboards or in their old mattresses,' Casey said.

John Evert's eyes flashed to Casey, but he had turned away and was folding laundry.

'You ask Mr Rivers, that's your best bet,' Casey said.

'Thanks, Casey. I appreciate it,' John Evert replied.

As Casey predicted, Quincy did not mind vouching for John Evert. Indeed, he seemed delighted. John Evert looked him in the eye and said that he wished to put aside a little each month for a new set of clothes, and Quincy commended him for his good sense, then added loudly, for the benefit of the rest of the staff, that he would prefer to see them all saving, rather than spending their wages in the Bella Union.

John Evert felt as though he were learning new things every day. When he saw the young boy who had taken on his junior role at the *Star*, he felt as though he was in possession of a great wealth of knowledge in comparison. He liked his new-found intelligence: it made him feel stronger, more capable; and with Bill at his side, he always felt safe, for there was no man more confident than he. But there were yet things in the world that were confusing to John Evert.

To date, on the jobs he had done with Bill, they had stayed in a saloon, or lodging house, but on the next one they stayed in a place that seemed to be occupied only by women. It was evening when they arrived, and the women in the parlour must have been feeling the heat, he thought, for they were scantily attired. They smiled a great deal at him and made him feel uncomfortable. He was glad when he was able to go upstairs. Bill had disappeared off somewhere, which was quite normal. John Evert sat down upon the bed, pulled off his boots and threw himself backward with a sigh.

He got a shock when the door opened, and a blowsy woman in a low-cut black lace dress entered. She had reddish hair and her skin was very white, like tissue paper. 'Well, hello,' she said.

'Hello, ma'am,' John Evert replied.

'Is there anything I can get you?'

'No, thank you, ma'am. I ate.'

'Would you like me to stay and keep you company a while?'

'That's all right, ma'am. I'm waiting for my friend,' he said awkwardly.

She giggled. 'Oh, I don't think you'll be seeing him till morning.' John Evert did not know what to say to this. 'How old are you?' she asked.

'I'll be sixteen soon.'

'Sixteen, huh? Little man, huh? Little big man.' She giggled again.

John Evert did not smile back. There was something about

the woman that he felt very strongly his mother would disapprove of, and the thought made him grave. 'If you don't mind, ma'am, I'm pretty tired. I'd best be getting some sleep,' he said.

'Oh, all right,' she said, and stalked out.

He was relieved when she was gone, taking the sickly smell of perfume with her. He undressed, got into bed and was about to fall asleep when there was another knock at the door. 'Bill?' he said.

'No,' said a quiet female voice. It was not the woman from before.

'Who is it?'

'Can I come in?' she whispered.

'Okay,' John Evert said reluctantly.

The candle by his bed still burned, and when the door opened he could see a mousy blonde girl. She was wearing a long white nightdress. She could not have been any older than him. 'Who are you?' he asked.

She dropped her gaze shyly. 'I been tol' I have to sleep in here.'

'Why?'

'There ain't enough beds in the girls' rooms. I'm new.'

John Evert sat up, wondering what was going on. He was sorely tempted to tell her to beat it, but she looked fair pitiful and he could not bring himself to do it. Also, it was not his house, so who was he to say what was right? 'Can you turn around?' he asked.

She faced the wall. He got out of bed and put his breeches back on.

'Here,' he said, holding back the warm blanket.

'What about you?'

'I'll sleep on the floor.'

She was panicked. 'Can't you sleep in the bed with me?'

'Why?'

'Because I'll get in trouble with Miss Cee if she finds you on the floor.'

John Evert felt intensely awkward at this. 'I can't,' he said.

Her eyes welled with tears. 'Oh, please. You can keep your clothes on if you like.'

'Of course I'll keep my clothes on,' he said angrily. 'What'd you think . . .?'

Eventually, moved by her unhappiness and the dark circles under her eyes, he put her into the bed, and climbed in after her. He tucked the blanket down between them, and tried to keep away from her as much as he could, but she kept coming over to his side of the bed. He felt a great confusion, and was torn between wishing her gone and an uncomfortable excitement at her nearness. She put a hand upon his chest, and then she moved her fingers lower to his belt and tried to undo it. There was desperation in her fluttering hands. To John Evert's dismay, he found himself growing hard.

It was not that he did not understand how things worked, but he knew that this was for married people, and there was in his mind a faint recollection of something he had heard once that had involved the daughter of a neighbouring family and a pregnancy out of wedlock. His mother's reaction had made clear to him the disgrace involved. And yet he felt himself consumed by the tingling in his body that made him want her to touch him. She moved her head close to his, and kissed him. To his surprise, her mouth was open. She put her tongue against his and he could not help but respond, and he could no longer stop her putting her hands on him. She stroked him in a way that was different from how he had, often enough, touched himself, and it was only a matter of moments before he convulsed and, to his shame, soaked the sheets.

To his relief, she said nothing, seeming simply calmed by this occurrence. She stroked his arm absentmindedly, and soon her breaths slowed and deepened, and she slept. She turned away from him but pressed the whole length of her warm body against him, and he put an arm round her. In her sleep, she settled herself more comfortably, squeezed his wrist, and held on to it the whole night long.

In the morning, they were startled awake by the door bursting open and Bill striding in.

'Come on, kid, it's late,' he said, rubbing his drowsy eyes with the heels of his hands. He yawned loudly in the direction of the window, then looked down at them where they lay. The blankets had slipped half off them and Bill took in their clothed state, the girl resting her head in the crook of John Evert's arm. An amused smile broke across his face. He shook his head. 'I don't know, kid,' he said. 'You are one of a kind.'

'You won't tell,' the girl said, dragging the blankets back up over them.

'It matters not to me what you do or don't get up to, little miss,' he said.

When Bill left, John Evert sat up to put on his boots. She lay in the bed, staring at him.

'What are you looking at?' he asked, not unkindly.

'Your face.'

'What about it?'

'I like your nose.'

John Evert blushed. 'I don't know why. It isn't straight.'

'That's what I like about it. How'd it happen?'

He shrugged. 'A fight.'

'Look at me,' she said. He did as he was bade. 'You've the prettiest green eyes I ever saw.'

'Boys' eyes can't be pretty.'

'Sure they can.'

'I gotta go.'

'Will you give me a kiss?' she asked.

He fiddled with his boots as he pulled them on, embarrassed by the memory of the night before, then bent down and kissed her forehead. Then he pulled the blankets up to her chin and tucked her in, the way his mother used to do.

'What's your name?' she asked.

'Kid,' he said.

She smiled sadly, 'Well, you're the nicest kid I ever met here.'

He tried to imagine of what her life consisted. Then he nodded at her, and left. Bill was waiting by the front door.

'Did you give her some money?' Bill asked.

'Money? What for?'

'Jesus,' Bill said, under his breath. He went back up the stairs.

When Bill returned, he said, 'For reasons I fail to understand, it appears you made a great impression upon that girl.'

'Do you always give a girl money?' John Evert asked, perplexed.

'Only the cheap ones, kid, never the ladies.'

'What do you give ladies?'

'A dress, gloves . . . a new hat.'

'That's no different from giving them money.'

Bill chuckled as he put on his hat and straightened the brim. 'No, kid, it isn't really, but that is one of the beautiful subtleties of womankind.'

'Hmph,' John Evert said, as he followed Bill outside.

As they walked along, John Evert noticed two men coming toward them. They wore white men's dress but they were Indians. John Evert drew up short and, without a word to Bill, he dropped down off the boardwalk and crossed to the other side of the street, aware of what felt like a cold, hard piece of metal in his chest.

Bill took a while to catch up with him and, when he did, he walked at John Evert's side for a while in silence. Then he said, 'How would you feel if I crossed the street when I saw Casey coming?'

'That's different. Casey's a good man.'

'No, it isn't. It's no different at all. You want to watch that about yourself, kid. I don't ride with bigots.'

John Evert, surprised by the tone of Bill's voice, turned, and saw that he was very angry. They tightened their horses' girths in silence. He resolved to make his feelings less obvious in Bill's presence, but could not bring himself to try to change them. Bill's opinion mattered terribly to him, but on this one thing it was just too hard.

John Evert did not expect his sixteenth birthday to be different from any other day. He was surprised, therefore, when Quincy wished him well that morning.

'How did you know it was my birthday?' John Evert asked.

'Hector Featherstone informed me of it. Take a few days off, why not? What'll you do?'

'I . . .' John Evert thought for a moment. 'I'll go to my ranch, if that's all right.'

'No bother to me what you do. How far away is it?'

'A day's ride.'

'Well, I'm sure Bill will lend you a horse.'

Bill let him have the roan, and John Evert set off out of town, his dog loping along at his side.

Most unexpectedly, Hector had handed him a gift – a book, which he had inscribed to John Evert – while Bill had given him a pistol: a shiny, brand-new Colt. John Evert rode out of town with his treasures in his saddlebag, considering himself very fortunate.

There had been a few days of rain, and the ground was a riot of purple wildflowers that undulated all the way to the horizon in a violet carpet, interspersed here and there with patches of yellow, as though the sun had spattered molten droplets of itself to earth. The air was alive with the hum of bees that worked busily, heavy with pollen, so that the air about him vibrated like a plucked string, and as dusk began to fall, the music of the bees was replaced by the drier strigil saw of crickets.

He rode slowly for he did not wish to rush his arrival, and he made camp at a small *cienaga* where groundwater had swelled to the surface to form a small, marshy pool, overhung by willows. He did not bother with a fire, enjoying instead the light of a full moon that bathed the landscape about him in a pale blue light, which he viewed from safe behind the dark curtains of the willows. His dog sat next to him. It was full grown now, all puppyishness gone; it was tall and very muscular in the shoulder, with a big, square head. He watched its profile as it studied the night, its big ears lifted wide at the night noises.

'You can go see. Go on,' John Evert said.

It turned its head to him, then back in the direction of the plain, and remained where it was, its cheeks puffing out gently as it sniffed the air. It never left his side.

The next day, he rode the last of the way, the contours of the country becoming familiar. It was a strange feeling, coming home. In part, it was wonderful, and he was thrilled at the idea of seeing his land once more, but a great part of him wondered how he should feel to see it without her. With every step toward the ranch, memories came thick and fast.

At the border of the property, he was in two minds whether to go first to his special place – the spliced oak – or the ranch house, but of course there was no longer a ranch house, so he directed the roan toward the tree, and skirted round the back of the pastures to get there. When he saw its peculiar, lumpen shape in the distance, he hesitated, then dismounted and walked the remainder on foot, as though he were approaching something sacred.

When he reached the tree, he was flooded with the warmth of familiarity. It was just the same, the twisted, hollow trunk cradling the holly bush within. He circled it, running his hands around its puckered girth, the wood dry and reassuring to his touch. He shut his eyes for a moment, and listened to the faint breeze and the song of a warbler hidden somewhere in the branches. His dog sniffed the tree, put its great paws upon the bowl of the split trunk and looked within.

'Pretty fine, isn't it?' John Evert said, stroking its neck. The dog pressed itself against him.

He lay down in the long grass, and closed his eyes against the sun. The song of the ascending warbler mingled with the whir of the crickets and the occasional stamp of the roan's hoof as it shooed away a fly. It was heaven.

Eventually, he got up and walked down in the direction of the ranch house, with a blade of grass hanging out of the side of his mouth. He came through the woods and stopped dead.

He had expected the scene to be just as he had left it, but that was not the case. Instead of the piles of cinders, or charred ground, fresh grass had covered the area that had been burned black; where once the ranch house had stood, there stood now a brand-new house, set very much along the lines of the original. Complete confusion stopped John Evert in his tracks. His dog sensed his bewilderment, and whined.

He approached the building slowly, stepped up on to the porch and looked in at a window. It was very bare, with just a log-burning stove in the corner, and a single chair at a table. He tried the front door, and found it open. There were two oil lamps and a couple of splints for lighting them, which had been used. At the rear, two rooms; one empty, the other containing two single beds and a couple of saddles. It was impossible to explain.

He went back outside, and walked around the property, looking for an answer. At the back of the building, he found it.

Branded into one of the low sleepers that had been used for the foundation was the double letter G, back to back. Phineas Gunn's brand.

Something in John Evert caught fire, as though someone had set a red-hot coal in his belly. He kicked furiously at the wood, and when his boot made no impression upon it, he ran to the roan's saddlebag, took out the Colt Bill had given him, and placed a shot in the middle of the letters. The resounding blast brought him to his senses, and he wrestled his emotions under control.

His dog sat watching him, alert, its ears pricked. He looked back at it, wondering what to do next. He decided to ride around the ranch and see what else was going on. He mounted the roan and cantered off to make a circuit. He found fences in good order, and he found cattle, some with the Burn brand, a lot with the Gunn brand. He rode along the Gunn boundary a good while and, after about an hour, he spied a lone rider. The other rider saw him, paused and put his hand up to the brim of his hat. They were too far apart to be able to get a proper look at each other. John Evert turned the roan about and trotted away.

He returned to the ranch house, and wondered what to do. As it was, his mind was made up for him as two men appeared in the distance. John Evert wished very much then that Bill was with him. His dog spied the riders, and growled softly. He bade it get under the porch steps and lie down in the shade while he awaited the riders' approach. Out of habit, he tucked the Colt into the back of his breeches, for he had no holster.

'Good day,' he said to the riders, when they drew up and halted some yards away.

'What's your business here?' one asked. 'This is private property.'

'I know it.'

'Well, if you know it what are you doing?' the man retorted. He dismounted and walked toward John Evert. He was a tall man, thick in the neck and stupid in the face.

'It's been a long time since I was here.'

'Who are you?' the man demanded.

'John Evert Burn. This is my place.'

The man squinted down at him. 'No, it ain't. It's Phineas Gunn's.'

'Listen—' John Evert began, but he was silenced by the man striking him lazily in the stomach. The blow folded him to the ground, all the breath knocked out of him.

'Hey, Sam,' the other man on the horse said chidingly. He might have continued, but a liquid blue shade poured with unnatural speed from beneath the porch, leaping at the man who had struck John Evert, burying its teeth in his forearm. The man yelled in pain as the dog knocked him to the ground, worrying his arm as though it were a rabbit.

'Holy shit!' cried the man on the horse, taking his gun from his holster, and aiming at the dog. John Evert sat up, taking a roaring intake of breath into his emptied lungs, but, unable to speak, did the only other thing available to him: he drew his Colt from his belt and fired at the man's hand, shooting the pistol right out of it. The man cried out in surprise, and as his horse reared in alarm he was unseated and fell. The terrified horse bolted.

John Evert was still seated upon the ground, taking gasping breaths. As soon as he was able he bellowed brokenly at his dog, 'No, leave it!'

Reluctantly, the dog did so, and took a few steps back from the man, blood around its muzzle and a crazed look in its eye.

'No,' John Evert said breathlessly at it. 'No.' He got shakily to his feet, and stumbled over to the man on the ground. 'You okay?' he asked.

'What the hell?' wailed the man, cradling his bloody forearm.

'I'm sorry,' John Evert stammered. 'He thought you were . . .' John Evert found himself shaking and having trouble speaking, but no more so than the two men on the ground, who looked fearfully at the dog. John Evert snapped at it, and it skulked back to the porch. John Evert went over to their remaining horse. He coaxed it toward him, stroked its neck and calmed it, then led it over to the man who had fallen and was now standing, brushing the dust from his trousers.

'Here,' John Evert said, handing him the reins. 'I'm awful sorry.'

The man stared at him confusedly. John Evert went to where he had seen the man's pistol land, and retrieved it. He emptied the cylinder of bullets and handed it back to him.

'What did you say your name was?' the man asked.

'John Evert Burn.'

'Hey, Sam,' he said to the other, who was also getting to his feet, 'you okay?'

'No, dammit, I ain't,' he said.

'Come on,' said the other, boosting him on to the rear of his horse, before mounting in front of him. He looked down at John Evert, his eyes alight with curiosity. 'This was your place, weren't it?' he said. John Evert nodded. 'I heard you were dead.'

'No,' John Evert said. 'Look, it was an accident. Gunn can't—'

'For pity's sake, will you get us outta here?' the injured man cursed, clutching his arm.

'I'd better take him to get that arm fixed,' the man said. He turned the horse and they began to trot away.

John Evert watched them go. When they were out of sight, he went back to the house.

His dog was watching him, wagging its tail, still with that deranged look in its eye. He felt disturbed. Perhaps Casey had been right; perhaps he did not know the dog, after all. He stared at its bloody muzzle. Under John Evert's stern gaze, the dog's ears slowly drooped. Then it lay down and crawled toward him a few paces on its belly. Suddenly it was once more the puppy he knew. With relief, he whistled to it. It skittered to his side and gazed up at him adoringly.

He took the dog down to the river, washed the blood off it and went for a swim. He had planned to stay that night but he was filled with foreboding at what had happened, and at Gunn's building on his land, and he decided he had better return to town with all haste to seek advice.

10

It was Bill he went to first. He told his tale and Bill, who was polishing a boot at the time, winced. 'Now, that wasn't very smart, kid. Using your pistol and, moreover, in such a handy way. You and that damn dog. You need to learn when's the time to sacrifice something you care for.'

Appalled, John Evert replied, 'I was defending myself. The man had a gun pointed at me.'

'It's not you having a gun that's the rub. It's how an inky kid who works on a newspaper would come to shoot so well. What are you going to do if Gunn and his men come after you?'

Bill trundled his cigarette from one side of his mouth to the other. 'It's important to plan for every eventuality.'

John Evert chewed the inside of his cheek.

'Don't worry about it too much, though.' Bill sighed. 'I've got it.'

John Evert glanced at him hopefully, but Bill gave no further explanation, saying simply, 'You'd better get back to work, hadn't you?'

John Evert returned to his desk, and picked up where he had left off reading. Politics did not impinge upon his day-to-day existence, but even he was not immune to the fact that seven cotton-growing states in the South had asked for secession. He did not really understand what it was all about, but he knew what he did not like about the South.

He cast an uncomfortable glance at Casey, where he was hunched over the print machine, tinkering with something. It just did not seem right to him to keep another man as a slave just because of the colour of his skin. Quincy might not be the definition of a principled man, but John Evert liked him greatly because he employed Casey, paid him a wage and treated him no different from any other man at the *Star*.

An errand boy appeared at the door, with a soft knock, and shuffled about. 'I got a message here for Mr John Evert Burn,' the boy said.

It was from Hector Featherstone, and it requested an immediate interview. John Evert reached into his pocket and handed the runty kid five cents.

'Thanks, mister.' The boy beamed.

'You can tell Mr Featherstone I'll be right over.'

'Hey, have you finished that article?' Quincy demanded. 'Before you go off on your personal business in the middle of the working day.'

'It's been on your desk this half-hour,' John Evert replied.

'Oh, well . . . off you go, then.'

'Is this true, that you shot a gun out of a man's hand?' Hector asked, peering at John Evert over his spectacles, eyebrows raised, keen eyes boring into him in the uncomfortable way he had when his interest was piqued.

'I guess so,' John Evert replied, looking somewhere over Hector's left shoulder.

'Lucky shot?' Hector enquired.

'Yeah.'

Hector studied him, and John Evert had the uncomfortable sensation that Hector was looking right through him to the wall beyond. He resisted the urge to shift in his chair. Bill had been right. Perhaps it had not been such a good idea. Why had he not thought to aim wide and just scare the man?

'What do you do in your spare time, John Evert?' Hector asked, opening a hand toward him, as though to draw out the truth. 'When you are not at work at the *Star*, I mean.'

John Evert hesitated for a fraction of a second. 'I go riding.'

'Bill has lent you a horse, I understand.' John Evert nodded.

'That is generous of him. What do you do for him in return? Someone has told me that you run errands for him. Sometimes you are gone with him for several days at a time.'

'Who told you that?'

Hector did not reply, merely raising his eyebrows as he awaited an answer.

'Yes. I go away with Bill sometimes.'

'What do you do on these trips?'

'Bill meets acquaintances of his.'

'And you? What do you do?'

'I gather news for Mr Rivers on things – auctions, local news and such.'

'I see. Does this business happen to take you to saloons, or gaming houses, perhaps?'

John Evert said nothing, figuring silence better than a lie. Hector's gaze scoured John Evert, his eyes like flints. 'What has got into you, John Evert? Your mother would not approve.'

The blood rushed to John Evert's face, and his hands, which rested upon his thighs, gripped the flesh tight enough to pinch. 'What are you going to do about Phineas Gunn building on my land?' he demanded.

'Mr Gunn told me that he wished to erect a shelter for his *vaqueros* when they were working your land. I gave him a written dispensation to do so, which you may see here. Clearly, if he had built anything on your land without permission it would constitute a hostile takeover. Gunn is not a fool. He also signed this document, which confirms that he is paying a token rent for grazing his cattle on your land. When I told you that I would look after your interests, I meant it.'

John Evert chewed his thumbnail. 'I've a mind to go back there and burn that house down.'

'If that is your attitude then why not sell the ranch and be done with it?' Hector snapped, to John Evert's surprise. 'Is that what you want?' Hector threw open his hands, as though framing for John Evert a picture.

'I came to you for help,' John Evert said.

'And I am giving it. Now, listen to me,' Hector said, his arched brows drawn into sharp angles. 'There is more. Gunn is furious about your dog savaging his man.'

'He didn't savage him. He roughed him up some, but that man had knocked me down.'

'Gunn wants you to pay for his man's treatment at the infirmary.'

'I won't,' John Evert replied.

'It would be unwise to antagonise Gunn.'

'Why? Because he plans to play my stepdaddy?' John Evert spat the word. 'Because he's telling you he and my ma had plans to marry? You know if Phineas Gunn got me out of the way, he could claim my land as his own?'

'Be reasonable.' Hector sighed.

'I've heard of this sort of thing happening before,' John Evert said.

'Where? From your desk at the *Star*? You seem very worldly for a young man of sixteen years. Where have you become so familiar with the ways of the world? On your trips with Bill, perhaps?' Hector was smiling, but his eyes were not.

John Evert had the distinct feeling that he had fallen into a trap of some kind. He decided to get away from Hector's line of questioning as fast as possible. 'I'm sorry, Mr Featherstone, I have to get back. Mr Rivers can't do without me. Good day.' He got to his feet and swiftly made his exit.

He spent the next couple of days in a low-lying state of anxiety, which was compounded by the daily news, which spoke of fresh unrest across the country. On 4 March 1861 Lincoln had stated that his administration would not initiate civil war, but still the ugly prospect hung heavy about Los Angeles. John Evert would have liked to talk to Bill, but he had disappeared, with no word of his expected return.

A day later, he was walking down Main Street with his dog

when he was met with the disturbing sight of mounted figures outside the *Star*. They comprised Phineas Gunn, the marshal and three other men. Quincy spoke with them. At John Evert's approach, they turned to him.

'Good day, Marshal,' John Evert said.

'Good day, son,' the marshal said, as he dismounted. 'I'm sorry to say that Mr Gunn here wishes to press charges against you.'

'What for?'

'Attacking his men.'

'I was on my own property.'

'You were, but there's no excuse for setting your dog on a man.'

John Evert looked up at Gunn on his horse. A smile played upon Gunn's dry pink lips, and an insufferable smugness hung about him, like an odour. John Evert's eyes smarted with hatred.

'I don't want to be unfair,' Gunn said. 'I'm prepared to accept that that animal is wild and out of control.'

John Evert looked down at his dog, which sat at his heels, panting calmly. Sensing his eyes upon it, it put its head back and gazed up at him, its ugly brick face split in a happy grin. 'He doesn't look savage to me,' John Evert said.

'Me neither.' The marshal chuckled.

'But the fact remains that it attacked my man,' said Gunn. 'It is within my rights to ask for the arrest of John Evert Burn . . .' John Evert looked at him in alarm 'or . . .' Gunn paused '. . . to demand that the animal be destroyed.'

'You'll have to kill me before you kill that dog,' John Evert said.

'That won't be necessary,' Gunn said, with a smile. 'Marshal.'

The marshal put his hand upon John Evert's shoulder. 'I'm sorry, son,' he said, and unravelled a thin rope that he had held coiled in his hand. 'What's his name?'

'He doesn't have a name,' John Evert said.

'How come?'

John Evert had been planning to name it, but he had noted that Bill had not named his horses. When he asked why, Bill had said that as soon as you named something you would not be able to let it go. John Evert had not understood this at the time, but in his admiration for Bill's ways he had figured that he would follow suit. It was only now, to his dismay, that he commenced to understand Bill's thinking. 'He never needed one,' he said miserably.

The marshal took a step toward the dog, which, sensing the change in its master's mood, emitted a very faint growl. As the marshal continued to move toward it, the dog's lip twitched and then curled back to expose its teeth.

'I wouldn't, Marshal,' John Evert said.

The marshal hesitated, but continued to advance. In response, the dog opened its mouth to snarl and saliva dripped from its jaw. The ridge of hair along its back stood up on end, and, all of a sudden, it did look wild.

'You see!' cried Gunn. 'It's out of control.'

The marshal bent down with the rope looped in his hands, and the dog splayed its front paws in the dust, lowering its front end as though tensing to spring up at the marshal. 'Jesus,' the marshal said, and unbuttoned the holster that held his gun.

'No!' John Evert cried, leaping forward between the marshal and the dog. The dog, sensing danger to John Evert, tried to lunge past him at the marshal. John Evert whirled around to face it and caught its paws in his hands. The dog scrabbled at him and John Evert pushed forward into it, so that it stood right up on its hind legs, its paws resting upon his shoulders, its heavy head against his cheek. John Evert put his arms around its muscular neck, his fingers clutching its smooth fur, and tears began to fall down his face. 'Don't you dare,' he said. 'He's all I've got. You kill him, you have to kill me, too.'

A small crowd had now gathered to watch the spectacle of the huge dog standing up on its hind legs in an embrace with the boy, who appeared to be holding on to it for dear life, while the marshal pointed a gun at them.

'Mr Gunn,' the marshal said. 'There must be some other way.'

'No,' Gunn snapped. 'The dog must be put down. Take that boy off him,' he said to his men, who began to advance on John Evert. The dog snarled as they drew nearer, then gave a couple of deep, fearsome barks. A watching woman shrieked.

'Wait!' rang a clear voice. Everyone stopped and looked for who had spoken. It was Casey, standing like a pillar in the shadows of the porch of the *Star*.

'What do you want, nigger?' Gunn demanded.

'Don't you speak that way to my man,' Quincy roared. 'What is it, Casey?'

Casey came down off the porch. 'I know that dog, sir. If Mr John will let me, I can lead him. I can take him off quiet, without a fuss.'

'Capital idea,' Quincy said.

'I agree. This is turning into a circus,' the marshal said, gesturing at the gathered crowd, a few of whom booed at the prospect of the show drawing to a close.

Casey walked to where John Evert stood, still hugging the dog, which had stopped snarling. Casey put his hand on the dog's head. It licked his wrist. John Evert looked at Casey, through his tears, 'Oh, Casey, please don't,' he sobbed.

'I told you this would happen,' Casey replied.

'Please.'

'Ssh,' he said soothingly. 'You've two choices. Either you let him be killed here in the street, frightened half to death, or you let me take him out for a nice, long walk and we go catching us some rabbits. Then, when he's sleeping, he'll go off right quiet, just like he's dreaming.' John Evert shook his head. Casey nodded reassuringly in response, then said under his breath, 'You trust me, John Evert?'

John Evert thought about this. He thought about the money in his mattress, and how Casey had somehow known about it, and how he had kept John Evert's secret for him. He nodded slowly.

'Then trust I know best,' Casey spoke very quietly. His dark eyes, with their faintly yellow whites, were intense.

John Evert remained silent for a while, then said brokenly, 'All right,' loudly enough for everyone to hear.

'Thank the Lord for that,' the marshal said.

Gunn seemed disappointed. Casey took the rope from the marshal, made a slip knot and looped it over the dog's head. 'I'll need a gun,' Casey said respectfully.

'I'm not trusting a nigger with a pistol,' said Gunn.

'I've had just about enough of this,' the marshal said. He wrenched a gun from one of Gunn's men and handed it to Casey. 'Thank you – Casey, is it? – for helping us out here. You bring that gun to me when you're done and I'll see it back to Mr Gunn's man.'

Casey clucked at the dog, which was now quite calm, and began to walk away. The dog followed him happily, but when it realised John Evert was not following, it paused and looked back at him, forcing Casey to stop. It wagged its tail once or twice, confused.

'Go on,' John Evert said tremulously. 'Go on with you.' The dog trotted away with Casey.

The marshal put his arm around John Evert, and John Evert put his face briefly in the marshal's shoulder, breathing in the reassuring smell of leather and sweat.

'Not so brave now, eh?' Gunn said superciliously.

'Go about your business or I'll have you for breach of the peace,' the marshal snapped.

There was a silence, then the sound of hoofs trotting away. Slowly, the usual noises of the street resumed.

The marshal held John Evert at arm's length. 'I'm sorry, son,' he said. John Evert did not trust himself to speak. 'That Phineas Gunn's a mean son-of-a . . . Well, if there's anything I can do for you?' John Evert shook his head.

Even Quincy was quiet for once, and gestured for John Evert to go inside.

He trudged upstairs, fell on to his bed and passed out.

*

When he awoke, John Evert felt as though a great stone had been placed upon his chest once more. He put his hand down the side of the bed and found an empty space where his dog should have been. He rolled on to his side and curled into a ball.

Later, Meriweather came into the room. 'John Evert,' he said softly. John Evert gave no answer. Meriweather sat down on the edge of the bed. 'I'm awful sorry about your dog. That Phineas Gunn's a piece o' shit.'

'Is Casey back yet?' John Evert whispered.

'Nope. I reckon he might be gone all night. It's dark out now.'

'I can't believe he offered to do it.'

'Sure you do. That dog went off with him happy as anything. You'd rather it were that way, wouldn't you?' John Evert stared at the wall.

'Hey, I've an idea,' Meriweather said. He went downstairs and John Evert heard him leave the building. He returned some time later, placing two bottles on the table next to John Evert's bed. He lit the oil lamp and turned it up gentle. 'Look, here's liquor and some food.' He poured John Evert a cup and John Evert sat up, folded a blanket against the iron bedstead and leaned back upon it. He took a drink of the liquor, which burned his gullet. Meriweather waved a folded paper in his hand. 'Lincoln's latest speech,' he said. 'You want to hear it?'

'Go on, then,' John Evert said.

Meriweather took a swig of liquor and sat on the floor, propped against the side of John Evert's bed, and began to read. John Evert had to hand it to the man, he had a way with words, and he was lost for a while in the beauty of the language and the warm feel of the liquor.

When he awoke the next morning, his head was pounding. Meriweather was asleep face-down, still fully clothed, on the other bed. One empty bottle stood upon the table, and the other lay on the floor, on its side. John Evert got to his feet, massaging his throbbing temples. He gave the other bed a kick, at which Meriweather let out the groan of a dying man.

John Evert went to the water pump and washed his face. The city was dead quiet all around. It was Sunday, he remembered. When he returned, Meriweather was sprawled upon his back, an arm over his face. 'Man,' Meriweather said. 'I feel like a possum's pissed in my mouth. D'you wanna go to the Union for some breakfast?'

They stumbled downstairs and were about to leave the building when the telegraph started up with its distinctive clack-clack. Meriweather groaned. 'Hold your horses. Let me hear the message.' He took a seat, tilted his ear toward the tap of the Morse code and began to copy out the message on to a sheet of paper.

John Evert rolled himself a cigarette while he waited.

'Hell,' Meriweather said suddenly.

'What is it?' John Evert asked. 'Meri?' Meriweather was sitting bolt upright, still scribbling the message, with his mouth half open. 'Meri?'

At that moment, shots rang out in the distance. John Evert sprang to the door and threw it open. He could see nothing in the street.

'We've got to find Quincy,' Meriweather said, getting to his feet and snatching up the piece of paper from his desk.

'Why? What is it?'

'Ricardo Urives, and there's rangers too.'

The two of them bolted out of the *Star* and toward the centre of town. As they reached the central plaza, they ran into the back of a small crowd.

'Here, let's get up the top of the Union so we can see,' Meriweather said.

They ran inside the Bella Union, ignoring the angry bartender who bellowed at them, leaped up the stairs and out of the spring door on to the veranda that commanded a view of the whole plaza.

The commotion was spilling out of the street that ran into the plaza from the north side. People were shouting in Spanish and English. John Evert and Meriweather craned their necks to see what was happening, but then the crowd flowed into the plaza, obscuring their view. People were bubbling around a brawl, and they could just make out a great bear of a man with a preposterously large handlebar moustache. His torn shirtfront was covered with blood and he was staggering. Facing him was a slight man who held a knife in his outstretched hand.

'Is that Urives?' John Evert asked.

'I reckon so. I've never seen him but everyone says he's big.'

John Evert was transfixed. Urives was the finest specimen of a desperado he'd ever heard of: a multiple murderer, thief and general villain whose wanted posters frequently appeared around town. It was his name that mothers used to frighten naughty children into bed, his name that was bandied around every saloon, along with wild tales of his exploits.

'Who's he fighting?' John Evert asked.

'Who knows?'

Urives lumbered forward. The small man swapped his knife to his other hand and darted at him, quick as a rat. Urives swiped at him with his bowie knife, but the small man was too quick, ducking under Urives's arm and stabbing him as swiftly as a Spaniard would spear a bull. Urives let out a roar and lashed at him. One successful connection of his huge paw would have broken the man's neck, but the small man danced away. A shot sounded and Urives lurched. Another man ran out of the crowd, but Urives spun around and slammed his fist into the side of his face. The man fell backwards and hit the dirt with an awful snap. He did not move again.

Two more men ran at Urives with just their fists. Urives ploughed and thumped his way through them, the crowd swirling about him as he progressed across the plaza. John Evert noticed there were women in the crowd too, half of them dressed for church, but all too fascinated to move away. Doors and windows opened all over the plaza until the whole town seemed to be watching the spectacle.

Urives seemed invincible. As John Evert watched, Urives was

shot twice and stabbed some eleven times, yet still he did not fall. The bartender of the Union joined them on the veranda and spat. 'Two bucks that he falls in two minutes,' he said.

John Evert was disgusted. 'It doesn't seem fair, one man against them all like that,' he said.

'He killed a boy in Arcadia Alley,' the bartender replied. 'They won't rest till he's dead.'

More shots rang out. The crowd parted. Two mounted rangers and a small group of cavalry entered the plaza from the west. The crowd fell silent, and, at that moment, a flash caught John Evert's eye. Bill was in the crowd. He stepped out, towards Urives.

'Leave him alone,' Bill commanded, his voice ringing through the silent plaza. The man engaged in fighting Urives must have recognised Bill for he fell back. Urives stood, heaving like an exhausted animal. He wiped sweat and blood out of his eyes with his sodden shirt sleeve and squinted at Bill.

Bill carried no weapon, but one of the rangers, seeing Bill, called out to him, 'This man is to be taken alive.' Bill did not acknowledge him.

Urives was staring at Bill, and said something in Spanish that John Evert could not make out. Then John Evert heard Urives say distinctly, 'You!' in disbelief.

Urives bent down and pulled a tiny pistol from his boot and aimed shakily with a bleeding hand at Bill who, John Evert knew, had a small pistol in his sleeve. He had taught John Evert early in their acquaintance that, if you wanted to be sure of getting the draw on a man, you had to learn to draw from the sleeve.

'Draw!' Urives shouted at him.

Bill said calmly, 'Ricardo, you're surrounded. Don't act stupid.'

Urives cocked his pistol, and Bill, in a single fluid movement, drew from his sleeve and fired, hitting Urives in the chest.

Urives stared at him, looked down at the place where his heart should have been, then fell face down in the dirt.

'Holy Mother,' said Meriweather.

'Four minutes,' the barman said, with a tut at his pocket watch.

'You!' cried one of the rangers. 'What right have you to fire upon this man against our order?'

Bill put his gun in his holster, removed something from his shirt and held it outward. 'I am a Texas Ranger,' he said.

The lead ranger dismounted, marched up to him and snatched the item from him. John Evert caught the glint of silver in the sunlight. 'A Texas Ranger is not above the law,' the ranger said. 'What is your name?'

'Bill Gosling.'

John Evert could make out the great transformation that took place in the ranger's posture, the satisfaction in him as he said slowly, 'No, I don't think so. I believe your real name is William Adair-Wilson, isn't it?'

Bill went very still, his profile, which so lent itself to statuary, seeming now as though carved of dark marble under the all-seeing eye of the midday sun.

The ranger continued, 'William Adair-Wilson, I have looked forward to this meeting, long overdue. I hereby arrest you on behalf of the British Crown.'

An audible gasp went up from the spectating Angelinos, who, while living an excitable existence, had never yet seen such entertainment.

The marshal stepped forward and spoke to the rangers. 'I know this man,' he said. 'I can confirm he is a ranger. There must be some mistake.'

'How long have you known him?' one asked.

'Eight years or so.'

'He's wanted for theft and murder, and long before you knew him he was wanted for piracy, too.'

'In all seriousness?' Bill said, his voice lazy with disbelief. 'After all this time?'

'The British Lion never forgets,' the ranger said.

'Don't I know it,' Bill replied. 'I simply cannot believe they have nothing better to do.'

'Take him,' the ranger ordered the cavalry men.

With remarkable speed, Bill was cuffed and hauled away. The marshal and rangers followed, deep in discussion. The crowd dispersed, and all that was left was the body of Urives, in a darkening stain upon the dust of the plaza.

John Evert was all at odds with himself as he tried to piece together the revelations of the last minutes. Meriweather stood silent until, eventually, he said, 'Did you know anything about this?'

'About Bill being a Texas Ranger? Yeah, I knew,' John Evert admitted, relieved, at last, that he could be honest.

'What about the things he's been involved in, though? Theft? Murder?'

John Evert did not reply.

'Because the thing is,' Meriweather continued slowly, as though speaking the thoughts as they occurred to him, 'I see how often Quincy's in on news before it comes down the wire. You know, some outlaw meeting his just deserts, being robbed or suchlike, and Quincy always seems to know about them after you and Bill have been away . . .' Meriweather frowned at the ground for a while before continuing. 'Some of these things, you'd have to be a mind reader, unless, of course, the person who was telling Quincy was one of the people caught up in those things, someone like Bill, say . . .'

'You reckon?' John Evert said thickly, his throat awful tight.

'You haven't just been looking up the price of steers when you've been out of town with Bill, have you?'

John Evert's face grew hot. Meriweather let out a low whistle of disbelief.

'It was my choice,' John Evert said. 'I needed the money, for the bounty, for my ma . . .' He trailed off. 'You must despise me,' he said.

'It'd be mighty hard to despise you.'

'Why?' John Evert asked.

'After what happened to you, you're still the decentest person I think I ever met.'

John Evert swallowed, unable to speak.

Finally, Meriweather said, 'I'm not gonna tell anyone you gone rogue with Bill.'

John Evert rubbed his temples, awash with relief.

'But what are you going to do if Bill talks?' Meriweather asked.

'He won't.'

'You sure?'

'Yeah.' And John Evert knew that was true. His trust in Bill was implicit. His next thought was not concern that Bill might implicate him: it was how he was going to set about getting him out of this mess, and get him out he must, for he knew full well that the only place Bill was heading otherwise was that wooden scaffold, and then his mother would be lost for ever.

His feelings toward Bill had always been confused, but he remembered that first moment in San Gabriel when Bill had had a knife to his throat but had chosen not to use it, had chosen instead to believe John Evert's story about his mother and the bounty, and how Bill had given him a chance. And because of that decision of Bill's, he felt a loyalty and kinship to the man. Perhaps it was for no more than the banishment of loneliness but, in a lonely country, what greater bond was there than that?

A preliminary hearing was set for two days hence. John Evert attempted to gain access to the jail so that he might talk with Bill, but the deputy would not admit him. All visitors were refused. Wild rumours flew about the Bella Union, the drugstore and every front parlour.

The only person who seemed strangely unmoved was the man to whom news of any kind was usually the spice of life: Quincy Rivers. The other curiosity was the disappearance of Casey, who had still not returned from the task of dispensing with John Evert's dog.

'You don't think he's run off, do you?' Meriweather asked.

'With no money on him, no clothes, no food?' Quincy replied. 'Besides, it's not Casey's way to run off.'

'He had that gun.'

'He knows no one would buy a pistol off a Negro and not report it.'

Quincy sat back in his chair. Legs splayed, arms behind his head, he bore an uncanny resemblance to a toad that had come off worst in a run-in with a wagon wheel.

'Where is he, then?' Meriweather pressed. 'And what about Bill?'

Quincy made no answer, merely sucking his bottom lip meditatively.

Meriweather turned his attention to John Evert. 'Can I trouble you to run an errand for me? Will you take this note down to the rail master and find out if he knows any more about when that overdue mail train's expected?'

'Sure,' John Evert replied, welcoming the distraction.

He left via the front of the *Star*, and began to walk toward the station, but it was hot and he regretted leaving without his hat, so he turned back to retrieve it. Taking the alley, he meant to enter by the side door, but as he put his hand to the latch he was drawn up short by the sound of raised voices within.

'You never asked Bill why he wanted John?' Meriweather said. 'Why not?'

'He said he needed another pair of hands,' Quincy retorted, 'and I needed someone out there looking up stories anyhow.'

'Another pair of hands? To do what? You never asked *anything*?'

'Well, did *you* ever ask?' Quincy asked.

'No, Quincy, because I thought you were in charge, not Bill. I thought the only reason John was out there with him was because he was running errands for you.'

'You're damn right I'm in charge around here!'

'Yeah, so why are you getting so hot under the collar?'

'Christ, Meriweather, will you leave me alone?' Quincy cried.

'No. How long have you known Bill?' Meriweather demanded.

'I don't know – a good seven, maybe eight, years.'

'And what do you know about his history?'

'Nothing. Same as everyone else. I don't know the man that well.'

'But he knows you, doesn't he? How well does he know *you*, Quincy?'

There was a crash, as of something being overturned. 'Let it go, will you, Meriweather?' Quincy roared. 'Just leave it!'

'Jesus. He has something on you, doesn't he?'

'No, he does not,' Quincy bellowed. John Evert pressed his eye to the gap at the hinge, and saw Quincy standing, sweating like a runaway horse, his chair knocked over backwards. He stood on one side of his desk, Meriweather on the other.

Meriweather leaned forward, putting his hands flat on the desk as he said, 'What if I was to go to the marshal and tell him that you let John go off with Bill all those times? That you knew they were up to no good, and that part of the reason you did it was because Bill was feeding you stories for the paper?'

John Evert drew back at the door, startled by Meriweather's threat, then put his eye back to the crack. All the fight went out of Quincy. He pulled his chair upright and sat slowly in it, as though he were deflating, pulling off his kerchief to wipe his brow. He put his face into the material, and was still. 'All right, all right,' he mumbled. 'He has something on me. I never asked him where he went with John, or what they did. I owe Bill. I owe him. He asked for John, so I let him have him and I asked no questions. That was the deal.'

'And what about John?' Meriweather hissed. 'Did you think what sort of trouble you were getting him into? You sold him for stories and to protect yourself. How could you?'

'I know, I know,' Quincy said, his kerchief balled up in one fist. 'He's an all-right kid too. Don't think I don't feel bad about it.'

'Well, I'm sure that'll make John feel a whole lot better, that you feel bad about it.'

John Evert was too shocked to know what to feel. The realisation that Quincy had known all along was too disturbing to comprehend. John Evert had always believed that it was he who had sought out Bill. It had never occurred to him that it might have been the other way around.

'Pull yourself together,' Meriweather said. 'I'm not going to say anything to anyone. I just wanted to hear the truth from your own mouth, that's all.'

'Really?' Quincy said. 'Oh, Meriweather, you're a good man.'

'Save it,' Meriweather replied. 'I don't want your gratitude. I'm ashamed of you, Quincy Rivers. What a Goddamned mess.'

John Evert slipped away and ran all the way to the rail master's office, his thoughts colliding with each other, like frightened steers.

Bill had engaged Hector Featherstone to act in his defence. Cyrus Lyne, as district attorney, acted for the state of California.

Knowing that the court would be besieged with onlookers, Quincy, Meriweather and John Evert arrived just after dawn.

Quincy had not been able to look John Evert in the eye since he had returned from the railmaster's office the night before, and John Evert had kept his distance from him also. Now, however, he pushed all that business to the back of his mind, determined to focus on Bill's predicament before his own.

With the assistance of the clerk, Quincy secured the right for the newspaper men of the *Star* to occupy front-row seats. John Evert sat next to Meriweather, his pencil and notebook at the ready. As the public filed in, the room came alive with speculation. Spanish ladies fanned themselves against the heat and smell of hot bodies, the clack of the spines of their fans signalling excitement or irritation. The grizzled old pipe smokers sat in a silent row. The only ones not deep in conversation, they had been witness to so many years of perjury and confessions that there was nothing for them to do but tap their pipes out and murmur that it put them in mind of that case back in 'fifty-two.

Hector entered with his briefs. He was immaculate, his slim frame encased in a well-tailored black suit that hugged his angular shoulders. Cyrus Lyne came in, with the two rangers who had accosted Bill in the plaza two days earlier. Lyne cut nothing like the figure Hector did, but as he glanced about the room, his small, close-set eyes sparkled like those of a terrier scenting a rat.

'All rise,' ordered the clerk of the court. There was a scraping of chairs and benches.

Judge Ogier took his place at the bench, taking some time to arrange his papers before him. When he settled his glasses upon the bridge of his nose, and surveyed the packed building, he did so with the air of a man engaged upon any ordinary business.

'Gentlemen,' he said, 'I would ask Ranger Colbert to take the stand to read out the charges against William Adair-Wilson. The charges originate from outside the state of California, and must be read in full to be entered into the record. As this is a preliminary hearing, we have no jury at this time. The purpose of our proceedings today is to formalise the charges and determine whether the defendant is to be tried here or elsewhere. Ranger Colbert.'

The clerk whispered something to the judge.

'Oh, yes,' said Ogier. 'We should have the defendant first.' He shook his head at the clerk and smiled. The courtroom tittered.

Bill, in chains, was led in by the bailiff. There was an ugly graze on his left cheek, but his expression was as unconcerned as ever, his sleepy gaze wandering about the courtroom. He caught John Evert's eye. John Evert was careful to keep his expression neutral, and could only hope that Bill could read his thoughts.

Bill turned his back and took a seat next to Hector. His huge, shaggy crown was a stark contrast to Hector's sleek, otter-like head.

The ranger removed his hat and took the stand. The clerk approached him with a Bible, and the ranger laid his hand upon it as he said, 'I swear to tell the truth, the whole truth, and nothing but the truth, so help me, God.'

'Can you confirm your full name?'

'Joshua Colbert.'

'Would you be so kind as to tell us the reason for your presence here in Los Angeles?' Ogier said.

'Yes, sir. My predecessors have been on the trail of William Adair-Wilson for some sixteen years. We believe he first arrived on these shores in 1844. He arrived by boat for he had spent the last three years engaged in piracy. He was at that time being pursued by British ships from Hawaii . . .'

John Evert's mind reeled as the ranger spoke. 'I got sick of the sea,' Bill had said, when John Evert had asked him why he had left it. He shook his head at his own naivety.

'Upon reaching California,' the ranger said, 'he scuttled his ship. Then he and the remainder of his crew struck into the interior. He was able to evade the British soldiers pursuing him, and disappeared. The British contingent was not in a position to remain in California, and was recalled elsewhere. At that point, the responsibility for the search was passed to the state of California.'

John Evert thought about the time he had asked Bill what had first brought him to America, and realised now how deftly Bill had deflected the question.

'After his disappearance, Adair-Wilson lived under assumed names throughout California. He also spent time in Texas and the New Mexico territory. He has been involved in criminal undertakings everywhere he has been domiciled, and is wanted for murder and theft in numerous jurisdictions. I should also add that for several of the latest crimes committed, Adair-Wilson appears to have had an accomplice.'

John Evert's gut lurched. He squeezed the pencil he held so tightly that it mashed his fingers.

'We have a description of the accomplice, who is but a youngster. We have strong evidence to indicate that he is also in Los Angeles, and I believe we are soon to secure him.'

John Evert felt the reassuring press of Meriweather's thigh against his own but his attention darted to Hector, who had turned his head. Hector was not imprudent enough to glance at the public gallery, but John Evert read in that profile all the disapprobation he needed. Was he also aware of other eyes upon him from around the courtroom, or did he simply imagine it?

'Thank you, Mr Colbert,' Ogier said. 'You may return to your seat. So, there is much to consider and to hear. There has been debate as to whether this trial should take place here or whether we should await an application by the British to have Mr Adair-Wilson returned there. As the accused is to be tried for crimes committed in the state of California, I adjudge that he is to be tried here, in this court, for those crimes. Court is adjourned while a jury is formed.'

Meriweather propelled John Evert out of the courtroom and back toward the *Star*. 'Right. We'll get you out of here tonight,' Meriweather said, once they were seated in a threesome in the centre of the print room. 'I can give you fifteen dollars. Quincy, how much have you got?'

But Quincy seemed frozen into immobility, sitting in a heap in his chair, his hands lying useless in his lap.

'Quincy, wake up!' Meriweather barked. 'How much have you got?'

'I've seventy-five dollars in the safe here,' Quincy said, his voice flat. 'There's more in the bank, but I can't get a hold of it until tomorrow, and that's maybe too late.'

'No,' John Evert said, his head in his hands. 'I can't take your money and have you be guilty of helping me. I'll go and hand myself in to the marshal.'

'Don't talk crazy!' Meriweather cried.

'I don't think I've got a whole lot of choice,' John Evert said. He was lost. He could not think straight. He wished so much that his dog was by his side to put its comforting head upon his thigh, as it had done so often when he was troubled. Then he remembered that his dog was dead, and with that numbing thought he figured he might as well go and turn himself in.

'Do you have any idea what it's like in jail?' Meriweather said softly.

'No. I don't care.'

Meriweather kicked the leg of John Evert's chair. 'Well, we do. Now pack your things. I'm going over to the Union. That crooked bartender owes me a few bucks.' Meriweather marched to the door.

'No, Meriweather,' John Evert said, his own voice stronger than he expected. 'I won't run.'

Meriweather turned from the door and came back to where John Evert and Quincy sat. With a pained expression, Meriweather said, 'Do one thing for me, then, John. Don't turn yourself in. Wait and see what happens. If you turn yourself in, you're as good as dead already. Waiting never killed anybody.'

Two days later they were all back in court, with a jury assembled, and ready to begin. John Evert felt like a marked man sitting in the courtroom. He had expected to be summoned by Hector but there had been no communication from Hector's office or the marshal's. An ominous silence reigned. But whatever was yet to

come, John Evert was glad that he had not run away. He wanted
to know what would happen to Bill. He wanted to be present to
see it.

'Mr Lyne, you may open,' Ogier said.

Cyrus Lyne got to his feet, and treated the court to a most
enticing slice of Bill's history. Just as Bill had told John Evert,
his father had been a distinguished member of the East India
Company, his mother the daughter of a powerful Indian begum.
John Evert had been intrigued by the idea of Bill's mother. Bill
had told him a little about her. John Evert remembered now the
conversation, which had taken place upon a yellow grassy bluff
with a fine view across the forest that carpeted the valley beneath.

They had been seated beneath a string of poplar trees; a strong
wind shivered the leaves from green to silver and back again,
while the smoke from their fire was tilted on its side and spiralled
away. It had been a day of particular splendour, and grateful,
perhaps, to Bill, for reuniting him with the land he loved so well,
John Evert had felt given to confidences, so he had told Bill about
his own mother, and Bill had turned upon him a long look. There
was no pity in it, John Evert had been glad to note, for that he
could not bear. It was simply a look of understanding.

Their talk that day had been solemn, and something Bill said
had caused John Evert to ask of him, 'Was it difficult? Being a
half-breed?'

Bill had studied the ground in front of his crossed legs before
replying. 'Yes. You're looked down on by everyone, but especially
by the British. You would not believe the hypocrisy of that race.
It makes it hard to know where you belong.'

'I feel like that,' John Evert had said, aware of a need to reward
this intimacy of Bill's. 'Sometimes I just don't think I like people
that much.' He was silent for a moment. 'I think I prefer them.'
He had tilted his head in the direction of the horses and his dog.

Bill had found this highly amusing for some reason. 'Very wise,
kid.' He had chuckled.

The court learned how Bill had joined the East India Company, aged eighteen, and had risen successfully through the company ranks for several years before, without warning, he had turned pirate.

John Evert listened carefully, noting the great loyalty that Bill had evidently inspired in his men, for the entire crew had turned pirate with him. He had abandoned only the captain and first mate upon an atoll in the Hawaiian archipelago, and they were left uninjured. In his voracious reading, John Evert had come across tales of the high seas and understood that shipboard life was no simple adventure. Knowing Bill as he did, he had the feeling that surely something must have been amiss with the way the captain ran the ship, something that was not, perhaps, Bill's fault. But then he remembered Bill's observation that people tended to judge things on how they seemed, as opposed to how they were, and he had to admit, the story of his mutiny did not look at all good.

The years that followed were rich with incident. Bill had been an excellent specimen of a pirate, managing to steal plenty of cargo without much damage to man or property, and successfully evaded capture, despite large bounties upon his head. But, finally, his pursuers were too hot on his heels for comfort, which precipitated his flight to America.

He had lain low for a couple of years, but then emerged in a brawl, and was later identified in a robbery, before disappearing again, at which point he was presumed to have turned Indian. John Evert already knew that Bill had spent time in Indian company: no white man could possess the tracking skills that Bill did without having been instructed by Indians.

Lyne's story raised more questions about Bill than it answered. If he had made so much money, where was it when he lived so frugally? In trying to make head or tail of things, John Evert had a notion that Bill had blazed and shambled his way through his colourful past much as he conducted his life in and around Los Angeles: with a different hat for every occasion, a loyalty founded on the spur of the moment, depending upon how much he liked an individual, and very little plan at all – like the time they had stopped for victuals at the house of a young widow, whom Bill had paid three hundred dollars for the meal because she had been distraught about a creditor. John Evert wished he could take the stand and attempt to communicate to the courtroom that woman's face, her disbelief and joy as she held on to Bill's stirrup-leather, clutching the bills to her breast as tears ran down her face, aged before its time.

Once Lyne had concluded, Hector Featherstone got slowly to his feet. John Evert wondered what on earth Hector would find to say in the face of this vast catalogue of wrongdoing. Hector stood very erect, and opened his hand to place his fingertips upon the pile of paper before him on the table.

'Sir,' he said gravely. 'The defence has no intention of arguing that Mr Adair-Wilson did not spend several years engaged in piracy.'

Murmurs rippled through the courtroom. Even Ogier appeared surprised, and frowned over his glasses at Hector, who continued, 'Mr Adair-Wilson acknowledges his years of piracy.'

'Mr Featherstone,' Judge Ogier said, 'are you sure this is the line you wish to take?'

'Yes, sir. In doing so, I intend to prove the absolute necessity of my client's turning to illegality, the impossible position he was placed in, which necessitated a drastic course of action. Furthermore, I wish to disclose Mr Adair-Wilson's involvement with an organisation called the Military Order of the Lone Star, from which he has often taken orders.'

'What's the Order of the Lone Star?' John Evert whispered to Meriweather. 'Is that the Texas Rangers?'

'No,' Meriweather whispered back. 'I don't know what that is.'

Hector then requested that the court be adjourned so that he might have time to muster his key witnesses. It being late in the day, Ogier agreed.

Back at the *Star* that evening, Meriweather said to John Evert,

'You see? Nothing's happened yet. It might all be a bluff what the rangers said, about knowing the identity of the accomplice.'

'Yes, maybe,' said Quincy, who half sat upon the edge of his desk, wiping his brow with his kerchief. 'Go get us some liquor, Meriweather,' he said, putting some coins into Meriweather's outstretched hand. John Evert took a seat and rested his elbows on his knees, rubbing his eyes. He was so tired. The last few days he had been coiled up tight as a spring.

Meriweather opened the door of the print room, and marched straight into the marshal, whose hand was just up to knock.

'Hello, Meriweather,' the marshal said.

Meriweather threw a desperate look over his shoulder. The marshal stepped around him, and entered, taking his hat off as he did so. 'Hello, John Evert,' he said.

'Marshal,' John Evert said. He had been expecting this moment and was surprised at how calm he felt now that it had come.

'I guess you know why I'm here?' the marshal said. John Evert nodded. The marshal took a breath and then said, 'John Evert Burn, I am arresting you in connection with offences relating to the recent arrest of Bill Adair-Wilson.'

'Bunkum,' said Quincy, suddenly galvanised into action. 'This boy has no connection to Bill. I am willing to stand up in court and swear it.'

'So you'd perjure yourself, would you, Quincy?' the marshal said. 'There are witnesses, I'm afraid. Well, son,' he addressed John Evert, 'I don't know how you got yourself into this trouble, but considering your age they'll maybe go easy on you. And if you were prepared to testify against Bill, of course, that'd make all the difference. Might just be a few years behind bars.'

'A few years,' Quincy echoed. He slumped back against his desk and bit his knuckles savagely.

'I guess I'd better come with you,' John Evert said, getting to his feet.

'Can I come?' Meriweather asked.

'If John Evert would find that helpful,' the marshal replied.

'Yeah. Thanks, Meri,' John Evert said.

Quincy could not bring himself to say goodbye. He put his kerchief over his eyes as John Evert went and stood in front of him. He could have been furious with Quincy, maybe he should have been, yet he felt only sorrow. 'It's all right, Quincy,' he said. 'It's not your fault. I could have said no. He gave me the choice, you know. I've no one to blame but myself.'

Quincy squeezed the bridge of his nose, and said nothing. John Evert put on his hat and the three of them walked out of the print room of the *Star* and into the darkness.

'You thought we'd try to spirit him away,' Meriweather said. 'Is that why you came?'

'No,' the marshal replied, 'but I wanted to be the one to do the arrest. I thought it being someone he knew would make it easier, and I didn't want a fuss. These out-of-town rangers seem to like to do things at high noon, with an audience. That's not my way.'

They walked on in silence. The night was cool and pleasant, and John Evert was particularly aware of the smell of the dusty street, and the leathery odour that came from the saddler on the corner at the crossroads. He figured he might not smell these things again for a long time, and sadness overwhelmed him. He pushed aside the feeling, set his jaw and put his shoulders back.

'That's right, son,' the marshal said.

When they reached the jail, the marshal filled out a line in the big ledger on the desk before him. 'You'd best say goodbye to Meriweather,' he said. 'I'll make sure he's able to visit, to bring you anything you might need.' He moved away to give them a moment.

'Hell,' Meriweather said, biting his lip. 'I wish you'd run like I wanted you to. We weren't very smart on this one.'

John Evert managed a half-smile. 'You're a newspaper man, not an outlaw, Meri.'

'Not like you. You're both.'

John Evert did not fail to detect the faint note of admiration in the other man's voice.

Meriweather slapped him on the back and turned to go. 'I'll be back tomorrow. Quincy and I'll get going on a front-page case of mistaken identity.' Meriweather was still talking as the marshal gently shut the door on him.

He led John Evert down a corridor to a cell and unlocked it. 'There's no one else?' John Evert asked, craning his neck to peer into the empty cells as they passed by, wondering where Bill was being kept.

'I didn't want to put you in the main jail. There's some noisy, unsavoury characters in. You need anything, you holler. There's a guard here all night. Tomorrow, the rangers will know you're here, but not before I've let you have some legal advice.'

'Thank you. Will you . . .' John Evert spoke haltingly. 'Will you let Mr Featherstone know I'm here and ask him . . .'

'I told him before I came to get you. He'll be here tomorrow.' The marshal locked the door and walked away.

John Evert was alone in the cell, with nothing but a bed, a bucket and a tiny barred window to keep him company. A couple of stars were visible through it, very high up. That was all.

12

Awaking cold at dawn, John Evert was torn between anticipation at seeing Hector, and shame at what he had done. The thought of looking him in the eye made him blush. He paced around his cell, then sat upon the bed, then got to his feet and paced again. The guard brought him water and dry bread, but he could eat nothing.

After what felt like an eternity, he heard Hector's unmistakeable English accent, and stood at the rear of the cell, taking an awkward stance against the wall. When Hector appeared with the marshal, John Evert scoured his face to ascertain his feelings, but Hector was composed.

'Here, Mr Featherstone, a chair for you,' the marshal said. Having set the chair inside the cell, the marshal locked the door again and left.

'Well, John Evert,' Hector said simply. John Evert studied his feet. 'Have a seat.' Hector gestured at the bed. John Evert sat down upon it. Hector pulled up the chair to the side of the bed. He took his watch out of his waistcoat pocket and consulted it, then returned it to his pocket, folded his arms and looked up at the ceiling. Finally, he spoke: 'Why don't you tell me about the first time you went somewhere with Bill?'

John Evert cleared his throat. 'Sure,' he said. Very factual, he relayed that first trip to the San Gabriel valley.

Hector listened carefully. When John Evert had finished, he asked, 'Did Bill pay you?' John Evert nodded. 'And that's why you continued to, ah, *work* for him?' John Evert nodded again. 'Did Bill force you to do anything? Ever threaten you?'

'No, and I won't ever say that he did,' John Evert said firmly.

'And I won't give evidence against him. Even if it means I go to jail.'

'That is a credit to your integrity *now*,' Hector said wryly. 'My only advice to you is that you should, you *must*, tell the truth on the stand. At all times, John Evert, be totally truthful. You will be under oath. You will have no other option.'

'Yes, sir. I understand that.'

'Your age will be taken into account, but as there was no coercion, there can be no suggestion that you were under duress. Now, this is important, did Bill ever tell you that he was a member of the Order of the Lone Star?'

'No. He told me he was a Texas Ranger, but not about that other thing. I wish someone would tell me what it is.'

'From what I have recently learned, it is a secret masonic organisation.' Hector paused a moment, and John Evert had a notion he found what he was talking about unpleasant in some way. 'It was founded about a decade ago. Its original purpose appears to have been to free Cuba from Spanish rule, but now it looks to expand slaveholding territories outside the United States. Its primary focus is to create a federation of slave states.' Hector's distaste was evident.

'Like the South wants?'

'Yes. It is predominantly a Southern organisation.'

'But Bill's not a slaver.' John Evert was aghast. 'Why would he want to be a part of that?'

'A good question, and one that is yet to be answered. I do not know how Bill, how any right-thinking man, would wish to become involved in that sort of organisation. Freemasonry . . .' Hector sighed. 'Anyway, it appears that the Order *began* with a nobler purpose. Its object was, apparently, to assist people in their fight for freedom, to assist those engaged in revolution for a good cause, but that appears to have become lost amid greed and lust for power. Some of the men who form part of this organisation are powerful, and are seeking to destabilise our own government.'

John Evert's eyes widened. Taking in his reaction, Hector changed tack. 'Never mind that now. To return to Bill, he paid you. Am I correct in supposing that you are now therefore of some means?'

'Yes. In the bank I have about—'

Hector put up his hand. 'No need to tell me. Have you spent any of this money or have you, as I suspect, been saving it to raise a bounty?'

John Evert nodded, and Hector studied him with an expression that was both sympathetic and exasperated.

'I know that doesn't excuse any of the things I've done,' John Evert said, feeling the weight of Hector's judgement keenly. 'I've never killed anybody, Mr Featherstone, but I must have helped Bill kill people. I'm very sorry for everything. You're right to be angry at me after all you've done for me.'

'I'm not angry with you. Surprised, yes. Angry, no.'

'You're not?' John Evert said, bewildered. 'So, will you defend me, too?'

'That is the purpose of this meeting, is it not?'

'I wasn't sure if you would.'

'This is my job. To provide a defence. All men deserve a fair trial, no matter what they may have done. As your attorney, I will defend you to the best of my ability.'

Hector stood and called for the marshal, but just before the marshal reached the door of the cell, Hector turned to John Evert, raised his eyebrows and smiled briefly. John Evert's chest swelled with gratitude.

Later that day, John Evert was interviewed by the rangers. Hector was with him, and had already advised him on how to handle the questions that were put to him. His answers were as general and noncommittal as possible, which irritated the rangers.

'We have witnesses who can identify you,' said Colbert, 'so it does not matter if you admit to these crimes or not. We can prove that you were there with Adair-Wilson, but it will help you if you testify against him.'

'No, sir.'

Colbert's face flushed. He turned to Hector. 'Are you going to make it clear to him what that will mean?' he demanded.

'My client is fully aware. Mr Burn will make no testimony against Mr Adair-Wilson.'

'Both of them will hang,' Colbert said.

'Judge Ogier will be the one to decide that,' Hector said, unperturbed.

John Evert was in a cold sweat, but Hector's cool, untroubled presence at his side was comforting.

'Can I see Bill?' John Evert asked Hector, when the rangers were gone.

'I'm afraid not.'

'Where is he?'

'In another part of the jail.'

'Can you give him a message from me?'

'No, I cannot. Nor can I pass you any message from him.'

'Okay,' John Evert said, and fell silent. After a time, he asked, 'Will I hang?'

'I think it unlikely,' Hector said, and John Evert marvelled at Hector's honest levelheadedness when it came to discussing even the most outrageous things. He could not decide whether it was reassuring or terrifying.

'What about Bill?'

Hector paused. 'If Bill is found guilty he will hang for certain.'

'But he won't be found guilty. You're going to get him off.'

'John—'

'But you will. I've watched you in court plenty of times. I've never seen anything like you. If there's any man in the whole country who could get him off, it's you.'

Hector's face contorted wryly.

When Hector made to leave, John Evert said, 'I know you can't pass any message to Bill but, if you *were* able to, I mean, if you could, I'd only want you to tell him that I'm okay, and that I'll never turn him in, that he can trust me.'

'I believe he is very well aware of that fact. It's all the more reason why he should feel guilty for having exploited you in the way that he has—' Hector cut himself off abruptly and frowned. 'Forgive me. Now, get your rest. I will see you tomorrow in court. It's a big day for us, for America, too.'

'America?'

Hector looked at him in surprise, then leaned against the bars lightly, as though suddenly tired. 'Of course, you haven't heard.'

'Heard what?'

'Fort Sumter fell to the Confederates. Lincoln has just issued a decree calling seventy-five thousand militiamen into national service. The country is at war.'

That evening, before it got dark, John Evert became aware of unrest about the town. The jail was situated on the outskirts, and during the short time he had been there, it had been dead quiet, but that evening there was plenty of noise and activity, which filtered down to him through the high window.

John Evert wished very much that he could see what was going on. He knew that Quincy and Meriweather would be busy composing headlines about the war, and reflected for a moment on how the disastrous upheaval of his own circumstances would, for everyone else, be dwarfed by what now faced the whole country.

A familiar sadness settled upon his chest, threatening to suffocate him. He had not felt it for some time, not since his first nights in Los Angeles. What chance now of rescue for his mother? If he went to jail, he would lose the ranch. He considered what it would mean for him to be imprisoned, to be kept from the outdoors and the things he loved most in the world. In a moment of clarity, he knew he was not the sort of fellow who would be able to bear a life in prison, and dark thoughts enfolded their dusty wings about him.

He heard the clatter of horses trotting by, followed by the heavy wheels of wagons. It was not until well after dark that the streets fell quiet. John Evert did not think he would sleep a wink, with his day in court ahead but, at some point, he must have, for he was jolted awake in the darkness, his heart racing.

'Who's there?' he said, disoriented.

He could hear a scraping noise, so loud and close it seemed to be inside his own head. He reached to his waist for his pistol but, of course, it was no longer there. He leaped off the bed and flattened himself against the wall, wondering who or what was in the cell with him, the blood thudding in his ears.

There was the distinct sound of metal on metal, and John Evert's eyes darted to the barred window. It was too dark to make anything out, but his senses told him that, whatever it was, it was from the street outside. There was a low moan and then a thump.

'Who's there and what do you want?' John Evert demanded.

'Hey,' said a deep, familiar voice.

'Casey?' John Evert breathed, in astonishment and delight.

'Yep.'

'What the hell are you doing?' John Evert nearly sank to his knees with relief at Casey's voice.

'Brought someone to see you.'

'I can't see out, Casey. The window's too high.'

'There something you can stand up on?'

John Evert dragged the heavy wooden bed frame as quietly as he could beneath the window, then felt his way in the dark to stand upon the bedhead and grasp the base of the window. His hand met a large, dry, leathery palm that squeezed his.

'Oh, Casey, it's good to hear you,' John Evert said.

'Not as good as who else I've got.' Casey pulled his wrist up higher, so that John Evert was on tiptoe. His hand met a wet nose, and the hot breath of a delighted whine.

'Hello, boy,' John Evert said, his voice cracking as his dog tried to shove the whole of its wide head through the bars, licking his hand furiously.

Casey chuckled, his voice deep and pleased. John Evert found he could not say a word. 'Hold up,' Casey said, as the dog scrabbled about. 'I can't hold him here long, he's so damn heavy.'

The dog's nose vanished from the window, then Casey's hand returned. 'Now, listen, you stand back from this wall, far back as you can. Maybe you take that bed over with you and get behind it.'

'Why? What's happening?'

'We're getting you out.'

'How? And who's we?'

'Who'd you think?'

John Evert dragged the bed to the far wall, and got down on the floor behind it.

'Cover your ears,' Casey said, and his hand disappeared.

John Evert saw a bright, white light flicker through the window, and jammed his fingers in his ears. A few seconds later, there was an enormous *whoomph*, and a shockwave rebounded off the walls, knocking the breath clean out of him and leaving his ears ringing.

When he opened his eyes, the air was thick with smoke and dust. And the wall was gone.

There, in the flickering light of a torch, was Casey, covered from head to toe with white dust. 'You there?' He coughed.

'Here, Casey.' John Evert clambered out from behind the bed. He could hear distant shouting. 'Damn,' he said, spluttering at the dust that clogged his throat, 'that was mighty—'

'Come on, we've got to be quick.' Casey snatched John Evert's hand and hauled him over blocks of stone into the cool night air. He tossed aside the torch, and they ran across the bare ground to the nearest building. They paused there as a bugle rang out in the night, then darted from building to building, avoiding standing out in the open. The dog kept close to John Evert's heels.

There came the sound of horses, and men on foot. One called instructions to the others. They held lanterns, and the light from them dappled the ground, spilling around a building to where John Evert and Casey were pressed against a wall. Some of the men began to come down the side of the building.

'Go, boy, go get 'em,' John Evert said to the dog. It whipped around the building.

'Jesus!' a man cried.

'It's just a damn mutt,' called another. A shot rang out, but John Evert was not concerned: in the darkness, the dog would be far too quick to get hurt.

'Leave it,' one of the men said. 'Come on, back here.'

Casey dragged John Evert on. 'Where we going, Casey? The *Star*?'

'No.'

'Then where?'

Casey made no answer as they zigzagged on. An alarm bell had begun to toll and shutters were opening. 'It's getting hot,' Casey said, his voice low and anxious. 'Come on, there's no time.'

After what seemed like hours, Casey led them to a warehouse in a part of town that John Evert did not know. He shut the big double doors behind them and lit an oil lamp. They were both out of breath. Casey's brow glistened with sweat. There was a thud and rapid scrabbling at the doors, making John Evert jump. Casey cracked open the door and the dog raced inside.

'What're we doing here?' John Evert asked.

'We've got to wait for things to die down,' Casey replied.

In the rear of the warehouse, Bill's grey and the roan pony were tethered, already saddled. John Evert went to the pony, which nickered and thrust its soft muzzle into his pockets in search of sugar. His dog twisted around his legs, rubbing its face against him. Despite his confusion and fear, John Evert smiled and held onto his two friends' noses, delighted to be reunited with them.

There was another thud at the door, and Bill, hair standing on end, head and shoulders white with dust, marched in like some noble marble statue brought to life. He nodded at Casey, who ran to the corner and pulled a blanket off a chest. Bill kicked the lid back, reached in and drew out his gunbelt and pistols, which he buckled on. Then he went back in for his Whitworth and slung it over his shoulder. He tucked an armful of rifles under one arm and came to John Evert. He put his free hand on John Evert's shoulder, squeezed it, and gave his lopsided grin. John Evert felt his chest expand with joy and relief: everything was going to be all right.

Bill handed him three rifles; John Evert buckled two of them behind the saddle of the roan and the third he slung over his shoulder, its cool weight comforting against his back. They mounted the horses, John Evert opening his saddlebag to glance inside. There was a change of clothes, food and a couple of books.

'Casey, I thank you,' said Bill. 'I'll see you right in this life or, more likely, the next.'

'He's not coming with us?' John Evert asked, dismayed.

'Too easy to spot,' Casey said. 'Two whites and a black. I'll be all right. I'll get out of town tonight.'

'And then what?'

'Don't worry about me.'

'No way, Bill,' John Evert said. 'Casey comes with us. If they catch him—'

'No,' Casey said firmly. 'This is the way I want it. I owe Bill.'

'Since when?'

'Since a long time. How'd you think I made it out of Carolina?'

John Evert looked from Casey to Bill. 'You never said.'

'You never asked,' said Casey.

'There's no time for stories now,' Bill said. 'Casey, the door.'

Casey pushed open the double doors and let out a low exclamation of surprise at a disembodied head floating in the darkness. He crossed himself.

'Abraham?' John Evert said. Abraham slowly lowered the lamp that he was holding aloft, so the rest of his body came to light. John Evert's heart sank: he knew who would next appear.

'Abraham,' Bill said in exasperation. 'How the hell did you know to come here?'

'It is my job, sir, to know such things.'

'Then I wish profoundly that you would take a day off.'

'I beg you to wait for Mr Featherstone. He is on his way here now.'

'There's no time,' Bill snapped. He kicked the grey to move past Abraham, but he was too late. Hector appeared in the doorway, his collar loose and his shirt half buttoned. Where his hair was usually slicked back, now a lock fell over his forehead, making his appearance unusually youthful.

He ignored Bill, moving swiftly to the side of the roan, and put his hand upon its neck. 'John,' he said, with an urgency John Evert had never heard from him before, 'don't do this. I beg you to stay. If you leave, you will be hunted for the rest of your life. You will lose your ranch for good.'

'Mr Featherstone, it's too late. I'm already a criminal.'

'Not until you're convicted, you're not. Give me the chance to get your name cleared. How can I if you leave with Bill now?'

Moved by Hector's plea and feeling rent in two, John Evert appealed to him, 'But what is there to keep me here, Mr Featherstone?'

'Your job at the *Star*.'

'All due respect, sir, but working at the *Star* won't get me what I need.'

'John, consider, even Lincoln himself was a labourer once. "Just what might happen to any poor man's son", remember?'

'I'm sorry, Mr Featherstone, but it won't be fast enough.' He looked down into Hector's anxious face, the wide arched eyebrows and piercing gaze. 'I'm sorry.'

'What about your mother?' Hector demanded. 'What would she think of your activities?' John Evert's heart dropped, and he was assailed by the most intense memory of her, as though it were she, not Hector, imploring him to stay. He looked at Bill, uncertain.

Bill said firmly, 'Kid, if we get out of here alive, I will help you find her. I swear it.'

'You promise?' John Evert said breathlessly, his heart hammering against his ribcage.

'I do,' Bill said.

Hector turned. 'Goddamn you, Bill,' he said quietly, stepping away from the roan.

'I think we can safely say that that event has already occurred, Mr Featherstone.'

John Evert pulled his bandanna over the bridge of his nose. He could not help but feel a flush of excitement dance in his belly. Bill put the grey into a standing canter and John Evert dug his spurs into the roan, which sat back on its haunches and bolted after the grey.

Away to the right, John Evert saw soldiers on horseback travelling at speed away from them; they neither saw nor heard the two horses galloping across the junction behind them.

John Evert turned in his saddle and looked back. The figures of Hector and Abraham, lit by the glow of the lamp Abraham held, stood like gatekeepers on either side of the yawning doors. John Evert shivered involuntarily then whipped his face front once more as he followed Bill into the night.

Part Two

A Belt of Fire

1861–1862

13

Pursuit was inevitable, and it took all of Bill's cunning for them to evade their hunters. The moment they reached the Los Angeles river, Bill nosed the grey into the water and John Evert followed, to cover their tracks. When they spotted cattle, they rounded them up and stampeded them into the river and out the other side. John Evert expected they would ride on with the cattle, to disguise their passage in the churned-up ground, but Bill shook his head, directing him back into the water.

'But why?' John Evert said. 'They can't be far behind us.'

'They'll expect us to have gone with the cattle. We need to get behind them.'

Later, they watched, hidden by the sheltering curtains of a bank of willows, as cavalry pounded down to the water's edge. John Evert's heart was in his mouth as every noise – the creak of his saddle, the jingle of the grey's bit as it threw its head up and down impatiently – seemed magnified a hundredfold. Yet it worked: the cavalry deliberated over the crazed path of the cattle, located where the herd had left the river and galloped away after it.

They left the water where the cavalry had entered, and rode back in the direction of Los Angeles, atop the messy trail that the cavalry had left behind. Once they reached stony ground, upon which only a master tracker could follow them, Bill turned the grey north, then east, before heading back south, toward the Mexican border.

The next few weeks were not a fine state of affairs. They lived like the hunted men they were. They could enter no town nor call on the hospitality of any ranch. They lived off the land, which was no difficulty, it being spring, and where the land could not provide, they pilfered from homesteads, a bucket of milk here, a swift hand through a kitchen door there.

It would have been a lie to say that John Evert was not sometimes filled with doubt as to the wisdom of going on the run with Bill, but Bill had made him a promise, and John Evert had more faith in that promise than he had in anything else in the world. And when he was trotting along upon the roan, the desert light pure and bright, his dog loping at his side, it did seem that he had made the right choice. He was free, no matter what else, and as soon as it was safe to do so, they would set out on the trail after his mother.

He had many questions for Bill, mostly about the Order of the Lone Star, whose nature was but ghostly to him.

'It's about independence from government. These politicians, they don't listen to what the people want. Well, they say they do, at first, when they want your vote, but once they have a little power you find they're not working in the interests of the people,' Bill said. 'Take the Mexican War – the idea that Mexico started it. Nonsense. Our government wanted that war because it wanted more land for settlers. The government may say its hands are tied to prevent injustices, but the hands of the individual are not. So the Order was formed. If we see oppressed people in need of aid, we give it. If we see people abusing their power, we strike them down. Or that was the plan anyway,' he added wistfully.

'So those men you've killed or taken captive . . .' John Evert began.

'Men with power who were causing disruption in society, men that the Order felt, or I felt, should be brought to rights.'

'What about Ricardo Urives? I thought he was just a thief and a brigand.'

'Well, in his case, no. With him it was something personal between me and him. I can't pretend all I've done was for the Order,' Bill admitted.

'And who started it? Who runs it?'

'It was founded in Texas by a group of wise and wealthy men who saw the way things were being run and felt it could be done better.'

'And they're friends of yours?'

'A few of them but, I'll be honest, the direction they're heading in is not one I agree with.'

'And what do you get out of it? Hector Featherstone told me it wants to create more slave states. I can't believe you . . .' He trailed off, unsure of how to finish his thought without sounding critical.

'I don't want that any more than you do. When I became a brother of the Order, the founding principles were fair and just, and I needed them at the time because I was in hot water and those men are powerful. If you have them on your side, it wouldn't matter what sort of trouble you'd got into, they'd be able to help you out. It's a brotherhood of like-minded men, who won't be ruled by others, and I enjoyed that.'

'You joined it to get away from the British?'

'Yes, in more ways than one. And before you ask, because I can see it writ large on your face, I didn't turn pirate for no reason. The captain of that ship was a despot, and when there was mutiny, I was elected to lead it.'

John Evert nodded. 'And the Order of the Lone Star will protect us now,' he said confidently, liking the sound of that noble band of brothers.

'I don't know, kid. Maybe, maybe not. War's going to change everything. The Order is Southern. It will fight for the South. And that will decide whether it survives or not. If it picks the wrong side, that will be the end of it, and us.'

'How come?'

'Because what we're doing isn't something you can turn your back on.' Bill sighed. 'Once you're in, you're in.'

Bill's cryptic statement confused John Evert but he did not ask more, and Bill changed the subject. John Evert figured he would let Bill deal with the details now, and save his own energies for what might lie ahead. It was a great comfort to him to know that Bill was applying himself to their future, for with him there was always a way. There was only one other person who had ever made John Evert feel as safe, and he experienced a pang of guilt.

He tried to imagine then, as he often did, what his mother might be doing in that very moment, where she might be, but it was impossible: his imagination only ever took him into the past. And it was the strangest things he remembered, not great events, but the small and everyday.

He saw in his mind's eye the white muslin sacks she would hang in a row from the rafters, filled with the pulp of fruits that had been boiled for hours, the juices left to drain, with painstaking slowness, one pure drop at a time through the fine muslin mesh into the bowls below. She would boil the crimson drippings with sugar, leaving them to cool and set into perfectly clear jellies. It was like magic for him. Sugar was expensive, but she would sell quantities of the finished jellies to the general-store owner, who would ride over to collect them. In the fall, the whole house would be filled with the rich, sweet smell of the sugary fruit, and the low sunlight would creep through the window and be dispersed into every shade of red and orange through the glass jars upon the window sill, better than any church's stained-glass window.

Once they had slipped over the border into Mexico, they were able to enter small villages and bunk up for a night or two, but they never stayed longer. They followed in a zigzag trail along the Mexican border, always in an easterly direction, toward Texas.

They stayed off the plains, where they would be visible, favouring instead the slower routes through cobalt-blue hills. Storms followed them. Giant cat's paw clouds bowled along above, and silent flickers of lightning shivered down onto the plain. Then the rain would come, quiet, thick and incessant. They had oilskins in their saddlebags, but it was not long before runnels of water poured off the brim of John Evert's hat and down inside his collar. The roan put its ears back and tucked its muzzle into its chest. And then, as quick as it had come, the storm would clear and they would ride again through thirsty desert.

They reached Texas weeks later, by which time Bill had cultivated a beard of Old Testament proportion. They rode for many leagues across yellow sandy soil, through wild onion and verbena, the air tart with citrus fragrance, and cherry-red sumac drupes stained their wake, like drops of spilled blood. Above, immense, indifferent skies looked on.

They halted at a small town in Texas, where Bill dispatched a message in search of the Order. They remained there for several days, holed up in a dingy lodging house, until he received an answer.

Then, for the next few days, they rode hard, with no rest at all.

John Evert was bone-tired and ravenous, their rations down to just a few rank pieces of dried beef, when, in the middle of a sweltering afternoon in which even the trees seemed to droop listless in the heat, they rode up on to a scrubby rise, and looked down upon a sprawling ranch that was bigger than any John Evert had ever seen. Several men were gathered outside the long ranch house. Smoke curled from the chimney, and there was an air of activity. John Evert made to kick the roan on down the hill, but Bill stopped him.

'No, not yet,' he said. 'I need an idea of who's there.'

John Evert sighed as they pulled back off the ridge, and he slid off the roan on to wobbly legs. 'Lie down and sleep if you're tired,' Bill said curtly. John Evert saw that Bill was tense, a novelty he was not happy to witness.

John Evert fell into a twitching sleep in the shade of a cottonwood. Bill did not rest. He had crawled on his belly back to the rise, and there he remained, gazing down on the ranch.

When John Evert next awoke, it was dusk. June bugs hissed sickly in the grass. He reached for his canteen, but it was empty. His tongue was thick in his parched mouth. Night fell, bringing a welcome coolness, then Bill was at his side bidding him wake.

They led the horses down the long slope, John Evert stumbling occasionally, still half asleep. The faintest glimmer of light squeezed through chinks around the windows in the log walls of the ranch house. It gave off a lowering strength, like a fortress.

'That dog stays out here,' Bill whispered. He knocked loudly at the door. There was no response. He knocked again.

'Who calls?' said a voice from within.

'One who wanders and asks for shelter.'

'Under what name?'

'The nameless name.'

John Evert shot him a quizzical look but Bill ignored him. The door opened silently. John Evert could make out only the outline of a man, but he did not miss the unmistakeable sound of a gun being cocked. He reached instinctively for his pistol, but Bill pushed him firmly behind him. John Evert was more than awake now. The hairs stood up all over his body.

'Your business?' the faceless man said.

'My business is the lonely state. I seek my brothers.'

'From where have you come?'

'Nowhere. Like the turtle, I carry my home upon my back.'

'Brother, you are welcome,' the man said, standing back. Bill walked forward, and John Evert followed.

The place was high-ceilinged, with great beams forming hollow triangles all along the eaves to the back of the room where a mighty fire burned under a heavy mantel. The space was filled with men, and candles flickered all about its perimeter.

'Our brother returns,' said the man. A ripple went around the room as others appeared to recognise Bill. A few approached and clasped his hand, murmuring greetings.

'Is Thaddeus here?' Bill asked.

As if in answer, someone threw a log upon the fire with great force, and red embers exploded out of the fireplace into the room. The man responsible stood up from where he had been bent over the hearth. He was enormous, a bear of a man. He walked over to them slowly. When he reached them, he surveyed

Bill thoughtfully, then delivered him a right hook in the face. Bill sank to his knees. Startled, John Evert made to go to his aid, but Bill put out a hand to keep him back. He held his cheek for a moment then got to his feet and looked the man in the eye. 'Hello, Thaddeus,' he said evenly. 'We're hungry. Will you feed us?'

Thaddeus stared at him for what seemed a very long time, then replied, 'Be fed.' With that he turned and walked back to the fire, whatever having passed between him and Bill apparently concluded. 'It is good you are here,' he said, over his shoulder. 'We have need of you now.'

A young man brought them some bowls of steaming food. John Evert wolfed his down without tasting it, burning his tongue. Afterward, Bill spoke quietly with a couple of men in a dark corner. Then he walked up to the front of the room, by the light of the fire, and took a seat in the midst of a row of men to one side. Receiving no sign from Bill, John Evert remained where he was, glad not to have to sit in front of the company.

Thaddeus went to the fire, and gazed into it for such a long time that he seemed to have fallen into a trance, but finally he let out a long breath, and took a dagger in a scabbard from the mantel. He made the sign of the cross with it in front of himself then did the same to the other three sides of the room. John Evert watched with interest. There was no talking, and the warmth and silence, combined with his full belly, commenced to make him feel drowsy again. His eyes began to smart. He thought it was the smoke from the fire, but then he saw that two long pipes were being passed from man to man, and that each was taking long draws. The man sitting nearest to him held a pipe out to him. John Evert took it. The tobacco tasted pretty good, but the smoke smelt sweet and strange. Soon after, he felt deeply relaxed.

Thaddeus began to talk. He seemed to be outlining a set of rules, which made little sense to John Evert. His mind began to wander, and he wondered, of a sudden, what was in the pipe. After Thaddeus had finished, another man spoke and then another. Despite his drifting attention, John Evert realised that they were discussing the war.

'The North talks of subjugating us,' one said. 'Are we to submit to despotism?' Murmurs in the negative rumbled around the room.

'We have the right of self-government just as the North does,' said another. 'It's a sacred right.'

'Sacred . . .' The word was picked up and echoed by several in the room.

John Evert's drooping eyes were drawn to the fire, which seemed unnaturally bright. He heard the odd word or phrase as it was spoken: 'Never alive until now . . . Something to fight for . . . die for . . . Domestic foes . . .'

Later, the debate must have become heated as he was snapped out of his drowsing state by Thaddeus bellowing, 'Justice and liberty!'

Momentarily awake, he also heard Bill's voice, 'The word "liberty" used by the keepers of slaves . . .'

There was a furious response, but John Evert did not hear it. A golden bird had walked out of the fire. He leaned forward and squinted at it, then rubbed his eyes. When he looked once more, it was gone. Bill was speaking again, and John Evert forced himself to attend to what he was saying: 'Any revolution that does not fight for freedom for *all* men . . .'

'This isn't England!' cried another. 'This is America.'

'Our way of life . . .' began another.

John Evert wondered if he was the only one feeling strange. A lot of the men looked kind of odd. One was on his feet, his mouth slowly forming the words, 'The glorious cause . . .' John Evert thought he had better lie down, and tilted to lie upon the bench he was sitting on. Almost immediately, he fell asleep.

He awoke to the sounds of movement. When he opened his eyes, he saw that many of the men were departing, and those who remained were gathered in small groups, muttering to each other. He had no idea how the meeting had ended. He lay back again and shut his eyes. Some time later, he was aware of people standing near him. 'Your son?' a voice murmured.

'No.' Bill snorted under his breath. 'I own him.'

John Evert kept still. It was quite normal for Bill to profess no intimacy with him – it happened all the time when they were on the road – but for some reason, on this occasion, it cut something in John Evert. He tried to examine his feelings. Was he jealous of these men and their brotherhood? He did not consider it much of a brotherhood from the way Thaddeus and those men had treated Bill, yet Bill seemed to set great store by them. John Evert did not like it, not one bit.

John Evert waited until he was sure Bill and the other man had gone, and then he opened his eyes. It was dawn. Cold blue light seeped in around the edges of the windows. Men lay about the place, asleep. When he sat up, his head ached and he felt wretched. He walked outside slowly. His dog was curled up in a ball against the wall of the house. When it saw him, it pricked its ears and raised its head. He flicked his hand at it and it got to its feet, stretched, then lolloped to his side. He went to the horses, unbuckled his saddlebag and slung it over his shoulder. He left the rifles for they were not his, but he took the Colt for that had been a present. He stroked the roan's head, breathed in its familiar grassy smell, then turned and walked away. He was not sure where he was going, but he had to get away from that place. He felt the sliding sensation of despair and knew it was only in movement that he might find escape.

It was only a few hours later, when the sun was fully up, that he heard the sound of galloping horses. He did not bother to turn.

'Where in the name of Jesus do you think you're going?' Bill demanded. John Evert said nothing, and continued walking. Bill fell silent and John Evert sensed confusion in him. Bill dismounted, took him by the arm and turned him about. 'What happened?' he asked, unfamiliar concern in his face. 'Did one of them say something to you?'

John Evert struggled to form the words. 'I don't like those men. They don't give a damn about you. You said they did but they don't.'

An expression John Evert could not interpret passed across Bill's face. 'No doubt, but so what?'

When John Evert did not reply, Bill took his chin in his hand and turned it toward him. Bill studied him in silence, and then something dawned upon his great, sleepy face. If John Evert had had to put a word to it, he would have said he looked almost humble. 'This isn't about them and me,' Bill said quietly. 'It's because I said you weren't my son.'

John Evert had not allowed himself to admit it, but it was so.

Bill unhanded him, leaned against the grey's shoulder and took out his tobacco pouch. 'Kid,' he said slowly, 'do you think it'd be in your favour for people to think I'm your pa? Don't you see what that makes you? They want to hurt me, so they hurt you. You care that much what other people think, then the whole of life is going to be a disappointment to you.'

John Evert stood rigid, feeling foolish.

'Now, will you come back with me so I can finish up and get out of here?'

'You're not staying with them?' John Evert asked.

'No,' Bill replied. 'You're not the only one with the ability to exercise good judgement.'

John Evert mounted the roan and kept it far behind Bill, so he did not have to look at him. Back at the ranch house, Bill asked him to stay put while he spoke to a couple of the men. John Evert was sitting the roan, chewing his nails, when a voice arose at his side. 'Where's Bill?'

John Evert did not turn. 'Dunno,' he said morosely. Curiosity got the better of him eventually, and he shifted in his saddle to see who had spoken. It was Thaddeus, who was observing John Evert intently, in a way that would have made him uncomfortable if he had not felt so thoroughly surly. He glared back at Thaddeus, until Bill appeared.

'This boy's on the road to a hiding,' Thaddeus said.

'I know it.' Bill sighed. 'What's he done now?'

'Nothing particular, just has a way about him I don't like. He's a lot like you.'

'How's that?' Bill asked carelessly, as he mounted the grey.

'Insolent,' Thaddeus replied.

'Atta boy.' Bill beamed. 'Does his father proud.'

John Evert was startled by this statement, but not as much as Thaddeus, whose eyes darted from John Evert to Bill and back again. Delighted, John Evert sat taller in his saddle.

'I'll be seeing you, William,' Thaddeus said, 'and you,' he said to John Evert pointedly.

'I certainly hope that is not the case, Thaddeus, but I wish you well regardless,' Bill said. They kicked the horses on and trotted away.

When they were some distance from the ranch, Bill said, 'I'd quit looking so pleased with yourself. You'd better hope neither of us meets him, or any of those other characters, on the battlefield.'

'Battlefield?'

'The Order will fight with the South. They've refused me protection if I don't do the same. Well, screw them. I won't side with bigotry. We'll fight with the North.' To John Evert's shocked expression, he added, 'We have no money and, worse, we're wanted. The only safety lies in the army, so it's the Union for us.'

'How long . . .' John Evert began.

'Not long,' Bill said breezily. 'Just till things die down a bit.'

John Evert digested this, then asked, 'Why does he hate you?'

'Thaddeus? Oh, plenty of reasons. He'd say it's a difference of ideology. I'd say it's because of a woman. It wasn't my fault.' Bill sighed. 'Actually, that's not true, it was my fault. You'd have hoped such things could be overlooked, considering our supposed bond, but in the end it always comes down to the same thing – personality.'

John Evert cleared his throat. 'Why did you say that – about my being your son?'

'Because I'm sick and tired of your worry,' Bill replied. 'You wanted in with me. Well, now you're in.' He tutted. 'If I'd known you'd be this much work, I'd have left you in jail.'

And with that he kicked the grey into a canter and then a gallop. John Evert smiled at Bill's slouching shoulders as the pair of them charged away over the brush, into the east.

14

On the road, John Evert had ample time to consider his situation. Where once the notion of leaving California to go to war would have been unthinkable, he found himself now in a position of no security, with no hope of ease, and thus he figured he had but one option to embrace: heroism. He had little notion of the politics that had led to war; his stance was but a simple one – what he had seen of Southern attitudes at the Order of the Lone Star had convinced him that that way was wrong, and thus to fight for the North was to fight for good. The guise of soldier had to be more respectable than that of outlaw. Holding to this idea gave him a sense of purpose, that not quite all had yet been lost. These were the thoughts that occupied him as they arrived at Fort Monroe, Kansas.

The fort consisted of an interlocking grid of white buildings and tents that stood out starkly against the deep green of the surrounding pines. A sentry pointed them in the direction of the enrolment officer.

'Names?'

'William and John Jetsun.'

'Ages?'

'Forty-one and sixteen.'

The enrolment officer scribbled something in his ledger and waved them on. They were sworn in perfunctorily, after which they led their horses past a neat drill field and row upon row of tents. There were men everywhere, busy about their tasks. Most wore the blue uniform, with soft flat caps upon their heads. They headed toward the quartermaster's tent where they were equipped with uniforms, shoes and knapsacks. Rows of Enfield rifles and bayonets stood behind the quartermaster, but Bill indicated to him their guns, and asked only for cartridges for John Evert.

'A fine piece,' the quartermaster said, looking at Bill's Whitworth. 'You've seen action before?'

'In the Mexican War.'

'Where's enrolment sent you?'

'E Barracks.'

'I'd suggest you seek a word with Colonel Ewing. He'll welcome someone like you.'

As they left the quartermaster's tent, the sounds of the encampment swirled around them: the hoof beats of cavalry trotting by, the thin call of bugles being sounded, shouted orders and the chime of a blacksmith's hammer. John Evert took it all in, as did his dog, which trotted alongside him with its ears pricked. They located their barracks in one of the nondescript rows of white tents. John Evert made the horses comfortable in the shade of a tree, and studied the men collected nearby. A lot of the younger ones had clearly come straight off the farm, some still wearing rolled-up breeches and floppy straw hats. They did not look much like soldiers.

The day might have seemed dutifully busy, but it was at night that E Barracks came to life. There was arm-wrestling and card-playing; one man had set himself up as magician, and was busy stripping the unwise of a dime; another had with him a viola, from which he scratched out a pretty tune. All the men introduced themselves. They were rough, simple folk, filled with enthusiasm, every one of them a volunteer.

'Hey, why'd you join up?' a sandy-haired boy asked John Evert, as he sat outside his and Bill's tent, cleaning the horses' filthy bridles.

'My pa,' John Evert replied, the word still awkward in his mouth.

'Sure. Bet you couldn't wait to come along and see some action. I can't wait to shoot my first Rebel,' the boy said.

John Evert noticed the way he carried his Enfield idly across his shoulder, like it was nothing more than a dead branch. 'You know how to shoot that thing?' he asked.

'Sure.'

'Accurate?'

The boy looked down. 'Kinda.'

He must have been around the same age as John Evert and yet inside, John Evert could tell, he was a whole lot younger. 'I was going to get myself some target practice tomorrow, in the woods,' John Evert said. 'You can join me, if you like.'

'Hey, thanks, I will,' the boy replied, smiling a gap-toothed grin. His carefree optimism troubled John Evert. Dinner was fine, though: there was bacon and beans, and plenty of coffee. John Evert gorged himself, making up for the long weeks on the road. He fell into his camp bed early and was half asleep by the time Bill entered.

'Hey, Bill?' he mumbled. 'How much training do these men get before they see action? There are boys out there have barely handled a gun.'

'The men aren't much better. All full of the "glorious cause". They've no idea what's waiting for them, but that isn't a bad thing – they'll make good soldiers after training.'

'How?'

'When you're under fire, it's not clever men you want around you, it's willing. The safest man to have next to you is the one who'll do exactly what you tell him, without asking why. You would do well to remember that, kid.'

John Evert felt somewhat reassured by Bill's words, but hoped if he was under fire he would always be next to Bill.

The next morning, they were blasted awake by bugle calls, and headed to the drill field. Bill's uniform fitted immaculately. He had shaved, and his face was smooth and handsome under the peak of his cap. He quickly ran through the drill commands with John Evert, so that they would be familiar to him. Other youngsters upon the drill field were not so lucky. The sandy-haired boy, Orville, fumbled his rifle and almost dropped it. The drill sergeant roared his displeasure.

Bill never did seek out the Colonel Ewing the quartermaster had mentioned. In the end, however, Ewing came to him. He entered Bill and John Evert's tent one afternoon, and doffed his cap politely. He seemed a pleasant character.

'Good day to you, gentlemen. May I speak with you?'

Bill saluted him. 'Of course, sir.'

Ewing waved his hand absentmindedly, as though being saluted were faintly tiresome, and took a seat on the fold-out stool. 'I understand you saw action in the Mexican War.'

'I did.'

'Well, we should have you as an officer, man. I am surrounded by the enthusiastic and untrained, as you see. I have need of someone like you.'

'That is kind of you, sir, but I prefer to remain in the ranks. Time will tell whether I prove myself officer material.'

Ewing inclined his head. 'I admire your scruples, although I see no need for them.' He studied Bill with interest. 'Very well, then,' he shrugged amiably, 'but I hope, for our sakes, that you prove yourself quickly.'

He turned his attention to John Evert. 'Hello,' he said genially.

'Sir,' John Evert said, saluting him.

'I hear from Orville Renton that you are something of a crack shot, young Jetsun. He tells me you have prevented him from posing a grave danger to himself and others when he is in posses- sion of his rifle, which can only be a good thing.'

'I've given him a steer, sir.'

'Well, perhaps you'd do the same for the other boys. They have little notion of what they face, whereas you strike me as having a fair idea of what you will see on the battlefield.'

John Evert was pleased at the compliment. 'I'd be happy to offer my help to any man who wants it.'

'Thank you. Well, Messrs Jetsun, I look forward to seeing more of you.'

After Ewing had gone, John Evert asked, 'Why'd you say no to being made an officer?'

'It doesn't do to leapfrog, kid. You want the men around you to be loyal, and for that you need to prove that you're made of the same stuff. You have to march through the same mud, the same shit. Then, when it comes to it, maybe they'll be prepared to give their lives for yours.'

John Evert suspected that news of Bill's refusal of a commission got around for, two days later, when the men of their regiment were given the opportunity to elect their own non-commissioned officers, they unanimously voted him as their sergeant.

Bill proved an excellent organiser. He was professional when it came to training: any man who was not up to scratch, Bill had him alone on the drill field, under his personal supervision. He instilled pride in the uneducated farm men and turned recruits into soldiers. Around the fire at night, he told them of great battles and generals, and those rough cobs came alive to his tales, so remote from their own experience. They could not get enough of Hannibal and his elephants, but their favourite was the Trojan Horse, which had them shaking their heads and slapping their thighs at the double-crossing.

After a few weeks' training, there was an admiration toward Bill that no other sergeant on the field could instil in his men. John Evert, meanwhile, had tutored many of the men in shooting, selecting for Bill those who had any skill with a rifle. Orville Renton became John Evert's constant companion, following him everywhere. John Evert did not mind it, but oftentimes he found himself longing to be alone with his thoughts. At night he lay awake and traced the rough edges of the scar on his shoulder with a restless finger, thinking of his mother and promising her, in his mind, that it would not be long, that they were still coming, however far away they might be just now. He thought of her so hard he wondered that she must feel it too, that she must know somehow he was out there, flung far away upon the earth but thinking ever of the day they would be reunited.

They broke camp and began to march to Springfield, Missouri.

Men were packed heavily, with fifty pounds of equipment and rations, and on foot the soldiers took days to cover a short distance. John Evert was thankful that he and Bill were cavalry and did not have to march. The winding train of the army on the move wound like a centipede, a mile in length, in fits and starts about the countryside. There were endless halts. Cicadas whirred insanely as the heat bore down like an anvil upon heavy woollen uniforms. The heat haze shimmered along the trail they pounded. There were constant stops for water. Many vomited from drinking too fast. Others grew bored waiting around in the blazing sunshine, and wandered off in search of berries, which delayed progress yet more.

At day's end, the men quit marching with relief, and sat smoking, shaving or washing their stinking shirts in the river. Lice were a problem. Everyone itched and scratched, and gave themselves red sores. Those not besieged by insect infestation were at the mercy of blisters. John Evert was appalled by the sight of the surgeon treating a man's heel that had been worn to bleeding pustules by ill-fitting boots. Tears poured down the soldier's face as the surgeon patched him up, then had him put his boot back on and keep marching. There was no respite.

'What's happening at Springfield?' John Evert asked Bill, after they had been on the road for several days.

'Our General Lyon is meeting the Rebel armies of McCulloch and Price.'

'Why're we being driven there so damn fast?'

'Because Lyon only has about five thousand men, whereas McCulloch and Price have around thirteen. Even if the numbers were equal, Lyon would have plenty to worry about. I knew Ben McCulloch in the war. He's a hard-bitten son-of-a-bitch. His men will fight like dogs for him. I like him a lot.'

'How come you're on the way to fight a man you like?' John Evert asked, confused. 'There's a boy in our regiment who has one brother fighting for the Union and the other's fighting for the Confederacy. It doesn't make sense.'

'No, kid, it doesn't. But that's people for you. We're always at our most righteous when the opportunity for killing or dying arises. One of the Good Lord's little jokes.'

Many days later, they halted for the last time, five miles north of Springfield. The men seemed enthusiastic that they were finally to see some action, but one or two were very quiet, and John Evert overheard more than one man having a few words with his maker in advance of the battle. Orville was one of those who seemed suddenly to appreciate what might await him the next day. He came and sat in John Evert's tent, saying nothing, petting the dog.

It was a balmy August night. Through the open tent flaps, the stars were many and brilliant.

'You all right?' John Evert asked, as he cleaned the barrel of his rifle by the light of an oil lamp.

'Yeah. Kinda. I keep thinking of home. My ma. Funny things like the cornbread she makes. She makes a fine cornbread.'

John Evert's eyes flickered to Orville. Thankfully, the brush he held between his teeth released him from the duty of a reply.

'Do you miss home, John?' he asked. John Evert shook his head. 'How come?' John Evert shrugged, the lie sitting like bitter gall in his chest.

'I wish I was like you.' Orville sighed.

John Evert raised his eyebrows in surprise. 'Why?' he mouthed around the brush.

'Cuz you ain't afraid of nothing. It's like you don't give a damn what'll happen to you. You're the best shot I ever saw. You ride like you were born in a saddle. You've got nothing to worry about tomorrow. I ain't so sure myself. I got a terrible feeling I ain't going to see my farm again.' Orville blanched at the honest rush of his own words.

John Evert was not sure what to make of Orville's confession. He had never considered how other people might see him. He removed the brush from his mouth and cleared his throat. 'The reason I'm not afraid is I don't have anything to go back to,' he said. He was surprised how much it hurt to say it out loud.

Orville considered his words seriously. 'I'm real sorry,' he said. 'There's no call for it.'

Orville nodded sagely in the half-light, seeming strengthened by this knowledge.

'Why don't you take my dog to sleep with you tonight?' John Evert said.

'Oh, he won't come with me.'

'Sure he will.' When Orville got up to go, John Evert bade his dog go too. To Orville's pleasure, the dog followed him, after a few concerned looks back at John Evert.

The next morning, there was a fast breakfast before they were on the move. According to Bill, General Lyon had proposed a bold plan: rather than launch an anticipated attack with his full five thousand men, he would split his forces, launching a surprise two-pronged attack, early in the morning.

'I thought it was a bad idea to divide your army,' John Evert said.

'Usually is,' said Bill, 'but we're outnumbered anyway. The only advantage we have is surprise. It's a gutsy move. I like it.'

John Evert wished that he were capable of such optimism.

That night, they approached the northern hill of Wilson's Creek in dead silence. A light, misting rain fell, muffling all sound, but it ceased once they reached the hill, giving way to a clear night. The ground and foliage remained soaking wet. It was a long night, sitting or lying on the sodden ground, gazing up at the stars or down upon the sleeping Confederate camp that was spread either side of the wooded creek. John Evert could not sleep. He was surprised to find he had no fear of death; instead, it was the idea of dying as an outlaw who had brought disgrace upon the family that disturbed him. If his mother were to learn of his death, and the last she knew of him was that he had been imprisoned and gone on the run, with no attempt made to clear his name, it would be a terrible thing for her. How things had come to such a pass as this, he could not figure. It was hard to tolerate.

Rare for him, he prayed that night to a God who was but ill-formed in his imagination. While doing so, he travelled in his mind to the ranch, saw there the split oak tree, and prayed to that, too, prayed that he would survive the day and have the chance to see it again.

He felt relief at the first twitter of the birds – anything was better than the interminable waiting. A whisper went down the line to mount and ready. John Evert settled himself upon the roan's warm back, while dew and raindrops spattered down from the trees.

As the sky began to brighten, there came the deep bass *whoomph* of cannon from the south as the Union forces launched their assault. The ground shook underfoot. The Rebels awoke to the fact that they were under siege, and hysterical tongues of orange flame leaped out from the dark woods in crackling response. Cannon and gun spoke to each other as the two Union hills fired down upon the creek. Lyon appeared upon the north hill where they stood with the cavalry. As the general cantered down the line, John Evert was surprised by how small and slim he was: he had expected a giant. 'Speed, men,' he called. 'Maintain the element of surprise.' With that he galloped on.

'Stay close to me, kid,' Bill said, from where he sat nonchalant upon the grey.

'Always do,' John Evert replied, but realised that his hands were shaking. 'Orville,' he said, looking to his other side where Orville sat on his father's knock-kneed nag. 'Stay close to me and Bill.'

A Union battery behind them fired, and John Evert and Orville ducked instinctively as the shot whistled by. Bill stayed right where he was. 'They want to be faster than this,' he said.

The first line of blue Union infantry charged down the hill toward the still unready grey-clad Confederates. Musket fire joined the bass boom of the heavy artillery, the noise akin to material being ripped from top to bottom. The whole valley was now alive with strange percussion. 'Form the line!' cried a cavalry officer.

They fell into line, side by side. At the cry of 'Advance!' they commenced a juddering trot. John Evert leaned back in his saddle to take the weight off the roan's shoulders as it shuddered down the hill and, quite suddenly, the horses broke into a canter. His heart was hammering and his mouth was filled with bitter bile. The noise as they came down into the valley was immense. A huge whooshing sound shot by John Evert's ear. Not far ahead, several infantry were blown sky-high, along with clods of black earth. The creek-bottom was dense with smoke. Only when they were almost on top of them did he see the straggling line of men in grey, firing muskets at the advancing Union line. The tongues of flame streaked irregularly out of the guns up and down the line, over and over, yet few men fell.

'Fire!' came the order, and a staccato volley was let off. Once they had fired, the Rebels were held up for a good half-minute as they reloaded. Bill dropped his rein, took aim and felled a Confederate instantly. John Evert fired also, but his aim was wild and he hit nothing. He slung his rifle back across his shoulder and drew instead his curved sabre. The horses were covering the ground so fast they were practically upon the Rebels. The roan mowed down a grey-clad soldier who was bent over, desperately reloading his rifle. The horse swept on. In a matter of seconds, the line of Union cavalry was through the Rebel infantry.

They wheeled about to return to help the Union infantrymen who were locked in musket fire or hand-to-hand combat. It was chaos in the smoke. It was all John Evert could do to stop the roan mowing down Union and Rebel alike. In the heat of battle, he could see men losing their heads completely. He had to duck as one of his own infantry took aim at him and fired. John Evert shouted, but the man's eyes were raving mad. Artillery hailed in on their heads, Union and Rebel alike. One of the horses near John Evert reared up, squealing, as it was hit in the chest. Its rider fell over backwards and was promptly bayoneted by a waiting Rebel. John Evert yanked the roan to a stop. As the agitated animal fidgeted beneath him he awkwardly reloaded his Enfield, aimed and dispatched the Rebel. The roan let out a high-pitched whinny of alarm as another Rebel leaped up and caught the bit at either side of its mouth. The pony tossed its head in fright, and reared up, lifting the man off the ground. In fury, John Evert threw his Enfield to the ground, drew his sabre and slashed it with all his might down the side of the roan's head, taking the man's left arm clean off, just below the shoulder.

Something strange happened to John Evert at the sight of the missing arm, the blood: he went completely deaf. He heard no more of the cannon fire, the shouting and screaming. All he heard was a thunderous rushing in his ears. He looked around him in the smoke. He could see none of the cavalry, only infantry skirmishing. He dismounted, picked up his Enfield from the mud, remounted and kicked the roan on. He cantered forward through the dark woods, branches whipping into his face, but he felt nothing. He ran into the back of the Union cavalry.

Bill's grey was whirling around in fright beneath him, and even Bill was wide-eyed. When Bill noticed him, he beckoned him over urgently. John Evert rattled to his side and his hearing thickly returned as though he was surfacing from under water. Bill spoke quickly, 'We must keep moving forward and make another charge further into the camp.'

'Where's Orville?' John Evert asked, his own voice sounding hollow to his ears.

There was no sign either of the staff officer who had been with them. Bill took command and cantered up and down the ramshackle line of cavalry.

'Hold, men. Look! Look at me!' he commanded. 'Listen to me. Do as I say. We have nothing to fear if we stay together. Their cavalry isn't mounted. Let's tear down as many of their infantry as we can.'

A shell exploded close to Bill and the grey plunged in terror, but Bill brought the horse under control. All the panicked men's eyes were fixed upon him, including John Evert's.

'Are you with me?' Bill cried, as Rebel bullets peppered the trees around them.

'Aye, aye,' cried the terrified farmers, released from having to think for themselves.

Bill wheeled about, raised his arm and charged forward, and they charged, shoulder-to-shoulder, after him. John Evert leaned forward over the roan's withers to avoid low-hanging branches. The woods reeked of black powder and the dank, exploded ground. They galloped across a shell hole, and John Evert caught a flash of dead bodies and missing limbs, figures contorted in impossible sickening shapes. He could never have anticipated the horror. He had imagined battle to be an ordered and ritual thing with two armies advancing neatly across a field. This frenzied carnage was beyond belief.

He passed a Confederate standing over a fallen Union infantryman, holding aloft a log, with which he must have planned to bludgeon the man. John Evert pulled the roan to a stop, turned it about, lay flat along its neck and fired his rifle. The Rebel fell down with a neat, black hole above his eye. John Evert stared at the fallen body, numb. He shook himself, swung the rifle back over his shoulder and galloped after the cavalry. Quite suddenly, they were out of the woods and on to open ground, in a field of chest-high grass. Ahead was a Rebel barricade.

'Break left,' Bill shouted. The line did so, following his lead, so that they galloped one behind the other, along the edge of the woods, to the corner of the field. Bill called a halt, and they slithered in a panicky concertina, one into the back of another, panting hard. 'All right. All right,' he said soothingly. 'Noah, Joseph, you keep on through here and see if there's a way round for us, so we don't have to cross that field. Quick at it!'

The two men trotted off through the trees. Bill sat calmly, studying the ground. John Evert and the other men were jumpy, listening to the artillery fire outside the safety of the wood. Nobody spoke. Suddenly, two foot-soldiers ran pell-mell into the side of their line. One man raised his rifle.

'No, wait! We're Union!' cried the men, as they threw their hands into the air.

'Hold your fire,' shouted Bill. John Evert could just make out the Union blue beneath the mud that coated their uniforms. One foot-soldier leaned forward, put his hands on his knees, and spat heavily. Behind them the sound of heavy shelling continued.

'What's happened?' Bill demanded, above the noise.

'It was all going pretty well but they rallied. We're licked. We need help. Can you flank around with us?'

'That's what we're trying to find out.'

The two scouts returned. 'No good. There's a huge ditch, full of fallen trees. There's no way round, the woods are too thick.'

'Then we go through the field,' Bill said.

'You'll be riding right through the centre of them,' the foot-soldier replied.

'Yes. Where are you in most trouble?'

'The base of the hill. They're all over us.'

Bill turned his attention back to the cavalry. 'Right, men, re-form the line but not side by side. I want every man one behind another.'

The soldiers raised their voices in protest. Only John Evert moved forward to get behind Bill.

'Quit your jabbering!' Bill bellowed. 'You heard me, one behind another. If we ride single file they won't be able to see how many we are.'

'But they'll pick us off one by one,' cried one of the men.

'That's as may be, but I'll go first. The first volley will be for me, then there'll be the reload, giving you time to gain on them. Raises all our chances.'

'Except yours,' one wit responded.

'Ha! Just so,' Bill spat. 'Now, you can come with me and take your chances, or you can stay here and get picked off by the Rebels. Keep those nags nose to tail, you hear me. Not a man out of place till we near the barricade. When we're close, I want you to fan out, you understand, shoulder to shoulder again.'

'Then what?'

'Then we jump the barricade.'

The men nodded dumbly. They began to line up behind John Evert, snaking back through the woods until they reached the point at which they had first entered the field.

'Stay here a minute,' Bill said.

John Evert's eyes never left Bill as he cantered out alone along the edge of the smoke-wreathed field, half obscured by the edge of the woods, riding in a curiously sloppy fashion. Rebels from the barricade fired bullets at him, and he bounced and slithered in his saddle, crying out in mock fear. He turned one way and then the other, doing his best impression of a man lost in panic. There was laughter from the Rebel line as he wobbled back into the woods, elbows flapping at his sides.

'Right,' he said, as he re-joined the cavalry. 'There'll be one volley when we're single file. After that you fan out and you all ride like hell, you hear me?'

Another round of shells slammed into the field, filling it with smoke.

'Charge!' Bill shouted. The grey galloped forward, John Evert's roan tucked neatly behind it, the rest of the cavalry in a line behind them. As they charged through the smoke, the first Rebels spotted Bill coming, but seeing only one horse they did not act fast. One sharp-shooter took a leisurely shot, but missed. Another Rebel fired a wing shot that took off the tip of the grey's left ear. The horse squealed but did not break its stride. Bill roared out an unearthly yell, stood up in his stirrups, his rifle at his shoulder, and neatly took down the sharp-shooter. At this, several Rebel shooters in the centre fired at Bill. All were unsuccessful.

Meanwhile, Rebels at either end of the line saw through the smoke that there were horses behind Bill's. They shouted at each other and began to fire, but the horses were in full gallop now, and as they bore down upon the barricade the rear riders tore to either side to catch up with Bill's horse, fanning out to ride shoulder to shoulder, so that shots from the ends of the line could now only hope, at best, to take out one rider. The Rebels in the centre of the barricade were unready as the grey launched itself over the barrier, Bill swinging his sabre and felling a man. Horses careered over the barricade on either side of him: one horse leaping clear sideways, putting a hoof in a Rebel's face; another couple falling and taking out several Rebels as they did so. Once over the barricade, the cavalry cut a swathe through the infantry, trampling them underfoot and scattering them. That was when John Evert happened to look around, and saw Orville entering the field, but behind the line.

Most of the Rebels in the centre had scattered, but sharp-shooters remained at the far ends of the line.

'Orville!' John Evert cried. 'Get back in the woods.'

But the boy was in panic. Seeking the shelter of the cavalry, he did not notice the Rebels still hidden by the barricade, and charged across the field. John Evert booted the roan, leaped back over the barricade and turned to the left, drawing Orville away from the shooters at the other end of the line.

'This way, Orville!' he cried. Orville saw him and began to turn toward him. 'That's it!' John Evert yelled as he galloped along the side of the barricade. At the same moment, he saw two Rebel shooters ahead, embedded in the barricade, about a hundred yards apart, both busily reloading. 'Shit!' he breathed.

He dug his spurs into the roan, and galloped hell for leather toward them. He reached the first man, just as he raised his rifle to his shoulder. John Evert took his left foot from his stirrup and kicked him, hard as he could, in the face. The man fell back. John Evert drew his sabre as the roan covered the ground to the next man and, balancing all his weight in one stirrup, he slammed the butt of his sword into the man's head. He re-found his stirrup, yanked the reins hard, so that the roan spun on the spot, and sprinted back toward Orville. Then he saw why Orville had come out of the woods: Rebels were coming toward them from the rear.

Bullets were whizzing past, the two of them forming an easy target out in the open field. John Evert flanked Orville. He was headed for the side of the woods but John Evert slammed the roan into his nag to prevent him and they veered off together.

'No, there's no way through there,' he cried. 'We have to jump.'

'Jump?' Orville wailed, as he bounced around on the back of his horse.

'The barricade.'

John Evert leaned down and grabbed Orville's horse's rein, turning its head back toward the barricade. They could not have chosen a worse spot to try to clear: where the centre of the barricade had been just logs and artillery boxes, this far end was made up of cannon wagons, as wide as they were high.

'I don't think he can!' Orville shouted, wide-eyed, as they galloped toward the obstacle.

'Yes, he can,' John Evert cried. The two horses careered toward the cannon wagon. The roan, sighting the obstacle, pricked its ears forward. John Evert still had hold of Orville's rein. He switched it to his left hand, drew his sabre again with his right, guiding the roan with just his legs. Bullets whizzed behind them, pinging off the metal of the wagons they were galloping toward. Orville's horse had seen the obstacle ahead, and put its ears back. John Evert knew it was going to refuse.

'Hold on tight!' John Evert shouted, and with that he let go of Orville's rein and spanked the animal's flank with the sharp edge of his sabre, wincing at what he did. The horse screamed, but in its pain and fear it jumped. The roan followed, making a huge leap that carried it clean past the barricade. Orville's horse mangled it and half slithered over the wagon on its belly, stumbled on the landing, but, miraculously, kept its footing, and Orville his seat. They charged along the level ground into the wooded base of the hill, the Rebel fire behind them too far away now to be a danger, John Evert letting out a whooping cry of success.

Their horses cantered laboriously up the steep hill, and made it to level ground at the top, where they drew down to a shuddering walk, both animals dripping with lather, steam curling out of their nostrils.

Orville was struck dumb, and John Evert winced again at the blood pouring from the flank of the boy's horse. He seemed to be having trouble breathing, so John Evert thumped him firmly on the back, saying cheerfully, 'Jesus, Orville, did you see how high your horse jumped? You'll have to tell your pa. He'll never believe you. Never.'

Orville opened his mouth: 'He . . . he did. He did, didn't he?' He reached down and patted the horse's neck, saying over and over again, 'He did. He did.'

The woods were surprisingly quiet. The noise of fire from the field below gradually ceased. Eventually, they wound their way into the remains of the Union army.

'What's happened?' John Evert asked an infantryman.

'It's over. The Rebels had us.'

John Evert blinked. It seemed impossible, after all they had done, that they did not have the victory.

They made their way back round to the northern camp. Their progress was slow, Orville's horse dragging its hoofs in the dust, the roan badly lame. John Evert wondered where Bill had got to. It did not cross his mind that anything could have befallen him. Sure enough, on the last leg of the trail, they found him.

Bill looked like a devil freshly spat out of Hell, his mouth and jaw black from all the powder cartridges he had bitten open, hair stuck up all over the place, matted with dried blood from a flesh wound to his head. When he saw John Evert, a look of relief crossed his face then was gone – so quickly that John Evert thought he might have imagined it. 'All right?' he said, his voice casual.

John Evert nodded. 'Where are the others?' he asked, surveying the depleted cavalry.

'They didn't make it.' Bill shook his head.

John Evert remembered the jump over the barricade, and the sight of falling horses, falling men. Something sour rose in his throat, and he swallowed.

They limped into camp, and made the horses as comfortable as they could. Bill sponged the grey's head of dried blood from its damaged ear, but its white face was stained blue-grey all down one side. John Evert cleaned the roan of the mud caked right up to its chest, and brushed out its mane and tail. He coaxed it to put its lame foot in a pail of cold water and let it stand with its exhausted head pressed into his chest. He tethered it loosely, so that it could lie down. Only then did he trudge, bone-tired, to his tent.

The men in their barracks were silent. Only Bill seemed capable of talk. John Evert caught sight of him in discussion with the drill sergeant, who stood with his arms folded across his chest, angrily digging up earth with the toe of his boot.

John Evert's dog was twisting itself around where he had tethered it firmly to a stake in the ground. He let it loose and the dog tried to play with him, but he pushed it away. It slunk into a corner of the tent. He took off his boots, his jacket and pants, and lay down on his bed. To his bruised body, the camp bed felt like a bank of the softest grass. He closed his eyes, but sleep would not come. He kept seeing the soldier whose arm he had severed, and the one he had shot. Every time he shut his eyes, terrible things assaulted his memory, things he did not even remember seeing at the time: the contorted postures of the dead, a horse with its hind leg blown off by a shell. He began to shake. He got under his blanket, and curled into a cold, shivering ball.

Later, when Bill came into the tent, he was stripped to the waist, having washed himself of all the blood and powder. He sighed heavily, and sat down to remove his boots.

'I guess he's pretty pissed,' John Evert said flatly.

'Who?'

'Lyon.'

'He's dead.'

'Oh.'

'You okay, kid?'

'Uh-huh.'

'You were great today.'

'It didn't feel great,' John Evert said. He wished then so very much that his mother was there, and at the same moment he caught a waft of the soap Bill had used. By some trick of the senses, it smelt just like her, or maybe it was just the smell of cleanliness and goodness. He began to weep then, silently, not sobbing, just hot water pouring out of his eyes as though they were bleeding. He turned away to face the canvas.

Bill did not say anything. He simply brought his own blanket, and lay down beside John Evert, letting his body warm John Evert's shivering frame. Eventually John Evert fell into a fitful sleep, but in the night he awoke, sitting bolt upright, shouting.

'Lie down, kid,' Bill said sleepily, patting him as he might a horse. 'It's all right. No one's coming to get you.'

John Evert did so, and Bill put an arm around him, keeping it there until he slept again.

15

The shattered Union troops beat a retreat north the next day. They had suffered more than a thousand casualties, and the medical tents were full of the maimed and the dying. Bill went in to take a look, and advised John Evert against doing the same. Their regiment had suffered, but not as badly as others, and Bill's calm, redoubtable leadership had made him a hero among the men.

John Evert was quiet and withdrawn, and preferred to go walking in the woods with his dog than to talk with anyone. He felt as though he were wading through a fog. When anyone spoke to him, he seemed only to hear an echo, as though they called to him from leagues hence. He wondered whether he should ever feel normal again.

At parade, Colonel Ewing inspected the men, offering words of reassurance and encouragement. When he reached Bill and John Evert, he paused. To John Evert's surprise, it was not Bill to whom Ewing spoke, but himself. 'Private John Jetsun.'

'Yes, sir,' John Evert replied, saluting.

'For putting yourself in mortal danger to rescue the life of a fellow comrade, I am promoting you to private first class.'

John Evert said, 'But I didn't think to do it, sir.'

'There is often little strategy in battle, only courage, and you have plenty of that.'

John Evert wished that he felt more pleased, or felt anything at all.

Ewing turned his attention to Bill. 'Well, Sergeant Jetsun, I trust you feel you have proved your worth. I will think it churlish of you to refuse to allow me to make you an officer now.'

There broke out some unrestrained whoops of encouragement and cries of 'Jetsun!'

The drill sergeant called for order, but Ewing only smiled. 'I think your men speak for you,' he said, as he handed to Bill his new rank insignia, then stood back, saying, 'Second Lieutenant Jetsun,' as he saluted Bill.

'Sir.' Bill saluted him smartly.

Ewing took his place in front, and addressed them all as one. 'The Confederates may have had a tactical victory, but scouts tell us that their losses were as heavy as ours. You have acquitted yourselves well in battle, particularly when this was the first action many of you have seen. You have done the Union proud. Make no mistake. We will regroup, rest and await reinforcements. Let us remember briefly our fallen, then that we have lived to fight another day. Thanks be to God.' Ewing gestured at his adjutant, and they left the field.

Bill and John Evert walked back to their tent. 'You don't seem so pleased,' John Evert said a few minutes later, as Bill tossed his new insignia upon his bed.

'No, kid, this is just the beginning. This won't be any ninety-day war.'

Over the next few days, John Evert considered what Bill had said. It gave him no pleasure. More than anything he longed to saddle up the roan and ride back west, but a new development gave him cause for a whole new kind of disquiet.

He was walking with his dog through a quiet area of camp when he rounded a corner and came upon a band of Indians. Instinct alone had him reach for his pistol as a surge of nervous emotion flushed through him, and he was transported back to the nightmare of the raid on his ranch. Fortunately, before he cocked his pistol, he had the sense to notice that they were being addressed by a soldier. He drew back and studied the men, who stood but ten yards away. It was their hair that first struck him: unlike the Indians he had known in California, they wore it either loose and long at their backs, or braided with beads or feathers, while a couple wore it shaved at the sides, leaving only a strip of hair down the middle of the scalp. Most wore pale buckskin trousers; a few wore blue Union jackets, but the rest were bare-chested, sporting only strings of beads or scraps of leather as decoration. They were all armed with rifles or small axes and knives thrust into their belts. John Evert could make neither head nor tail of what he was seeing; he wondered why some alarm had not been raised, and what the Union man could possibly be saying to them. As he stood there watching, his fear turned to anger. One of the Indians, as though hearing his thoughts, turned and looked at him. John Evert stiffened. The other was a young man, but something about his ready stance, the muscular solidity in his frame, made him intimidating. His expression was placid. After studying John Evert for a moment, he turned away again.

John Evert immediately sought out Bill in the mess tent, and interrupted his conversation. 'Did you know there's Indians in this camp?' he demanded.

Bill swivelled lazily toward John Evert, 'I did. What of it?'

'What are they doing here?'

'They're employed as trackers. There's none better than Indians for that.'

'You're going to trust them?' John Evert was quivering with rage.

Bill's brow knitted, then cleared. 'Kid . . .' he began, making to get to his feet, but John Evert was so hot he barrelled out of the tent before Bill could say more.

He thought he had hidden himself quite well, but it took Bill less than an hour to find him in the woods. 'Is a man not entitled to any privacy?' he burst out, as Bill sat next to him upon the fallen tree where he had set himself up to hurl rocks at a broken can, for the satisfaction of the ugly noise it made.

'A man, is it?' Bill said wryly. 'This doesn't look much like manly behaviour to me.' John Evert ceased throwing stones, and jammed his hands into his pockets. 'Kid, I appreciate your feelings toward the Indians, but those men didn't have anything to do with what happened to your mother.'

'They're all the same.'

'No, all men are not the same,' Bill said, his voice sharp. 'You can't judge a man on his skin or his pattern. Until you've spent time with a man and got to know him, you're not entitled to judge him at all. You may not like it but we need those men as trackers. They may be all that stand between us and a Rebel bullet in the face. There's more at stake here than your prejudices, understandable as the root of them may be.'

'I can't bear it,' John Evert said. 'The way they look, what they make me think of.' His voice was almost a whisper.

'You can bear it. I'm not going to force you to fraternise with them, but you will keep yourself in check. That isn't a request, it's an order.'

Bill departed, and John Evert was left to burn with injustice. Not until darkness began to fall was he able to talk himself into returning to camp.

John Evert was not alone in his suspicion of the new additions to the men. Only a few of the Union soldiers had had dealings with Indians, but most had been brought up on tales of the pernicious nature of their red-skinned brothers, and that was all that mattered. Bill called an assembly to deal with the grumbling.

'What have they come here for?' someone demanded. 'Why don't they keep their noses out of the white man's business? It's got nothing to do with them.'

'I expect this war will prove as important to them as it will to us, but I agree they do not yet know that,' replied Bill. 'The straight reason they've come is that they have no place else to go. Many have been driven off their lands into reserves.'

'Why don't they just stay there, then?'

'There isn't enough food, and what do you think they would do there? They're hunters, fighting men, proud people. We should be thankful they're enterprising enough that, rather than scalp

Union stragglers, they've come to look for honest work, work at which they are exceptional.'

'How can we trust 'em not to turn on us in battle?'

'It's not in their interests. Anyway, you're better off entering a battle with all the knowledge that they can bring you, and the small risk of them turning, than to enter battle with no knowledge and no risk. Choose that last option and your chances of ending up dead are a lot higher – that's simple probability.'

Confused, the heckler fell silent, and Bill had his way: the cavalrymen and scouts were joined by Indians. John Evert did not talk to Bill for days. Bill gave no sign of being bothered by his silence.

In the meantime, the scouts were kept permanently busy and spent all day engaged in gathering information about Confederate positions and movements, and often there was unexpected skirmishing.

One bubbling stew of an afternoon, John Evert, Bill and a small band of scouts were sweating in a heat haze that shimmered over a dirt road that wound through some straggling woods. They had axes in hand, and were busy felling telegraph poles to cut the wires. Afterward, they planned to drag the poles to the nearby railroad and put them over it to cause disruption to Confederate supply lines.

It was the Indian who had accompanied them who got wind of something. He did not say anything, merely came to Bill and gestured up the road with a toss of his head. Bill signalled to the men to stop their work. They stood silent, dissolving, it felt, in the liquid eddies of the humid air. A fat bead of sweat ran from under John Evert's hat and down his neck. Even the birds were silent. Nothing moved.

John Evert looked to the Indian. Kusox was his name, not that John Evert had ever had call to use it. He was the one John Evert had first noticed. He was stripped to the waist, with only a rifle slung over his sinewy torso. His long hair was tied back, and around his forehead he wore a dark blue bandanna that must once have been part of a uniform. His ears were pierced from tip to tail with so many metal rings that the lobes hung long and heavy. His features were blunt, dramatic: slanted eyes, thin lips, hooked nose. His expression put John Evert in mind of a cold-blooded vulture. He looked away in distaste.

Bill said something to Kusox, who moved lightly off the road into the bushes and disappeared. They waited, but there was no further sound or movement. One man impatiently let his axe blade fall on to a pole, the knock of its blade hitting home echoing down the empty road. Bill gestured angrily for him to cease.

The bullet that came from the trees seemed to fly directly over Bill's shoulder, and hit the man beyond before they even heard the shot. The others threw themselves to the ground, fumbling with rifles in the dust. Bullets were flying out of the trees, but it was impossible to tell how many shooters there were.

John Evert lay at Bill's side, mercifully sheltered by a small pile of felled poles. 'Can you see them?' he asked, panicked.

'Not yet,' Bill replied, with his eye to the sight of the Whitworth. 'Hold on.' He squinted hard. 'There's one. See him? Look carefully.' He spoke calmly, unconcerned by the bullets whizzing past his head, or the cries of two injured men. 'Concentrate, kid. See that tree with the kink?'

'Yes,' John Evert said, forcing himself to focus.

'Look down and right a little. See him?'

John Evert just made out a solidity that was not natural in the shadow of the tree Bill had pointed out. 'Yeah, I see him.'

'Take him out.'

John Evert got a sight on the shadow, aiming for chest height. He breathed deeply, trying to match Bill's steadiness. The noise of gunfire about him fell away. He squeezed the trigger gently, and the shadow in the woods vanished.

Bill began firing into the trees. John Evert kept his eyes peeled for more sharp-shooters in the shadows. Slowly, the chaos about them abated, and eventually all fell quiet. A moment later, there was the sound of a hasty retreat being beaten through the woods. It appeared that the Rebels were fleeing.

Bill was the first to stand up. He walked into the middle of the road where two of his men lay dead. 'Come on,' he said to the rest. 'Let's get in there and look for their dead – they'll have guns, maybe horses, too.'

'Where's that damn redskin?' said one of the men.

'Never mind him,' Bill snapped. 'Get on in there.'

The six of them gingerly made their way into the trees, jumping at every crack of twigs underfoot. They came across a fallen Rebel and relieved him of his gun and cartridges. Bill found two tethered horses. It was as he was untying them that a hidden Rebel jumped up behind John Evert and got a hand around his throat. John Evert yelped. His surprise was but momentary, however, for just as he saw the blade in the Rebel's hand, he also saw, melting out of the trees, the figure of Kusox, who, with one smooth motion, slit the man's throat. He did not break his stride as he walked past the falling man, as though he had done no more than brush away a bothersome fly.

John Evert, breathless, looked at Bill, who rolled his eyes. Kusox said something to him, after which Bill marched toward John Evert and the others. 'There's more coming,' he said. 'Leave the poles and head for camp.' As he passed John Evert, he said, under his breath, 'Still unhappy with those trackers?'

John Evert made no reply.

Back in camp, he reluctantly asked Bill whether he should thank Kusox. Bill shook his head. 'It's his job to protect you. Your gratitude means nothing to him.'

John Evert made no more comment, but later that night, he wandered from their tent and, under cover of darkness, peered across to the edge of the treeline where the Indians had made their own camp. They had a fire going inside a tall, triangular tent, and he could just make out the shadows of seated figures. He wondered what they talked of, and what they did with their long nights.

There was little question as to what the Union soldiers did with their nights: the card games and singing, the bets and competitions knew no end. Tedium had become the mother of invention. The soldiers were not without contact from the outside either: enterprising, impoverished locals were drawn to the camp like wasps to spilt syrup. Drinking was officially forbidden, but liquor-sellers wheedled their way past the guards to flog moonshine, old knives, duck eggs.

Women of dubious character, black and white, had set up a camp of their own, a mile away, in an abandoned settlement. The commanding officers turned a blind eye to the existence of what the men called Smoky Row.

John Evert was no longer naive. He did not require the educative nude photographs that changed hands among the men to know what the women in Smoky Row were selling. Whenever Bill went missing, John Evert knew where to find him, and so when a summons for Bill came from Ewing, he headed down the trail in that direction. He did not hurry along the rutted track. It was hot, and there were blackberries ripe for the picking all along the way. Ewing would never know how long it might take him to locate Bill anyway. Mosquitoes whined about his head. He removed his hat to rub his sweat-drenched hair.

The small black fruits hung swollen from the brambles lining the trail. He popped them one by one into his mouth, savouring the sweetness as they burst open upon his tongue. In his eagerness, he pulled too roughly, and caught his finger on a thorn. A tiny, bright bead of blood sprang from the tip.

Once he had stuffed himself, he took out his handkerchief, for he thought to fill it with fruit for later. Lost in the simple task, he fell to contemplation, and it was to the Indians that his thoughts were drawn. The other day, he had come across two on that path, engaged in the self-same task as he was now. They had nodded at him before continuing to converse in their own language. One had laughed quietly, and they had seemed so easy and companionable there. He had surprised himself by wondering whether, perhaps, they were not so different from him after all. They talked, they laughed, they stirred food in a pot over an open fire, just like everyone else.

And then his thoughts inevitably flew to his mother. Was she harvesting berries this month, too? And who was she with? The thought was unbearably painful.

John Evert had never really known any woman but his mother. Now there were nurses, cooks and seamstresses, who formed an essential part of the regiment, but they all seemed old and unapproachable, not to mention ugly. He had mentioned this to Bill, who smiled and said they had been expressly chosen that way so as not to distract the men.

Lost in thought, John Evert had not been watching where he was going, and walked straight into the sharp end of a long stick that was being pointed at him. 'Ow!'

The stick was held by a ragged-haired blond boy in faded, ripped clothing. He had pointed ears, a small, jutting chin, and looked aggressive, but his eyes were frightened. John Evert noticed then the scattered blackberries all over the ground, and that the boy held in his free hand a sodden bit of bark that he must have been using as a basket. Before he could say anything, the urchin let out a filthy curse, then fled on bruised, skinny brown legs.

John Evert rubbed his stomach where the stick had hurt him. He looked about for a way of collecting the berries the boy had dropped, but there was none; his own handkerchief was already full, stained purple and bleeding, so he left the fallen berries, carried on down the path and soon arrived at the shoddy string of broken dwellings and sheds, with dog roses growing over them. A long droop of the pink blooms had been severed by the closing hinge of a door, and lay now like a funeral wreath upon the ground. The place was silent but for the whir of the cicadas.

'Bill!' he called. All remained quiet, but a woman appeared in a doorway.

'Excuse me,' he said awkwardly, 'have you seen Bill?'

She gestured toward the far end of the cluster of buildings.

John Evert made his way down the row. As he walked, he looked to right and left, and down a long, narrow gap between two sheds, he caught sight of the boy again, in an open space. John Evert stopped and watched him through the dark corridor where he stood, grubby and straw-haired, in the sun. He was carrying a large bucket that must have been heavy, for he leaned his weight away from it to balance it and it sloshed as he walked.

Just then there was an angry utterance and a man appeared behind him. From his dress, John Evert could see he was not a soldier. He cuffed the boy around the ear with such force that he fell to the ground, upending the bucket. Then he kicked him hard in the legs. John Evert flinched at the thud the man's boot made as it connected with them. The boy cried out and reflexed into a ball with his arms over his head. The man spat and ambled away.

John Evert deliberated for a moment or two, but then went down between the sheds to where the boy was getting to his hands and knees. 'You okay?' he asked.

The boy leaped to his feet, fists balled at the ends of pathetically skinny sun-baked arms. 'Go to hell!' he hissed. He ran to a tiny shed, half hidden in the trees, slamming the door shut behind him. John Evert heard the sound of a clumsy bolt dropping. He also became aware then of a bad smell. He looked down at the contents of the bucket, and his nostrils curled in disgust. He tipped the bucket over to cover the mess.

He went to the door of the shed. Inside, he could hear weeping. He thought better than to knock. Instead, he left his handkerchief full of fruit on the ground outside the door and went in search of Bill.

The boy occupied his thoughts for the rest of the day. There had been something strange about him. He was small and fragile, delicate of feature, and radiated the kind of anger that had been learned. It put John Evert in mind of a cornered bobcat, hissing and snarling, and all the while looking desperately for a way to run. He pondered going to check upon the boy, but a day later he had a nasty accident with his Enfield when it half blew up in his hands, thanks to something lodged in the muzzle.

He suffered a wicked burn and was grateful he had not been more seriously injured. A nurse bandaged his right hand, which put him out of action. He could do nothing useful so had to content himself with rereading the two books that Casey had slid into his saddlebag so long ago.

In the airless heat of the tent, he drifted in and out of sleep. Suddenly he saw the crow he had rescued as a fallen nestling. He knew he must be dreaming but it felt real. It used to bring him things – shiny beetles, old nails – and this time it had brought him something silver. It was terribly bright and John Evert wanted it very much. It was important. He held out his hand, but the bird would not give it. Every time he approached it, it hopped away. Seized by unexplained urgency, John Evert ran at the crow and tried to grab the object, but the bird seemed to swallow it and went for John Evert's hand, pecking him savagely. It was agonisingly painful, and he awoke suddenly, hand stabbing, heart pounding.

He held up his bandaged hand to draw the blood away from it, and closed his eyes, waiting for the pain to subside, wondering what it all signified.

16

Overall, the camp was a peaceful place, so it was a surprise when a vicious brawl broke out late one night. The alarum bell jolted John Evert awake. He stumbled from the tent, and overheard Bill, who had recently been promoted to captain, being spoken to by a youngster who rattled out, 'I'm sorry, sir, but there's been a fight and there's a man dead.'

John Evert pulled his boots on and hobbled after Bill as he hot-footed it to the other side of the camp. When they arrived at the scene, there was confusion in the semi-darkness, but one thing stood out clearly in the circle of light from the lanterns: a group of soldiers, who were undeniably drunk. Their uniforms were awry, and they stumbled about as they hurled obscenities in the direction of the ammunition tent. Two even had rifles clumsily pointed that way.

'Put up those weapons!' Bill yelled. 'What's gone on here?'

'A girl done kill Bob Flynn, sir,' replied a bystander.

'These men are drunk,' Bill snapped. 'Where did they get liquor?'

'Seems they found a batch of moonshine in a barn.'

'And who started the fight? Dammit, man, speak.'

The man shuffled his feet. 'This girl, sir.'

'What girl? Be quiet!' he roared at the drunkards who, even in their well-oiled state, had the sense to fall into hiccuping silence.

'Renton?' Bill shouted. 'Where's Orville Renton?'

'Here, sir,' came the nervous reply, as Orville stepped from behind the spectators.

'Renton, I hope I don't find you drunk?'

'N-no, sir,' Orville stammered.

'Good. Do you know what happened? Tell me.'

Orville pointed at the ammunition tent. 'I don't know it all, sir, but she's in there, with a flint and steel.'

Bill stared at the ammunition tent, and his face became grave. He ordered all the men back, relieving one of his lantern, and moved slowly to the tent.

'You there,' he said, in a clear voice. 'I am the commanding officer. I give you my word no harm will come to you. I am going to open the flap. I won't come in. I just want to talk with you, all right?'

There was no answer, but Bill very slowly drew back the flap of the tent. Nothing happened. He did not enter the tent or withdraw. John Evert thought he could just make out Bill's mouth moving, as though he was speaking softly. After a while, curiosity got the better of him. He walked over on soft feet and peered around Bill.

There, in the shadowy midst of a lot of gunpowder, clutching a flint and steel in each trembling hand, was a crouched figure in a ragged shirt. At first, John Evert could make out little more than a pair of eyes that glittered in the light of the lantern, but then he recognised the face. The figure saw him at the same moment, and tensed. Bill, sensing John Evert behind him, kicked him in the shin, hissing at him to get lost, but when he refused to leave, Bill let the flap fall closed.

'What is it?' he said.

'It's the boy from Smoky Row,' John Evert whispered in Bill's ear.

'What?' Bill whispered back. 'Is it a boy or a girl?'

'I don't know. I saw him there. I thought he was a boy but maybe not.'

'What about Bob Flynn?' blurted out one of the men.

'Where is he?' Bill said.

Several soldiers led Bill and John Evert some distance away, and showed them the body of Flynn where he lay sprawled in the dirt, his pants around his ankles. A deep wound to his neck had soaked the ground beneath his head black with blood. They returned to the circle of light, where the men remained gathered around the tent.

Bill sucked his teeth. 'What passed here to result in this?' he asked, of no one in particular. 'That creature in there looks like a boy to me.'

'It's a girl,' one of the men replied.

'How'd you know?'

'Half her clothes were off, sir.'

Bill frowned. 'Why?'

The man shuffled his feet and mumbled, 'Seems these men were coming back to camp and came across this girl and, uh . . . thought they'd—'

'I see,' Bill cut him off icily. 'And did they?'

'No, sir. She screamed and that brought us all real quick. By the time we got here Flynn was dead. She must've had a knife.'

'Well, I'm glad of that,' Bill said. He stalked over to where the group of intoxicated soldiers leaned against each other for support.

'Hey, sir, we didna—' slurred one, but he had no time to finish before Bill's fist connected with his mouth. John Evert saw two teeth fly out of it. Once Bill had thoroughly beaten the man, he turned his attention to the others. For several minutes there was no sound but that of Bill's fists connecting with bodies. When he finally stepped away, the drunken soldiers were nothing more than slack heaps upon the ground.

Bill turned to the watching soldiers. 'If I ever hear again of women being molested in this camp, I'll have every one of you court-martialled and hanged, do you hear?'

There was not a word from anyone.

Bill returned to the ammunition tent, and sat down cross-legged on the ground outside. John Evert made to go to him, but Bill gestured him away, and called instead for a blanket, which he pushed into the tent. He spoke through the canvas for a long time, so long that the men began to disperse and return to their beds. But John Evert stayed and watched until a hand appeared through the tent flap, then another, and finally a small figure crawled out, and squatted on its haunches looking at Bill, the blanket knotted around its waist. Bill held out his hand for the flint and steel. With some reluctance, she gave them up.

She wore only a thin, ragged shirt above the blanket, and she put her arms about her chest, cradling her shoulders. Bill called to a man for his coat, and, ever so gently, put it around her shoulders. He helped her to her feet and took her to the medical tent, where he entrusted her to the hands of the nurses. It was so late by the time he returned to his own tent that neither he nor John Evert had it in them for talking, so they slept.

'What'll you do about last night?' John Evert asked Bill the next morning.

'I'm not sure,' Bill said, uncharacteristically. 'She's from Smoky Row?'

'Well, I saw her there.'

'Let's go down and see about a few things, then.'

It did not take Bill long to learn the story. Friendly with several women who made the place their home, he had only to ask to be told. The facts did not surprise him: orphan, in the sort of service that might just as well have borne the title 'bonded servant', abusive master who bullied, beat and half starved her, safe in the knowledge that she had no place else to go.

'Why's she done up like a boy?' Bill asked the man whom John Evert had seen kick the girl.

The man, dough-featured and slack in the belly, was having trouble answering this question, due to the blood pouring from his nose. 'I dunno, she's allers been like that.'

'You ever put her to work with the other women here?' Bill asked.

The man shook his head, spraying blood down his blue overalls.

'You piece of shit. How old is she?'

'Fifteen, maybe. She's small for her age.'

'What was she doing on the road at night?'

'I dunno.'

'Running away, I reckon,' Bill said. 'Little wonder.'

Bill and John Evert went outside to discuss the matter.

'She's not our responsibility,' Bill said.

'We can't leave her here,' John Evert replied.

'Where do you propose we put her?'

'I don't know but we can't leave her here.'

'Why not?'

'We just can't,' John Evert said tightly.

Bill studied him dispassionately, but something about John Evert's intensity must have persuaded him, for eventually he nodded. John Evert had not been able to bring himself to tell Bill that what he had seen in the bucket on the day he had first met the girl had been a blue, dead baby.

At a summary meeting with Colonel Ewing, it was debated how the drunkards should be disciplined, but it was decided that Flynn was the main culprit, and since he was dead already, there was little more to be done. Ewing left it to Bill to decide the punishment for the others.

'I mean to set an example to the men, sir,' said Bill.

'I expect you're right,' Ewing replied.

John Evert stood in a corner of Ewing's tent while Ewing and Bill spoke. He should not have been party to such a meeting, but Ewing ran a relaxed show, and seemed to view him as a necessary appendage to Bill.

'And the girl,' Bill said. 'You couldn't call it intentional murder.'

'Of course not,' Ewing agreed. 'Flynn deserved what he got. She won't face any charges from us. But I wonder why she was out in the open at night.' He shook his head. 'It's hardly safe.'

'It appears she was running away,' Bill said.

'Well, she'll have to go,' Ewing said dismissively.

'Sir, I think it impossible for her to return to – that life. Would you consider my trying to find her employment in the medical tent, with the nurses, perhaps?'

'She's too young. You know the rules on nurses. Certain age and, ah, lack of physical attributes.'

'She looks like a boy. She could be mistaken for one. Could an exception be made?'

'I appreciate your gallantry,' Ewing laughed, 'but this is not the time or place for it. It's highly irregular.'

'I know, but I sometimes find the irregular pays dividends,' Bill replied.

Ewing frowned, but it was hard for him to suppress amusement. John Evert knew that Ewing favoured Bill above all the men. 'Well, you may try, but one sniff of trouble and she's got to go.'

'Yes, sir.'

'Thanks,' John Evert said, as he and Bill walked away.

'I hope I don't come to regret this, kid. Got a feeling I will,' Bill said. 'How's that hand?'

'I still can't use it.'

Bill snorted. 'What about your eyes? They okay?'

'Yeah.'

'Well, if that's so, go check the horses. The men are too lazy to be good grooms.'

So John Evert went to look over the horses, while Bill took care of the girl.

The next day, Bill appeared in their tent in a state of exasperation. 'What is it?' John Evert asked, sitting up with interest, for he was mighty bored of feeling useless.

'That girl.' Bill sighed.

'She wasn't with the nurses when I went to get my bandage changed,' John Evert said.

'She won't have none of it, won't even go in there, like she's frightened of something,' Bill said. 'She's all quiet and wouldn't say boo to a goose, but you turn your back and she's disappeared. I tracked her down to the woods and hauled her back here.'

'Did she say why she went there?'

'She won't say anything. I wonder whether she might not be soft in the head.'

'What's her name?'

'Funny you ask – it's the only thing she's said. Calls herself Robinson, but that can't be right.' Bill squinted at John Evert. 'Why don't you try talking to her?'

'Me? Why me?'

'You're the one who insisted we encumber ourselves with her. It's about time you learned to take responsibility for your actions. And you're good with wild creatures,' Bill said, gesturing at John Evert's dog. 'You're not much use to me any other way, with that damn hand of yours.'

John Evert, mildly offended, stalked out with his dog for a walk.

The woods were unremarkable, row upon row of pine, the ground a needle-covered carpet of silence. His dog loved it there and streaked off in search of rabbits, while John Evert ambled along in the gloom, admiring the occasional break in the canopy where a shaft of sunlight struck down to gild the leaves of the tiny saplings that were seizing their chance in brilliant lime-green.

Something was nagging at him, but he was not sure what. He guessed it was probably to do with the girl. How was he supposed to know how to persuade her to do anything? He did not even know how to talk to a girl, particularly one like her. He remembered the curses she had flung at him. He would never have thought girls would know such language.

His dog barked somewhere up ahead, and he followed the sound, walking into an open clearing, and was surprised by what he saw: the girl, as though he had summoned her merely by thinking of her, was engaged in a tug-of-war with his dog over a long, thin stick. The animal shook its head to and fro, putting its weight back, trying to pull the stick from her grip, while she let out a rusty chuckle.

When she saw John Evert, she let the stick go, and the dog bounded off with it. Her eyes were wide with alarm and she lowered her body slightly, as though she might make a dash for it. Without thinking, he held up his bandaged hand, and said, 'It's all right. Look.'

What had he meant by that? he wondered. 'I can't do anything to you,' he continued. 'I can't do anything with this hand.'

She looked him up and down. Her eyes were less frightened now, more suspicious. He wondered what an ass he must seem. She moved to a stump, upon which she had made a pile of sticks, and began to gather them up. He noticed the tips were sharp, and he saw her slip a blade into her pocket. One stick was longer, and had a sinew tied at one end.

'You making a bow?' he asked. She glanced at him, her eyes fast and wary, above cheekbones you could have cut yourself on. He walked slowly toward her, and she moved around the other side of the stump, keeping a close eye on him.

'It's the wrong wood,' he said, taking up the piece she had been trying to fashion into a bow. She stiffened and her eyes narrowed. 'I'm sorry, I don't mean anything by it,' he said. 'See?' Holding either end, he bent the stick. 'It's too springy. You won't have any force in that.'

She looked at the bow and at the ground. Her expression suggested disappointment. She moved her right arm at the elbow, like she was using the handle of a water pump. She might have been gearing herself up for something, but said nothing.

'I can find you a better kind of wood – ash or mulberry, maybe,' he said. She was watching him through the choppy mess of her blonde hair, her expression undecided. 'Only if you want,' he said, setting the bow down. He glanced about the clearing, and spotted a suitable tree. 'That one'd be better.'

It probably would not, but he figured he was on to a good thing with her not running away, so he prattled on, like he might talk to a skittish horse. He made his body unthreatening, too, as he would with a horse, dropping his shoulders, and turning away from her, so she did not feel she was being watched.

He broke a sapling at the side of the clearing, and took out his knife to whittle the splintered wood. The work was awkward with his left hand. When he was finished, he handed the strip of wood to the girl, who had approached him quietly, saying, 'Will you take that while I fetch another?'

There was a pause, but after a while, gently, the sapling was pulled away from his hand. He cut a few more, then sat on the ground to assess them. She sat a safe distance away, her elbows resting on her bent knees. She wore the same rolled-up, oversized breeches he had first seen her in. He made sure not to stare at the bruises and cuts on her lower legs. There were a lot. He wondered how she felt about having killed a man, but something about her told him that was the least of her worries.

He inspected her childish arrows, none of which were fletched. 'You'll need feathers if you want those to fly properly.'

She threw a stick for his dog a few times, and out of the corner of his eye he watched her smile as the dog brought it back, cantering on the spot as it did when excited. It was a very brief smile. Her face quickly fell back into repose when she looked away from the animal. He thought she had one of the saddest faces he had ever seen.

'You like dogs?' he said. She did not reply. 'I heard you don't want to work in the nurses' tent. Maybe you could help with the horses, if you like. If we can't find something for you to do, I don't think they'll let you stay.'

Still no answer. He took out his knife and began awkwardly to strip the green bark from another sapling, using his foot to keep it steady.

'Robinson,' he said. 'Where'd you get a name like that?'

He noticed a few moments later that the air felt different. He did not need to turn to know that she was gone.

He was frustrated with himself for not doing better but, still, it was a start.

He finished the bow as best he could. It was not perfect, but she would be able to give someone a shock with an arrow shot from twenty yards, which he figured was what she hoped for. He left it on the tree stump for her to find.

Later, when he saw Bill, he said, 'You should try getting her to work with the horses.'

'Who?'

'That girl.'

'Oh. Spoke to you, did she?'

'No.'

'Then how do you know?'

'I just do.'

They were sent on a reconnaissance mission for several days, and upon their return they learned that the girl had run away.

John Evert did not hesitate but asked to see where she had been sleeping. To the matron's consternation he took his dog into the nurses' sleeping tent and had it scent the bedding where she had lain. He had not used the dog much for this purpose, and was glad it had not rained, but it had little trouble picking up her scent. John Evert expected she was barefoot, too, which helped. Once he knew which way she had left the camp, he begged Bill to ride out with him.

'Why can't you do it alone?'

'You're better with words than I am,' John Evert said.

It took them only a few hours to catch up with her.

She did not hear them coming over the grass behind her as she walked with her bow slung crossways over her shoulder, her arms swinging at her sides. Something about the valiant, wrong-headed little figure striding out to God only knew where cut John Evert.

When his dog barked, she whirled around, nearly falling over in her anxiety. She looked about wildly, but there was nowhere to run. They trotted towards her, slowed to a walk, and halted some little way off.

'Well, missy, I don't know where you think you're going, but I wouldn't advise it,' Bill said. He leaned forward, crossing his forearms over his pommel. 'We've gone out on a limb for you and this is how you repay us.'

That must have touched something in her, for she said something quietly.

'What?' Bill said, craning forward.

'I don't want to be no trouble,' she said, in a low voice that had a catch to it, as though from lack of use.

'You're no trouble, but you could be useful. You could work with the horses. How's that strike you?'

'I never did plan on staying,' she said. There was an edge of frustration in her tone.

'Maybe you didn't, but what are you going to eat? You don't know what's happened to the country round here. People are desperate. And summer's over. Give it a month and they'll take your eye out as soon as look at you. You thought of that?'

She frowned, caught between a rock and a hard place. Oh, John Evert knew how that felt.

'It'd sure be a help to me,' John Evert said, 'if you'd stay. Just in case you would, I got you some clothes. They're not new, but they're about your size.' He dismounted, removed a bundle from his saddlebag and held out to her the small blue uniform of a fallen drummer boy. He had paid a man to wash out the blood stains.

'Is it a dress?' she asked suspiciously.

'No. Look.' He shook out the jacket and the pants, and held them up against himself, the breeches coming halfway down his shins.

The uniform seemed to decide it for her: she nodded, her shoulders drooping, and walked towards them. Bill held his hand down to her and, reluctantly, she took it. He swung her up behind him on to the grey, and they trotted back to camp.

Around them, the trees were beginning to turn, leaves shrinking and drying into fiery yellows and oranges, as the trees battened down the hatches for the dark times to come.

17

There was a chill in the air that morning and fog lay dense upon the surface of the lake near which they camped. John Evert was standing ankle-deep in the shallows. He bent forward and scooped up a handful of cold water, throwing it into his face. On the other side, three duck took flight and beat skyward, quacking flatly. Usually such a sight would lift his spirit, but not that morning. The day before, Bill had announced that the scouts must study with one of the Indian trackers to improve their skills, and it was Kusox whom he had chosen for the task.

John Evert, disgusted at the thought of working with the Indian, had not appeared at the stated time and had thus missed the first exercise. He had not reckoned with how furious Bill would be at his insubordination. Today he could not do anything but attend.

'Why him?' John Evert had asked.

'Kusox? Because he speaks the best English,' Bill replied. 'He lost his parents when he was young, spent some years in a Mission school. Something you two have in common.'

John Evert had been incensed by Bill's words. He had nothing in common with a redskin, and he never would.

He stepped out of the water on to the cold wet grass and walked barefoot to his tent to dress.

Later, standing at the back of the group of scouts who clustered in a semicircle around Kusox, John Evert continued to seethe. Kusox was wearing his usual combination of buckskin leggings topped with a Union jacket. Around his neck was knotted a red scarf. John Evert knew that if any of the other men had dared to flout regulation uniform in such a way they would have been punished. He did not see why Kusox was allowed to sport this flamboyant accoutrement, along with all the brasswork in his ears. He glared at the ground and mashed a tuft of grass flat with his heel.

Kusox soon had them busy, following a trail he had set earlier in the morning. John Evert made the best of it, following it further than the others, but in the end he, too, was defeated. Kusox wrinkled his nose at their ineptitude. He clearly thought all of them utterly hopeless. John Evert was glad of Kusox's disdain: the mutual antipathy made it easier to hate him. The only person Kusox appeared to have a shred of respect for was Bill, who walked along beside him, assessing the scouts' progress. Bill joked to the men that Kusox was, quite literally, their 'Left Hand', which was the meaning of his name, presumably given him, somewhat unoriginally, because he was left-handed. John Evert found himself wondering how he would come off in a fight with Kusox.

He was determined to do better in the next exercise. This time, Kusox did not set a trail. Instead, he walked out into the long grass ahead and wandered a long way before dropping earthward, out of sight. Bill gave the signal that the scouts should follow, and they set off.

When they reached the place where Kusox had disappeared, they did their best to follow his trail, but the grass was high and resilient, and it was hard to discern where a man had lain or crawled. The scouts were defeated. As they stood in a huddle, conferring, a small stone hit John Evert just above the right ear. It stung like hell and he cried out, clamping his hand to his head, looking about for the culprit, but there was naught except the wind riffling the soft tips of the grass. Another man was hit with a pebble and shouted, and the others laughed at his discomfort and began to seek where Kusox was hidden.

In the commotion, no one noticed Kusox rise up fluidly, as if he had grown out of the ground, at John Evert's side. John Evert jumped, unnerved. 'You Goddamn snake,' John Evert said, his lips curling.

The violence of the words was not lost on Kusox, who stared at him equably. 'Sore loser.'

John Evert narrowed his eyes to angry slits. Kusox watched him with eyes that sparkled as bright and hard as black agate. It was not until Bill called them both to attention that they broke off.

John Evert had once believed there could be no worse thing in life than the battlefield, but there were other horrors afoot. No longer on the move, the thousands of men encamped in one place quickly fouled their water supplies: dysentery and typhoid were rife. Orville came down with raging tonsillitis. John Evert sat in the medical tent with him each day, reading to him as he lay silent, unable to utter a word. It was the book Hector had given him that he read to Orville. He thought of Hector sometimes and would flick to the front of the book, where the attorney had inscribed it to him. He wondered whether Hector ever thought of him, and if he would even recognise him now, no longer a boy but a tall man with spurs on his boots and a sabre at his side, whose knuckles, once ink-spattered from the print room, now bore the scars of blade and shot.

It gave him great pain to consider that, now he was an outlaw and his mother lost, Phineas Gunn would have moved successfully to press his suit for ownership of their land. More than ever before, everything hinged upon John Evert finding his mother alive. But he and Bill were on the wrong side of the country, in the midst of a war. It might take a lifetime to find her. With each day that passed, John Evert grew increasingly aware of that. He had strange dreams at night: the twisted oak standing black and stark against a midnight blue sky, the stars above it whirling across the heavens as though the very earth itself were being pulled onward by some great indifferent hand. He would wake shivering.

The girl Robinson remained an elusive conundrum. She exhibited no gratitude either to Bill or himself for removing her from bondage. If anything, the language of her gestures seemed to imply that she found her new surroundings merely a different prison. She was not troubled by the men: Bill's articulate threat of what would befall anyone who interfered with her was clear in their minds. If anything, they showed her an awkward deference as she walked about them in her boy's uniform, a few wisps of blonde hair protruding from under her blue cap. She gave no sign that she even noticed them, keeping her eyes fixed to the ground, a small line vertical upon her otherwise unsullied brow, as though a blade of worry had been pressed deep enough to score her for ever.

John Evert had instructed her on how to look after the horses. He spoke. She did not. The way she moved about the animals suggested to him that she was unfamiliar with the work, but she was polite with the horses, respectful, and she did not make mistakes.

After a couple of weeks, she had grasped that John Evert really was no threat to her. He might toss brushes at her, or bundles of hay, and she was there to catch them, unlike the first days when she had startled him by bolting when he accidentally touched her waist while passing her a saddle.

'Jessamy's got a saddle sore,' John Evert said, 'so give Collins another horse to ride today.'

They were in the hayrick, tossing bales from the top to the ground. They both sneezed for it was dusty work, the air filled with tiny golden motes that rose and fell, drifting slowly earthward, like weightless gold rain.

'I think Blue's lame, too,' John Evert added.

She nodded, then said, 'How come your horses don't have no names?'

'Bill always said not to,' John Evert said, hurling a bale down with a soft thump.

'He ain't your pa,' she said. It was a statement, not a question.

He shot her a glance. And, for once, she looked back at him. Light fell through the wooden slats of the walls on to her face, turning her eyes from plain amber into wheels spoked with rust and gold. 'How'd you know?' he said.

'You get along too well.'

John Evert smiled at the candour. 'Your name's not Robinson,' he said.

'It's Beth,' she said awkwardly. 'I hate it.'

'It's a fine name.'

'I prefer Robinson.'

'All right,' he replied. 'That's pretty good too.'

From that moment on, she was easier around him.

New horses had been requisitioned and were now stabled with the regulars in a large barn that the regiment had commandeered. Most were the usual broken-backed farm creatures that caused no trouble, but there was one, a black mustang, that must have been cut late and within which an angry fire burned. A horrible beast, it bit and kicked and rattled up the other horses no end.

Robinson was afraid of it and in her wariness she made the mistake one day of looking it in the eye too long while unbolting its box door to fill its water trough. It went for her, teeth big and yellow. She leaped back and it shot past her to the other horses that were loose and minding their own business in the main body of the barn, and soon had them all cantering around wildly.

It took John Evert a good while to get the horses calmed and a rope around the black mustang, but once he did, he pulled it close to him, got an arm over its nose and stopped its wild tossing of its head. He stood afront of it and forced its head down so that its forehead was to his chest. It tried to shake him off, but he leaned his weight into it and held it fast.

'Come over here,' he said to Robinson.

'I don't want to,' she said.

'Come over,' he said.

Reluctantly she came nearer. The mustang, sensing her fear, squealed and tried to pull away from John Evert, but he held it fast. She finally stood next to him, trembling.

'You're riling each other up,' he said. 'Make your feelings steady.'

She frowned, not understanding him. Holding the mustang around the muzzle with one arm, he pulled her by her shirt front so she stood closer to the animal and tapped the centre of her chest with two fingers. 'In there,' he said. 'Make it steady in there. Breathe slowly.'

She made an effort to still her shallow, panicky breath and inhaled deeply. Slowly, both she and the horse quieted a little.

'Stroke him,' John Evert said. 'Calm, though.'

She tentatively put out her hand and stroked the horse's tensed black neck. John Evert had her do it for a long time, until the mustang had quite forgotten what its fuss was about. Eventually, he released its muzzle. It snorted and shook its head a little but did not pull away. John Evert put her hand on the rope at its neck. 'Take him back into his stall,' he said.

She did as she was told, releasing the horse as it ambled back through its door. She quietly shut the bolt on it and remained there, leaning on the half-door, watching as it paced a few times round its stall, then got down on its knees and tilted over to roll.

John Evert came and stood next to her, and they watched the mustang twisting to and fro in its straw bed, kicking its legs up at the ceiling. After a while, he became aware of her eyes upon him and turned to her.

'How'd you learn to do that?' she asked.

'I don't know,' he said honestly. 'I've always been good with animals.'

She studied him, and while he would not have described it as a soft look, it was a more restful one than her usual sharp gaze.

Winter came, and with it hardship. The men shivered in their tents; holes had to be hacked in the ice to free up water for the horses; food supplies were scarce and full of weevils. It was during this winter of 1861 that John Evert became convinced he would not see the sunshine of California again. He ached with longing, and the surroundings seemed to reflect his own emptiness back to him.

He stood one day at the edge of a snowfield, the landscape

freshly baptised under a cloak of white that temporarily masked the unforgivable violence that had beset the land. Distant trees were black scratches upon the canvas. A rabbit had written flat-footed, staccato messages across the snow. He was supposed to be following the tracks of a deserter, but his eye wandered instead to a herd of elk in the distance. Smooth-kneed, they ambled across the snow like grey ships upon water of arsenic white, heads thrown back to balance their weighty masts of bone. They seemed to him so ancient, so regal, that he longed to erase himself and all his fellow men, and give the land back to the beasts, under whose rule it must be kinder.

Uncertain how long he might be away, he asked Robinson to look after his dog while he was gone. He had thought she would be pleased, but she merely shrugged. 'It's just a dog.' He was surprised: he had seen her several times, when she thought herself unobserved, playing with it, but she seemed determined never to show a liking for anything. He wondered why. He tried to ask her questions – where she was from, how she had lived – but she always evaded them, resorting to sullenness.

'How come you never ask me any questions?' he asked her one day.

She thought about this for a while. 'I figure it's rude.'

'It isn't,' he said.

She carried on with her work in silence, but just before they parted ways, each of them leading a couple of horses destined for different parties, she said, 'It wasn't mine, you know.'

'What wasn't?'

'That baby.'

John Evert was so wrong-footed he knew not what to say.

'Ain't got no more questions today?' she asked innocently, but the corner of her mouth twitched. He blushed. Thus they parted company.

John Evert went out on reconnaissance with three scouts and Kusox. Typically, Bill would have been with them, but Ewing wanted him for something, so John Evert led the group. They rode through close woods, in single file, the men in the middle talking among themselves, John Evert at the head and Kusox at the rear in silence. They had been going an hour when the sound of something large moving in the undergrowth made John Evert pull up short, raising a silencing hand. The men ceased their talk. He put his Enfield to his shoulder for, whatever it was, it was moving fast. He checked his trigger finger just in time as his dog burst out of the undergrowth in front of him, grinning, trailing a piece of rope around its neck that it had evidently worked loose from the stake to which it had been pegged.

'For God's sake.' John Evert sighed. The men behind him snickered. There was no dissuading it now that it had found them, so John Evert let it be. They rode on, the ground beginning to slope downward, full of boulders, so the horses had to pick their way carefully. Before long, they heard the hissing sigh of the river. It was in full flood, a treacherous, swirling morass of recent snow melt. As they followed its path, banks rose steeply on either side of them, the water having chiselled a steep-sided valley. Forced into a narrower stream, it roared deep and angry, colliding against the rocks that projected from the flow in sprays of white foam.

So compelling was the flood that all their eyes were drawn to it, away from the opposite side of the valley, and that was the great mistake they made. Something hissed past John Evert's ear and he twisted in his saddle to see the man behind him fall from his horse. He saw Kusox's thigh bloom with blood and Kusox somersault backward off his horse as it shied beneath him. Rebels hidden in brush on the other side of the river were picking off the men of their line. John Evert threw himself from the roan to the ground and landed heavily, winding himself. The roan turned on a dime and jumped clean over him, galloping back the way they had come. The other horses followed it. John Evert crawled back down the path on his belly as fast as he could, hidden from the Rebels by the low rocks and brush that lined the riverbank.

He put out a hand over the nose of a fallen man but felt nothing. He crawled on to Kusox, who was alive and silent as an angry, injured snake on the earth, blood pouring from his thigh.

'Are you—' John Evert began.

Before he could finish, a smattering of bullets around them indicated that there were Rebels on their side of the river too, bearing down upon them from ahead. Instinctively John Evert and Kusox hurled themselves into the raging, freezing swell of the river.

The shock of the cold water was enough to take John Evert's breath away. He was immediately dragged down by the force of the current and his heavy uniform. He wrenched his jacket open and wriggled frantically to free himself of it, and the current mercifully swept away the heavy fabric. His boots were weighing him down as well, but there was no way to kick them off and swim at the same time. He surfaced with the roar of the water in his ears. Over the swirling surface, he saw Kusox being dragged like a rag doll in the white water. His injury would make it hard for him to swim, and John Evert could see that he was struggling to keep his head above water. He could see the strike of bullets against rocks, but they had been whipped so rapidly onward by the river that bullets were no danger to them now. John Evert used the current of the river to push himself forward, toward Kusox, whose black hair fanned out around him like reeds.

With a single almighty effort, John Evert reached him and grasped him by the waist.

'My leg!' Kusox gasped, spitting water.

'I know,' John Evert said. At that moment, something ploughed into them from behind. John Evert barely had time to register that the dog had plunged into the water after them, then realised they were rushing toward a boulder that was projecting, bluntly lethal, from the middle of the river. He grabbed Kusox's hand and closed it around the rope that still trailed from his dog's neck, braced himself momentarily against a smaller rock, and pushed with all his might. The current caught Kusox and the dog and they whirled away, looking to pass safely one side of the boulder. He kicked again, but some eddy in the current caught his heavy boots and the force of the water sucked him clean under, down the jagged side of the boulder, which was indented below the surface. He was pounded downward and bashed into solid rock, then spun upside down and something played the drums on him, tossing him from right to left, refusing to let him free. He lost all sense of which way was up or down, and yet, even as his lungs began to ache, he was surprised to discover that he was not afraid. He had heard once that drowning was a peaceful way to go, and it was, the press of the water all about him strangely comforting in its embrace. It was growing dark and everything was slowing and John Evert opened himself to it.

Something in him snapped. No, death would not take him today. His foot connected with something solid, perhaps the bottom of the river, and he kicked off with all his might and was pushed or pulled upward, back into the light.

His head broke the surface and he gasped for air, the sky above him bright and white. The river had opened somewhat, which had taken some of the force out of it. He could see Kusox and the dog, paddling toward a sandbank. He splashed in their direction, hoping the current would help carry him there, which it graciously did. He drew up with a crunch on the sand next to Kusox and the pair of them lay, exhausted, face-down on the edge of the river, while his dog stood with its head low, hacking up water.

After his initial relief at being alive, John Evert became aware that he was freezing. His skin was white as porcelain and he was shivering from head to foot, teeth chattering. Kusox was the same. They could not stay out in the open, for there might be Rebels anywhere. He got Kusox to his feet and slung his arm about his shoulder so that they were able to limp awkwardly up into the trees for cover. Once hidden, he left Kusox and jogged ahead. They must find shelter: it was mid-afternoon, there were not many hours of light left, and they had to get dry. Kusox could

not walk, and John Evert would likely have to leave him and go
for help. He had seen small caves in the steep banks of the river
before they had been attacked, and now he hoped to find one
large enough to shelter them. He muttered a prayer of thanks
when, soon after, he found what he was looking for. He went
back for Kusox, who had removed his buckskin leggings and used
his bandanna to make a tourniquet for his leg, and helped him
make his way through the forest to the cave.

It was cold but dry, and there were the remains of a fire. There
was a risk Rebels might use the place still, but they had no choice
but to hope for the best. He helped Kusox strip out of his wet
clothes.

'How bad is your leg?' John Evert asked him.

'The bullet is in deep. It will have to come out later,' Kusox
said, his teeth chattering.

Dry leaves that had been blown into the cave by the wind
carpeted the floor. John Evert scooped them up into a great pile
and half covered Kusox with them to try to warm him, then went
in search of wood. When he returned to the cave, he set about
making fire, but Kusox tutted at him. 'I'll do it.'

He began the fire more quickly and ably than John Evert could
have done, though his leg must have pained him a great deal. At
the first spirals of smoke, he placed a couple of dry leaves against
the heat and soon had a weak flame going.

Once they had a good blaze, John Evert wrung every drop of
water he could out of their soaking clothes and propped them
up on sticks, steaming next to the fire. Their hands shook with
the cold and John Evert's whole body stung with goose bumps
and scratches. The light was fading fast outside the cave and both
men were suddenly overtaken with tiredness. Kusox lay down,
his head near the fire. John Evert put a hand upon his shoulder
and, feeling how chill he was, whistled to his dog, which trotted
over. He put a hand to the dog, which was already quite dry. He
bade it lie down next to Kusox, who twitched at the feel of the
animal's fur against his naked skin.

'If you told me I would sleep next to a dog, better a bullet.' Kusox sniffed.

'I expect sleeping with an Indian was not his first wish either,' John Evert snapped back, as he piled more dry leaves on top of Kusox.

There was a pause, before Kusox said, over his shoulder, 'You are the son of a skunk.'

'Takes one to know one. I can smell your stinking breechcloth from here,' John Evert said. He lay down too, pressing his back against the dog's thick fur and rubbing his arms vigorously, trying to encourage the circulation.

'Hmph.' Kusox snorted, communicating a great deal in that short sound.

They huddled there, in their pile of leaves, shivering, like new-born creatures, and fell eventually into a deep sleep.

They were woken later by noises outside the cave. They turned to each other to speak at exactly the same moment. John Evert put a hand over the dog's muzzle to stifle its growl. Kusox spoke so quietly that John Evert could barely hear him. 'Take your chance,' he whispered. 'Leave me. Get out before they bring light. They won't see you.'

'No,' John Evert whispered back.

'Why not?'

'Shut up.'

They listened long in the dark, but the noises died away, and no one came. Perhaps it had been but an animal. The fire had died down and John Evert stoked it up again, piling it up with wood. Kusox's buckskin trousers and undershirt were quite dry so he was able to put them on, crying out as he pulled the trousers over his thigh, which was angry and swollen around the tourniquet. The uniform jacket was still sodden and no use at all. But the cold kept them awake now, and there was nothing to do but talk.

'You spent time in a Mission school, I heard,' John Evert said.

Kusox's eyes met his across the fire. 'Bill told you. Yes, I did, after your people murdered mine.'

'*My* people? You say it like I did it.'

'You maybe did. Or someone just like you,' Kusox said dismissively.

'If you hate us so much why did you join up?'

'Nowhere else to go.'

'Not the reservations?'

'Have you been to a reservation?' Kusox asked. He shook his head. 'I thought not.'

'Wouldn't you rather have stayed with your—'

Kusox narrowed his eyes in annoyance. 'You think just because my skin is the same colour as another Pawnee it makes us family? What if I say you look like one of those soldiers in grey that you fight against, so you must all be family? My family died. All of them, not only my parents, uncles, cousins, everyone. And because I spent time in the Mission, because I can speak English, the Pawnee treat me differently. I *am* different. Why not come and fight then and be paid, instead of sit in a reservation and die a slow death?'

'Who taught you how to track so well? If you weren't with the Pawnee—'

'After I'd been in the Mission five years I was allowed to go back to the Pawnee, to people my father once knew. It was hard. I didn't belong to them and I had picked up your ways. But one of the men was kind to me. He taught me how to track, and plenty of other things, too. He was like Bill . . . like Bill is for you.'

John Evert wondered how Kusox knew Bill was not his father. Perhaps Bill had told him. He seemed to treat the Indians differently from how he treated all the regular soldiers. John Evert had long wondered why that was. He studied Kusox's countenance as the other man gazed into the fire.

His black hair hung in two smooth wings at either side of his head. Looking at him now, in the flickering light, John Evert realised for the first time how striking the face was: the great symmetry of Kusox's brow, the deep-set eyes. It was a proud face, angry, but handsome still. John Evert had been too busy hating it to notice. With one smooth motion, Kusox pushed his hair back behind his ears, and the fire shone gold on the long rows of brass earrings, which glinted in the light.

They sat in silence for a long while until John Evert spoke again: 'I've a question for you.' He swallowed. 'You people always scalp those you kill. I've seen you do it with my own eyes. I fought Indians once, in California, and I lost but they didn't scalp me. Why's that? They took all I had but forgot to scalp me. Why?'

'You people think that only you lose things,' Kusox replied, his voice rich with contempt. 'We lose everything – land, people, all the time. Stolen, murdered. All by you.'

'Damn you. Answer my question,' John Evert said hotly. 'Why didn't they scalp me?'

Kusox sniffed, then spat into the fire. 'I don't know. Seems strange to me. I can't tell you about the people in California. I can only tell you about my people, the Pawnee. But maybe you fought well. They thought you were dead. If you die bravely, the Pawnee don't take the scalp. We only take from the weak. Maybe your California people are the same.' He shrugged and then, some moments later, asked, 'What did they take?'

'My mother.'

Kusox said nothing.

'I followed them but . . .'

'How?' Kusox said, after a while.

'What do you mean how?'

'How did you follow them?'

'On a mule.'

'They left a trail? That you were able to follow with your dead-beat skills? I don't know who these people are you speak about—'

'Paiute.'

'Well, no Pawnee would leave a trail that you would be able to follow.'

John Evert ignored him. 'When all this is over, I'm going back to California to find her, no matter how long it takes.'

Kusox cast him a look as though he were deranged. 'I tell you one thing. If the Pawnee took her, you will never find her again. Never. But those people don't sound very smart to me. With those people, maybe you could find them again.' Kusox moved his leg and winced with the pain, taking a hissing breath.

'It's not long till dawn,' John Evert said. 'As soon as it's light, I'll send the dog for help.'

The moment the sun was up over the horizon, John Evert roused Kusox and said, 'Give me one of those things in your ears. Just give it,' he added, when Kusox hesitated. 'I need something to send to Bill that he'll recognise and I've got nothing.'

John Evert bent the brass earring open, then wound it tightly around one of his bootlaces, which he tied around the neck of his dog. Then he took the dog to the entrance of the cave, took hold of its big head so it looked into his eyes, and said to it clearly, 'Bill.'

He stood and bade it go. It took a few steps, then looked back at him. 'Bill! Go!' John Evert said sharply, and the dog cantered away.

When he returned to the fire, Kusox was watching him. 'Why didn't you go?' he asked.

'I'm not going to leave you here on your own. The dog will get back fastest anyway. Bill will send horses.'

Kusox watched him thoughtfully for a while. 'I do not know. I do not know how your people have beaten mine.'

'Guns,' John Evert replied. 'That's the only reason I can see.'

'We have guns.'

'But not as many as we do.'

Several hours later, cavalry came for them. 'Like a Goddamn carrier pigeon!' one of the cavalrymen said, pointing at the dog, which cavorted in excitement at seeing John Evert.

'He has his uses,' John Evert replied, his voice casual, although inside he knew damn well that without the dog Kusox would probably have died one way or another.

When they returned to camp, John Evert went to Bill, and Kusox to the medical tent and then to his people. They separated without a word, but somehow things were different.

After giving an amused, but evidently relieved, Bill the details of the event, John Evert went in search of the liquor man. He had only lately discovered the benefits of moonshine. The hangovers were wretched, but when that first shot of it hit his stomach and seeped out into his body, well, it was pretty much the only time he felt half way to all right. He was very secretive about his new-found vice, for he knew Bill would thump him if he suspected he was developing such a weakness, possibly because drinking was something Bill was a tiny bit ashamed of. Although, being a man of taste, Bill would never have stooped to moonshine.

John Evert had spent the night craving liquor, and was not sure why he wanted it so much but he wanted to forget and, short of being under fire, that was the best way he had found so far.

18

The Union Army had been shipped to the mouth of the James river as part of the Peninsula Campaign and was now a few miles east of Richmond, Virginia. On a muggy afternoon, John Evert's regiment had been pulled back from a swamp to high ground, where John Evert was entrenched with several thousand men in tangled woods that stood behind a deep ravine. As cavalry, he and Bill should not have been in with the foot-soldiers, but sharp-shooters were most needed there. They had been assigned a man each to load for them so they had a new rifle within reach the moment they had fired.

Fighting got off to a lethargic start around midday. There seemed little order to the Confederate attack, which made things easy for the well-placed Union defenders. John Evert had not slept and was in a trance, firing automatically at the moving figures that no longer seemed human. He had to pause to wipe the sweat out of his eyes and slap at the mosquitoes that sucked greedily at his neck. The sunshine beat down like a hammer, and was answered in ringing response by the ground as it shook with artillery fire. They must have been at it for six hours. There came a point when, battered by the Union defenders, the Rebels pulled back, and both sides rested. Bill and John Evert lay back against the fallen tree they had been using as a cover to shoot over. Bill lit a cigarette. John Evert shut his eyes and wondered whether he would ever sleep again. It was eerily silent in the woods, all the birds terrified away; even the crickets were still, as existence held its breath in horror. By now John Evert was inured to it all. He did not think about the men at the base of the ravine. He thought about Robinson.

A few days previously, they had been cleaning saddles together. He had watched her as she bent at her work. She had put on some weight, but not much. She was clearly just very light of bone – like one of those horses you could feed and feed but which would just sweat it off in nervous energy. Her skin was sunburned to olive and she was peppered with moles, a perfect circular constellation decorating one cheek.

'Is Robinson your family name?' he had asked.

'No.'

'Why do you call yourself that, then?'

She was silent for a long time, then said, 'Some fella told me a story once, about a man who was on a ship. The ship sank and he got himself on a . . . I don't remember the word. What is it when there's a piece of land and there's water all round?'

'An island?' John Evert said.

'Yeah, that's it. He got himself on an island. He was the only person there. And it was a hot land and there was green everywhere, all full of trees and animals. He caught fish to eat and there was fruits and all good things. And he was completely on his own.'

'Robinson Crusoe,' John Evert said, with a smile.

'Yeah.'

'And you liked the story?'

'Yeah. I think how good that'd be. In that place. No one to bother you. All that—'

'What?'

She did not reply, merely plunging the filthy rag she held in the bucket of water at her side, and continuing to rub at the leather before her.

'Where do you want to go? When the war's over, I mean,' he asked.

'I dunno.'

'You don't think about it?'

'Not really.'

'What do you want to do?'

She stopped rubbing at the leather then and looked him in the eye, with such melancholy that he was taken aback. 'I want . . .' she said hesitantly. 'I don't want to be told what to do by nobody no more. It ain't that I don't want to work. I'll work. I'll work all the day long. But I won't be told what to do. I want to be free.' Her voice upon the word was so wistful that it hung like a bird on the wing.

'I can help you. If you want,' he said, surprising himself.

'What do you mean?' she asked. Her voice was suspicious again.

'When this is over, I'll go back to California. I know people there. I reckon I'd be able to find you something to do.'

She was already shaking her head. 'I have nothing to give you,' she said firmly.

'You don't have to give me anything,' he said, with a frown.

'Like hell I don't,' she said. She jumped to her feet. Just before she turned to walk away, he thought he saw her eyes filling with tears. He had no idea what he had done wrong. He wondered whether all girls were so confusing.

He must have fallen asleep for he was jolted awake by the sound of the eerie Rebel yell from across the ravine. Bill turned over on his stomach, and squinted between the branches of the tree. 'Well, I never,' he said ruminatively. 'It's Thaddeus.'

Wide awake now, John Evert flipped over on to his belly and squinted down to the base of the ravine where he made out the shape of the man he had met in Texas a lifetime ago, a high hat upon his head, seated upon a large black horse. A sudden shiver passed through him, though he could not say why the presence of that character should be more chilling than that of a thousand Rebels. John Evert slithered the muzzle of his Enfield along the top of the branch, but Bill put a hand upon the barrel. 'No, kid, he's out of range.'

Thaddeus led a line of soldiers, who all wore the same distinctive dress. They held themselves in a noticeable order that was missing from the shambolic formations of the Rebels they had encountered over the last three days.

'Texans,' Bill said.

'Do you know those men?' John Evert asked.

'Hard to tell from this distance. Some, probably.'

John Evert studied Bill's profile but it was impossible to tell what he was thinking.

It was an hour before sunset when the Texans suddenly led a charge, and there was a surprise in store for the Union. The Texan horses were in excellent, grass-fat condition; a different story from the plank-ribbed, broken-down nags of the Union cavalry. They raced toward the Union line at a cracking pace, and Thaddeus and his men opened fire early.

The Texans aimed deliberately, and John Evert noticed how their rifles seemed smaller than standard. They pumped bullet after bullet into the Union lines, their rifles speaking out in neat unison again and again, without pausing to reload.

'What the hell are they?' John Evert asked, bewildered, as he counted a sixth successive shot out of one Texan's rifle.

'Seven-shot Spencer carbines, repeaters. I've heard of them but never seen one,' Bill replied.

Thaddeus took out two Union soldiers, whirled his horse around and fired behind himself at a third. After each shot, John Evert caught the glimmer of sunlight upon what must have been empty shells falling. 'How's he getting new bullets into that?' John Evert asked.

'Into the breech. It holds seven cartridges at a time.'

The Texans fired with such speed and efficacy that the point of the Union line that defended against them was soon unmanned, the exhausted Union troops demoralised by those dazzlingly fresh men. Union cavalry tried to move upon the advancing Rebels, but they had no chance against the remarkable weapons the Texans held. With surprising speed, the Texans penetrated the Union line.

'Here,' John Evert said, passing Bill his Whitworth. 'You can take Thaddeus – he's close enough now.'

'No, kid. That's not the way to do things.'

'But you've been up here dropping Rebels all day!' John Evert cried.

'Not him, not like that. We were friends once.'

'Then what are we doing here? Why are we even fighting at all?' John Evert asked. 'I'm not fighting any more. They can court-martial me and shoot me,' he said, his voice breaking.

Bill sighed, and rubbed his eyes. 'Shut up, all right?'

'No, I won't.'

Bill turned his bloodshot eyes upon him, and made to thump him, but John Evert, quick as a flash, brought down his rifle on Bill's knuckles. Bill yanked his hand away and massaged it, then studied John Evert. 'Very well,' he finally said. 'I'll tell you why.'

'Here, you two,' Bill said to the men who were loading for him and John Evert. 'Go and get us more cartridges.'

'Both of us, sir?'

'Yes.'

Once they had gone, Bill rolled himself a cigarette. 'She was . . .' Bill began, and stopped. 'No, no point comparing her to daft things. Those blue eyes . . . you had to see them. Impossible for me to describe in any way near sufficient. Anyway, she was young and she took a shine to me. Before you know it, she's decided she's in love with me. She was a good girl. Maybe I was in love with her, too, for a little while. But I got distracted. There were a lot of things going on at the time. And settling down was no possibility when I was on the run. I couldn't take her with me. I didn't want to take her with me, either. If I'd known what was going to happen I would have done it all differently. Thaddeus really cared for her, far more than I. But she had no time for him.' He left a long pause, then took two drags of his cigarette. 'Not long after I went away, she went and found work in a hospital – to take her mind off things, according to her sister – and she caught typhoid. It killed her. It would never have happened if she had stayed at home.'

John Evert considered Bill's story in silence, deflated. He heard the catch in Bill's throat as he continued, 'I've done some poor things in my time, but that was the worst. They're not like us, women. We have all manner of things that are important, but they . . . they put all they have into us, to their own detriment.' By the time Bill had finished talking, it was too late: Thaddeus and his men had disappeared into the undergrowth at the base of the ravine, and were now skirmishing, well hidden, with the Union soldiers. 'Enough of all this.' Bill tossed aside the butt of his cigarette and called to a messenger to ask for reinforcements from across the river.

After many days of battle, Bill and John Evert were promoted again, to major and second lieutenant. John Evert said it was only because there were so many dead that they were running out of men. Bill did not contradict him.

John Evert might have made it safely through another day, but the same could not be said of Orville, who had come down with dysentery and missed the whole battle. John Evert found him the next day in the new medical tent to which he had been moved. Orville lay deathly still under the sheet, pale and sweating. When John Evert spoke to him, Orville did not know him. John Evert collared a passing nurse. 'What's wrong with him? This doesn't look like dysentery,' he said.

'No,' she said. 'It's malaria. A lot of them have it. It's inevitable when we're here in the swamps at this time of year.'

'What can you do for him?'

'We're doing all we can. We're giving him quinine.'

John Evert took a seat next to Orville. He was sweating so much that the sheet that lay over him was soaked through. He twitched and mumbled in his delirium. Later, another nurse walked by and studied John Evert. 'You really shouldn't be in here,' she said. 'You'll catch something.' Orville was in no state to understand that John Evert was there so he allowed the nurse to usher him out.

In the morning, Orville was calmer, and for a moment he seemed to know John Evert. Soon after, he quieted and slipped away. John Evert gently closed Orville's eyes, then sat back and closed his own.

Orville had already entrusted to John Evert his letters, in which he spoke warmly of him to his mother, calling him his best friend, telling her that when John Evert was upon the field with him he just knew that all would be well. John Evert rubbed his eyes a while, then opened them, blinked, stood up and walked out of the tent into the nauseating humidity. He steadied himself against one of the struts of the tent, feeling sick, tired. He needed a drink.

He was determined that Orville should not be interred in a common grave, side by side with men he might not have known. He dug the grave himself, but there was not even the dignity of a coffin; Orville's only covering as he went into the ground was his uniform.

Noting his absence from the horse lines, Robinson came looking for him. She watched him digging, then disappeared. By the time he was filling in the hole, she reappeared at his side, and laid a crudely made wooden cross upon the ground.

He studied it. 'Did you make that?'

'I asked a man to do it.'

He knew asking anything of anyone would have cost her dearer than if she had made it herself, and he was grateful. 'I wish I could bury him somewhere better than this,' he said.

'We've all gotta be buried somewhere,' she said flatly. Then she said, in a more thoughtful tone, 'You got someplace special?'

He was on his knees, screwing the cross into the ground at the head of the mound. He thought for a moment, then said quietly, 'Yeah.'

'Where is it?'

'California. On my ranch. By a tree I love. When I die, it's the only place I'll rest.'

'You got a ranch?'

He heard the interest in her voice and glanced at her. She had taken a seat on the ground and was hugging her knees to her chest. Her cap was pushed back on her head, framing her neat, elfin features.

'Yeah, though it's kind of complicated. The way I left it, I'm not sure it will be mine to go back to.'

'How big is it?'

'About a thousand acres.'

'A thousand acres!' she cried. She stifled her excitement, and said more calmly, 'Really?' He nodded. Her interest piqued, she demanded, 'Is it true the sun shines there every day?'

'Every day,' he acknowledged, with a faint smile, and wondered whether Orville would have minded them having this conversation over him, then decided he would not, which made him miss good, simple Orville more.

'You must be able to grow most everything,' she said.

'Sure. Oranges, lemons, whatever you want, provided you have the water.'

'Well, how about that?' she said appreciatively, lost in the imagining. 'I'd like that. I always wanted—' She stopped herself.

'Always wanted what?'

She blushed. 'You'll think I'm foolish.'

'I won't.'

'I always wanted to grow some things of my own.'

'That doesn't sound foolish,' he said. 'That doesn't sound foolish at all.'

John Evert had not thought life could ever surprise him again, but a few days later, he and Bill were called to see Colonel Ewing, and he was proven wrong.

Ewing stood with his back to them, staring out of the rear of the tent. The flaps were open so that he had a view of the parade ground. He did not turn around. Something in the set of his shoulders made John Evert stiffen.

'Sir,' Bill said, and John Evert could hear he was also on his guard.

Ewing turned about. 'Major Jetsun,' he said thoughtfully, 'my most trusted and able commander. But that is not your name. Is it, Major Adair-Wilson?'

The image of Judge Ogier's courtroom flashed through John Evert's mind: the memory of Hector's profile; the din as Casey blew him out of gaol. After everything, so many miles, so many things done, they were right back where they had started.

Ewing turned to face them and his gaze was ice. John Evert knew the betrayal of his trust must seem double for the very fact that he had relied so heavily upon Bill. The retribution was likely to be double also.

'That is my real name,' said Bill calmly, 'but I am the same man, whichever you use.'

'No, you are *not*, dammit!' Ewing erupted. 'One of those men is a decorated officer of the Union. The other is an outlaw wanted in three states and abroad for piracy and murder.'

Bill's expression was serene. 'I suppose you're right, sir. What will you do?'

'I find your callousness nothing short of abhorrent. Have you no wish to explain yourself?'

'None, sir. You seem to believe yourself in possession of all the facts. One thing I would ask, how was my identity discovered?'

Ewing tossed a photograph upon the table. Bill had taken an interest in the new-fangled portable machines, but had had the good sense to stay on the other side of the camera, studying its mechanism. However, he had been caught unawares in this photograph, in which he was seated in profile in the background of a group portrait.

'Some bright spark, motivated by jealousy I don't doubt, started asking questions about the man who had served in the Mexican War and was making such a name for himself here. No one had heard of Bill Jetsun, but they'd heard of Bill Adair-Wilson. The deceit you have practised upon me and your men is indefensible.'

'The men don't give a rat's arse.'

'I should have you sent back to California immediately or simply court-martial you here. I am undecided. Get back to your regiment, and if you even think about leaving I shall have you hunted down and hanged for desertion.'

'Sir,' Bill said. He and John Evert saluted and left.

'Now what?' sighed John Evert.

'Now nothing,' Bill replied. 'Let him cool off. We're in the middle of a war. All this *abhorrence* he feels,' Bill tutted, 'will wear off at the first sound of artillery.'

John Evert wished he shared Bill's confidence. He slept little that night. The army might not have been an easy life, but it was a life. He had grown used to the order and structure of his days, the companionship of the men, the varied, skilled tasks they had to perform in pursuit of the enemy, which were not so different from what he and Bill had been practising together for a long time, only now it was legal.

And then something else unexpected occurred: in a moment of spite, or just a well-aimed fit of reorganisation, Ewing declared that all unnecessary hangers-on to the camp be despatched back whence they came. This applied to a couple of boys who had attempted to join up but, proving too young, had been allowed to stay on to help with menial tasks, several escaped slaves, who had sought shelter amid the Union lines, and the imposter drummer boy named Robinson.

'But where'll she go?' John Evert demanded of Bill, once the news was handed down around the camp.

'I'm writing to a friend of mine in Missouri,' Bill said, from his desk, where he was bent over, with paper and pen, in the light of the oil lamp. 'He lives in Kansas City. He'll take her on as a maid or some such. I'll give her enough money to see her straight till she gets there.'

'I can't see her managing work as a maid,' John Evert said.

'She'll have to,' Bill said, with an edge to his voice. 'It's all I can think of.'

'This is happening so fast.'

'Life does. All you can do is run to keep pace, kid.'

They had been demoted and were confined to their tent until

the next battle, with a guard keeping watch, but any attempt at keeping them in solitary confinement failed from the beginning. Kusox or one or other of the men was invariably to be found sneaking up behind it at night to give them news. There had been fierce grumbles of discontent among the men at Bill's demotion, but Bill had sharply called them to order, via the sergeant, and forbidden insubordination.

The day of Robinson's departure drew near, and John Evert still had not seen her. He sat upon his bed, morose. Early that evening, Kusox slapped upon the canvas to ask to enter and John Evert took him to one side. 'Kusox, do something for me, will you? Fetch that girl.'

Without a word, Kusox slipped off in the direction of the horse lines and, not long after, returned with Robinson. Bill stepped out of the tent to smoke with the guard. Robinson entered from the back and stood awkwardly, brushing the dust from herself. She wore her old breeches and shirt from when they had first met.

'What happened to your uniform?' John Evert asked, for want of anything else to say.

'They made me give it back to the quartermaster,' she said, 'but I went in there when he wasn't looking and took it back.'

'Good. It'll be useful to you.'

She looked at him, uncertain, obviously waiting for him to speak. Her eyes flitted nervously around the tent, the inside of which she had never seen.

'I wanted to say I'm sorry,' he said.

'What for?'

'For you being sent away.'

'It ain't your fault,' she said.

'Aren't you worried about leaving?'

'I guess not.' She shrugged. 'I always was on the move.' But then her expression changed to one he had not seen before, and she said in faint wonder, 'And I thought you were so *good*.' Then the most remarkable thing happened: she laughed. A great

creasing up of her face, so that her eyes squinted, her nose wrinkled, and her upper teeth appeared in a neat little row.

'You think this is funny?' he asked, bewildered.

She was trying to stifle the sound. 'I'm sorry. It's too bad, ain't
it?' Then she scratched her head vigorously, rumpling her hair.
'I think I got lice,' she said matter-of-factly.

'Do you want me to write to you?' he asked.

'Hell.' She looked appalled. 'No.'

John Evert was taken aback. 'Then, listen, when this is over,
I'll come find you.'

'What for?'

'To see you're all right.'

'I'll be all right. I'm always all right,' she said firmly.

'I'll come anyway, just to be sure.'

'No, you won't.'

'I give you my word.'

'What's that?'

'A promise.'

'I don't believe in no word or nobody,' she said flatly.

'Even between friends?'

'I don't have friends. Easier that way,' she said, but there was
a very faint tremor in her voice. 'Look, I gotta go,' she said.
'Good luck.' She grabbed his hand and shook it before scooting
out of the tent the way she had come, giving him no time to
reply.

Ewing ignored Bill and John Evert until they were called to
march again, to Harper's Ferry, to assist the isolated Union troops
there. He had Bill and John Evert marching at the rear of the
column, making plain their disgrace. News filtered back to them,
however, about what they went to face. The Rebels were tightening
the noose around Harper's Ferry. It fell before they arrived. They
pushed on hard to Sharpsburg, where General Lee's Confederate
Army awaited them.

As Bill had predicted, at the first sniff of battle, Ewing had
their confinement suspended, puffing something about war

changing things and second chances. John Evert even overheard him say to Bill, 'If you acquit yourself well, I'll see what I can do to fight your corner once this is over. I need you now. This battle may determine the whole course of the war.'

They spent a restless night under light rain, and the spatter of droplets on the canvas of the tent reminded John Evert of the night before his first battle. He wished he knew now what he had known then: nothing about what he was likely to face. To distract himself, he considered sending a letter to the place where Robinson was headed so she might feel not entirely alone when she arrived. But she had told him not to, and it might annoy her. He figured it probably would annoy her. He would think on that one further. He could not keep himself from worrying about her, while knowing she would hate him for doing so.

The Union troops attacked at dawn, sweeping south through the cornfields, where Rebel and Union fought with fire in their bellies, annihilating each other. As cavalry, John Evert and Bill were held back, but eventually the cavalry were let loose, and wretched excitement constricted John Evert's throat and tightened his muscles. The roan felt it too, for it bucked splendidly and snorted, snatching at the bit. The cavalry was fast over the river and into the low-lying cornfields. There was no sign of the Rebels, and they maintained a trot as they got their bearings. Through the first of the cornfields, nothing seemed amiss. They had simply to press on to catch up with the infantry. And then, while passing through a narrow gap in a tumbledown stone wall, they discovered what had become of the first regiments.

Every single stalk of corn in the field they were passing through had been snapped clean off, as neatly as though with a scythe. So thick had the bullets flown that not one head of corn remained standing. It was so wet with blood it was as if a bloody hailstorm had fallen. Amid the fallen ears lay row upon row of bodies. The horses refused to walk over the strewn dead. The roan put its nose to the ground, and shook its head unhappily.

'Come, we'll have to go around,' Bill ordered quietly.

They filed about the edge of the field, gazing at the sorry sight underfoot. It was eerily quiet. 'Have they retreated?' John Evert asked.

'Unlikely.'

Their eyes darted about to thick tree trunks, bits of stone wall, a collapsed barn – all of them providing perfect Rebel sniper positions. The Union cavalry could not have been more exposed. And when the hit came, it was, as expected, from Rebels masked by the landscape. They leaped out from behind collapsing walls, firing in rapid unison, melting out of the rocks and trees like grey and brown wraiths. The horse next to John Evert went down heavily, crushing its rider. John Evert crouched low to the roan's withers and set it into a gallop, his sabre drawn. With no warning at all, cavalry appeared, not just to the front of them but also behind – they were surrounded. The state of the horses, the skill and dress of the riders, was all they needed to be sure that it was the Texans they were up against. Bullets flew thick as rain. John Evert could hear the awful sound of men's heads popping like exploding watermelons.

The roan took a bullet in the neck and squealed, twisting its head to the right. Unable to let go of his tight reins in time, John Evert accidentally encouraged the pony's fall, and it crashed down on its left side, trapping his leg beneath it. The shock stunned him. He lay still for a moment, until the roan staggered back to its feet, releasing him. As he tried to sit up, a Rebel leaped toward him. He brought his right foot up to meet the man's chest. The man let out a strangled cough as the wind was taken out of him. While he stumbled, trying to catch his breath, John Evert reached for the sabre that lay on the ground at his side and ran him through. He kicked him away, then looked to the roan, which stood bravely by his side, refusing to run away but trembling. Blood poured out of its nostrils. He dared not ride it.

He whirled around at a rapid tattoo of hoofbeats. A Texan was riding hell for leather toward him, sabre in his left hand.

John Evert watched his approach, not looking at the rider, but rather at the horse's head. At the last moment, he jumped up and snatched the head piece of the bridle behind the horse's ears, pulling it clean downwards, snapping the throat lash, so the bit crashed out of the horse's mouth. As the horse reared up in fright, John Evert ducked down and rolled under its leaping body. The horse hopped a few strides, tangled itself in the loose bridle that flapped about its legs, stumbled and unseated its rider, pitching him headfirst on to the ground. John Evert ran toward the prone man, kicked him over, and pulled the Spencer from his side. He fired it once, twice, three times at Rebel cavalry that were flying past. The Rebel's horse was stumbling about, but it had not broken anything. John Evert got the bit back in its mouth and vaulted into the saddle. Fighting raged on every side. He scoured the melee for Bill and finally spotted him, far away, at the end of the field, skirmishing with three Rebel cavalry.

Bill was keeping them busy enough with his sabre to prevent them reloading, but he could not keep it up for ever. John Evert dug his spurs into the fresh horse, which sprang forward, its long strides eating up the ground. He crashed the horse directly into the first Rebel, and slashed horizontally through the man's middle, so that he doubled over and slid forward off his horse. The second Rebel, a grizzled man with white whiskers, gave him a dashing run of steel, and John Evert knew himself outmatched. He did the only thing he could: he dropped the reins, drew his pistol and shot the man in the chest. Bill was locking steel with the remaining Rebel, and looked to have the upper hand until, out of nowhere, a bullet thudded into Bill's stomach, and he slumped forward.

'Bill!' John Evert cried. He snapped his head about to where the bullet had come from, and saw Thaddeus upon his black horse, his left forearm still held horizontal with his rifle braced across it. A tinge of red descended over John Evert's vision, so that even the air itself was painted with a wash of blood. He dug his spurs into the horse and charged toward Thaddeus, screaming wordlessly. Thaddeus sat still, waiting for him, watching him come. As John Evert galloped near, Thaddeus raised his rifle again, but John Evert slid off his horse at the gallop, firing in mid-air. Thaddeus's bullet missed him, but John Evert's found its way home. The man let out a bellow of pain, and looked down at his left shoulder, astonished. John Evert was alone now on the open ground. Thaddeus took aim at him again, close enough now for John Evert to see his face a twisted snarl. John Evert reversed his grip on his sabre handle and, using an action Kusox had taught him, hurled it like a spear. It quivered in its flight, and sank into Thaddeus's thigh. John Evert was shaking all over. He had landed awkwardly when coming off the horse. His ankle felt strange; he could only hobble forward when he attempted to run toward Thaddeus. He was forced to stop and stood still, panting.

Thaddeus dismounted slowly and limped toward him. He towered over him, his eyes dead of all feeling. 'Get on your knees, traitor,' he said.

'I will not,' John Evert said.

'Get on your knees,' he said monotonously, kicking John Evert in his wounded ankle, so that he cried out and fell to the ground.

Thaddeus drew his sword. Taking it in both hands, he swung it up behind his right shoulder. John Evert, kneeling at his feet, looked him in the eye, burning with rage. Thaddeus opened his mouth and began the down-swing – but something strange happened, for he suddenly convulsed and all the power went out of his arm. The sword dropped harmlessly to the ground.

Thaddeus looked down at the centre of his chest where a blue-black flower was unfolding, petal by petal. John Evert twisted around to see Bill, who must have crawled a long way to get so near, and who now sat, splay-legged, only maintaining an upright position by leaning upon the rifle he had just fired.

'You son-of-a-bitch,' Bill said, 'you leave that boy alone.' Then he fell over backwards. Thaddeus began to topple, and John Evert slid out of the way as he came to earth, like a felled tree.

John Evert's ankle was screaming with pain and his vision was filling with tiny gold sparks. He had to crawl over to Bill on his hands and knees.

'Bill, Bill, Bill,' he said, over and over again. Bill lay on his back, his eyes only half open, his hands resting upon his stomach. 'Bill,' John Evert said again.

'Yes, kid,' Bill replied.

'Are you all right?'

'No.'

John Evert took Bill's hands away from his stomach. Blood oozed unhindered from a hole in his gut. To John Evert's horror, a large bulge of intestine swelled out of the wound.

'By God, this is it—' Bill gasped.

'No, no, no,' John Evert said desperately. 'We'll see you back to the nurses and they'll patch you up just fine.'

'No, kid. We know what this is. Better to let me go here than have those butchers stitch me up and go slowly with the gangrene.'

'No, no,' John Evert said, weeping now. 'You can't. You can't leave me.'

'Aw, come on, kid,' Bill said, exaggerating his adopted twang, as he liked to when fooling about. 'I taught you everything I got. To tell the truth, I was beginning to worry you'd get bored of me some day.'

'Bill, please, I can't do it without you.'

'Sure you can. You learned real well. I never had any kids. Well, I never met any of them . . . Jesus, this stings,' he gasped, 'but I'd have no complaint if they'd turned out your way.'

'Bill, stop it, you bastard.' John Evert's tears fell into Bill's blackened and powder-blasted face. 'What about my mother? You promised.'

'I know. I'm sorry. Take Kusox with you. We had a word.'

'I don't want Kusox. I want you.'

'He'll be more use to you.'

'He won't,' John Evert cried.

'Always talking back.' Bill sighed, then he smiled. 'Hey, kid, do you remember when we first met, when you said God sent me?' He gave a wheezing laugh, which turned into a cough. 'God didn't send me, you know. You chose me. There is no God. There's only you. Remember that. Remember . . .' He coughed blood and he could speak no more. He squeezed John Evert's hand and smiled his lopsided smile, then closed his eyes.

John Evert threw back his head and let out a strangled cry that went on and on, until he had no more breath to sustain it. He sat there, cradling Bill's shaggy head, until eventually the fighting died out around them. Dusk fell and, at last, the field was empty and theirs alone.

The next day, John Evert removed Bill's body from the blood-wagon, put him up over the grey's back and took him into the woods to a bluff that commanded a fine view away from the battlefield. He buried him in the shade of a large oak tree, and fashioned a cross, upon which he carved 'Bill'. Then, feeling as though he had not yet completed the burial, he collected smooth stones from the river and made a pyramid of them to weigh down that huge heart. He sat next to the grave, his hand upon it, as the wind shook the leaves of the oak tree and the purple shadows of clouds skimmed the yellow ground. His mind, arching all the way to the horizon in search of comfort, remembered the time Bill had told him that, when people died, he figured they became ghosts inside of the people who loved them. John Evert had thought that sentimental, as Bill often could be after whiskey, but now he felt certain a thin rope was running up through the earth, along his arm, deep into his breast, raising the hairs upon the back of his neck, making his whole body sing.

He stayed like that a long time, watching the play of shadows upon the land, then finally released the ground. He picked up his crutch from where he had set it, and limped slowly down off the bluff.

Part Three

The Long Green Grass

1864–1865

19

The road was pink in colour, some mineral in the soil rendering the earth and its dust incarnadine. Cracks ran deep through the bone-dry ground, and the vegetation, what there was of it, was scrubby, clinging to the sere landscape by sheer force of will.

John Evert rode the grey, while the roan trotted at its side, at the end of a lead rein. It seemed miraculous that the two horses should have survived nigh on four years of warfare but, like John Evert, they bore their scars. The roan's wind would be forever broken by the bullet it had taken to its neck, while John Evert's ankle had a tendency to sprain, which at times resulted in a slight defensive limp. The only one of them to remain untouched was his dog, which ran at his side. He watched its loping gait for a while, then turned his gaze back to the road.

After Bill's death, almost two years earlier, Ewing had offered John Evert release from the military for he had served due time, but he had declined, saying he owed it to Bill to see the job through to the end. Ewing had been pleased, and he had been good to John Evert, who at but twenty years of age rode now a major. Partly due to this elevation, but more so to the loss of Bill, he had withdrawn into himself; he formed no more attachments to his fellow men. It had made him a better soldier, but also a solitary figure.

In search of consolation for the loneliness he felt after Bill's death, he had lost his virginity to a prostitute. While the discovery of such pleasures provided him with escape, it was a temporary one, and brought him little comfort, save for the few seconds of release. So, after doing it plenty, just to be sure, he gave that up, too.

The only thing he had not given up after Bill's death was his fledgling fondness for drink. Without Bill's guiding hand to prevent it, he indulged himself. It came on in slow degrees, one sip at a time, until he did not pass a day without a drink and there was never a day when he was quite sober. Given the choice, he would probably not have left the army even now, but when his ability to soldier came into question and his weakness became impossible to ignore, Ewing had insisted that he be honourably discharged. The war was over now anyway. The Thirteenth Amendment to the Constitution had been passed: slavery had been abolished. And Lincoln had been gunned down at the theatre less than a week after General Lee's surrender at Appomattox. It was all over. There was no choice but to leave. And John Evert had nowhere to go but home.

There had been a time when all he had wanted was to rush back to California and get on the trail after his mother, but the experience of the war had made him let go of his childish dream of her recovery. He would pursue her regardless, but he knew that the great likelihood was that he would search for a lifetime without success. The knowledge weighed upon him so heavily that he found himself reluctant to return to the land of his birth.

Upon announcing his plan to return to California, he was surprised by Kusox's request to go with him. He looked over now to where Kusox rode a dun pony, some way behind him. John Evert had refused to allow it, but Kusox had been adamant that he would accompany him. John Evert had spoken his mind plainly. 'I do not doubt that before Bill died he extracted some sort of promise from you that you would look out for me. I don't know what he can have offered you to persuade you, but I tell you that I do not want you, nor do I need you. I release you from this nonsense.'

Kusox had looked down his nose at him.

John Evert had threatened him when he found him riding behind him by half a mile, but the man would not be put off. In the past, John Evert might have been tempted to shoot him, but

Kusox had served the regiment loyally, had saved many lives, and he could not bring himself to do it. So he drank his liquor and ignored Kusox when he took a seat at the fire night after night, still wearing his blue uniform jacket, unbuttoned over his bare chest, above buckskin leggings.

That night, John Evert made camp and, as always, Kusox joined him. Kusox prodded the fire with a stick and then spoke. 'Bill didn't offer me anything. He said you would.'

'What the hell are you talking about?'

'Bill said you have land and that maybe you'd give me some, if I helped you.'

'I'd give you some of my land?' John Evert asked, in amazement. Kusox did not reply. John Evert shook his head at Bill's presumption; that outrageous bastard, making promises he could not keep. 'And you believed him?'

'Are you telling me he lied?' Kusox said.

John Evert thought on this, took a swig from his hip flask and looked into the fire. He knew he needed someone to help him if he were ever to have any hope of finding his mother now, so many years later, and there was the glaringly obvious fact that Kusox possessed skills he lacked. No one was better equipped for the task.

'I don't know,' John Evert said slowly. 'There might be a chance of land if you come with me. *Might be*, but you'll have to make yourself of use to me. You hold me up in any way and I'll have no more to do with you.'

Kusox had no quarrel with the arrangement.

Ever since, they had ridden side by side through the cracked landscape, heading ever westwards. What they travelled through was devastation. There being no territory or tangible goal, but for the hearts and wills of men, victories had been measured in loss of life, the destruction of property and society. The once fertile lands of Georgia, of all Tennessee, were laid waste as though by biblical plague. Houses and farms lay in ruins. Women and children scavenged in the dust. Crops had been burned or left to rot. No steer, hog or ewe was left living. Only the birds remained, singing emptily in the branches of the thorn trees.

They met the casualties of war on the road: injured soldiers making their way home; emancipated slaves; a group of hollow-eyed women and children, led by a preacher. The road was not a safe place. Gangs of hungry men wandered it, starvation turning them feral. Only the foolish or the untouchable journeyed in the open. But they were safe: the gold leaves on John Evert's shoulder straps and Kusox's demeanour were enough to intimidate opportunists. Also, John Evert carried Bill's Whitworth and two Spencers; Kusox carried his own gun and a large bowie knife.

John Evert had not given much thought to what might greet him in Los Angeles; after all he had seen and done, the threat posed by a Los Angeles courtroom seemed but trivial. His only notion was to return to the ranch, see how things stood there, then set out on the stone-cold trail of his mother. Raising the money for the enterprise was no longer an issue: Bill's idea of a last will and testament had been to bequeath to him a detailed list of the many places about California in which he had stashed his riches. No banker's hall had ever been blessed with his presence, but many caves and sheltering tree roots had known his trust. No, it was not money that worried John Evert now, it was his mother alone.

To his dismay, he had found he could no longer call her face to mind. It was as though the war had erased all that was good in him. All he could recall was the feeling of her: her warm humour, her teasing him for his seriousness, her impatience at what she perceived as dawdling in others. For his own sanity, he forced his mind down other avenues. And, presently, he was engaged in worrying over his route to California.

Their progress was absurdly slow. Every bridge they came across was burned; every river had to be forded. They entered Missouri, and travelled through the mountains of the Ozark plateau, a land of forested canyons and shallow green rivers.

One night, they slept in a cave, the roof of which was rimmed with fang-like stalactites. The flickering light of their fire cast ghastly shadows upon the walls – it was as though they were held in the mouth of some dreadful beast. The rain hissed down outside. John Evert thought of the other time he and Kusox had slept in a cave. He had spent time in Kusox's company since then, but he would not say he knew him any better. But he felt easier beside him, that much was true. The old hatred in his breast had long since died down. John Evert helped himself readily to the liquor he carried, to keep warm, he said to himself, but it filled his belly with only cold fire. Through narrowed eyes, he spoke to Kusox about a subject that had been nagging him for weeks.

'What if I can't give you any land when we get to California?'

Kusox regarded him calmly. 'We will see when we get there.'

'You must have some place else to go.'

'No. I have no family and what were our lands have been taken.'

'I don't think an Indian can legally own land.'

'I do not need a piece of paper.'

'And why the hell would I give you anything anyway?' John Evert drawled, vaguely aware that he was slurring his words.

'Because I will help you look for your mother.'

'You don't think I'll find her, do you?' John Evert said.

'No,' Kusox said. 'But you will not listen to what I say. You confuse stubbornness with strength.'

'That's not what you said before, when you told me why those Indians didn't scalp me,' John Evert retorted. 'You said I must have been brave.'

'Maybe you were then but now . . .' Kusox gestured pointedly at the flask in John Evert's hand. 'Now, you can't even rise in the morning without a drink. It's made you weak. The way you are now, I would take your scalp.'

John Evert threw a log violently into the fire so that a shower of sparks fell over Kusox, who did not flinch.

*

They rode on, through the collapse of law and civilisation. John Evert had finished the last of the moonshine and, without it, sleep was fugitive. He awoke in the night, shouting, in a pig sweat. Whatever hideous memories marched across his mind, their steps were deep. At the first small town they reached, he filled two canteens with liquor. His hands trembled as he tied them to the saddle. He took a swig from his hip flask to steady himself.

After Bill's death, John Evert had written to Robinson, at the address of the friend to whom Bill had sent her, to inform her of his passing. She had shown no liking for any person, but for Bill she had always maintained a respect that seemed as close to liking as she was capable of. He felt she should know he was gone, and he had expected a response. None had been forthcoming. Knowing that letters often went astray, he had written twice more. There had never been a reply. He had been angry at first, then concerned. He wondered whether something had happened to her. And so their route to California was through Kansas City. He had told her that he would find her after the war, and he had been taught never to break a promise. That last bit of his mother he could carry with him forever.

They rested up in a lodging house upon their arrival in the city. There was a time when an Indian would have been refused accommodation, but in these straitened times, the sight of money was sufficient to procure anything.

John Evert found the address with no trouble. The house was seated upon a wide, leafy thoroughfare, away from the centre of town, and must, in happier times, have been an address of some distinction. He straightened his uniform upon the veranda as he prepared to knock. He had half expected her to greet him, but when the door was opened by a young woman in servant's garb, who was not she, he was not surprised. He took off his hat.

'Good day,' he said. 'I'm sorry to trouble you, but I'm looking for a lady by the name of Robinson, or Beth.'

'I'm sorry, sir, but there's no one of that name here,' the young woman replied.

John Evert nodded. 'May I speak with your master, then?'

She bobbed, begged him wait, and closed the door. He examined his boots.

The maid returned, and he was shown into the house, then a study, where an elderly man in a pink waistcoat, with grey hair that curled under his ears, greeted him. 'You are a friend of Bill's?' the man asked, with a warm smile. 'How is the man?'

'He's dead,' John Evert said.

The man's face fell, and he sat down heavily in his chair. His eyes shone, and he sat silent as he attempted to collect himself. 'You were friends?' he asked eventually, his voice hopeful.

'I knew him but little, sir,' John Evert said, unmoved. He felt nothing, incapable even of wonder at that.

The man sighed gently. 'Well, then, what may I do for you?'

'I'm looking for a young lady by the name of Robinson or Beth. Bill sent her here.'

'Yes.' The man nodded slowly. 'Yes, he did. I did my best for her but she found it impossible. Service, I mean. She left. I wanted to help her find another place or position, but, to my regret, she refused my assistance.'

'Do you know where she is now?'

'I did have someone look for her. I, too, wished to know what had become of her. She . . . took up residence in an insalubrious part of town.' The man seemed embarrassed. 'I can write down the names of the streets where I believe she might be found.' He took up his pen, and scribbled a few lines in a wobbly hand. He held out the paper to John Evert, who folded it and put it into his pocket. He made to take his leave, but the man stopped him. 'Wait,' he said, reaching down to open a drawer in his desk. 'Your letters.' He held up to John Evert the slim packet.

John Evert did not take it. 'How do you know they're from me?' he asked.

'I may be old, but I am not senile, young man,' the man said wryly. 'I have not read them. The first was opened. The rest, naturally, were not.'

'Naturally?'

'Miss Robinson cannot read,' the man said gently, the letters still held in his outstretched hand. John Evert took them. 'Forgive me for pressing you,' the man said, 'but I feel that you and Bill did not know each other but little. Truthfully, I think you knew each other well. There is no need to hide this from me.'

To John Evert's discomfort, the man's eyes welled with tears. He stood and held out his hand to John Evert, who could not bring himself to take it. Instead, he stood to attention, saluted and made his way with all haste from the room.

Back in the street, he paused to kick himself mentally. Of course she could not read, and she would have been too proud to ask for anyone's assistance. He rubbed his eyes in exasperation at his own idiocy. Her strange behaviour in that final conversation of theirs – all was explained. Well, not all: some. He returned to the lodging house in search of Kusox.

They rode to the part of town where the streets that the old man had indicated could be found. It was clear at once why he had been discomfited to mention the place: it was a broken, wretched neighbourhood, with filth in the streets, decrepit wagons left where they had fallen, dirt-smeared children and stray dogs skulking through the shadows. John Evert's dog bared its teeth at the skinny curs, which gave it a wide berth.

They turned a corner, and were met with a barricade manned by a small party of militiamen.

'You can't come through here,' a slight young man said.

'Why not?' John Evert asked.

'Street's closed.'

'Under whose orders?'

'Mr Allam.'

'I will see him.'

'Tomorrow,' the man said.

'Today will do just as well,' John Evert replied, staring him down.

'Er . . . maybe,' the man mumbled. When John Evert continued to stare at him, he relented. 'I'll go find him,' he said, and jogged off.

John Evert dismounted and followed him into a nearby house where a greasy-haired man with watery eyes sat behind a desk.

The man stood and saluted vaguely. 'What can I do for you, Major?'

'I need to enter the street to look for someone.'

'Impossible, I'm afraid.'

'Why?'

'Sickness.'

A cold hand trailed across John Evert's shoulder. 'What kind of sickness?'

The man shrugged. 'If you value your life, stay away.'

'I must ask permission to enter anyway.'

The man's face contorted and his eyes hardened. 'If you enter, you do so at your own risk. I cannot vouch for your well-being. No one is allowed to enter or to leave.'

'I will enter,' John Evert said firmly.

The man let out a nervous laugh, then shrugged again. 'It's your choice.'

As he remounted, John Evert voiced his thoughts to Kusox. 'If I didn't know better, I'd say that man is hoping some accident befalls us. Why do you think that might be?'

'All these men here, they're Confederate. I'd say every one of them wishes us ill,' Kusox observed. John Evert narrowed his eyes at him.

The militiamen opened a gap for them at the edge of the barricade and they entered. The poverty was appalling: children, horribly emaciated, stared at them with empty eyes. John Evert went from door to door, asking after Beth Robinson. Those wretched souls he spoke to seemed half dazed. He had little hope of getting any useful answer out of anyone. Small fires burned at regular intervals along the road, heaped up with recently incinerated material.

'What is this sickness?' John Evert said to Kusox uneasily, noticing then how many doors were painted with a long red cross.

'I want to look,' Kusox said impatiently. 'Here.' He gestured at one of the doors.

Night was beginning to fall, shadows lengthening, when Kusox pushed open a red-crossed door. The smell emanating from within was putrid.

A woman blinked up at them from where she sat among bodies lying upon the ground, but said nothing. The place was lit by two tallow candles, and they had to squint close to see anything at all. Kusox took up one of the candles, and knelt at the side of a body. John Evert stood at his shoulder. Kusox flipped back the corner of the blanket covering it. He hissed at the sight of the face beneath, which was a scarlet porridge of weals and ulcers. The sight chilled John Evert to the bone. He seized hold of the back of Kusox's jacket and pulled him away. 'Don't touch anything,' he hissed, as he dragged Kusox backwards out of the house. They stumbled into the gloom of the street where John Evert released him. 'Stand still!' he ordered. 'Stand still and do as I say – keep your hands out in front of you.'

For the first time, John Evert saw fear on Kusox's usually impassive face. 'What is it?' he asked, his hands stretched open before him. John Evert ran to a nearby fire, and pulled out a half burning log. A few wraith-like figures on the street stopped to watch, drawn by the commotion.

With his free hand, John Evert removed his hip flask from his belt and unscrewed the lid, tossing it on to the ground. 'Put your hands together,' he ordered. He approached Kusox, poured the spirit over his hands, and immediately touched the burning end of the log to them, at which Kusox's hands burst into flickering blue flame. Kusox stood, appalled, staring at his burning hands. 'Stay still. Trust me,' John Evert said. Kusox's nostrils flared, like those of a horse, but he stood his ground. After a moment, the flames disappeared, leaving him looking from one hand to the other in wonder. 'It's smallpox,' John Evert said quietly. 'I'll look for her. You can leave now. I don't expect you to put yourself in danger.'

Kusox drew himself up and scowled. 'No.'

'You're a crazy, stubborn son-of-a-bitch.'

John Evert did then the only thing he could think of: he walked the length of the street, calling her name. After a while, Kusox took up the refrain also, taking a parallel road, and they walked the desperate grid of the lost, the damned watching them from windows and doors. To John Evert's eyes, it was as the dead might observe the living when they came to visit Perdition.

When John Evert had finally shouted himself hoarse, a slight figure came walking through the smoke-choked fires and the gloom to meet him. The first thing he noticed as she drew close was that she had grown a few inches taller. Her hair was longer, but the messy, boyish cut remained; she pushed it roughly to one side, trying to tuck it behind an ear, as she stopped in front of him and demanded, in her strange throaty voice, 'What the *hell* are you doing?'

She was very thin. Her cheeks were sunken, the bones jutting. And she was angry. 'What business is it of yours to come calling my name for everyone to hear?'

'Are you all right?' he asked, his insides flipping at the sight of her. It had been two years since last they had met, yet it seemed like yesterday.

'Fine,' she said, trying to be dismissive, but he could see she was rattled. 'Why are you here?'

'Because I told you I'd come see you were all right.'

She compressed her lips tightly as though holding something in.

'You can't stay here,' he said. 'It's smallpox.'

'I know it.' She shrugged.

He was taken aback by her indifference. 'But you'll – you'll die.'

'I've been here ages and I ain't got it. Don't reckon I will now, neither.'

The wind had been taken out of his sails. He was not sure what he had expected from her, but it had not been indifference.

'I also . . . I came to tell you something,' he said haltingly. 'Well, I tried to tell you, but you can't read. I know that now.'

Her eyes narrowed into furious slits. 'If you've come here to tell me I'm uneducated—'

'No, no, listen, I'm sorry,' he gabbled. 'I came to tell you Bill's dead. I wrote to you.' He took the sheaf of letters from his pocket to show her.

'Well, what's that to me?' she said, but she looked away as she spoke, trying to hide a frown.

'I thought you'd want to know, or maybe I just wanted to tell you. I don't know why.'

She was silent for a few moments.

'Because he meant so much to you, that's why,' she said. 'I'm sorry for it. Really, I am.'

The unexpected tenderness in her voice made something quiver and break inside him. He looked at his boots, fighting back the emotions that threatened, after such long restraint, to come barging out.

His dog appeared then, sniffed at her legs and wagged its tail. It sat down between them and looked up at them, a daft grin on its face. She stroked its head while John Evert studied her profile. Eventually, she met his gaze.

'Why are you in this place?' he asked, casting a glance over her shoulder at the scene.

'I'm helping some kids,' she said briskly. 'Well, I was . . .' She trailed off.

'They're all dead?'

She nodded once, biting her lower lip.

'They will all die, you know,' he said. 'You'll be on your own here. Please, come with us.'

'Come with you? Where to?'

'California. I've had an idea. Well, it was more Kusox's idea actually. I have land there. You know I have. I thought you might like to have a small piece of your own.'

She raised both her eyebrows in deep surprise, but said nothing.

'You could grow some things, you know, like you wanted to.'

She itched her brow a while. When she spoke, her voice was not even. 'Why'd you try so damn hard to help me when I don't ask for it?'

He gazed at her small, sharp face, and sought the answer inside himself. Eventually, he said simply, 'I guess I just like looking after things. Come with us. Give it a try. If you don't like California you can go on any place you want. What do you have to lose?' He glanced about the wretched street.

He had her lie face down across the grey's haunches, behind his saddle. Kusox tied her on, so that she would not slip off. 'It's going to be uncomfortable,' John Evert admitted, 'but it's got to look convincing.'

She did not complain or utter a sound as she lay with head and feet dangling down either side of the grey. As they began to ride out toward a barricade at the other end of the quarantined area, opposite the one they had entered by, they were brought up short by a shot fired in warning. John Evert called out, 'We are here by the permission of Mr Allam.'

'What's that you're carrying?' the sentry called.

'A body.'

'You can't bring that through here!' the voice shouted back.

'I can and I will. If you want to stop me, you'll have to shoot me. My name is Major John Jetsun. I'm sure you'll have no trouble explaining why you shot an officer of the United States Army to anyone who might ask.' John Evert extended his arms palms out, to demonstrate that he was unarmed. 'You may come here and look at the body, but we have been among the sick and the dead. If you let us pass, we'll ride straight and not stop for a day. Or you can come arrest us yourself.'

There was a thoughtful silence, and John Evert coaxed the grey forward into a walk once more, keeping his hands in the air. As they drew near the sentry post, he could make out the militiamen staring at him across the sandbag barriers, their rifles at the ready.

He sat straight in his saddle, daring them to approach or shoot, but they parted slowly and let him pass. Once he and Kusox were well beyond, John Evert took up his reins once more, and soon they were gratefully hidden in the dark streets. They collected the roan and their belongings from the lodging house and beat a hasty retreat out of the city.

20

They did not talk at all for the first few hours, each lost in their own thoughts. John Evert wondered what she thought, and what Kusox thought about the fact that they were now three. He himself was not at all sure of the wisdom of having two people to think about, but he figured it was too late now, and he knew that he had been right to get her out of Kansas City. He glanced over to where she sat the roan. She could ride, but not very ably, and she certainly had not ridden for a long time: when they stopped to water the horses, she walked stiffly after dismounting. When they reached a farm, John Evert purchased a sheepskin from the farmer, and tied it over the roan's saddle to cushion the seat.

When they moved off again, Kusox rode ahead, uninterested in conversation, preferring to keep an eye on the surroundings. John Evert was glad of it for he wanted to speak to her, and figured she would be more likely to talk if it was just the two of them.

'Why did you leave the house that Bill sent you to? He seemed like a good man. He wasn't unkind?'

She shook her head. 'No. I just wasn't no good at that work. I kept getting things wrong.'

'Like what?'

She shrugged. 'I dunno.' She was silent for a while, then said, 'The woman who worked in the kitchen, she kept telling me I was doing things wrong.'

John Evert immediately hated the woman who worked in the kitchen.

'And he kept being interested about me, that old man,' she

271

said with a frown, 'asking questions. It made me feel funny, so I left.'

'Why'd you go to the part of town where we found you? It didn't seem very . . .' He was not sure how to phrase what he wished to say.

She cast a sidelong glance at him. 'I wasn't doing that kinda work.'

He blushed. 'But why that kind of place?'

'It's what I know,' she said simply.

'You deserve better,' he said.

'What do you know about that?' she said, brushing her hair out of her eyes crossly. 'You don't know nothing about me, about the things I've done, I had to do. I don't deserve no better.'

'Life doesn't have to be like that,' he said gently.

'Maybe not for you with your book learning and your big ol' piece of land,' she retorted. 'For someone like me, low work and thieving is all there is. You think I don't want to be good like you? Maybe it's easy to be good when there's been good things in your life so you know how to do it. Me, I don't know about all that.' And then she would say no more, so he let her be. He took solace in the idea that she remembered him, and that what had been between them might have passed for friendship.

There was a great risk that either he or Kusox had been infected with the smallpox, and he knew it but did not share it. He contented himself with keeping a close eye on Kusox, in case of any sign of fever. For himself, he felt like he had a fever most all the time, but he just drank through it. Robinson's gaze followed his hand whenever his hip flask appeared, the pale, shifting sands of her eyes missing nothing. She looked away just as fast.

They rode hard for a few days, each driven by the same need to put distance between them and Kansas City, but when they rode into a landscape of green meadows with hummocks of cushiony grass and a river meandering through, they halted to rest.

The grey had a swollen fetlock, so John Evert led it down to the river and had it stand up to its knees in the cool water. When it got restless, he let it go, and it clambered up on to the bank and wandered back to the other horses, its lead rope trailing through the long grasses. He took off his clothes and swam in the tea-dark water that was chilly but vitalising. He pulled himself out on to the bank, and lay flat among the reeds, allowing the sun to return the warmth to his cold skin. He half dozed, eyes closed.

After a while, he heard a soft plop in the water that he took at first to be a fish, but the sound was followed by a second splash that was too big to be any fish. He rolled on to his stomach, and looked through the reeds. Possessed of the same idea, she had followed the same animal track that he had to the water. She must have seen the grey back with the other horses, and assumed he was with it. If he had thought quicker, he would have made a noise immediately to alert her to his presence, but it was too late for she had already, with one smooth movement, pulled the shirt he had given her – he had made her burn her clothes back in the city, for fear of the variola they might hold – over her head, and stood now, waist deep in the water, naked.

She was so slender that the circle of water she broke was small enough, he would have thought, to encircle with his two hands. Her breasts were very small and high, the nipples dark and tiny against the chill of the water. She turned her head to one side, and he noticed how slender her neck was, like that of a deer. Then she swirled away from him, and he saw the lean length of her back, the lovely folded wings of her shoulder blades, and the pattern of *cigarrito* burns that echoed almost perfectly the constellation of moles upon her cheek. All of a sudden he figured he knew why she dressed like a boy: to protect herself from interference. The confusing combination of desire and pity that flooded him was shocking. Mortified, he pressed his face into the marshy ground to stop himself watching.

She and Kusox had not spoken to each other once during their journey, and they did not speak now, but John Evert watched her gathering kindling for the fire that evening and placing it in a bundle at Kusox's feet. Later, Kusox passed her things to hold while he fed a skinned rabbit on to a spit, all of it done wordlessly. John Evert found himself wondering, not for the first time, about the dealings between Indians and their womenfolk.

That night, by the fire, once Robinson had curled up in a tired ball to sleep, he said to Kusox, 'You ever been married?'

Kusox seemed faintly surprised by the question. 'No,' he said, 'but there was a woman.'

'Someone you cared for?'

'Yes.'

'Why didn't you marry her?'

'I did not have enough to offer. Her father would not accept me.'

'Did she care for you?'

'Yes. She was never my wife but she came to me as a wife, at night, right up until she married.' Kusox spoke matter-of-factly, then looked at the girl curled up in the glow of the fire. 'Is that why we came for her – for you?'

'No, no,' John Evert said hastily. Kusox's eyes never left his face and there was, perhaps, the smallest flicker of amusement in them.

'A woman is good for a man,' Kusox said. 'She makes him less hot in the head, but she makes him weaker too.'

'How?'

'When a woman is involved, he fights but he does not fight purely for love of the fight. He fights to protect, and he is no longer happy to die.'

The next day, the smoke from the campfire hung close to the ground and flies bothered them incessantly. John Evert had learned from Kusox that both of these were signs of imminent rain. They rode to woodland, where Kusox slung canvas over a branch to make a shelter. It was but an hour later that the downpour came, closing in as a soft yet implacable sheet that flattened the warm air to the ground. They made a new fire, just inside the shelter entrance, and the breath of the rain blew smoke within, filling the interior with cloudy warmth. John Evert lay in a rear corner, reading. He leaned comfortably against the grey's saddle, with his dog close and warm at his side. It was a book that he had found in a grand, abandoned house they had passed many weeks earlier. Robinson sat just inside the entrance to the tent, a blanket about her shoulders, re-plaiting the leather cheek strap of one of the horses' bridles. Kusox was outside in the rain, engaged in some business of his own.

'How come you two's together?' she asked, peering out at the billowing sheets of rain as her fingers worked over the leather.

John Evert looked over the top of his book, 'He asked to come with me.'

'Why?'

'He wants me to give him land.'

She was silent for a time, then turned her head to regard him. 'You're really going to give us both some place to live? Why would you do that?'

'Kusox has to help me find someone, and while we're gone we'll need someone to look after the place. You could do that, then have your own place, too. You'll be on your own. You won't mind that?'

'No,' she said. 'I reckon that'd be a fine thing.'

There was a faint smile upon her lips, and although he felt a stab of guilt at raising her hopes when the ranch was quite likely lost to him, he could not resist adding, 'You'll be able to do what you like all day long. If you want, you can just lie by the river with a piece of fishing line tied around your big toe.'

She smiled properly then, lines scrunching up at the corner of her eye and her small teeth momentarily visible. She certainly had a good smile and he liked to see it.

She made an appreciative noise, and then, serious again, she turned her back to him once more and stared out at the rain. 'Who'd you have to go find?' she asked.

'I'll tell you another day.'

At that moment, Kusox became visible, some way off.

'Don't you reckon he'll be lonely,' she said, watching Kusox, 'with no folk of his own?'

John Evert noticed the concern in her voice, and she turned fully to look at him. It was an unusually vivid scene: her face, made bright by the soft light falling through the white canvas, and, beyond her, the figure of Kusox, walking toward them, through the rain.

'I reckon he'll be all right,' John Evert said, letting out a long yawn. In the warmth of the tent, he soon dozed off.

When he awoke, the rain had ceased and the sun had burst out. He was alone. He stretched, and walked out into the fresh brilliance. A soft breeze shook a branch above him and it rained down a benediction of droplets upon his shoulders. 'Where are they?' he asked his dog. It looked at him in anticipation. 'Seek 'em,' he said, at which it bounced off purposefully, nose to the ground. John Evert followed, his gaze trickling over shining foliage. A blue jay skimmed across his path, the azure flash startling.

After a while, the path he was following came to an abrupt end, where the ground gave way to a sheer drop. His dog trotted along the edge of the short cliff, taking a long slope down to the side. John Evert became aware then of a low hum in the air. As he descended, the hum grew louder. At the base of the slope, his dog turned to look back at the cliff face. It caught sight of something, and bounded forward, but drew up short as though struck. Then it began to behave in an extraordinary fashion, leaping about, snapping at the air and biting itself. He whistled to it, but it ignored him. It was only when a small, black creature thumped softly into his face that he realised the cause of the dog's commotion, and the noise – bees.

As he had not been looking for them, he had been blind to them, but now he made out that the air was swarming with them. Their deep drone filled his head and echoed from the walls of the cliff, making the air vibrate around him. He kept still, but the bees seemed otherwise preoccupied and did not bother him. Looking into the back of the natural amphitheatre, he saw the reason: Kusox, stripped to the waist, was balanced precariously halfway up the rock face, smoke spiralling from a bundle he held with one hand while, with the other, he reached deep into a cavity in the rock. John Evert watched as Kusox withdrew his arm, which was a writhing mass of bees. Carefully, he slid the thing he held into a bag he had slung across his shoulder.

Robinson was sitting on a rock to one side, watching. John Evert walked over to her, and saw that her face was alight with wonder.

Gradually, Kusox began to make his way back down the rock face. When he reached the ground, he turned, with painstaking care, and headed toward them. He was still covered with the creatures that formed a curious, moving carpet about his chest and shoulders. As he took one slow step after another, they began to lift off in skeins, spiralling away. As he drew near, she got to her feet, a nervous smile hovering on her face.

Very carefully, Kusox unwrapped a soft piece of leather and held out to her a jagged, dripping piece of honeycomb. 'Take it,' he said, and made a soft blowing sound. Without hesitation, she did so, blew gently to disperse the bees that had alighted upon it, and put it whole into her mouth. She let out a delighted sound at the taste.

Kusox held out a second piece to John Evert, who broke it in two. He put the first piece into his mouth, the liquid outrageously sweet around the soft waxiness. 'How did you . . .' John Evert began, but in his distraction he fumbled with the second half as the melting honey began to slide from his fingers, so that he had to catch at it with both hands. The sudden movement alarmed the bees, one of which stung him roundly on the wrist. 'Ah!' he cried, the spell broken. Kusox rolled his eyes and walked slowly away.

'Gee,' was all Robinson said, her eyes following Kusox.

*

They travelled west across Kansas, and as they did so, John Evert learned more about both his companions. He had noticed Robinson watching him whenever he picked up his book. 'Do you want to learn to read?' he asked her.

'Nope,' she said immediately, turning back to what she was doing.

He thought for a moment, then said, 'Do you want to know what it's about?'

She did not object, so he gave her the outline of the story, and then, he was not sure how, he found he was reading some to her, and this became a habit most evenings.

'Hmph,' she said, at one point. 'I don't believe that. A man like that acting so soft, somebody's gonna have his pants.'

'How do you know?' he asked, for she was correct.

'I can tell, is all. You know a lot of words but you don't know people. The people in them books ain't real. Real people are dirty-dog-sons-of-bitches.'

'That's one way to put it, I guess,' he said. Her lips twitched.

More instructive yet was an evening when, pie-eyed, he had gone to his saddlebags, only to find the last canteen empty. He was confused: he knew for certain that it had been full when they had left the last general store. He pulled out the plug, put the skin to his mouth and blew. A faint hissing indicated the two small holes, low down in its side.

He returned to the fire where she sat, staring into the embers, poking them gently with the bit of iron they used to stir the cook pot. 'Do you know anything about this?' he demanded. She looked at the canteen in his hand, and shook her head a little too quickly. 'Rattlesnakes round here keen on hooch, are they?' He was filled with an unaccountable rage. He moved swiftly around the fire, at which she, quick as a flash, was on her feet, with the glowing end of the iron stirrer pointed at him. The sight brought him up cold.

'What are you doing?' he said, his rage strangled by her fear. He dropped the canteen.

She flinched at the sound of it hitting the ground. 'I don't want that you have to hit me to make me do right,' she said bitterly.

'Hit you? What do you think I—'

'Leave me alone!' she cried, hurling the stirrer back into the fire, and fleeing with her bedroll to the safety of some nearby trees.

Kusox watched silently, smoking his pipe. John Evert was almost tempted to ask his opinion, but he was too proud. How could he explain the necessity of the liquor, that without it he had to contend with the sliding sensation in his stomach, the dread, the demon voice whispering in his ear that spoke of failure, and loneliness, and something so dark there was no name for it?

He passed a wretched, sleepless night, and was never more pleased to see the dawn.

John Evert left her to her own devices for the morning, but after a couple of hours' riding, he tilted the grey's head to catch up with her where she rode away off to one side. She did not look at him as his horse fell into step with the roan. 'I'm sorry,' he said quietly. She did not reply, merely scratched her nose, and then her cheek, a familiar gesture. He had thought once that it was the short locks of her hair tickling her, but he had begun to realise that awkwardness made her do it. 'You need to know I'd never hit you, not ever. Do you understand that?' She made no sign that she did. He guessed that there was little point in saying such a thing to her: he would have to show her.

'Will you tell me about that baby?' he asked, surprising himself with the question. She seemed to freeze at the recollection. 'You told me once it wasn't yours. But whose was it? It's been bothering me.'

Frowning down at the roan's neck, she said quietly, 'All this time?'

'Yeah.'

She did not say anything for a few minutes, but then she cleared her throat awkwardly. 'It was one of the girls who worked round that place. She'd tried to get rid of it, like they all would, but it wouldn't be got. He was so angry about it.'

'The man Bill and I spoke to?' John Evert asked, but she appeared not to hear him.

'When she had the baby, it went on all night. The noise she made . . .' She shuddered at the recollection. 'When it came out she didn't want to see it or nothing. It was hollering for its mama and she just let him take it out in the woods. After he came back, a while later, I went out looking for it. I don't know why. I figured he'd have killed it and I wanted to see it. But he hadn't. It was just laying there on the ground. Not making no sound at all. It was like it knew no one was coming for it. I wrapped it up and hid it. I couldn't bring it back with me. He'd have gone crazy. I did my best to feed it, but all I had to give it was a little bit of milk, and it was hard enough getting that. I think I didn't go see it often enough. A few days later when I came to see it, it was dead. I should've buried it but I couldn't. I brought it back with me. I didn't want to leave it out in the woods there, all alone. He found out about it in the end. He was making me go bury it.' Her voice had grown ever quieter and slower as she spoke, as though she were winding down, like an exhausted clock. He was so sorry for her, but knew not how to tell her.

'Was it a boy or a girl?' he asked.

She sighed, 'Oh, what does it matter?' but after a moment, she tilted her head back and said to the sky, 'It was a boy.' Then she wiped her face with the back of her hand and clicked at the roan, slapping the reins against its neck, so that it broke into a ragged canter, leaving John Evert behind.

What a strange-soldered thing she was, he thought, so strong, but touch her in the wrong place and she just fell to pieces.

They rode the yellow plains of the New Mexico territory, their profiles silhouetted against striated, dark blue hills, so that they appeared to ride the tiny lines of a book. Sudden five-point peaks thrust up out of the desert floor, as though some giant, drowning in the dust, had thrown up his desperate hand for rescue. Sometimes the sky was nothing but blue; other times it was dabbed furiously with tiny, circular clouds, a buttermilk sky from one horizon to the other. In the mornings, the hills were blue; in the evenings, red.

John Evert had tried again to talk to Robinson. The roan had shied at a ground bird that had flown up suddenly in its face, and she had fallen, with ill luck, upon the pincushion of a cactus. He and Kusox had been forced to lay her flat and cut her shirt off, so they might remove the spines from her skin. She had said not a word as they worked across her back, pulling out hundreds of tiny black needles. When working around the circular burns on her skin, Kusox flicked John Evert a glance, before dabbing an ointment from his saddlebag upon the puncture wounds. Then they had given her a new shirt and got her back on the roan.

'What's that stuff you put on her?' John Evert asked later, when the two of them were riding side by side and she was some way behind, obviously awkward after having been so exposed to them.

'It will make the skin heal,' Kusox replied. 'It takes out the poison.'

'Where'd you get it?'

'I made it from a plant.'

His interest piqued, John Evert asked, 'How do you know which plant?'

'The one who was my friend, the one who taught me to track, he was a medicine man.'

'You're a medicine man?'

'No,' Kusox said sharply, as though insulted. Then he added, in a low voice, 'I know how to give medicine, some kinds of medicine, but I could never be a medicine man. I am not pure,' he said. He had put great stress on that last word, and John Evert thought on this, trying to understand, but then light dawned.

'Because you spent time with the whites,' John Evert said. Kusox nodded once. 'But that's not your fault.'

'What has that to do with it? It is the way things are. It is the law.'

'I don't reckon laws make much sense,' John Evert said, thinking particularly of his ranch and Gunn's claim on it. 'I don't reckon people make much sense either sometimes,' he added.

'People come and go. They leave, they die.' Kusox shrugged. 'But the land never changes: it is always there and will be for ever, long after me, long after you.'

'That's why having a piece of land to call your own is so important.'

'Of course.'

John Evert looked down at the grey's mane, his feelings conflicted. But there was no help for it. He had to tell the truth.

'Kusox, I'm not sure I'll be able to give you any land when we get to California. I haven't been straight with you. I let you come along as I thought you'd be a use in finding my mother, but the truth is there may be no land. My ranch was under threat when I left California and someone else might own it by now. I can't let you come along under false pretences. It's not right.'

For a while Kusox did not say anything. Finally he spoke: 'I will stay. When I first met you, I didn't trust you. I thought you spoke with two tongues in your mouth, like most of your kind, but now I see why Bill took you with him. I think the land will be there still.'

'You reckon?' John Evert said, filled with relief that Kusox would remain. Despite himself, he was glad of his presence.

'There will be a fight in California, for the land?' Kusox asked.

'I would say most definitely,' John Evert replied.

'Make sure you fight well.'

'I will. I can promise you that.'

'That is enough for now.'

That evening, when they made camp, and Kusox left to hunt, John Evert turned his attention to Robinson. Those scars of hers bothered him too much and he wanted to know how she had got them.

'While we were pulling out those cactus spines . . .' he began clumsily.

'John Evert!' she interrupted, and it gave him a strange jolt, her saying his name. 'There's things I can't never talk about, with you or nobody.'

She could not bring herself to look at him, and stared instead at the ground, her jaw clenched tight. 'You got scars too,' she said. 'I see that thing in your shoulder, but I don't go asking about how you got it.'

Of course she had noticed his scar, he thought. He was branded with that for ever. 'I'll tell you,' he said.

'I don't want to know!' she cried.

Moved by her distress, he said, 'All right. I'll not ask you again.' He knew it was risky, but he stepped closer to her and, ever so gently, put his arms around her. She stood stiff as a board but, after a while, she let her cheek rest lightly upon his chest. He put his nose to the top of her head. She smelt of hay or apples.

She let him hold her for a few moments, but as soon as she moved, he let her go. They did not speak of it.

A few days later, she was running a high fever, so high they stopped at a cave in an isolated rock island to keep her out of the sun. She sweated and shook a great deal.

'Is it smallpox? The cactus?' John Evert asked anxiously, but Kusox gave him no answer. Instead, he lit a bunch of dried sage, and fanned the smoke around her where she lay. After that, he lit his pipe, sucked at it and blew the smoke over her.

'I don't think that's going to do her any good,' John Evert said. Kusox glared at him with such vitriol that John Evert was chastened.

She drifted into a feverish sleep. Kusox did not leave her side, which began to worry John Evert.

During the night, she awoke, frightened, and called out. Kusox gently pulled her up into a sitting position, and the two of them studied her. Her eyes sparkled feverishly in the embers of the fire. John Evert put his hand to her forehead. She was roasting hot. They could smell that she had emptied her bowels. John Evert stoked up the fire, so they could see better. Kusox stared into her face and listened to her breathing. He turned her over and they saw beneath her the dark pool of liquid. Kusox went to his bag and returned with a small gourd.

'Wait. What is that?' John Evert demanded, as Kusox prepared to let her drink from it. 'Don't do that. We should find a doctor.'

Kusox curled his lip. 'You have no idea how often I want to cut your throat. There are no doctors here,' he said curtly. 'Either she takes this or she will get sicker and then maybe she will die.'

John Evert's stomach tilted unpleasantly. 'Is it that bad?'

She sat between them, not saying a word, trembling. Kusox took her chin in his hand so she looked up at him, and said, 'Drink this.'

Her eyes slid to John Evert. 'You don't have to,' he said. 'We should ride for help.'

She looked back at Kusox, who put his face closer to hers. 'Trust me,' he said quietly.

She reached for the gourd herself. Kusox tilted it back for her.

She vomited a while later, and was delirious for much of the night.

John Evert chewed his fingernails savagely, furious at having let Kusox take charge, convinced he had poisoned her. Kusox paid him no attention, focusing only on giving her repeated doses of the liquid, whatever it was. It was as though John Evert did not even exist.

All the next day, she was painfully weak and the water they gave her – almost all they carried – seemed to go straight through her, but by nightfall, the fever had broken.

John Evert thought they should stay another day in the cave, but Kusox insisted they ride on in search of water. To John Evert's disbelief, she nodded her agreement, and walked, with a wobbling gait, outside to prove her mettle. She asked for privacy, so that she might give herself a dust bath, ashamed at the state of herself. They let her be. John Evert was mumbling his concern still when Kusox turned around to face him and shook his head. 'You,' he said, eyes narrow, 'I give you a horse and you want to know how old it is, how many teeth it has, you want a different horse. Her,' he jerked his thumb at her, 'I give her a horse, she rides it.'

John Evert scowled at him.

It was not so long before they passed into the Arizona territory. Their constant companions were the heat and the dust. The smell of hot earth invaded their senses, coating the insides of their noses thickly, leaving a crusted layer upon their skin and in the corners of their eyes. They dreamed of pools in which to bathe but there was barely enough water in the canteens to allow for more than the smallest swig every few hours. John Evert gave Robinson a pebble to suck, to draw some saliva into her parched mouth.

Suddenly, incomprehensible in the empty vastness, they spied a herd of horses. Their legs zigzagged in the heat haze, such that John Evert thought they might be a mirage, but no, they were real. They were driven by a *vaquero* who glanced at them but had not even the energy to nod a greeting. They took stock of the animals that loped by.

'That's a nice horse,' John Evert said, of one tall, bright chestnut with a lot of thoroughbred in its veins.

Kusox sucked his teeth dismissively. 'I would take five of the small pintos for one of those shiny, useless things.'

Suspiciously, John Evert regarded the short-necked, scrubby little brown and white blotched creatures that Kusox indicated. 'Why?'

'You choose a horse on its beauty,' Kusox replied, 'which stands for nothing. How often has that big grey of yours gone lame?'

'A few times,' John Evert acknowledged.

'Mine,' Kusox said, patting his dun pony, 'never. Short pasterns,' he said, indicating on himself the area between his ankle and his heel. 'Much better.'

'This grey would outrun your dun in a minute,' John Evert said.

'And put its pretty foot in a prairie-dog hole and fall down so I can walk past you any time I want,' Kusox replied.

'Let's see, shall we?' John Evert said, putting his heel to the grey and drawing his reins up tight, so that the horse drew itself up, ears pricked, and gallantly danced on the spot, despite the lead weight of the heat on its back.

Kusox shortened the reins on the dun pony so that its neck bunched into its shoulders, like an irate turtle.

'Hey!' Robinson shouted, directing the roan around to stand in front of the two of them. 'What the hell d'you think you two roosters is playing at? You remember the last time those horses had water? Well, I do. You want to race each other to prove how long your damn horns are, be my guest, but you leave those horses with me and you do it on foot.'

John Evert let his reins drop and fell into step behind her. After a moment, Kusox followed. John Evert looked back at him and they exchanged a quick smile.

They broke for rest at a rocky butte that cast a shadow, and sat in a row in the thin sliver of shade. It was silent all around, but for the noise of the dog panting and the blood pulsing thick and languid in their veins.

'Hey, there's water at your place in California, ain't there?' Robinson asked, licking her dry lips.

'Sure,' John Evert said.

'Tell us about it.'

So he told them about the river, about the serpentine bend of it all the way through the property. He told them about the pool where the fat trout fed, the limpid green of the water where it flowed lazily around the rocks, about the tiny sticklebacks that darted like flashes of silver in the shallows. He told them about the great broken oak tree and its mysterious immortality that had seen it survive lightning strikes. He told them about springtime and the blue haze of the lupins and the checkerspot butterflies that dotted the yarrow. He told them about fall and the spilled sunbeams that were the aspen leaves. He told them everything.

'The piece you're gonna give us,' she said, 'me and Kusox, that is. I don't mind how small my piece is but can I have a bit of river in it? Just a real small bit.'

The fact she asked for so little touched something inside him. 'Sure you can.'

'You know, I don't mind what happens 'tween now and then,' she said, 'so long as we get there.'

She shut her eyes and leaned back against the rock. John Evert studied her face. He had no doubt that they would get there; what possessed him was worry about how long they might be able to stay.

They were so tired they ended up spending the night at the butte, sheltering in a deep, narrow-mouthed indent around one side of it. It was cold in the desert at night. They burned some mesquite and the smoke from the fire was full of its sharp scent.

Coyotes visited them in the night, announcing their arrival with their despondent, collapsing wails. John Evert tied his dog with his lariat and handed the other end to Kusox. He took a burning piece of wood out of the fire and used it as a torch as he walked out of the shelter of the rocks. There were eight of them. They sat about fifty yards away, in a semi-circle around the rock entrance. Their eyes shone yellow in the light from the torch he held. He walked several paces toward them. Three stood and trotted back a few paces. He stopped and studied them, each in turn. One lay down and put its head on its paws. He felt very peaceful out there with them. He stayed a while.

When he returned to the rock, Robinson asked anxiously, 'Will they come in here?'

'No, they're not hungry,' he said.

'How'd you know?' she asked.

'They told him,' Kusox mumbled, from where he half dozed by the fire, and then, after a pause, 'Hey, did they tell you where there's water and a beefsteak?'

'Ass,' John Evert said.

'What's the point of being able to talk to animals if they can't tell you anything useful?' Kusox said, with laughter in his voice.

'You're not funny.'

'I am,' Kusox said.

'Idiot.' He repressed a smile.

John Evert shivered in the night and slept poorly. At some point, the coyotes departed, taking their song with them, and he was sorry for he loved to hear it.

21

They crossed into California on a bright, clear day, but before heading for Los Angeles, they visited one of Bill's caches for funds. They headed north and made for the gold country of the western sierra, a snow-capped Eden of meadows and lakes, of breathless waterfalls and crystalline pools, the banks of which teemed with grazing mule deer.

The problem with this paradise was that Bill, ever the lyrical man, had given the most cryptic cross-wise directions possible, and the landscape was all of a muchness. Even after narrowing the instructions down to a two-hundred-yard stretch of redwoods that lined a particular valley, they were left with a thousand spots to search.

It was a particular sequoia they sought, the shape, apparently, reminiscent of the female form. They scrutinised every goddamn tree trunk in the valley, and each time they made out two breast-like mounds they hurled themselves enthusiastically into ransacking the ground at its roots, but to no avail.

It was on the third day of desultory seeking that they sat upon the bank of a lake to rest. They had chosen to stay together, for as well as the numerous tracks of bear and mountain lion, they had come across moccasin footprints. It was impossible to make any prediction as to tribe, but Kusox was of the mind that their being discovered trespassing in anyone's territory would end badly, and John Evert agreed.

They were tired and hot. Robinson had her hat tilted back upon her head as she lifted the canteen to take a long draught. Her eyes flicked skyward, and she froze, before pulling the canteen away from her mouth, spilling water down her chin. She squinted at something above the sheer drop of the tall overhang on the other side of the lake, and said, 'It ain't bosoms we're looking for' – she was pointing up at a long, dark gash in a giant sequoia that clung by sheer effort of will to the crumbling stone edge of the overhang – 'it's a woman's privates.'

John Evert's gaze followed the trail of her finger, and she turned to him, her face triumphant.

Following a scramble up the cliff to reach the tree, Kusox made a pert remark as John Evert reached arm-deep into the wooden gully in the tree trunk. He rolled his eyes, but could not help smiling. Within seconds, his hand made contact with a cool, metal loop.

Not one of them said anything as they sat in the wide shade cast by the redwood's trunk, looking at the gold nuggets in the metal case. There must have been fifty pounds of gold. John Evert held one of the knobbly chunks and experienced a pang at the thought that Bill's hand must have touched it once, too.

He dreamed of Bill that night but, like all kind dreams, the wisp of its memory was spirited away as soon as he woke.

From that moment on, his mood took a more sombre turn. Their increasing proximity to Los Angeles and the ranch was beginning to stir up unwelcome emotion in him. With each swinging step of the grey, there was a growing murmur of recollection. He could hear the sound of his mother's heel upon the wooden floor, see her silhouette behind the white sheets she hung upon the wash-line, and the long, black snake of her hair draped over one shoulder as she sat with her back to him at her dressing-table.

He drank, as ever, to steady his nerves and take the edge off his thoughts. Robinson saw it and came to his side one day when he was tying a saddlebag on the grey. 'You're nervous, ain't you?' she said. When he turned to her she added, 'I ain't seen you like this before. You afraid of something?'

'Not afraid exactly. It's more dread, I guess,' he admitted.

'Dread of what? Failing?'

He was surprised by her sudden prescience.

'Kusox told me about your ma,' she said. John Evert found he was not annoyed that she should know it. He wondered at the fact that she and Kusox had become close and felt unhappy about it in some unidentifiable way. 'I'm sorry I've been tough on you,' she said. 'I thought you'd always had it easy 'cause of the way you are.'

'The way I am?'

'Those fine manners of yours. But I guess we've all had bad things happen to us. Ain't nobody had it easy all the time.' She put a hand on his forearm, ever so briefly, and then walked away.

Los Angeles was exactly as he remembered it: parched, dusty and raucous. They walked the horses through wide streets where chickens scratched in the powdery earth. Scrubby oak trees squatted, their stubby leaves cracking in the heat. Shadows extended but a finger's width from adobe walls. Lizards gulped in the shimmering haze. While every able-bodied man east of New Mexico had gone to war, the Angelinos had kept to themselves. All seemed in ruder health than the citizens of the eastern states. Children scuttled about, while women with sandpaper hands toiled at washboards.

Yet things were not quite the same, as John Evert discovered when the horses turned down Main Street. Every building seemed to have shrunk, the substantial structures he remembered from his adolescence revealed as modest frame houses. Now that he had his bearings, he was able to lead them to the plaza. His gaze fell upon the spot where Ricardo Urives's blood had once left a dark stain.

The Bella Union was the same, yet different: smaller, more worn about the edges. He bade Kusox and Robinson wait outside, amid the shifting pockets of people. He was grateful for the Angelinos' insouciance: his little band struck no incongruous note there, where a Spaniard in black and white studded suit talked lazily to a *vaquero*, who wore what must have been the remnants of a gown as his sash.

He pushed open the door of the Union, and entered the sawdust-padded gloom. It was quiet. Only a few men were sitting about, one solid back hunched over the bar. John Evert was sorry not to see the old barman; in his place there stood a younger man. '*Días*,' the man murmured.

'You still rent rooms?'

'*Sí*.'

John Evert asked for a shot of *aguardiente*. He placed a coin upon the bar. 'Keep it,' he said, when the man bent to make change.

He took two rooms: one for him and Kusox, one for Robinson. On the road they had all bunked together, but he wanted no questions asked about his unusual domestic arrangements. He delayed enquiring about Hector Featherstone or any of his old acquaintances, wanting to get a feel for the town once more. He bought a copy of the *Star*. Its lead pages were full of talk of land redistribution following the war, but there was also the local news of crops, and cattle, and small claims.

The door of the *Star* still rattled in its hinges when he pushed it open. There was a new handbell upon the counter. He rang it. A boy came through, to whom he named himself as Major Jetsun.

When Quincy appeared, he held a bunch of papers in one hand, and glanced up from them for just a second to say, 'How do?'

'Hello, Quincy,' John Evert said.

Something about his voice must have struck a chord, for Quincy put down his papers and studied him properly, his jowls wobbling as he chewed on a toothpick. He struggled to see beyond John Evert's beard and the low brim of his hat, but when he did so, his eyes widened.

'Well, I'll be damned. John Evert.'

The pleasure in his expression soon changed to concern. John Evert considered the things that might be passing through Quincy's mind.

'It's good to see you,' Quincy said. 'I thought . . . we all thought you'd been lost for good.'

'Nearly.'

Quincy eyed his uniform, and thrust out his hand. 'It's mighty good to see you again. Major, is it?' They shook hands. 'Can I buy you a drink?'

'I've thought about you a lot,' Quincy said, as they sat at a table in the Union. 'Wondered what happened to you. I kept Meriweather on the lookout for news of you and Bill.'

'Bill's dead.'

Quincy fell silent for a while. 'I'm sorry to hear that. Sorry indeed. Mad dog he was, but a good man, in his way – an honourable one, anyway. Was it a brave death in the field?'

'No. I'd say it was more of a murder.' John Evert waved away Quincy's next question. 'Another time.'

'But you're alive and you've come back. Though I don't know how swell an idea that is, son. Sorry, I oughtn't be calling you that any more – you're a grown man.'

'I can't be running all my days. I've come to reclaim what's mine.'

'There's a warrant out for you, still.'

'I know it, but I hope that I can clear my name.'

'You been to see Mr Featherstone yet?'

'Not yet. Any sign of Casey?'

'Hell, no. He'd have to be crazy to come back here after helping you two escape from jail. But he's all right. He wrote me from San Francisco.'

'I'm glad to hear that. Meriweather?'

'Got married and moved to San Antonio. John, I worry that as soon as the marshal finds out who you are, he'll send you straight up the river. If there's anything I can do for you . . .' He trailed off, hopefully.

'I'll tell you if there is.'

After Quincy took his leave, John Evert had three more shots of *aguardiente*, then went upstairs and knocked on Robinson's door. There was no answer. He was not surprised, for neither she nor Kusox liked to be cooped up. He wondered if they were together, and was surprised by a pang of what might have been jealousy. Pleasantly dozy from the liquor, he went to his room to lie down a while.

He was awoken by a soft knock at his door, which opened hesitantly. She stood in the doorway. 'Come in,' he said, 'I'm awake.' He sat up and rubbed his eyes, his mouth parched and unpleasant. She crossed to the window and looked out on to the street. Her shirt was tucked into her trousers, which were held up with a thick belt that he had cut short to fit her tiny waist. She wore new boots, and her freshly washed hair was tied back in a stubby, gold bunch at the nape of her neck.

'How long we staying here?' she asked.

'I don't know yet. Until I find out what I need to.'

'I don't like it.' She sighed. 'I liked it more when we were on the road.'

'We'll go to my ranch in a day or two,' he said. But would they? He was uncomfortable with the knowledge that he had brought her to Los Angeles without telling her that he might at any moment wind up in jail.

'Have you been with Kusox?' he asked. She nodded. 'Listen, I should have said this before, but if anything should happen to me, you make sure you stay with him. I'll tell you where Bill's caches are. You won't want for anything.'

He stopped talking then for she had turned to him, and a curious expression had come over her face. He could not read it, although there was certainly anger in her eyes. He joined her at the window.

'It's dangerous for you to be here, isn't it?' she said. He nodded. 'Then why the hell did we come?'

'It's difficult for me to explain.'

'No, it ain't. If you was going to leave me, you should've done it in Kansas City, you bastard,' she said.

He was taken aback by the bitterness in her voice. Tentatively, he put out an apologetic hand to her, but she leaped back, with the alacrity of a frightened rabbit, and darted for the door.

He sighed, then went back downstairs for another drink and to await his first visitor, for he knew Quincy would not be able to keep quiet for long.

Abraham flitted through the door at sundown, his eyes spiralling about the saloon until they alighted upon him. Abraham's reaction was similar to Quincy's, delight fading into concern, although, in Abraham's case, it was underscored with sadness, too.

Despite John Evert's reluctance, which was only partly due to the fact that night was about to fall, Abraham insisted upon taking him there and then to Hector Featherstone's house.

John Evert had never been to Hector's home on Aliso Street. It was dark by the time they reached it, but he could tell from the perfume in the air that roses grew in its garden. Abraham led him into the front parlour, the tidy arrangement of which suggested that Hector had a wife. Hector entered the room in his shirtsleeves. John Evert had been concerned what Hector's reaction might be at seeing him again but, to his relief, the attorney walked swiftly across the rug toward him, saying, 'How glad I am to see you again, Mr Burn.' They shook hands warmly. Hector looked him up and down. 'I should never have recognised you, John.'

'I'd recognise you any day. You haven't changed at all.'

'Ah, you flatter me. I believe I've gone rather grey since last we met.' It was the truth, for the wings of his dark hair were touched with silver. 'Does anyone else in town know of your return?' His voice was edged with concern.

'Only Quincy Rivers. I've not made the fact known to the marshal.'

'I think that wise,' Hector replied. 'The longer you can protract that situation so much the better. Shall we sit outside, perhaps?' he suggested.

They took seats in a couple of wicker chairs on the porch. Two oil lamps and the rising moon provided all the light they required. The night was warm. The odour of the roses bled up to where they sat. It was quiet, the neighbouring houses set some distance away.

John Evert had expected that Hector's first thought would be his status as outlaw, but he made no mention of it. Instead, he had many questions about the war. His reaction to Bill's death was muted; it was John Evert of whom he wished to know. John Evert's interest was the ranch, and Hector confirmed that Phineas Gunn not only still had custody of the place but, in John Evert's absence and presumed death, had taken steps to avail himself of the title.

The news that Gunn had indeed done everything John Evert had feared made him quiver with anger, but Hector's next words brought him up short. 'John,' he said. 'Your mother. I should have said this at the outset,' he continued, 'but I found I had not the courage. I must find it now.' He reached into the pocket of his waistcoat and withdrew a folded letter. He held it delicately, framing it with his fingertips. 'This came for you almost a year ago. It was addressed to me, in case you wonder why I have opened it.'

He handed it to John Evert who turned it to the light. The hand was his mother's.

He dropped the letter as though it had come alive. He fumbled on the floor for it then held it to the light again, unfolded it with shaking hands, and began to read:

My dear John,

As you must surely know to be the case, I have done everything in my power to reach you, to let you know that I am alive. It took a long time for me to attain a position in which I was trusted sufficiently by the people I found myself among to send word without fear of reprisal. You will be surprised to learn that I have not been without friends here; so much of what we have been taught to believe about these people has proved to be wrong – and the people I am with are not the ones who attacked us, but there is too much to explain and I have not now the strength – I tell you this with only the hope that it brings you some comfort.

I was permitted to speak to a priest who came to the tribe, and to ask him to seek word of you. I had to wait more than two months for his return, and the news he brought caused me great sorrow but, knowing you as I do, I need no explanation. I know that there can be no truth in what was said of you. Whatever the trouble you found yourself in there must have been good reason for you to flee.

I send this letter via Mr Featherstone, for I feel that if anyone may know of your whereabouts it would be he. My heart is heavy, for I must tell you that I am gravely ill. I begged the people among whom I have lived to bring me here to the house of Father Santi, so that I may be given Christian burial. They were good enough to grant my wish.

I know not how much longer I have for this world, but should you live, should you receive this letter, know that you are the light that God has held up for me to see my way. Be strong. No man may tell you that you are not the one to hold the right. My greatest hope is that you may come to me while there is still time. If not, know that, every day, you were my first and last thought since the day you were born.

I am your loving mother,
Maria

John Evert's hands were trembling as he looked to Hector, who cleared his throat.

'I sent Abraham at once to Father Santi in search of her. Abraham was able to speak with her, very briefly, but, John, it is my greatest regret to inform you that your mother died in November of last year.'

John Evert said not a word. He could not. All he was aware of was a faint roaring in his ears. He had no idea how long passed, but at some point he stood and stumbled down the steps of the porch. Hector made no move to stop him.

He could never after recall how he made his way back to the plaza, but when he reached the Union, he flung a glass of *aguardiente* down his throat, then another, and another. He did not stop until his senses blurred and welcome oblivion enveloped him.

22

When he came to, he was lying face down upon sheets that smelt of vomit. His tongue felt thick and rough in his mouth. When he raised his head, it throbbed with such violence he thought his eyeballs might burst. He rolled slowly on to his back, and studied the cracked ceiling, his mind swimming.

With agonising slowness, his conscious mind began to come to shore, scraping against something solid. Grain by grain, the thing grew, taking shape finally into the horrible memory of what he had learned before he got drunk. He did not hesitate. He rolled off the bed and staggered down the stairs, ignoring the explosions set off in his head by each step.

The bar of the Union was empty, but for the bartender, who sold him a bottle of whiskey without question. He trailed back upstairs, clutching it by the neck, like a club. He took three long swigs, which burned his scraped throat, fired through his empty stomach and seeped into his bloodstream. Then he lay back, taking occasional swigs, until everything grew cloudy and he passed out once more.

Later he became dimly aware of voices, figures about him, violence being perpetrated upon his person. He fought, vaguely. A muffled blow removed him from the proceedings. Then he was in darkness; something was over his face; he felt the sickening jolt of a wagon.

When he awoke again, there was flickering light everywhere. He put his hand up to shield his eyes. A breeze stroked his face. There was the sound of bells. Blinking, he forced himself to focus, and saw leaves above him, shimmering in the wind, their movement dappling his face with light. The bells crystallised into the calls of birds, far too loud. He rolled sideways and dry-heaved. He could smell a fire. Swivelling his eyes toward his feet, he was able to locate it. Kusox and Robinson were there. He opened his mouth to speak, but all he could get out was a moan. Robinson turned to him, then back to Kusox. Why did they not come to him? After what felt like an age, Kusox rose, knelt next to him and offered him water. He took a sip and blearily enquired where they were.

'That place would have killed you,' Kusox said. 'You had to come back to the land to get well.'

'Drink?' he asked. Kusox passed him the canteen again. 'No. *Drink.*'

'We don't have any,' Kusox replied.

'Get some.'

'No.' Kusox shook his head.

John Evert glared at him. 'How far are we from town?'

'A long way. Forget about that place. We will stay here until you are well.'

Fury rose in John Evert's breast and he writhed around to strike Kusox, who got to his feet lazily, easily avoiding John Evert's fists. 'You son-of-a-bitch!' John Evert spat.

Kusox shook his head, revulsion curling his lip. 'No more drink for you.' He turned on his heel and left.

Realising there was no hope of what he wanted so badly, and no longer with any shield, John Evert rolled into a ball and rocked himself as he had not done since he was a boy.

He must have fallen asleep for when he next opened his eyes it was dark. The light of the fire reflected in rippling waves off the overhanging canopy of leaves. He tried to move his hands but could not. When he looked down, he found his wrists were tied.

Kusox sat cross-legged in front of the fire, with his back to John Evert. Robinson was by his side, partly obscured, but when Kusox moved, John Evert saw her face. She looked anxious, her expression drawn. Kusox rose and came toward John Evert, carrying a bowl. He took a seat by John Evert and with a small spoon scooped up some thick sludge from the bowl. 'You have to eat this,' he said.

'What is it?'

'It doesn't matter. Either you eat it or I make you eat it.'

John Evert turned his head away defiantly. Kusox clamped a hand upon John Evert's forehead, and swung his legs across his stomach, pressing them down heavily so that John Evert opened his mouth to complain. As he did so, Kusox shoved the paste into his mouth, and moved his hand from John Evert's forehead to cover his mouth. The stuff was utterly foul and acrid, and John Evert moaned loudly in disgust. He wriggled but he could not move his arms, pinned as they were beneath Kusox's legs. He wailed behind Kusox's hand, and began to cough and splutter through his nose as the noxious paste mixed with his saliva and began to trickle into the back of his throat. He gagged and began to choke.

Desperately, he sought Kusox's eyes, but Kusox simply stared out into the darkness, as though something important held his attention. John Evert had no choice but to begin to swallow the paste. His stomach turned at the vileness as he forced it down. Kusox only removed his hand when John Evert's mouth filled with vomit, and he spewed his guts out onto the ground at his side.

To his disbelief, when he was done, Kusox loaded him up again. Bewildered, John Evert snatched a glance at the fire. Robinson had her face in her hands. That was when he became frightened, and in his fear he stopped complaining and did as he was bid. Eventually, Kusox ceased force feeding him. He had a few moments respite before he seemed to detach from where he was, became weightless and lifted into some other place. That was when the hell began.

He was assaulted by terrifying dreams. Hundreds of faces appeared to him, in quick succession, hideous to behold. Men he had known and seen killed on the battlefield, their twisted, mutilated faces falling in upon him as though he were being buried alive. It was monstrous. He awoke shouting.

His eyes sought the fire, in the hope of an ally. Robinson was there, sitting with a blanket around her shoulders, watching him.

'Robinson,' he called to her. 'Untie me, will you? Please.'

She ignored him, turning her back.

'Please,' John Evert begged. When he called to her again, she threw the blanket from her shoulders and walked away, into the darkness, where he could no longer see her.

He was sweating like a pig and began to feel feverish. He could hardly tell whether he was awake or asleep. One moment he was in a furnace, scorched by the flames about him; the next he passed under a waterfall and coolness flooded him, from his head to his feet, and he shivered. Then, all of a sudden, he was in a snow-scape, virgin and perfect. He was aware of his breath misting in the crisp air. His teeth chattered – it was that cold. A man was there, some way off, in the snow, walking away from him. It was Bill, and his heart turned over in relief at finding him there. He tried to follow him and, as he did so, he noticed that Bill's foot-steps did not break the snow. He called his name, but Bill paid him no mind. He did his best to chase after him, to keep up, but he was too slow, the snow getting deeper and deeper, thicker, until he was pinioned in it, unable to move another step. He fell forward.

When he was able to raise his head once more, there was a house ahead of him, rising up out of the snow. He was able to drag himself up the steps and stand. He put his hand upon the latch. There was something familiar about it. He opened the door, and silhouetted black against a snow-backed window was his mother. His breath caught in his throat. Then the floor of the house gave way, and he was falling, falling to the bottom of the earth, screaming.

Later, he was by the fire once more, and Robinson was at his side. She looked into his face. All his muscles were tense. He shook and twitched as though a snake had bitten him.

'What's happening?' he asked desperately.

She cupped his cheek with her hand, her eyes alarmed. 'I don't know,' she said. She spoke into the darkness beyond his head. 'Can't we untie him?' But it was too late, for he was sucked backward, away from her, into the darkness.

Mutilated soldiers crawled over him. Then it was night, and Indians appeared, hundreds of them, firing burning arrows, so many in number that they set the whole sky aflame. Somewhere behind them all, he saw his oak tree, but it was blackened and burned and stood in an empty wasteland. It juddered in his sight, as though the earth beneath it quaked. He cried out a good deal. He begged her for help, and somehow, in the darkness, he knew she was still there at his side.

The insinuating voice, the one he kept silent with liquor, visited him shamelessly now – 'Nothing to live for . . .' it whispered '. . . Nothing to live for.'

He was letting go, surrendering himself to the flames, when a small voice said, 'What about me?' He turned to his side and Robinson was there, in the nightmare with him.

'What are you doing here?' he asked.

'I don't know,' she said. He reached for her hand, but as he did so she began to melt before his eyes and turn to water. He tried desperately to catch her, but she slipped through his fingers, and turned into a lake. He, meanwhile, went back into the flames.

He awoke. It was day. His dog lay near him, watching him attentively. Unsure if it was real or a dream he did not call to it. He put his hand to his face and his person. His beard was thick; his stomach so concave it was halfway to his backbone. His mouth tasted bitter.

Kusox came and sat on his haunches next to him. They looked at each other, John Evert afraid to speak.

'You're awake,' Kusox said, answering the question in John Evert's mind.

John Evert sat up gingerly. They were by a stream, with willows lining the banks. The sunlight danced upon the water's surface.

'How long have we been here?' John Evert mumbled.

'Five days.'

'I've been asleep all that time?'

'No. You've been awake most of it – fighting.'

'With what?'

'With yourself.'

John Evert spat roundly. 'Ugh, my mouth. It's disgusting. What was that stuff?'

'Peyote.'

'What's that?'

'A plant.'

'I've seen some strange things, Kusox.'

He nodded. 'They're gone now. You live.'

John Evert blinked. 'My mother is dead.'

'Yes, but you are alive. And so are we. It's time to take back your land, for all of us.'

'Kusox,' John Evert said, putting his closed fist to the other man's knee. 'Thank you.'

'Don't thank me. Thank her.' He gestured over his shoulder toward where the remains of the fire lay in an ashy heap, still smoking gently. 'She found the peyote, not me.'

John Evert raised his eyebrows. He felt light inside after his purge, with a vague notion that there had been a huge, filthy weight sitting inside him, which, now that he had faced it, had been vanquished, leaving behind emptiness and a space for hope, perhaps.

He had felt it all: the bone-crunching guilt about his mother, his failure, yet one of the clearest visions during those strange, twisted nightmares had been of her. She had said nothing, only smiled, but her expression had been so beatific that he had known for certain that she was well. The last thing he remembered from his dreams was that the trees around him had come to life, bending down and embracing him. It was the most powerful communion he had ever experienced, and it had been with the land he loved more profoundly than he had even suspected. This was something to live for.

He stood and brushed his fingertips along the soft grasses that touched his thighs. He walked to the stream and watched the sunlight's revelry upon its surface. He took off his breeches and waded in, shutting his eyes in bliss as the cool water eddied around him. He became aware of how sweat-tacked he was, that he must stink, so he stripped and bathed, the water velvet to his skin.

He was still damp from the water, his clothes catching upon him, when he walked back to the camp. He wanted very much to see Robinson, but he was also shy, wondering what he might have said or done in those long days and nights. She was seated by the edge of the stream and he wondered if she felt the same bashfulness, for she did not meet his eye. But he was aware that, when he looked away from her to speak to Kusox, she studied his face.

When they were alone, he said, 'Where did you find that stuff? How did you know—'

'I bought it from a man in town. Every big place you go there's someone who can sell you anything you want,' she replied.

'You've used it before.'

'No. Never. But he said sometimes it's good for folks who've given up so I thought we'd try it. We didn't have anything to lose.'

'Weren't you worried it—'

'You're alive ain't you,' she snapped, but he could see she was trembling slightly.

'I saw you, you know.'

'I been here all the time,' she said.

'No, I mean in my dreams.'

'It was frightening,' she said, digging the toe of her boot into the dirt, 'watching you.'

'I'm sorry.'

She put up a hand to shade her eyes from the sun, and squinted at him. 'You won't touch no liquor no more.'

'I guess not.'

'That's not enough. You have to promise.'

'I promise.'

The three sat by the stream, in the shade of a willow, to discuss what they should do next. John Evert no longer felt as though he was in charge, if he ever had been: the crazed doings of the last five days seemed to have levelled their little band into a true democracy, and he was glad of it.

'There's enough money for us to leave here and buy land someplace else,' Robinson said.

'I don't want other land. I want my land,' John Evert said. 'I won't go on running. I may go to jail. I may be hanged.' Catching sight of her expression, he added, 'But I think that's unlikely. I have to try, though. Do you see?'

Kusox nodded his understanding. She frowned at the water.

'Why don't you and Kusox get out of here?' he said. 'I'll split Bill's money with you and you can buy your own land, if you want it.'

'An Indian can't buy land. You know that,' Kusox said. 'The only chance of land for me is if I'm with you.'

'I guess that's you settled then,' John Evert said.

Robinson chewed her thumb viciously, then locked eyes with Kusox, John Evert noticed, before nodding reluctantly.

They were riding along the short bends of a dry riverbed when they stumbled upon a group of Paiute. Some were mounted while others were on foot. The women wore long tunics that reached all the way to the ground, and around their brows were leather straps, which supported large water gourds held at their backs. They stopped dead at the sight of the three riders, who also drew up short. They all surveyed each other. There was obviously some confusion on the Paiute side at the sight of Kusox riding with a white man and woman, but some unspoken signs must have made clear eventually that they were not aggressive, for the Paiute women dropped their eyes earthward and walked on to pass them by. Those on horseback followed single file, giving the three of them a wide berth. Several, particularly the younger ones, watched the little party warily. After hesitating a while, John Evert raised a hand to them in greeting but not one acknowledged it.

As the last of the horses passed, Kusox looked back at John Evert. 'You see? Pintos.' He laughed at his own joke.

'Do you want to go talk to them?' John Evert asked.

Kusox stiffened. 'What for?' he asked, incredulous. 'What are *they* to me?' His head was thrown back slightly, the furious symmetry of his brows proudly raised.

John Evert supposed Kusox was right: they were as different as John Evert had been from Orville. 'Nothing,' John Evert said.

Kusox rode ahead of him, aloof, his back and shoulders tanned dark by the sun, his long hair, a black flag, unfurling triumphant in the breeze.

'He likes you, you know,' Robinson said, bringing the roan up alongside John Evert's grey.

'You think?' John Evert said. 'I say the wrong thing a lot. I annoy him.'

'That's just his way,' she said. 'He likes you.'

'Why do you think so?'

''Cause you tell the truth,' she said. 'You do what you say you're gonna do. You know how rare that is?' She scratched her cheek and then her nose absentmindedly.

'You look like a squirrel when you do that,' he said. Her gaze flicked to his face and she reddened slightly. He smiled at her. She looked away and made a point of keeping her hands on her reins. 'Well, he sure likes you,' he said, wanting to fill the sudden awkward silence between them.

She cast him a startled glance, which made things clear to him.

'And you like him,' John Evert said, feeling melancholy as he said it, although not knowing why.

She did not say another word and he figured he must have embarrassed her. After a while, she kicked the roan on a little so that it strode out ahead of the grey. John Evert let her ride on ahead, leaving him behind.

He struggled to untangle his feelings. He had a notion of being excluded by the two of them somehow, and it saddened him. But he chastised himself: it was perfectly likely that he would forfeit his freedom when he returned to Los Angeles and, that being the case, who was he to stand in the way of something between her and Kusox? He determined to put his feelings to one side, but he did not do it without a pang.

He looked back over his shoulder. The band of Paiute was invisible now, hidden by the vegetation of the river bends, but he thought on them, and upon something that had been nagging at him. What could his mother have meant when she said that she was not with the men who had raided the ranch? Who had she been with and why? He must find it out, then go, of course, to her grave and bring her home. He felt something upon his face and raised a hand, only to find tears streaking his cheeks. In that moment, he was glad the other two were far ahead and he was alone.

23

The first thing John Evert did upon their return to Los Angeles was to take his uniform to be cleaned, after which he paid a visit to a barber. If he was to meet his judgement, the least he could do was face it presentable.

The barber tutted as he cut away the matted length of John Evert's beard, then got to work with his cut-throat razor, first stropping it enthusiastically upon a piece of leather. When, with a flourish, the man flicked a mirror in front of him, he was taken aback by his reflection. His eyes were bright as spring grass against his tanned face, the lower part of which was paler due to the shade of his beard; the kink in his nose was not so severe; and while the scar to his mouth might have ruined its symmetry, it put something not unhappy in its place.

'Very good, sir,' the barber said, to the promising reflection. 'I expect you'll be going to that ball tonight, sir.'

John Evert's gaze swung up to the reflection of the man standing at his shoulder. 'That's right,' he said slowly. 'Can you remind me where it's to be held?'

'Don Carlos's hacienda on Aliso Street, of course. Those Ramones girls'll be a picture, I'll warrant.'

Several hours later, when John Evert walked down Main Street in his clean uniform, with polished boots and his sabre at his yellow-sashed side, he did not fail to notice the number of female eyes that flickered in his direction.

Robinson was unmoved by his transformation, seeming lost in her own serious thoughts. He asked her whether she would like to come to a ball. She replied that she would sooner have a tooth pulled. John Evert was sorry, for while there was nothing to be done about her broken fingernails and cussing, the haughty curve of her neck as she turned away from him would have shamed the finest lady in Los Angeles.

He was not sure why he wanted to go, except that he was inquisitive, and he had a notion that this might be his first and last chance to do such a thing before he turned himself in. He had been to fandangos with Bill, but a ball and a fandango were not the same thing. A fandango was a free-for-all, attended by gamblers and cow-punchers, with music from the guitar and flageolet, and the ladies of society never attended; a ball was invitation only. To attend a ball without an invitation was not the done thing, but John Evert was banking upon the fact that no one would expect such cheek.

This proved correct, for when he crossed the threshold of the gracious mansion on Aliso Street that evening, none thought to enquire whether or how he was acquainted with Don Carlos Ramones, the host.

The company was many and mixed. He heard Spanish, English, and many accents of each, and watched with interest as various men of business and two resplendently bedecked black men led ladies about the polished dancefloor with great aplomb. The ladies were dressed very fine, with full bell gowns in every colour of silk, the bodices displaying smooth shoulders framed with ruffles, bows and flounces. John Evert's uniform drew undisguised attention; the sentiments of Los Angeles as a whole had been with the South, but its citizens were not the kind to place politics above bravery. He was quickly taken up by two young Spaniards, who were keen to hear of his experiences in battle.

John Evert maintained the courteous manner he had learned under Colonel Ewing's stewardship. How trusting these fine folk were, he thought, when he might draw his Colt at any time, but the hospitality of Don Carlos was baronial, and wine flowed liberally, and while John Evert did not partake of the liquor – the thought of doing so aroused a great guilt in him – he entered into the spirit of the event.

It was at that moment that he caught sight, over the heads and shoulders around him, of Phineas Gunn. For John Evert, the room went still.

Gunn was attired in a swallowtail jacket, which hung uneasily from his angular person, as though the coat hook had accidentally been left within. He looked mighty pleased with himself, with two high spots of colour in his otherwise whey-coloured face, his sausage lips curled in a smirk. At his side hovered a mousy, obedient woman. The way she gazed at Gunn, and the way he ignored her, put John Evert in mind that she might be his wife.

He began to walk toward them, but a rotund Spaniard, his oiled hair gleaming, came between him and his goal. '*Buenas noches*,' said the man, extending his hand.

'*Buenas noches*,' John Evert replied, returning the firm handshake.

'It is a curious thing – I am in the habit of being familiar with the guests of my house,' the man said, his tone friendly.

'Don Carlos, I apologise,' John Evert said humbly, 'I am the guest of your daughter.'

'Ah, of course,' the Don said, with an indulgent smile, his eyes seeking and alighting upon a dark beauty in pink at the other side of the room. Sensing her father's eyes upon her, she turned and her eye caught John Evert's. She held it proudly, her head high, confident in her own splendour.

'May I introduce Mr and Mrs Gunn?' the Don asked, turning toward them, having ascertained John Evert's intention, but Gunn had already moved away. His wife curtsied rapidly, embarrassed, and turned to follow her husband. The Don was swirled away by other guests, and John Evert was left alone.

The Ramones girl was still looking at him. To her obvious astonishment, rather than going to pay his respects to her, he merely inclined his head and turned to follow the Gunns.

He followed them at a distance, and waited until Phineas was engaged in conversation, and his wife alone, before he moved casually to her side where she stood at the edge of the floor, watching the dancers.

John Evert studied her profile, before asking, 'Would you like to dance, Mrs Gunn?'

'Oh, heavens, no,' she replied, flustered, and then, looking askance at him, 'You don't want to dance with an old woman such as me.'

'In truth, I cannot find so much to say to these new friends of mine,' he gestured at the young Spaniards behind them, laughing among themselves.

'But you cannot be more than twenty,' she said. 'Such assemblies as these are for you, but, forgive me,' she countered, 'you are a soldier. We can only wonder at the things you have seen.'

John Evert liked her then, and held out his hand for her to take, which, after much deliberation, she did, and they moved to the floor, where John Evert was grateful to Bill for having taught him how to dance.

Afterward, he found her a seat, and brought her a glass of punch. 'Your husband does not care to dance?' he asked.

'Phineas? Oh, no,' she said, with a quick shake of her head. 'He thinks it silly.' She seemed suddenly concerned. 'In fact, I should . . .' And there Gunn was, at the other side of the room, eyeing her and tapping his pocket watch. John Evert stared at him, heat pooling in his guts, but Gunn did not appear to recognise him.

'Are you staying in town?' Mrs Gunn asked, as though desperate to prolong the moment.

'At present,' he said, 'but I plan to return to a property I own on the way to Anaheim.'

'Really?' she said, getting to her feet. 'We live in that direction also. Will you . . .' Glancing again at her husband's impatient gestures, her face fell and she made her excuses, then left John Evert's side.

He watched them go.

A moment later, the chair at his side was occupied once more, by the Ramones girl in pink. Sensing trouble, John Evert drew a breath to speak, but she cut across him. 'I understand that I invited you this evening,' she said pertly. 'What is my name?'

She ended his awkward silence by murmuring, 'Jacinta,' and holding her hand imperiously in the air between them so that he might lead her to the dancefloor.

It was very late, almost dawn, by the time he made it back to the Union.

As he was trying to enter his room, as quietly as he could, he heard another door open. He turned to see Robinson standing on her threshold, clutching a candle. She was fully dressed. 'Everything all right?' he asked.

She looked him up and down with a perplexed expression. He followed her gaze to his shoulder and saw that he was covered with tiny pieces of coloured paper from the *cascarones*, the empty egg shells that the women had broken over the men's heads at the ball's close. He could not know her feelings, but she seemed unhappy. 'It's—'

Without a word, she closed the door softly in his face.

He stared at the wood, leaned forward, rested his forehead upon it a moment and sighed.

The next day, they whipped about purchasing supplies and rode for the ranch. John Evert took them by a back route, so that they might approach via the woods. He needed neither sign nor border post to know the moment that the grey stepped upon his land.

'This is it,' he said. He knew Robinson and Kusox were watching him, but he had eyes only for the trees, the path he knew so well, and he travelled ahead in his mind to where the trail would open out into the pasture. They rode in silence, single file, until the land spread out before them, and there they paused, the three of them, in the shade of the treeline, to gaze upon the golden pasture where it swooped away from them into a broad valley, then up again to the treeline far on the other side. Ground water swelled to the surface in that pasture, giving rise to particularly lush green grass, and cattle meandered across it, heads to the ground. Overhead, two turkey buzzards wheeled in concentric circles on the warm air currents. It was beautiful and his heart sang for it.

Robinson broke the silence first. 'This is it?'

He nodded, and turned to them to see the land he loved through their eyes, and it was wonderful.

'Let's go down to the river,' he said. They wound their way up and down, over the further hill, and descended to the river, which looped across the land like a silver wire in the light of the sun. They stood on its banks, gazing into the water, and the light sparkled off it, making merry with dancing ripples.

'Kusox, I figured you could have a stretch north of here,' he said. 'The grazing there is not so good for cattle but the deer favour it and it's best for hunting.'

Kusox brought his dun pony to John Evert, so their horses stood nose to tail and the two men were facing each other. John Evert admired how tall Kusox sat in the saddle, the obvious thrill in him at this verdant land and the prospect of part of it being his, and John Evert was so very glad then that Kusox had come all this way with him.

Kusox frowned. 'But I did not earn it. I did not help you find your mother. I was not able to do what was asked of me. I didn't keep my part of the bargain.'

'You earned it,' John Evert said. 'You earned it a long time ago.'

Kusox studied his face. Then he held up his open fist, and John Evert took it. They squeezed each other's hands hard, and Kusox broke into a huge grin, let out a cry, spun the dun pony around and charged it right into the river, to the deepest part, and there dived headlong over the pony's neck into the water.

Robinson shrieked in delight and she and John Evert kicked their horses in after him. John Evert plunged into the water, which closed softly around him. He opened his eyes underwater and saw only light and bubbles. It was pure delight.

They horsed around in the water for a while, then pulled themselves together and got serious.

They made their way silently back through the woods a long way, and around to a spot in the treeline where they might watch the ranch house undetected. The place seemed deserted, but as dusk began to fall two men rode in from the east. They unsaddled their horses and led them into the barn, then entered the house.

Night fell, and the moonlight was bright enough to illuminate the stoop, and a man's shadowy shape as he sat there smoking. The irony of being camped out in his own woods, with an Indian, studying the ranch with a view to seizing it, was not lost upon John Evert.

'Do we take them now?' Kusox asked.

'No, not now. We'll wait till dawn when they ride out. There's to be no bloodshed – it would look bad for us.' He sensed Kusox's confusion in the darkness. 'Don't worry,' he added. 'There's to be a fight, just a different kind, that's all.'

They drew back from their look-out point, and hid themselves in a dip, away from any canopy that might reflect light, and made a fire.

Later, after they had eaten, Kusox took ash from the fire, mixed it into a black paste with grease and smeared it all around his eyes in a straight black band. The effect when he was done was as though he wore a black blindfold. He went to the dun pony and, using his fingers and palms, he covered its flanks and face in black patterns and handprints.

'Why's he doing that?' Robinson asked John Evert.

'I guess because he goes to battle,' he replied.

'You're going to battle too,' she said. 'You should do it.'

He looked down at her, astonished.

'We all fight together now,' she said, meeting his gaze evenly.

She was right. He deliberated a moment or two, then went to Kusox, who sat cross-legged by the fire once more.

'Do it to me too,' he said. Kusox looked up at him, not understanding. 'The paint,' he said.

Kusox was surprised, but when he went to add more ashes to

his mixing bowl John Evert could tell from his movements that he was pleased.

John Evert sat with his eyes firmly closed as Kusox painted a black band around them. When he was done, John Evert took the bowl, went to the grey and painted three long stripes along its haunches on both sides. He went to its face and drew black circles around its eyes. As he did so, a vision of the white-painted man on the white horse from the night of the raid all those years ago came to him. He stopped what he was doing. Something was gesturing dimly at him from deep in the darkness of his mind, something important. He concentrated hard but it was just out of sight.

He jumped at a touch at his shoulder. It was Robinson. 'Sorry,' she said. 'I didn't mean to—'

The light from the fire highlighted the angles of her face, her fine bone structure. He put out a finger, and dashed two black lines along her sharp cheekbones, which made her giggle.

The three lay as dark mounds upon the ground, gun-metal grey in the moonlight, and shivered in the cool of the night, as the grass rustled about them. John Evert found it impossible to sleep, and by the occasional noises he could hear coming from Robinson's direction, he suspected she was awake as well.

'Are you awake?' he whispered to her.

'Yeah. I'm cold,' she replied.

'Come here,' he said.

She wriggled over to him and he pulled her into the curve of his body, and bunched his knees up behind hers, so they lay like a pair of spoons until they warmed each other and slept.

At dawn, John Evert was awake and watching the house, smoking a *cigarrito* and sipping bitter cold coffee from a canteen. The two men emerged, saddled up their horses from the barn and made to go about their day's business.

Once they were out of sight, the three walked up to the ranch house and took possession.

As it had been the last time he had seen it, the new house was barely furnished, but it was well-made and warm. He made a thorough search of the place, pushing aside the memories that fluttered against him insistently, like butterflies awakened after a long winter. He gathered up the meagre personal possessions he found, walked them out a couple of hundred yards from the stoop, and placed them in a neat pile upon the ground for when Gunn's men returned.

He visited the new barn, and found all in good order. He also found another horse. He turned it loose from its box, stabled the grey and the roan in its place, and made them comfortable with water and oats. 'This'll be home now,' he said. The grey lay down and rolled, then got back to its feet, shaking from end to end to rid itself of the straw.

He returned to the house, where Robinson was unpacking their provisions, placing them upon a shelf, then moving them around. Her movements were jerky and he could tell she was worried. She wiped a surface with her finger and held it up. 'You want me to clean this place?' she asked, pushing her hair out of her face with the back of her hand. 'It's dusty.'

'You don't have to go to work.'

'I gotta do something,' she said, her voice thrumming with anxiety.

'Okay,' he said, 'I'll help you.' He wondered why he did not share her worry. Perhaps it was something to do with being home. He felt steady, becalmed, the sense of belonging growing up from the ground, like a vine furling itself around his legs and holding him steady.

Robinson had thought to put soap and lye and other useful things into the provisions they had bought, and now she set about scrubbing the place. She was no idler. John Evert wondered if she might take the grain right off the wooden shelves. Whatever she was scrubbing away, no speck was to remain. He tried to help her, but it was obvious he was doing little more than getting in her way.

The morning light was doing its best to filter through the grimy windows, and she set about those, too, until the house reeked of vinegar and white light filled the room.

The dust she was raising set John Evert to sneezing, so he went outside. Kusox was putting up a tent behind the house. He had never had much time for sleeping indoors. John Evert watched him work, and was mighty glad to have him there. But Kusox was still only one man, and there were only so many times one man could fire a gun.

Gunn's men returned mid-afternoon. They spotted their possessions piled in front of the house and the loose horse outside the barn. John Evert sat alone in the chair on the stoop, his dog lying at his feet.

'What's this?' one of the men called out.

John Evert stood. He had washed his face of his war paint and donned his uniform once more: full dress coat and sash, with his sabre at his side. 'I will save you a long speech,' he said. 'I am John Evert Burn, the legal owner of this property. I thank Phineas Gunn for his stewardship, but I am now returned. If there is any query as to my identity, you may visit my attorney Hector Featherstone, in Los Angeles, who will attest to it. In the meantime, I will have no compunction in shooting any squatters I find upon my land.'

His appearance and speech were enough to convince Gunn's men. They gathered up their things with no opposition. He gave them both a shot of the *aguardiente* he had found in the house, then handed them the bottle. 'You'll need it before you give Gunn this news, I expect,' he said.

The two men took their leave, and walked their horses away, one turning back in his saddle to look at John Evert.

After they had gone, John Evert threw off his coat and retrieved Robinson from the soap suds inside. She came out on the stoop with him, wiping her hands on her trousers. He handed her a gun. 'Do you know how to use this?' She shook her head. 'Kusox will show you.'

She swallowed, but he knew she would have no fear to use the piece when the time came.

That night they dined well on roast pigeon that Kusox cooked over an open fire. Robinson had baked bread. John Evert wanted to ask who had taught her to cook, but he knew she would not tell him. She was like a wiped slate, upon which so much had been written, none of which was ever allowed to remain. He wanted so much to know her, but doubted he would.

When they had finished eating, and were sitting by the fire, he said, 'Tomorrow, men will come for me. I will be arrested.'

She picked at her fingernails and gazed into the flames. Kusox smoked his pipe and looked at him. 'Your job,' John Evert said, 'is to protect the place until I get back.'

'You will go to fight for the land,' Kusox said.

'Yes, but not with a gun. I have to go fight in court. If I win, I'll come back. If I lose, I won't. If I don't return, you must make your way out of here. I'll tell you where Bill's gold is. You may not be able to buy land but Robinson can. She'll look out for you and you'll look out for her. Right?'

John Evert looked at her where she sat cross-legged in front of the fire, staring into its heart. It would be good for them to be together. He would have no need to worry for her if she was with Kusox.

He turned back to Kusox, and they considered each other in silence a while, until Kusox said, 'All right.'

When the fire died down, Kusox went to his tent. John Evert went to the chair on the stoop to smoke. He leaned forward, resting his forearms on the rail that ran along the front. He crossed his hands at the wrist, and stared at the tip of his *cigarrito*, which burned fractured orange against the blackness. The crickets were noisy. Somewhere an owl's voice trembled. The breeze brought the smell of hot earth and tinder grass. He shut his eyes and breathed deep.

The door opened and he heard Robinson's soft tread. She went to stand further down the rail from him. They did not say anything for a while.

'I don't want you to go,' she said finally.

'I don't have a choice.'

She came over to where he sat, and perched lightly upon the arm of his chair. He rested his arm along her legs, his hand on her knee. After a while, she put her hand on top of his. He turned his upside-down, and locked fingers with her. It felt very good, holding her hand, in the dark, as the breeze moved across the land.

After she left him, he sat for a long time on the stoop before turning in. He lay in the dark, wide awake. When the door to his room opened, he turned his head in the pitch black.

'Don't say nothing,' she said, as she got into the bed. He folded her into his arms. The touch of her body against his was so charged he felt as though he had been kicked in the loins by a horse.

When he awoke the next morning, he felt as though he had been asleep for all of five minutes. There was only empty space where she had lain. He stayed there a while, lying on his side, looking at the imprint she had left behind. Finally, he dressed and went outside.

She was there, with Kusox, who nodded at his greeting. She did not meet his eye, and went off toward the barn. He was surprised to find himself blushing. Did she regret it? There was unexpected torment in the thought, but he had no time to reflect upon it – a dust cloud was rising from the road to the east.

When the riders juddered to a lathered halt in front of the house, they consisted of Gunn, several of his men and a marshal, whom John Evert did not recognise. John Evert no longer wore his uniform, but simple farm clothes. Gunn, who sat a large bay horse, scanned his face intently. It was clear that Gunn recognised him now. The man was struggling to hide his guilt and alarm.

'John Evert Burn,' he said. 'Back again. I thought intelligence ran in your family, but I see I was wrong.'

'I'd say everything you ever thought was wrong,' John Evert replied. 'Good day, Marshal,' he added.

The marshal, surprised by John Evert's affability, touched his hat brim. 'My name is Austin,' he said.

'Is Marshal Randall no longer in authority here?' John Evert asked.

'We lost him to the typhus a couple of years back.'

'I am sorry to hear that,' John Evert said, with genuine regret.

'When we've finished with the pleasantries,' said Gunn, 'we are here to arrest you.'

'The marshal is here to arrest me but you are not,' John Evert corrected him. 'You are here in the hope of retaining illegal possession of my property.

'Marshal,' John Evert addressed him, 'I shall come with you with no fuss, on the condition that my workers remain in custody of my property until I am either convicted or released. Whatever Mr Gunn may have told you, the title deeds of this property are in my name, and are lodged in the office of Hector Featherstone in Los Angeles.'

Gunn looked over John Evert's shoulder at Kusox, heavily armed and appearing particularly murderous, and Robinson, who stood at his side, with a rifle held awkwardly in one hand. A range of emotions played across his face. Among them was fear, John Evert was sure of it, and he wondered why that should be when Kusox was but one man and Gunn had so many at his side. 'Strange company you keep,' was all Gunn said, before falling into a low conversation with the marshal.

John Evert noted the marshal's emphatic gestures, the repeated shaking of his head in response to whatever it was Gunn said. Finally the two men stopped speaking. 'Gather your necessities,' the marshal told John Evert. 'The other two may remain here for the time being.'

Gunn scowled and jabbed his horse in the mouth so it threw its head up and danced on the spot.

'Will someone saddle the grey in the barn for me?' John Evert said over his shoulder, as he went back inside and collected the saddlebag he had made ready. He walked quickly through the house, looking neither right nor left, for fear of what he might feel.

Back on the stoop, he bade Kusox farewell, with a nod and a weighty glance. Robinson had moved to the other end of the stoop and stood with her back to him, so he walked off the step into the bright sunlight without bidding her farewell.

He had his foot in the stirrup to mount when he heard the sound of running feet behind him and a voice saying, 'Wait.'

He took his foot out of the stirrup and faced her. Her mouth was a crumpled line.

'Here,' she said. She withdrew something from her pocket and put it into John Evert's hand. He looked down. It was Bill's Texas Ranger badge. He stroked the bright surface with his thumb. He had wondered what had happened to it – he had not found it among Bill's possessions after this death. John Evert tightened his fist around it, his throat constricted.

'It's lucky, I think,' she said.

Whether she had stolen it or been given it, he did not ask. It no longer seemed to matter. He reached out, took hold of her chin, tilted it upward and smiled at her. She turned away to hide her face.

And, with that, he was gone, his dog, chained in the barn, howling after his ghost.

24

Hector paced around John Evert's cell, his hands clasped behind his back. 'Why did you not come to me first?' he asked.

'I knew you would advise against it,' John Evert replied, from where he sat upon the end of the narrow bed.

'You are right. I would have. I will not pretend that you have made a wise decision in returning in this fashion or in taking possession of the ranch as you did. I understand your reasons for doing so, of course, but you know you may forfeit your freedom for ever, if not your life.'

'I know it.'

Hector stared at the floor, then looked up. 'Well,' he said, 'now that we find ourselves thrown into the arena, there is naught we can do but fight.'

Hector was treating him differently from how he had years before. John Evert was no longer a boy, but he figured it also had a lot to do with the fact that he had led men into battle. Hector might have been able to whip up a storm out of words alone, but John Evert knew he now possessed a quiet authority. Clearly Hector felt it, too.

Strangely, he enjoyed being with Hector, even though they met in prison; when he was in Hector's company, he was focused, even optimistic. The hours when Hector was not with him were not so good.

The claustrophobia he felt in the tiny space was severe. He thought constantly of the ranch, of Robinson and Kusox, and wondered what they did. There was so much riding on the outcome of his forthcoming trial, for all of them, and he felt the weight of responsibility. He was surprised by how often his thoughts turned to Robinson. The memory of their night together was intense. How many times had she lain with a man? Who had they been? Had it ever been of her own accord before? The questions tormented him.

Strange as it might sound, it was birds that saved him. A pair of fat, lazy doves would patrol the roof edge of a morning, and he took to leaving crumbs of the stale bread he was fed upon the high sill of his barred window. They were nervous at first, flapping away unless he remained completely still while they nervously pecked up the crumbs, but with patience, he persuaded them of his benignity. The female was always shy, but he and the male were soon on speaking terms. His heart lightened whenever he heard their throaty cooing.

He tried hard not to consider his future if the outcome of the trial was bad for him. He could be hanged, but the idea of death was not frightening: what he feared was a long incarceration, locked away from the land. Whether during peace or war, the majority of his days had been spent in the open air. For him, a life behind bars would be no life at all. He supposed that, if it came down to it, he would stage a break-out, and ensure it went badly and get himself shot in the process. It would be easy to do. It was not the first time he had thought about his own death, but this was the first time he had done so reluctantly. He found that, despite everything, he wanted to live.

The day of his trial dawned. He dressed in his uniform with great care. Hector had been keen on this, telling him, 'Your exemplary military career will make clear your true character.'

'What about the fact I served under Bill and he taught me all I know about soldiering?'

'Whatever else he may have done, Bill was a decorated and heroic soldier.'

Cyrus Lyne was prosecuting attorney and was pleased to be so, for Bill's case and escape remained a tale of renown. The rangers who had arrested Bill so many years before had been called back, but Ranger Colbert had been killed in the war, while the other, O'Donnell, made plain his irritation at being called to trial when the man he had chased for so long was dead. Such obstacles were of no interest to Judge Ogier, however: the law was the law, and it would have its day.

The jury studied John Evert suspiciously. They knew his story, or believed they did, and prejudices ran deep and strong in Los Angeles, but there were sympathetic faces about the court, too: the old pipe-smokers were there, spectating like owls; Quincy and one of his men from the *Star*, which had already made clear its position with a whipped-up leader piece in John Evert's favour; and Don Carlos Ramones's daughter, Jacinta, cast him a soulful look when he happened to cast his eye at the public gallery.

Cyrus Lyne opened for the prosecution and laid out the charges against John Evert: his role as Bill's accomplice, his break from jail and subsequent flight from Los Angeles.

The first prosecution witness was Phineas Gunn. He took the stand, and sat, bony and erect, as he attested to the wilful young-ster that John Evert had been, and to the day John Evert had set his dog upon Gunn's men and shot at one of them. 'It was no surprise to me to hear that John Evert Burn had fallen in with a man such as William Adair-Wilson,' Gunn said. 'From his earliest years, Burn has shown a love of violence.'

Then it was Hector's turn to cross-examine Gunn.

'Mr Gunn. Take us back to the day when John Evert Burn encountered your men upon his ranch. You were there to witness this encounter?' Hector asked.

'No, I was not.'

'So how do you know this was the case?'

'One of my men returned to my ranch with a fierce injured hand.'

'And the man relayed to you the tale of what had happened?'

'Yes.'

Hector turned to the judge and said, 'Your Honour, as Mr Gunn was not there to witness the event himself this is pure hearsay. I ask that his testimony be struck from the record.'

Lyne got to his feet. 'Your Honour, the men gave their testimony to the then marshal, Marshal Randall. I have here their written statements.'

'As we have written statements to this effect, I will not allow testimony to be struck from the record,' said Ogier.

Hector nodded his acceptance and turned his attention back to Gunn. 'Mr Gunn, do these men still work for you?'

'No.'

'A pity that there is, therefore, no opportunity for us to call them as witnesses.'

'I do not know where they are,' Gunn replied.

'Of course not.' Hector nodded understandingly. 'May I ask how many of the men who currently work for you have been with you for four years or more?'

Gunn thought for a moment. 'About five.'

'May I ask how many men you employ in total?'

'About fifty.'

'So many,' Hector said admiringly. Gunn inclined his head modestly. 'What are the reasons for such rapid turnover? Out of fifty men, only to have maintained five. Have you been employing an inferior calibre of man? Or is it that they do not find your employment to their liking?'

'Objection,' said Lyne. 'How many questions is Mr Featherstone going to ask my client at once?'

'Sustained,' said Ogier. 'Mr Featherstone, please frame your questions more carefully.'

'Mr Gunn,' said Hector, 'why is it that only five men remain out of fifty?'

'The work is hard, I suppose,' said Gunn. 'They leave to try their luck elsewhere.'

'Mr Gunn,' said Hector, 'in your testimony to Mr Lyne you said that you had known John Evert Burn since he was an infant.'

'Yes.'

'And for how many years did you know his mother, Maria Burn?'

'Eighteen.'

'You were fond of Maria Burn?'

'Yes. She was a very fine woman.'

'You were fond enough of Mrs Burn to make a proposal of marriage after the death of her husband?'

'Yes.'

'But she refused you?'

Gunn reddened. 'I made more than one proposal. The first times I asked her, she said no, but on the last occasion she accepted me.'

John Evert was white-hot with rage as he listened to Gunn. He could not believe the audacity of the man, that he could lie so shamelessly. His eyes bored into Gunn, but Gunn never once looked at him.

'And when was this occasion?' asked Hector.

'I'm not sure I can recall the exact date.'

'Let us set it in relation to the date of Maria Burn's disappearance. How long before her disappearance did she accept your proposal?'

'It was about a month before.'

'And why did you make the proposal of marriage to Maria Burn?'

'Why? Because I cared for her.'

'You loved her?'

'Yes.'

'There was no other reason to ask for her hand in marriage?'

'No.'

'Mr Gunn, may I ask whether there had ever been any dispute between you and Maria Burn with regard to the ownership of the Burn property?'

'Objection,' said Lyne.

Hector turned to Ogier. 'Your Honour, I must ask this question if we are to establish the nature of the relationship between Mr Gunn and Mrs Burn.'

'Overruled,' Ogier said. 'Mr Gunn, please answer the question.'

'There was a dispute about the way the boundaries of my property and the Burn property were drawn up.'

'Did you ever suggest to Maria Burn that you would take the matter to trial?' asked Hector.

'No. I always told her that we could resolve things another way.'

'By marriage, for example?'

'Objection,' said Lyne.

'Let me rephrase,' Hector said. 'Mr Gunn, did you ever say to Maria Burn that . . .' Hector consulted the papers at his side '. . . "If we were to marry then all of this trouble over the land would go away."'

'No, I did not,' said Gunn.

John Evert was infuriated by Gunn's lies, but things worsened as the prosecution went on to call witness after witness who had seen John Evert, if not committing any crime, then certainly present at the scene with Bill. Not for the first time, John Evert rued his broken nose and the scar to his mouth, for the passing of the years had done nothing to diminish those distinguishing features.

A day later, things brightened momentarily with the arrival of a long-awaited letter. It came from Ewing, now a general, who had been deposed from afar as a character witness for John Evert, but John Evert did not believe that Ewing's deposition would be enough to counteract all the prosecution-witness testimony. The portrait that the prosecution had been able to paint for the jury was not a pretty one.

'Will I not get a chance to tell the jury what happened at my ranch?' John Evert said, in his cell, to Hector that afternoon.

'You will, but Lyne does not want the jury to hear your history until he has had the chance to assassinate your character and attempt to make clear your guilt.'

'Our turn can't come a moment too soon.'

'You know that under cross-examination Lyne will ask you about the relationship between Gunn and your mother?'

'I know it.'

'And you know also that—'

'I must tell the truth, the whole truth and nothing but the truth,' parroted John Evert.

'Good man.' Hector nodded, and took his leave.

'Gentlemen of the jury,' said Hector, as he opened the defence on a bright, hot morning, 'you see before you Major John Evert Burn, decorated soldier of the Union, who has fought gallantly for almost the entire four years of the war . . . fought on your behalf for justice and liberty for all men. In doing so, he sacrificed much: the possibility to clear his name, his right to legal ownership of his property, his search for his mother, who was carried off in the most violent circumstances. The prosecution has painted John Evert Burn in an unflattering light, but I urge you to keep in your minds that John Evert Burn did not have to return to Los Angeles. He could easily have spent the rest of his life in anonymity, far from here, enjoying the fruits of his glittering military career. His return, of his own volition, highlights two essential facts: his courage and, most pertinently, his innocence. Desperate men do not return to the scene of their crimes. Only the virtuous or the insane take that risk, and it is my job to show you that John Evert Burn is not only sane but righteous, to show you that the charges against him have no merit, to show you that there is, in the end, no case against this individual.'

John Evert took the stand and looked around the sweltering courtroom. All eyes were upon him. He turned to Hector and kept his gaze firmly upon him to steady his nerves. In response to Hector's questions, John Evert told the court of the attack on the ranch, its burning and his mother's abduction. He spoke in a matter-of-fact tone, giving no more and no less than was asked of him.

When he had finished the story of the raid, Hector said, 'After your arrival in Los Angeles, what did you do?'

'I hoped to put up a bounty for the return of my mother but I discovered that there was not enough money for this. I took a job at the *Star* newspaper and put my trust in the soldiers who were sent to look for her.'

'Did they uncover any news of her?'

'No.'

'What did you do next?'

'I decided to raise as much money as I could and find a bounty hunter to take the job of looking for my mother. I discovered that William Adair-Wilson was a bounty hunter and I approached him to see if he would take the job.'

'And did he?'

'Not at first, for I did not have enough money, but we came to an arrangement that I would work for him and he would pay me. That way I could raise the necessary funds.'

'Did you know that William Adair-Wilson was a wanted man?'

'No. He told me he was a Texas Ranger. He showed me his badge.'

'And you believed he was a Texas Ranger?'

'Yes.'

'When you were with Mr Adair-Wilson did you ever kill anyone?'

'No.'

'Did you ever steal anything?'

'No.'

'What was your role, then?'

'I looked after the horses. I cooked. I did whatever things needed doing.'

'When Mr Adair-Wilson's true identity was revealed was it a surprise to you?'

'Yes.'

'He was arrested, and then you were arrested as his accomplice. Did you, upon your arrest, make contact with anyone to ask for their assistance in breaking you out of jail?'

'No.'

'Did you know that Casey Jones was going to break you out of jail?'

'No.'

'When he broke you out of jail, did you consider turning yourself in once more?'

'Yes.'

'Why did you not do so?'

'I knew that if I went to jail the search for my mother would be given up for good and my land would be forfeit. I felt that Bill was the only person who would help me find my mother. I felt I had no choice but to stick with him.'

'You were fond of Mr Adair-Wilson?'

'I was. He was the best friend I ever had.'

'You then travelled east and enlisted in the army. Why, after four years, did you return to Los Angeles?'

'The war was over. Bill was dead. I came to search for my mother and to pursue my rightful claim to my land, which I knew Phineas Gunn would be attempting to take possession of.'

'What did you think would happen when you returned to Los Angeles and were recognised?'

'I knew I would be arrested and would go to trial. I wished to be tried. I wanted to clear my name, then search for my mother.'

'Mr Burn, is your mother still alive?'

'No, she is not.'

'How do you know this?'

'I received a letter—' John Evert's voice broke and he coughed awkwardly '—a letter from her. She died just under a year before my return to Los Angeles. Had I known her whereabouts, I would have returned immediately. As it was, I was engaged in fighting, and by the time I returned it was too late. It will always be my greatest regret.'

Hector allowed the silence that followed this statement to hang for a moment, then said, 'No more questions.'

*

Cyrus Lyne rose to his feet to cross-examine John Evert. He approached the stand, briefly wiping the sweat from his forehead with his handkerchief. The room was intensely hot and the noise of beating fans thudded, like a soft heartbeat, in the background.

'Mr Burn, we have heard of the attack on your ranch and the abduction of your mother,' said Lyne. 'Would you say that this experience left you bitter?'

'At the time, of course,' John Evert said. 'I was robbed of all I held dear.'

'And you were angry?'

'Yes.'

'Your main goal in life was the return of your mother?'

'Yes.'

'You would do absolutely anything to ensure her safe return?'

'Yes.'

'Mr Burn, surely you were aware of the illegality of what you were involved in with Mr Adair-Wilson.'

'No.'

'When caught up in a gun battle?'

'I did say to Bill, the first time I went with him, that I thought he was a thief. He became angry and told me he was a Texas Ranger. Like I said, he showed me his badge.'

'And you believed a Texas Ranger was above the law?'

'I was but a boy. I did not know much. And, later, I learned that he was a member of the Order of the Lone Star, which does seem to have—'

'Ah, yes,' Lyne cut in. 'The Order of the Lone Star – the mysterious group of which we have heard, and yet about which we know so little. But you did not know that Mr Adair-Wilson was a member of this group until after his arrest, did you?'

'No,' John Evert acknowledged, 'but I was not surprised to hear it.'

'Would you consider yourself a gullible man, Mr Burn?'

'No, but I was a gullible boy. Most are, I believe.'

'You admit that you were a gullible boy. I believe you were also gullible when it came to your mother and the true nature of her relationship with Phineas Gunn.'

John Evert kept his face quite straight. Hector had made it plain to him that he must keep his temper in check and, thus far, he had been a model of decorum.

'Were you aware of the engagement between your mother and Mr Gunn?' Lyne asked.

John Evert cleared his throat. 'There was no engagement between my mother and Mr Gunn. My mother hated him.'

'On what evidence do you base this statement?'

'The fact that she actively disliked him, and told me so many times.'

'As we have heard, Mr Gunn has said, under oath, that he was engaged to your mother.'

'He is lying. My mother would have told me.'

'A mother does not tell her child everything. Did she tell you about the financial difficulties she was in?'

John Evert hesitated. 'No.'

'Mr Burn, I ask you again, do you have any *evidence* – firm evidence – that your mother did *not* have an arrangement pertaining to marriage with Mr Gunn?'

John Evert looked toward the window. Outside the courthouse, along the wall, there was a trough for horses to drink from. When the sun was at a certain angle in the sky, its light reflected off the water's surface to dapple the ceiling above the window. The appearance of that dancing light was one of the ways John Evert marked time during the trial. He studied it now, and remembered a similar light that used to be reflected on the wall of the ranch house at Christmastide. It came from a round glass bauble, terribly precious to his mother, for it had been a gift from his father. Each year, it was unwrapped with great care, and placed as one of several decorations on a long branch of spruce placed over the mantel – a convention John Evert's father had admired once on a visit to Europe, and which his mother abided by every year after his death. When the light caught the bauble, and the clever prism within, it was shattered into all the colours of the rainbow. It was magical. As a very young child, he had thought the bauble was the eye of God.

John Evert took a deep breath, and then, in honour of his mother and the things he did not and could not know about her, he turned his gaze to Lyne and said clearly, 'No. No, I do not.'

There was silence in the room until Lyne said, 'Thank you, Mr Burn. No more questions.'

Hector got to his feet once more and crossed to where John Evert sat. 'Mr Burn,' Hector said. 'Mr Lyne has suggested that, as a boy, you may have been bitter and angry after the kidnap of your mother. Would you say this of yourself now?'

'No.'

'Why not?'

'When you have served in battle and seen so many men die about you, childish feelings die, too.'

'You returned to Los Angeles with two companions,' Hector said. 'May I ask their names?'

John Evert was taken aback. 'Beth Robinson and Kusox,' he said, after a moment.

'Kusox? What sort of a name is that?'

'An Indian name. Pawnee.'

'May I ask what you are doing riding with an Indian after what occurred at your ranch?'

'Kusox was a tracker in the war. He gave excellent and loyal service and I would go so far as to call him my friend.' John Evert looked down a moment. When he spoke once more, his voice was strong. 'Every Indian is not the same. Kusox has nothing to do with the Indians who attacked my ranch. The Pawnee and the Paiute are very different, although' – John Evert smiled at the memory of Kusox's sniffiness – 'they do share some opinions on—' He stopped abruptly.

'Mr Burn?' Hector said, after a few moments had elapsed. 'Mr Burn.'

John Evert shook himself out of reverie. He must remember to say something to Hector when they were in private. 'I'm sorry,' he said. 'Horses. They share some opinions when it comes to horses.'

'I see,' Hector said, with a frown. 'Why did Kusox come all this way with you, to Los Angeles?'

'I said I would give him some land to live on.' There were audible expressions of surprise around the public gallery.

'Why would you do that?'

'Because I would not have him live out his days on a reservation. I consider him my friend.'

'Despite what happened at your ranch?'

'Despite what happened at my ranch.'

'Thank you, Mr Burn. No more questions.'

Hector and John Evert met afterward, in his cell. 'You did well today,' Hector said. 'What was that stumble? Did something occur to you?'

'Yes. It's strange. The horses. I suddenly remembered, the Indians who attacked the ranch, they rode the wrong horses.'

'What do you mean the wrong horses?'

'The white-painted man, he rode a big grey. And the others I saw, they rode tall horses, one bay, one black. Not one of them was on a pinto or a pony.'

'Meaning?'

'Well, I'm not so sure they were Paiute at all.'

'John, you assured me they were Indians. You swore to it to the cavalry.'

'Well, they certainly looked like them, and they had all the skill of an Indian with the bow, but I don't know what kind of Indian they were. And there was another odd thing: the tracks. Kusox put the question into my mind: the way they left a trail that I was able to follow for days. Indians don't do that, not Pawnee, not Paiute, not any of them. They're masters at covering their own tracks.'

'But, John, your mother told us by her own hand that she lived out her days with Indians.'

'She said they were not the ones who attacked the ranch, remember.'

'Yes, I recall. It raised a question in my mind, too, but once I learned that she had passed away it no longer seemed so pressing an issue. What are you suggesting?'

'I don't know, really. But there's something amiss. I never put it together before now.'

'There is often something amiss in this life,' Hector said. But he paced the cell a good while, deep in thought. Eventually he said, 'I must speak with Abraham. I am going to call for three days' recess. Lyne will do all he can to prevent it, but I believe I can persuade Ogier of the necessity.' At John Evert's dismayed face, Hector said gently, 'Three days' recess may save your life, John Evert.'

John Evert found the three days of waiting intolerable, all the more so for the fact that Hector neither visited him nor sent any message with explanation for his absence. The reality of what he was likely to face became more tangible for him and he awoke in the night sweating from fearful dreams of the gallows.

The day the court reconvened, Hector had still not found time to visit John Evert in his cell. The first John Evert saw of him was when they met in the courtroom. Hector tried to speak to him but John Evert turned his head away to make plain his frustration.

Quincy was called as a defence witness and attested to John Evert's upstanding morals. Upon being questioned as to the nature of the errands that John Evert had run for Bill, Quincy swore that his role had been that of innocent groom, and that neither John Evert nor himself had been aware of the illegality of Bill's activities. John Evert was grateful to Quincy for what he said on his behalf, but it was not enough to rouse him from his dolour or his increasing certainty that all was lost.

John Evert was in his cell, where he sat on the edge of his bed in a state of gloom. He barely looked up when Hector entered. 'Where have you been?' he asked.

'Active on your behalf,' Hector replied.

'Well, I guess none of it matters any more, does it?' he said. 'I'll be convicted, and everyone believes Gunn and my mother were engaged, so I'll lose all claim to the ranch, too. It's all been for nothing.'

'No, John,' Hector replied firmly. 'It has not been for nothing. Don't ever give up. You never know what may be just around the corner.'

John Evert looked up at Hector, who stood very taut, like a coiled spring, his eyes blazing. 'Tomorrow,' Hector said, 'I shall put Gunn back on the stand. I cannot say what may happen, but I have a plan. You must promise to keep your counsel. You must trust me. Will you do that?'

'I guess so,' John Evert replied, but his heart was not in it. He did not bid Hector farewell. Instead, he stood upon the bedhead and put some crumbs out on the window ledge for the doves. He was not sure how many more times he would see them.

The following day, Gunn took the stand once more.

'Mr Gunn,' began Hector, 'may we return to the raid upon the Burn property?'

'Of course,' replied Gunn, with a magnanimous air.

'Given the nature of your understanding with Mrs Burn, you must have been very aggrieved by her abduction,' said Hector.

'Indeed,' replied Gunn, humbly.

'The moment you learned of what had occurred at the Burn ranch, you and your men set off in pursuit, correct?'

'Yes.'

'How many days' lead did the Indian raiders have on you and your men?'

'Three.'

'So precise,' Hector said. 'How could you be so sure of how much time had elapsed?'

'The state of the bodies of the two men we found dead at the ranch. They were not fresh dead. An old cowhand such as myself always knows when something's been lying dead a few days. So we set off on the trail the raiding party left—'

'Yes, quite. May I ask you, Mr Gunn, how much you know of Indians and their ways?'

'Ha! Nothing, I'm glad to say,' Gunn replied.

'You are a church-going man, are you not, Mr Gunn?'

'I am.' Gunn nodded.

'Yes, you have been a staunch member of the church at Anaheim. I believe they have you to thank for their newest stained-glass window and the infirmary there. Am I correct?' Gunn inclined his head in assent. 'But is it also fair to say that your acts of charity are sporadic?'

Gunn's eyes flicked to Hector's face, sensing the criticism in his words.

'Yes, you went through a flurry of church-going after the raid on the Burn property, but have not been seen in church much since, until very recently. Until, in fact, the reappearance of John Evert Burn.'

'I don't see what that has to do with anything,' Gunn said.

'I suspect you are like many of us, Mr Gunn. You go to church when there's something on your mind, or your conscience.'

'Objection,' said Lyne.

Hector did not wait for Ogier to respond and said, 'Were you feeling guilty about the disappearance of Maria Burn by any chance?'

'I don't know what you mean. I was cut up about that woman being taken,' Gunn said, two high spots of colour in his cheeks.

'Oh yes you were. I cannot argue against that. You sat in my office just a few weeks after the raid. When you heard John Evert was alive. I remember it very well. How did you feel that day?'

'I was . . . I was distressed.'

'Because of your fondness for Maria Burn?'

'Yes.'

'Would it be correct to say that you were tormented?'

338

Gunn hesitated a moment. 'Yes.'

'Tormented by what you had done?'

'No, I didn't . . . I hadn't done anything. I was distressed about what had happened to her.'

'I will ask you again, were you feeling guilty?' Gunn said nothing but stared at Hector with a fixed expression. 'Mr Gunn?'

'No,' Gunn said, shaking his head.

'Did you have a hand in the raid on the Burn ranch, Mr Gunn?'

'Objection,' said Lyne, but Judge Ogier overruled him with a raised hand.

Gunn's face was puce. The courtroom was so quiet you could have heard a pin drop.

'The horses those raiders rode were not the horses that Indians ride. They were white men's horses. They were horses that you had provided, were they not?'

'No,' Gunn said, but there was a tremor in his voice.

'Indians don't leave tracks for all and sundry to follow but these raiders left a trail that could easily be followed. It was for you to follow, wasn't it?'

'No,' said Gunn. 'No, no.'

'Objection,' said Lyne, but Hector ignored him and continued.

'You may not have been there at the time of the raid, Mr Gunn, but you knew what was to happen, didn't you?'

'Featherstone,' said Ogier with a warning note in his voice.

'I ask you, Mr Gunn,' continued Hector, 'did you know the raiders who attacked the Burn ranch?'

Gunn was silent for a moment and then exploded. 'This is bullshit,' he said. 'I loved Maria Burn. I would never have harmed her.'

'Yes, you did love her. More, perhaps, than we can understand. But you were not dear to her. John Evert Burn did not lie when he said his mother hated you. She did. She would never accept your suit and you knew it. Did you organise this raid, this phoney abduction?'

'No,' Gunn replied, shaking his head.

'Did you arrange for her to be carried off, frightened half to death, so that you could then be the one to rescue her? Did you think that by being the one to rescue her from this staged abduction it would make her respect you and perhaps even love you?'

'This is a fantasy,' cried Lyne. 'You cannot let him go on.'

'Featherstone—' Ogier began, but Hector was like a wolf on the scent of blood.

'But you didn't bank on the desperadoes you hired double-crossing you, did you?' Hector said, his voice rising by the moment. 'Nor did you plan for Mrs Burn to be turned over to a distant Paiute tribe, did you?'

'Featherstone!' Ogier bellowed, bringing his gavel down to silence the attorney.

'All we lacked was evidence of the fact but you did not know that she wrote a letter!' Hector concluded at the top of his lungs, holding up in the air, between the first two fingers of his right hand, a piece of paper. Every eye in the courtroom followed Hector.

John Evert's heart was in his mouth. It was not the letter his mother had written him before her death, for he had kept it by his side ever since. This was something new.

Hector turned to face Ogier. 'I am sorry, Your Honour, for my outburst. I would like to enter this letter, dated the sixteenth of November 1864 from Mrs Maria Burn to her son, John Evert Burn, into evidence. May I proceed?'

John Evert noticed how pale Hector was: he looked as though he might faint, which was completely out of character. John Evert did not know what was afoot, but his heart was galloping.

'You may,' Ogier said, holding up a silencing hand to Lyne.

Hector advanced across the courtroom a few steps toward Gunn, who quivered on the stand. 'I do not doubt you loved Maria Burn, Mr Gunn,' Hector said, 'but what a terrible, destructive love it was that led you to do such a thing. You sowed the wind the day you hired those desperadoes to attack the Burn ranch and reaped the whirlwind. Shall I read it to you, this letter, so you may hear what Maria Burn thought of you?' Hector asked, unfolding the paper, but Gunn put a hand up and shook his head. He was fighting to keep control of himself. John Evert hoped desperately in that moment that Hector would not give Gunn a moment's peace. Hector did not.

Hector's voice was hard as he harried Gunn. 'You made several mistakes, Mr Gunn. First, you put your trust in desperadoes, which was foolish indeed. But much the greater error was that you underestimated John Evert Burn. You underestimated his hatred for you. Because of that hatred, he did not ride to you for aid as you expected him to do. And, most fatally, you underestimated his courage: the courage that led him to strike out alone although gravely injured; the courage that led him to seek honest work at this town's newspaper in the hope of slowly raising enough money to offer a bounty for his mother; the courage that led him not to give evidence against William Adair-Wilson whom he believed to be innocent of the crimes of which he stood accused; the courage that made him a decorated soldier, a major no less; the courage that brought him back to Los Angeles to turn himself in, knowing what he would face here but determined to see justice done. With all that you had in your armoury, Mr Gunn, John Evert Burn, with courage alone, has defeated you.'

'Goddammit I know it,' Gunn roared. 'That boy has been a thorn in my side since the day he was born. I wish those bastards had killed him!'

The courtroom erupted. Hector spun around to face John Evert, who was already getting to his feet, intent on strangling Gunn with his bare hands. Hector stared at him imploringly. John Evert, with the most enormous effort of will, forced himself back down into his seat.

Ogier brought his gavel down repeatedly to silence the gallery. 'If I do not have silence, I shall clear this courtroom,' he threatened.

Gunn was sitting with his face in his hands. Hector approached the stand. 'Mr Gunn,' he said, 'I do not doubt that you have no wish to prolong this moment. Make your peace with God and tell this courtroom the truth.'

'For God's sake, all right,' Gunn snapped, the fire in him not yet extinguished. He rubbed his temples, then sat upright in his chair. When he spoke, there was a savage pride in his tone. 'There was a meeting place where we were supposed to find the men I hired to attack the ranch, but when we arrived they weren't there. It was my mistake. They'd insisted on half the money up front, which I gave them, and they had good horses that I'd given them too. One of my men was acting suspicious, so I had the others rough him up some. He was in on the plan to double-cross me. He said one of those damn desperadoes had decided to take Maria off someplace for safe keeping – seemed he'd got it into his head that I was going to have her killed.'

'Hardly an odd supposition, given the circumstances,' Hector said.

'They misunderstood me,' Gunn said bitterly.

'We all in this room misunderstand you at this moment,' Hector said. 'You were not able to find out where they had gone? Where she had been taken?'

Gunn shook his head. 'I had to let her go.'

'But you were not so heartbroken that you could not pursue your interest in the Burn land.'

'It's a foolish man who comes away with nothing,' Gunn said, with a bitter twist to his lips.

'And these raiders, who were they? Were they Indian?'

'Some were, some not. I don't know who they were or where they came from. They were hired guns. What was it to me who they were?'

'What was it to you? Do you know the price the local Paiute paid for being blamed for this raid? There was a massacre of twelve of them at Sharps Spring. And not to mention those two young women who were carried off by raiding parties – raiding parties hired by you – and then released in the desert. Those two young women were simply pawns in your plan, to give credence to the kidnap of Maria Burn. Never mind the terrible fear they must have experienced. Their suffering was nothing to you in your insatiable greed, in your determination to seize what you wanted, whatever the price to others.'

Hector let his words hang in the air before turning to Ogier, saying, 'No more questions.'

Cyrus Lyne did not rise to his feet but said to Ogier, in a defeated tone, 'I have no re-examination, Your Honour.'

'How could you not tell me about this other letter?' John Evert demanded, almost leaping upon Hector when he came to his cell later. 'You did not trust me with it?'

Hector, looking very contrite, held out the folded piece of paper to John Evert, who snatched it and opened it. He studied the spidery scrawl a moment. 'But this isn't my mother's hand.'

'No, it's Abraham's.'

John Evert had to think about things. 'You mean you lied?' he asked in amazement.

'I didn't lie. I circled around the truth a little. Abraham is my notary. The letter is a true account of your mother's feelings, as outlined to him before her death. I hope never to have to take such a risk in a courtroom again,' Hector said, and, from his sapped expression, John Evert could see he meant what he said most fervently.

'Why did you not tell me of your suspicions about Gunn?'

'Because I did not trust your temper. I would not have you spout off on the stand about Gunn, and you would have if you had had any suspicion of what he had done. I needed you calm and ignorant.'

'Why did you go to such lengths to get me to admit to a possible engagement?'

'To make plain your honesty.'

John Evert sat in silence for a long moment. 'How could he do it?' he finally said. 'I can't believe it.'

'A moment of madness and bitterness,' Hector said. 'Unrequited love – it can be the unmaking of a weak personality. I believe he has been, in some ways, tortured by what he has done.'

'Not enough,' John Evert said.

'Well, prison or the hangman's noose will be justice served.'

'He'll go to trial?'

'Yes. But as to when—'

They were interrupted by the bailiff who had come to fetch them back to court.

Judge Ogier took to the bench. 'Gentlemen of the jury, have you reached a verdict?'

'We have,' replied the foreman. 'On the count of conspiracy to commit murder, we find the defendant not guilty.' The court-room erupted and Ogier hammered his gavel to quiet the room. The foreman continued, 'On the count of conspiracy to commit theft, we find the defendant not guilty. On the count of unlawful escape from custody, we find the defendant guilty.'

'Silence in the court,' Ogier barked, when the room again erupted. He did not speak again until the room was brought to order and silence reigned once more. He settled his glasses upon his nose, studied John Evert and said, 'Bearing in mind all the history of this case, in particular your courageous service in the late war, and bearing in mind that you have been in jail since your return to this city, I impose no separate penalty. Accordingly, Mr Burn, you are free to leave this court. Court is adjourned.' He gave an audible sigh of relief, then got to his feet and walked heavily from the room.

John Evert was still repeating the judge's words when he found himself having his hand pumped, first by Hector and then by members of the public who had reached over the rail to congratulate him.

Hector put his hand upon John Evert's shoulder and squeezed it hard. 'Well done, John. Well done,' he was saying. But John Evert did not hear much else.

'But what about the ranch?' he said to Hector in confusion.

Hector's surprise showed on his face. 'Oh, John, don't you see? Gunn admitted what he did in open court. He will be tried for his crimes and a convicted felon cannot hold land in the state of California. Your ranch will be yours, John, for certain.'

25

'And what will you do now, John?' Hector asked from where he sat behind his desk, his cheek resting on the prop made by his right hand. It was the morning after the trial and he seemed fatigued but deeply satisfied at their victory.

'I'll go back to the ranch,' he said. 'I can't tell you how grateful I am. I don't know how I'll ever be able to thank you.'

'Oh, I shouldn't worry too much,' Hector replied. 'Abraham will have a bill on the way to you. I expect it to be extensive.'

They laughed. John Evert shook Hector's hand and took his leave.

He was tightening the grey's girth when a buggy drawn by a black pony flew out of the traffic and slowed to a halt at his side in a little puff of dust. 'Mr Burn,' said Jacinta Ramones. She wore a bright blue dress and matching driving gloves. Her black ringlets were shiny as crude oil. In the rear of the buggy were several large, store-bought boxes wrapped in ribbons. She looked like a thousand dollars.

'I've been searching all over for you,' she said, in a superior sort of way, but then coloured in embarrassment.

He moved to the side of the buggy, and rested his hand upon its frame. 'To what do I owe the honour?'

'Well, I came to congratulate you,' she said, with a little toss of the head, which he found silly but, nevertheless, attractive. 'Where are you going?'

'To my ranch.'

'Then I shall accompany you,' she said. When he raised his eyebrows, she added, 'To see your tame Indian, of course. It is the talk of the town.'

This manner of describing Kusox did not sit well with John Evert, although he supposed she knew no better. 'I beg your pardon, ma'am, but I don't think today is the best day for it,' he said politely. All he wanted to do was get home, tell Robinson and Kusox the good news, and take a ride around his property.

'Oh, no, it must be today, for tomorrow the *feria* begins and then it will be a whole week before I may visit.' John Evert did not see that a week should make any difference but she continued quickly, 'I shall follow you,' jabbing her black pony in the mouth so that it threw its head up and reversed several paces. She would brook no opposition, so John Evert was forced to accept her company. She called a boy to her, gave him a few coins and bade him tell her household where she was headed.

She did not follow him but kept the buggy at his side, maintaining a string of uninterrupted chatter, which, he had to admit, amused him. She seemed to know everything about everyone in Los Angeles, and told all sorts of stories. It was only when they arrived at the boundary of the ranch that he saw she would have no way of returning to Los Angeles before dark.

His dog began to bark as they drew near the barn. At the sound, the door of the house opened, and he saw Robinson's white shirt, a pale smudge in the dark interior. His spirits lifted at the sight of her. She ran across the stoop and down the steps, then stopped abruptly as they trotted toward her.

When they drew up at the house, John Evert said, with a smile, 'Miss Ramones, this is Miss Robinson.'

The two women regarded each other suspiciously. 'How do you do?' Jacinta was the first to recover. Robinson said nothing, merely bobbed uncomfortably.

John Evert dismounted and went to Robinson. He wished suddenly to draw her to him, but that was impossible: he could feel Jacinta's gaze on his back. 'Miss Ramones is paying us a visit,' he said, trying to catch Robinson's eye, but she would have none of it.

Jacinta stepped down from her buggy. Robinson walked around

John Evert and said quietly to Jacinta, 'I'll take your horse.'

'*Gracias*,' Jacinta said, as though this were quite in the order of things.

At that moment, Kusox walked around the corner of the house. He wore only buckskin leggings. Jacinta took one look at his naked torso, the long hair and the earrings, and said, 'Gracious.' She took a step closer to John Evert.

John Evert went to Kusox. He did not offer his hand, but said simply, 'It's good to see you, Kusox.'

'Did you win?' Kusox asked.

'I did.'

Kusox smiled and nodded once. 'Very good.'

'Oh, and I need to thank you,' John Evert said, 'I think we only won because of what you once said to me. You were right about the pintos.'

'Of course,' Kusox said.

In the barn, Robinson released his dog, which now came galloping across the hard earth toward him. Jacinta let out a shriek, but the dog paid her no mind, hurling itself at John Evert, putting its paws on his shoulders and licking his face. He laughed as he fought it to the ground.

'What an extraordinary life you lead,' Jacinta said, looking from the dog to Kusox to the barn, where Robinson leaned, watching them.

'I guess so,' John Evert said, wondering whether she was regretting now her insistence on accompanying him. He tried again to catch Robinson's eye, to share the joke with her, but she disappeared back into the shadows of the barn. Never mind, he thought. He would get her alone later and explain things.

He took Jacinta into the house, and set about making coffee. The place was spotless, and smelt of something freshly baked. Through the kitchen window he noticed the neatly hoed rows of the vegetable patch, and smiled. Everything would be all right, at last. He was home.

When it was ready, he brought the coffee and chairs out on to the stoop. He and Jacinta sat, while Kusox took a seat on the top step and Robinson hovered beyond, outside, leaning against one of the wooden pillars of the stoop.

'So what happened?' she asked quietly, around the pillar.

'I was cleared,' John Evert said.

'It was magnificent,' Jacinta said. 'You should have seen the courthouse – packed every day. He was the hero of the town. The *hero*!' She let out a laugh.

Robinson's face darkened and she dropped her gaze to the ground. John Evert was aware that she was upset but he was not sure why or what to do about it. 'And the ranch is safe,' he said. 'Phineas Gunn will go to trial.'

'Of course it is safe,' Jacinta said. 'There can be no doubt.' She adjusted the lie of her dress where its open neck encircled her pale shoulders, looking pleased with herself.

Robinson pushed herself away from the wooden pillar with what sounded distinctly like a groan.

'Are you all right?' John Evert asked.

'You'll probably want supper,' Robinson said, her voice flat. 'I'll see about it.' She ascended the steps. As she passed Kusox, he put out a hand and took her gently by the wrist, so she paused. He looked up at her and she gave him the shadow of a smile before he released her. John Evert's eyes followed them, as did Jacinta's.

Robinson closed the door behind her. Kusox finished cleaning under his nails with his bowie knife then, to Jacinta's obvious relief, got up and walked away.

'What is your relationship to Miss Robinson?' she asked, as soon as they were alone.

'She's my friend,' he replied. He was aware that the situation must seem improper to this lady.

'Hmm.' Jacinta straightened a wrinkle in the fabric of her dress with one elegant hand. 'Where did you meet?'

'The sun will be down in a couple of hours. Why don't we take a walk to the river?' he said, in an attempt to divert her.

'Oh, yes. Let us do that,' she said.

They struck away from the side of the house and began to descend the slope, toward the river, his dog gambolling about beside them. John Evert was sure he felt a pair of eyes burning a hole in his back from the kitchen window.

It was the time of afternoon when the light had a particular splendour, when the edges of the landscape seemed to blur, and lacewings and dandelion seed heads tumbled about on rising and sinking air currents. The crickets sawed their endless song, and the ground beneath their feet seemed to throb softly as it returned the heat of the day to the sky.

Jacinta chattered gaily as they walked, but John Evert did not listen. He wondered how much of the ranch Robinson and Kusox had discovered while he had been away. He wondered whether they had found his oak tree.

Some little while later, when they were meandering along the bank of the river beneath the sycamores, a pair of egret took startled flight into the now purple blush of the sky. He and Jacinta stopped to admire the sighing white breaths of their wingbeats. And that was when they heard the crack of a gunshot.

John Evert's head snapped in the direction of the house, obscured by the trees, his thoughts scattering. His dog quivered at his heel, its ears standing up like pitch-fork prongs. 'Go!' he shouted at it, dread filling his chest, and forgetting Jacinta, he tore after it. He hurtled in and out of the trees, the setting sun blazing ruby into his eyes one moment, obliterated by the trunks of the trees the next, so that his vision flickered black and red, and he no longer saw where he was going. Instead, pictures flashed before his eyes: his mother, Bill, battle, Kusox, Robinson. His blood thudded in his ears so loudly that the world was inverted, and it was no longer his pulse thundering through his ears, but as though he himself were enclosed in the beating heart of a giant.

He made the edge of the woods, breath sawing his lungs, and took off up the slope to the house at a dead run, feeling as though he waded through treacle, wanting to bellow in frustration at his slowness. He could see the top of the house, the top of the barn, horses, a big bay that he recognised, and he thought that must be impossible, for surely Gunn was safe in jail. As he covered the last few hundred yards and hit the flat, he took in the terrible scene – Robinson standing out front of the house, like a thin reed against the earth, her hands above her head, a pistol at her feet; Kusox, several yards behind her, with a pistol in one hand and a gun in the other, pointed at Gunn and his men, all of whom had guns pointed back. He had time to see the two men closest to him turn and see him, saw their mouths moving as they shouted at him; and she turned her head and looked him in the eye, and he was glad of it, and he saw her mouth, 'Stop,' but all he could think was that it was happening again, that history was repeating itself, and he launched himself off the ground and dived toward her, carrying her off her feet, so that they flew through the air together, tilting left so that his body sheltered hers from the men behind. Looking back as he fell, he saw Kusox, face twisted in anger, guns blazing, and for the second time in his life, everything went black.

26

Everyone agreed that Mrs Gunn had handled things wonderfully. What a monstrous shock it must have been to learn that she had been married to such a man, and what a dreadful thing it was that, even after he had admitted to his terrible deeds in a court of law, he had come after John Evert once more. Eleanor Gunn, who might never live down the shame, had made it clear that she would mourn her husband respectfully, and those two poor, innocent men of Phineas's who had died in the crossfire, but she would hold nothing against John Evert, or even that Indian who had been responsible for her husband's death. The consensus around Los Angeles was that justice had been served, and what, after all, was one more dead Indian?

None of this made a great deal of sense to one wrapped in the woolly, white nimbus of a laudanum haze. White seemed the only colour John Evert knew these days: white walls, white sheets, white bandages, which were changed with monotonous regularity. Once, in a brief moment of clarity, he saw a pile of bloodied linen upon the floor. Was it something to do with him? A few times, he found himself close to speaking, but always someone came gently to nudge him back into oblivion.

Eventually, a day came when he awoke and felt more or less like himself. He looked around. He was alone. He lifted the sheet that covered him; his torso was swathed in bandages. He touched his stomach, which seemed undamaged, and then his sides, where he found sore points that made him wince. His left arm was numb and would not move and was bandaged elbow to shoulder. He lay back and waited for someone to come and tell him what had happened, and the person who came was Jacinta.

'Ah, you are awake!' she whispered, as she came to his side, her long skirt making a soft rustle as she moved. 'How is the pain?'

He cleared his dry throat. 'Where am I?'

'The Mission infirmary.'

'How long have I been here?'

'About ten days.'

He said nothing for a while, his mind struggling to catch up with reality. 'Where are Robinson and Kusox?' he asked.

'Don't make yourself anxious about them now,' she replied. 'Can I bring you water?'

John Evert swallowed. 'Yes. Where are they?'

Jacinta did not answer. Instead, she brought him a cup, and helped him to drink from it. Some water dribbled down his chin and she wiped it away. He searched her face.

'Answer me,' he said, and when she did not, a chill crept across him. 'Are they dead?'

Jacinta looked down, not meeting his eye, 'Your Indian friend, yes. I am sorry.'

He felt as though his whole body reeled. 'And Robinson?' he asked, his chest tight.

'No, she was not injured at all, unlike you.'

He smiled faintly, 'She's too skinny – it would be like trying to shoot a blade of grass. Why isn't she here?' he asked, trying to turn on his side, but hissing at the pain.

'I don't know,' Jacinta replied, her lovely mouth drooping slightly at the corners. 'But I can assure you she is alive and well. I have seen her with my own eyes.'

He lay back on the pillows and sighed, 'Forgive me,' he said, realising that he had upset her somehow. 'I don't know what's happened.'

She straightened the sheet over him. 'Do you remember anything?'

'I think so.' Sadness lapped, chilly and shallow at the base of his chest. 'So Kusox is really dead?' he said. She nodded. 'Who else?'

'Phineas Gunn and two of his men.'

'Jesus Christ,' he breathed.

'Don't concern yourself.' She shook her head, and her glossy ringlets bounced. 'There will be no charges against you.'

'I don't care about that.'

'Well, you should.'

'How was he even there? Why wasn't he in jail?' He lay back against the pillow and shut his eyes.

'I think you should rest,' she said, stroking his sweat-damp hair off his forehead.

He nodded and, within moments, he slept.

When next he awoke, Jacinta's perfume still lingered, and there was a nurse in the room. She had a gentle voice. She washed him and remade his bed.

Later, the same nurse appeared again, and asked if he felt well enough for another visitor. His heart lifting, he said that he did, but to his disappointment it was Hector who appeared.

'Good Lord, John Evert,' he said amiably. 'If ever there was a man that drama and near-disaster followed.'

John Evert managed a weak smile. 'The luck of the devil,' he said.

Hector looked rueful. 'Is it luck you call it, John?'

John Evert ignored this. 'I'm glad you're here,' he said. 'I don't know what has happened, and no one will tell me.'

'I'll fill you in,' Hector said, drawing up a chair. 'How much do you remember?'

John Evert frowned with concentration. 'I was in the woods, walking with Miss Ramones. We heard a gunshot. I ran back to the house. Robinson was there, Kusox with her . . . There was a stand-off . . . Kusox was armed, she was not, but there was a gun at her feet so . . . I don't know. Gunn and his men had guns on her. I made to get her out of there . . . That's all. I don't know who fired first.'

'We may never know. Gunn and your friend are dead,' Hector said. 'The last of Gunn's men say Miss Robinson fired the first shot you heard, but only a warning shot. As for who fired upon you first, who can say? But your man returned fire, and the rest is obvious to you.'

'What was Gunn doing there? Why wasn't he in jail?'

'It appears he was able to bribe a guard. I am so sorry. How it could have happened I just don't know. Ogier is furious. There will be hell to pay, but it is too late for some.' Hector paused and raised his eyebrows. 'One thing I will say for Phineas Gunn is that, despite his own deplorable character, he was drawn to virtue.'

To John Evert's quizzical expression, he said, 'I assumed Miss Ramones would have told you.'

'I couldn't make sense of what she said. But she has been very kind.'

'Miss Ramones would be a good match for you,' Hector said.

'I'm sorry?' he said. Hector raised his eyebrow at him and then John Evert understood and blushed. 'Oh, I don't think Miss Ramones . . .'

'. . . would be spending all day every day here tending you unless she felt a certain partiality,' Hector said.

John Evert promised himself he would reflect on the problem of Jacinta Ramones later, and went back to the matter in hand. 'What was she trying to tell me? About Mrs Gunn.'

'The very day after Gunn was killed, Eleanor Gunn signed over their version of the title deeds of your ranch to you, thus relinquishing any claim they had to the land.'

John Evert was struck dumb. Hector was smiling, but John Evert's gaze trickled down to Hector's feet, and remained there. After a while, he said regretfully, to those polished toes, 'I wish I had the chance to tell Kusox – he did not know it as I did, but that land would have meant as much to him as it did to me, I think.'

'Take solace in the fact that his sacrifice was not in vain,' Hector said quietly.

'I don't think he did it for me,' John Evert replied. 'He did it for Robinson. He always looked out for her. And what I want to know is,' he brought his gaze back to Hector's face, 'where is she?'

'Miss Robinson? That I do not know.'

A foreboding that had taken root in John Evert's mind blossomed. 'Mr Featherstone, I'm sorry always to be asking service of you, but please, I beg you, can you find out where she is?'

'Of course. If it is important to you, let me go to it.'

John Evert was left plucking restlessly at his sheet. He had done something wrong in Robinson's eyes, but he knew not what. He barely slept, and was so hot when he woke the following morning that his nurse worried about fever. The hours waiting for Hector's return were insufferable. When he finally did, John Evert tried to sit upright in the bed, wincing at the pain as he did.

'Calm yourself,' Hector said placidly. He put his hand on John Evert's shoulder, pressing him back against the pillows.

'Well?' John Evert demanded, as Hector took a seat.

'It is most odd,' Hector replied, folding his arms across his chest. 'From what the fathers and the nurses tell me, she was the one to bring you here, with Miss Ramones. They rode all night to do it. She was here with you every day. She stayed until it was certain you would live, then she entrusted your dog – which was injured, but not enough to warrant concern – to a boy who is attached to the Mission in some capacity, and then she left town.'

'How can you be sure?' John Evert persisted.

'You have a roan pony, do you not? She was seen riding out of town upon it some four days ago.'

'But why would she leave?'

Hector stood, went to the window, and looked out, deep in thought. 'You say she was not an educated woman. Is there any chance she could have been under a misapprehension that she would be in trouble of some kind over what happened?'

Dismay drew its oppressive leaden cloak about John Evert's

shoulders. Of course she would think that, with her suspicion of everyone and everything. It would only have taken one lawman to ask her a few questions to send her running for the hills, fearing that she would face incarceration if she stayed. He ground the heel of his hand against his brow. 'Can you try to find her?' he asked.

'I will do all that is possible,' Hector replied.

Jacinta continued to tend to him. She visited daily, moving very gracefully about the room, arranging things on his behalf, while he sat propped up in bed, bare-chested but for his bandages. But he was no good as a conversationalist for her, instead spending her visits looking out of the window, lost in reverie.

'You are hardly here,' she said to him.

He apologised. 'You've been so kind to me, Miss Ramones. Can I ask you? Did you speak to Miss Robinson at all, after what happened?'

'No. She would not speak to me. I don't think she likes me very much,' Jacinta said.

'It's not your fault. She's prickly,' he said.

'But she must be a good person,' Jacinta replied.

'Why do you say that?'

'Because you care for her,' she said. Looking into her dark eyes, he realised then that what Hector had said was true, that this lovely young woman held him in high regard. She also knew that his feelings lay elsewhere and, perhaps only now for the first time clearly, he realised it, too. A sudden image came to him, of Robinson with her hat high on her head, well back on her blonde mess of hair, her eyes creased up as she laughed at him after he told her off for cussing, and the thought that he might not see that humour again stung worse than the pain in his body.

'Has Mr Featherstone been able to uncover any news of her?' Jacinta asked.

'No,' he replied.

'Do not give up hope. What will be will be,' she said, with a sad smile. 'Shall I read to you?'

'Please. I'd like that.'

Anyone who has farmed the pioneer land of California knows there is but one true gift: water. When it came to his land, John Evert was blessed with good fortune, and he knew it. If it had not been for the fertile ground beneath his feet, and the river that fed it, his last most recent loss might have been enough to finish him off altogether; but some tenacity in him drove him to throw all his energies into the ranch. It became his overriding passion, and he worked himself like a dog to drown out the loneliness.

The water-pump by the house would no longer do for him: it was essential that he move with the times – he had read of hydraulic rams that used pressure to force water upwards. He purchased one and, with the assistance of some hired labourers, installed it in the river, building a long pipe that travelled all the way up to the house. The noise it made was like a mechanical heartbeat, thudding companionably upon the empty air.

He stood now, looking down at the ram, wiping the sweat from his forehead with the back of his hat. His stomach rumbled. He should go inside and make something to eat, but he could not raise the enthusiasm. Meals now consisted of a hunk of bread dipped into a pot of whatever was lying about, as he passed through the kitchen between his labours upon the ranch. He was thin. He did not care for himself. The odd times he looked in the mirror, he saw a body covered in the cicatrix of healed bullet wounds, all raised skin and suture dots, surmounted by the star-shaped wound to his shoulder. He was a mess, a half-dreamed thing assembled from the discarded limbs of so many dead men.

Robinson had always refused to look in mirrors. He had teased her about it, but she had not laughed; she had coloured and gone quiet. He had wondered what stopped her looking at her own reflection. Now, with hindsight, he thought perhaps he knew: shame. And the thought of her being ashamed of anything cut him.

He wondered, often, where and how she lived. He had laid out a lot of money in having men search for her, but it was as though she had evaporated into thin air. For years, he had been tormented with worry about his mother; now it was worry about Robinson. At least the news of his mother's death had brought with it some peace. He felt sore guilty even thinking it, but it was the truth. He could bear any knowledge, he felt, but not knowing was agonising.

He had travelled to his mother's grave with the intention of exhuming her to bring her home. Yet when he got there he found that the father who had given her burial had planted a rose bush upon her grave. Apparently she had requested it, and with the father's care, the rose had run riot in that rich earth, creating a heavy-headed beauty in the desert. The small act of kindness, and what Nature had done, had so touched him that he felt he should not disturb her rest. He had stayed beside her grave for hours, had told her all his story, and had wept for things that had not been.

Upon his return to the ranch, there had been a near crisis when he found a couple of bottles of liquor hidden in a cupboard. He had wrestled one open, had it to his lips, even, when something stopped him. He took the bottles out to the fencepost and shot them to pieces.

He had no desire to go into Los Angeles. Weeks went by without him speaking to anyone. Jacinta Ramones had come calling a few times but eventually she had ceased her visits, realising perhaps that nothing would ever come of them and that John Evert preferred his solitude. He read a lot, a hell of a lot – there was not much else to do in the evenings. He found that the only time he felt a remote sense of peace was when he was out of doors, surrounded by the living things, so he often slept under the stars. His thoughts regularly strayed back to those strange times under the willow trees, when Kusox and Robinson had tied him up and fed him that plant. He thought about the nightmare visions he had had, some terrible, some wonderful. He wished there had been the opportunity to thank Kusox properly for what he had done for him.

Kusox had been given desultory burial by Gunn's men, on the order of the marshal. Once John Evert was sufficiently recovered from his injuries he had asked to be taken to the grave, and had promptly exhumed the body, carrying Kusox to the river, to the spot where Kusox, Robinson and he had swum together on that happy day when they arrived at the ranch together. He buried Kusox at a bend in the river, in exactly the spot he had planned to give to him. He wondered whether Kusox, wherever his spirit might now wander, would know that he had done this; he hoped he did.

The local Paiute never came anywhere near his land, having been sent to barren reservations where they were no more than ghosts. Time was, of course, when John Evert would have applauded such a course of action, but not now.

Months passed before John Evert finally made his way back to Los Angeles, at Hector's bidding.

'Could you not have sent Abraham out to me with these,' John Evert asked, as he bent over Hector's desk to sign the papers Hector had laid out.

'I thought it would be good for you to have a trip into town and see your friends. You are very isolated out there, John. Besides, Abraham is away on an errand.'

'You seem cheerful today,' John Evert said, in response to Hector's smile.

'You catch me out,' Hector admitted. 'I am to become a father,' he said, colouring.

John Evert's smile rose involuntarily to his face, and yet as he clasped Hector's hand to congratulate him, he felt a weight settle in his chest.

'My wife has been with child several times, but each time she lost the baby,' Hector said, then rattled on. 'But she had an

operation and it seems certain that the child will survive this time
– she is nearly full term. Science and technology, John, the wonder
of the modern world. It makes the world smaller, and us larger
in it, the once impossible possible. It gives us all hope.'

Hector's eyes shone as he spoke, and he looked keenly at John
Evert. But John Evert could not quite bring himself to share in
Hector's optimism.

He left Hector's offices saddened, feeling more than ever his
own aloneness in the world. He resolved not to come into town
again.

The only other person he met with was Eleanor Gunn, who,
every now and then, would send one of her *vaqueros* to his ranch
with an invitation to visit her. He looked forward to those invi-
tations, not just because he had so much to be grateful to her
for. She was an intelligent woman and, like him, she was married
to her land. They would spend the afternoons discussing crops,
or the new design of a plough; when he needed men for labouring,
she was always happy to lend hers. He began to suspect that she
was relieved, even glad, to hold the reins of the Gunn ranch. He
admired her greatly for managing her estate alone.

He was alarmed when, the afternoon following his most recent
visit to the Gunn property, his dog disappeared. It was gone for
three anxious days and, when it had returned unscathed,
exhausted, looking pleased with itself, it had passed out for a
long sleep on the stoop. John Evert came across it there as he
walked up the steps to the water barrel. It tilted its head back,
and watched him as he removed the lid.

'Been out sowing those wild oats?' he said.

The dog thumped its tail up and down a couple of times in
response.

He raised a dripping scoop from the barrel and sipped the
clean water, his eyes travelling across the pastures. His attention
was snagged by a break upon the horizon line. He watched it as
it wavered like a blade of grass in the heat haze. God, it was hot.
It was too early for the mail coach, which had come but a week

ago. It would be one of the Mission fathers, he decided, who dropped in on him from time to time. He groaned. He took little comfort from their visits, preferring his hermit's existence.

He limped down off the stoop. His ankle, which had never fully recovered from the battle that had resulted in Bill's death, pained him more, these days, most often when it was about to rain, but there was certainly no sign of moisture in the air. Sometimes he felt terribly old. He was but twenty-one years of age. 'You have your whole life ahead of you,' the wretched father had said, the last time he had visited. Sometimes John Evert wished it were not so.

He dropped his gaze from the horizon and filled a couple of water buckets from the trough, took them into the barn and put them into the dun pony's stall. It nickered at him and walked over to see what he was doing. It was lonely. He had been forced to shoot the grey a month earlier when it had been in the throes of a colic that would surely kill it. The memory still pained him. He must get another horse, to keep the dun company. He would see to it some time.

When he walked outside again and glanced across the pastures, he saw that the blade had resolved itself into two horses, rather than one. Uninterested, he went inside, shut the door and bolted it behind him. He went to his bedroom and picked up his book, intending to pretend he was not at home.

Whoever it was, they were persistent with their patient knock. He thought he had exhausted them, when he was startled by a thud at his bedroom window, which turned out to be Abraham's cupped hands pressed to the glass, trying to see within. 'Ah, Mr Burn! You *are* at home.' His cheerful tone echoed through the glass.

John Evert smiled a little at being caught out so. He went to the front door, unbolted it and threw it open for Abraham while he made his way back around the kitchen, in search of some coffee.

He was rummaging in the pantry when he heard Abraham's

tread on the floor behind him. 'Mr Burn?' Abraham said, his voice tentative. 'Did you see . . .?'

John Evert turned to Abraham, clutching small sacks of coffee and sugar. 'Did I see what? How are you, Abraham?'

Abraham blinked at him. 'Truth be told, I am a little tired, Mr Burn,' he said. He did look tired, done in, in fact.

'Have a seat, Abraham. You're dead on your feet. What's been keeping you so busy?'

Abraham put his head on one side and gave him a quizzical look. 'Have you not seen Mr Featherstone, sir? Did he not say?'

'I saw him. He said you were on an errand.'

Abraham's mouth twitched. 'Oh, I see. I think you had better come outside, Mr Burn. Your visitor was reluctant to come in.'

'My visitor? Abraham,' John Evert sighed, 'I've no time for strangers.'

'Not a stranger, sir.' Abraham smiled, and something about his smile, about his ill-concealed enthusiasm, made John Evert's breath catch in his throat.

As though in a dream, he dropped the sacks of coffee and sugar, which hit the floor one after the other, with soft thuds, and strode toward the door.

There by the barn was the roan pony. Leaning against its shoulder, savagely biting her fingernails, her face shaded by a hat, was Beth Robinson. All of a sudden his ribcage was strangely compressed.

She glanced up at him for the briefest moment, then, in a paroxysm of embarrassment, turned to the roan's saddle.

John Evert had to put his shoulder to the pillar of the stoop to steady himself – he was not sure he could trust himself to stand without support.

After a moment, Abraham, who had come silently to his side, cleared his throat. 'I hope I did right, Mr Burn.'

'How did you do it?' John Evert asked in wonder.

'It appears Miss Robinson was not content at leaving you without assessing your return to health. She wired Mr Featherstone, enquiring after you, with strict instructions for secrecy as to her whereabouts. But Mr Featherstone felt his duty was first to you, his client, so he had me ride to where the telegraph was sent from. It was no great difficulty thereafter to locate her.'

'Science and technology,' John Evert breathed, in belated comprehension.

'I'm sorry, sir?' John Evert shook his head and gestured at Abraham to continue. 'I must say, I had a time persuading Miss Robinson to come with me.'

'I bet you did.'

'She was under a misapprehension that she was in trouble of some kind and that you would not wish to see her. I assured her this was not the case. I assured her that, in fact, you would very much wish to see her.' In response to John Evert's continued silence, he repeated, with a note of anxiety, 'I did do right, Mr Burn?'

'Oh, Abraham,' was all John Evert could manage.

A quick glance at John Evert's countenance seemed to be enough to reassure Abraham and a smile fluttered about his drawn face. 'If you'll excuse me now, Mr Burn, I think I must leave you. I am rather tired,' he said. 'Good day, sir.' And with that, he hopped down the steps, mounted his neat horse, tipped his hat in Robinson's direction and trotted away.

Still John Evert stood, for fear that movement of any kind might be his undoing. She, on the other hand, fidgeted, took off her hat and pushed her hair out of her face, then threw him an insouciant look of the kind she only adopted when something actually mattered to her a very great deal. And whatever she saw in his face, it must have been reassuring, because she began to take a few tentative steps toward him. And, as she did, the space around John Evert's heart grew wide, unimaginably wide, until it took in the pastures, the woods and all the land that hummed and sang in every direction.

John Evert had always considered himself pretty fast on the draw, but when it came to some things, he realised, he was not, perhaps, as quick as he might have hoped, for it was only now that he understood what it meant that she was walking toward him. Taking a breath, he quit the shade and stepped forward, into the light, and walked out straight, at last, to meet her.

Acknowledgements

Great thanks go to my deeply committed editor, Anne Perry, who never misses a trick. I am indebted to the brilliant Valeria Huerta, who first believed in this book, and to Suzie Dooré, who bought it on the basis of three chapters. Two fine editors, Kate Lyall-Grant and Sara Starbuck, provided editorial advice when I was first starting out as a writer. Without their early encouragement, I would never have kept going. It has been a pleasure to work with my clear-headed agent, Jane Finigan. I would like to thank the London Library, in whose stacks I found inspiration and where much of this book was written. I am grateful to the terrifically knowledgeable Pat Murphy of Holland & Holland, who advised on all things gun-related. Any errors that remain are entirely my own. Dr Adam Smith, Senior Lecturer in American History at UCL, took valuable time from the book that he was writing in order to read the civil war chapters of mine. Bruce Lee, whose ancestors fought on both sides of the civil war, helped me correct important details of the time. Thanks are due to an inspirational English teacher, Nicholas Van der Vliet, who first pointed out to me that I could write. Special thanks go to VJ Keegan, who has read every draft of everything I have ever written. For advice on all things legal, I thank my father, who prevented my love of story from breaking the law. Several people have generously provided me with places in which to write: particular thanks go to John and Catherine Hickman for the use of The Granary (and many logs during the winter months); to Brian and Helen Blythe for the use of their boat house; to Gina Schoff for the house on Ti Tree Avenue; to Amanda Davies for Crabbe Cottage; and to Manuel Pinto Ribeiro for the House on the River, near Silves, where the final draft of this book was completed.

For their support and encouragement, I would also like to thank the following: Benjamin Schoff, Olivia Pearey, Julia Young, Charlotte Cripwell, Talitha Stevenson, Andrew Dowler, Karun Thakar, Keystone Tutors.

Lastly, I would like to express the deepest gratitude to my parents and step-parents, all of whom have always supported me in my decisions, no matter how eccentric those decisions must, at times, have seemed.

The following books were used during the research for *The Brittle Star*:

Reminiscences of a Ranger by Major Horace Bell, which provided both the inspiration for this story and several of its characters
Battle Cry of Freedom by James M. McPherson
Rifles for Watie by Harold Keith